"The Man Called Kyril

just explodes before our eyes. The pounding of the heart begins, and we realize that down deep we will never really get over the thrill of a good spy story. There is such a labyrinth of plots and so many sudden turns that it is impossible to turn pages of the novel fast enough. The master touch, however, is the revelation of the traitor. No matter how good an armchair spy you are, you'll never guess his identity."

—COLUMBUS DISPATCH

"A brilliant debut . . . tremendously exciting."
—London SUNDAY TELEGRAPH

"Wonderfully tough and fascinating . . . keeps you guessing to the very end."

—NEWSDAY

"Skillfully embroidering an intricate pattern of deceptions, Trenhaile has written an espionage novel that slots near the Le Carré school."

—PUBLISHERS WEEKLY

John Trenhaile's meticulously plotted look at espionage from the other side "makes triple crossing seem rather amateurish."

—BOSTON HERALD AMERICAN

"Good entertainment."

—LIBRARY JOURNAL

"Trenhaile's characterizations of the aging Stanov and of Kyril, the loyal agent asked to do an impossible task, are brilliantly conceived."

—BOOKLIST

JOHN TRENHAILE
THE MAN
CALLED
KYRIL

A JOVE BOOK

This Jove book contains the complete
text of the original hardcover edition.
It has been completely reset in a typeface
designed for easy reading, and was printed
from new film.

THE MAN CALLED KYRIL

A Jove Book / published by arrangement with
Congdon & Weed, Inc.

PRINTING HISTORY
Congdon & Weed edition published 1981
Jove edition / February 1984

ISBN: 0-515-07633-3

Jove books are published by The Berkley Publishing Group,
200 Madison Avenue, New York, N.Y. 10016.
The words "A JOVE BOOK" and the "J" with sunburst
are trademarks belonging to Jove Publications, Inc.

PRINTED IN THE UNITED STATES OF AMERICA

To Vicki, my wife, with love

THE MAN CALLED KYRIL

1

The blue street lamps were extinguished one by one, conceding the snow-covered streets to the grey half-light of dawn. Across the city dogs spoke to one another, making the most of the early morning stillness before traffic and many human voices gathered to exclude them, but Dzerzhinsky Square was quiet. Nothing moved.

From his vantage point at the tall window the old man had an uninterrupted view of Marx Prospekt and the statue of 'Iron Felicks', who had given the square its name, but that was all. This tickled his sense of irony. The old man, who was paid to do nothing but watch, had nothing to do.

The room was growing lighter.

He turned away from the window and considered his spacious office. He thought he was familiar with it but he had never come to work as early as this; by spending the night there he had gained a new perspective.

The focal point of the room was a large, ornate, old-fashioned desk placed so that the natural light from the window fell directly on to its surface, bare except for a brass inkstand.

To the right stood a table with several telephones and a switchboard which the old man could work himself without going through an operator. One of the phones was the 'Kremlevka', direct to the Kremlin, another the 'Vertushka', his connection with the Politburo. He often wondered if even those two telephones were safe. But he knew that such things were only relative, that in his world nothing was ever truly secure.

To the left of his desk was another, smaller table for the more mundane requirements of office routine: a diary, paper and pens, two trays, one for outgoing and one for incoming documents. The latter contained such diverse snippets of information as the number of troops currently on the frontier with Pakistan, and the name of the winner of the sweepstake as to the date when the white lines on the British ambassador's tennis court would first be covered with snow.

One file, more bulky than the rest, lay on the desk awaiting its return to the 'Out' tray. His eyes lingered on it for a moment: 'Masked Shrike', the oldest of all his many projects and still his favourite. Years ago, quite by chance, he had met a delegate to a Party Congress; now that delegate was local secretary to the communist party of Albania, biding the old man's time, waiting for orders from Moscow. So many long-term plans, so many projects had evolved in this room, each contained in a master file with the line drawing of a bird on the cover. The achievements of a lifetime . . .

The old man had read many documents during his lonely vigil, cat-napping between bouts of work. This morning, however, papers no longer interested him. Nor did he care about the quartz clocks ranged on the wall opposite the desk, each showing local time in a foreign capital, nor the priceless Persian carpet, nor the portrait of Yuri Andropov which dominated the wall above the fireplace. At this early hour of greyness and shadows the old man's whole attention was concentrated on The Chair.

The Chair had become a legend for the men who worked in this building. The initials KGB officially stand for *Komitet Gosudarstvennoy Bezopasnosti*—the Committee for State Security (although within the KGB itself they traditionally represent *Kontora Grubykh Banditov*, or 'Office of Crude Bandits'). As the official name suggests it is a matter-of-fact organisation, not much given to sentimentality or myth. But there are exceptions.

For example, there is The Door. Access to the old man's room on the third floor of 2, Dzerzhinsky Square is normally gained through oak double-doors beside the fireplace. Opposite the desk, however, is another door which seems curiously out of place in such a splendid office. It is made of steel and held shut by twin padlocks. The old man's immediate predecessor, Andropov, hung a curtain over it and in his time the padlocks rusted. The old man did not use the door much either, but he abolished the curtain, wanting his visitors to be able to see what lay behind it.

Within the KGB many stories are told about this steel door. Shelepin, for example, was supposed to have treated it as his regular means of access; during his reign its hinges were oiled once a week. It is also said that, with the exception of the tenant of the large office on the third floor, no one who passes through The Door ever comes back; but these are only stories to frighten children.

The Chair, as it is always simply known, has an altogether different reputation. It is an old, heavy and extremely uncomfortable wooden throne, finely carved and polished to a high reflective shine. No one knows where it originally came from but it is presumed to be a relic of the Tzarist regime, once the property of an autocratic nobleman. Each tenant has his own way of trying to make it comfortable: blankets, cushions, foam rubber...But they all sit in it. No one could ever get rid of The Chair. It has become a symbol. For in it reposes supreme power, control over the daily lives of the citizens of the USSR, power extending into the heart of the Politburo itself. And in the eyes of Soviet law, The Chair is never empty.

Marshal Voldemar Pavlovich Stanov, at 73 the oldest man ever to hold the office of Chairman of the KGB, approached The Chair very slowly and lowered himself into its hard embrace. He laid his head against the carved rest and closed his eyes.

When the double doors opened Stanov did not look round. He knew it would be Colonel Yevchenko, his bodyguard and friend.

No one who was not expected entered this room. As Yevchenko placed the steaming glass of tea on the desk, Stanov's thin lips compressed briefly in a smile.

'Thank you, Nikolai.'

The old colonel grunted and sat down heavily in the nearest chair. For a few moments neither man spoke.

He's dying, people told Yevchenko, dying and under suspicion. You should get out while you can.

He's old, people said to Stanov (sometimes the same people), old and useless. You should let him go. Have someone young and fit to look after you.

But neither man had so many friends that he could afford to jettison the best.

Stanov finished his tea and sucked the flesh from the thick slice of lemon.

'We must be going, Nikolai. Is it time?'

Yevchenko nodded and hauled himself painfully upright.

'Everything's ready, just like you asked.'

'Nobody suspects I stayed here last night?'

'Just like you asked', Yevchenko soothed him.

They used the back stairs to the underground car-park, supposedly a fire escape but invariably kept locked 'for security reasons'. Yevchenko had gone to no little trouble to obtain a key without arousing suspicion. Parked close up against the basement door to the stairs was a black Zhiguli, indistinguishable from hundreds of similar vehicles on the Moscow streets. Yevchenko glanced right and left before signalling to Stanov that it was safe for him to leave the shelter of the stairwell.

'You must get down on the floor, old man.'

The endearment, permitted but rarely used, betrayed Yevchenko's anxiety, and Stanov smiled. It was painful creasing his old bones into such a confined space, but he managed it.

'You have the gun?'

In answer Yevchenko pressed a Stechkin into Stanov's hand, then covered him with a blanket.

'I'm going to put some empty salmon boxes over you. Don't worry, they're not heavy.'

Yevchenko took a last look round before settling into the driver's seat. There was no one about. Moments later the car was climbing the ramp to street level.

Notwithstanding his seniority and familiarity to the sentry, Yevchenko had to produce identification before they would let him out. The check was perfunctory, however, and Yevchenko had already begun to accelerate before the barrier was fully raised. When he was cruising comfortably along Marx Prospekt he said softly, 'It's all right.'

There was no reply, and for a mad second Yevchenko wanted to stop and see if Stanov was still alive. He resisted it and drove on. They were going against the rush-hour traffic and in 30 minutes reached the outer suburbs of the city. Yevchenko stopped in a deserted side-street and leaned back over the seat to tug away the boxes and the blanket. Stanov sat up, blinking.

'I said "It's all right" and you didn't reply, I thought . . .'

'Where in hell are we, Yevchenko? Why have we stopped?'

'I'll drive on, then.'

Yevchenko knew better than to fuss. They completed the journey in silence. A few miles further on the car pulled up outside a block of flats which Stanov eyed with distaste.

'Half-built rubbish. Look at that front area, it's like a building site.'

'You sent him to live there, remember?'

Stanov licked his lips. 'Have you got the file?'

'It's in the flap of the seat in front of you.'

Stanov reached out, but before he could take the folder Yevchenko spoke again.

'I still say you're wrong. Why lie to him? For the last time, think . . .'

'I have thought.' Stanov's voice was sharp with tension. 'Have I thought of anything else these last two years? And *I* say . . . and also for the last time . . . *I* say I will not trust this man with the whole truth. For his sake and for ours, I will not tell him all of what we know. So let there be an end to it.'

Yevchenko opened the door and climbed out of the car. From the back seat Stanov noted with approval that in his plain dark overcoat and ordinary shoes Yevchenko might have passed for a civilian; he didn't have 'soldier' written all over him any more. While Yevchenko leaned against the car Stanov opened the file on Captain Ivan Yevseevich Bucharensky and began to read.

Most of the details were so well known to him that he could

have recited them from memory. Age 42. Trained at Dietskoye
Selo. Specialities: disguise, languages, small arms. Cleared to
work for Department 13 of Line F, now Executive Action
Department ('Department V'). Twenty years in the field, prin-
cipally western Europe. Stanov skipped a few pages: he knew
there had been several notable successes, no glaring failures,
much competent work. Divorced 1971 (no children). Trans-
ferred to Centre 1979, Personnel Directorate. A poor fate for
an honest worker, therefore a reader of the file must assume
that this worker was not as honest as he looked. Stanov pursed
his lips. That had been a good move on his part.

He turned up the assessments. Until the transfer to Centre
these had been uniformly good; then they became guarded.
Bucharensky was a man under a cloud, reasoned the Personnel
Directorate; let us not do anything to dispel it.

Then, almost a year ago the sudden demotion; loss of pay;
removal to this shoddy apartment. And what must have made
it all so distressing to Bucharensky was that there had been not
the glimmer of an explanation: not here in his file, not in a
personal interview, not anywhere. Just the end of a career. A
year ago the assessments simply stopped.

Stanov put away the file. In fact Bucharensky had never
been assessed so thoroughly as over the past year. During that
time he was under 24-hour surveillance by hand-picked teams
who reported daily to Stanov or Yevchenko. Very few lives
could undergo that treatment and not show signs of cracking.
But Bucharensky had not cracked. As far as Stanov could learn,
no word of complaint had passed his lips over the last 12
months. Instead he had stoically endured what must have seemed
the worst thing ever to happen to him. Stanov was satisfied.
He was about to entrust this man with what remained of his
own life.

'He's coming.'

Stanov nodded to show that he had heard and squeezed into
the far corner of the back seat. Through the windscreen he saw
a man walking towards them, his arms laden with brown paper
parcels. The face was familiar to Stanov from numerous photographs. Bucharensky did not look up from the pavement until
he was almost level with the car. Then he became aware of
Yevchenko standing by the open door.

'Raise arms, please, comrade Captain.'

Bucharensky obediently put down his parcels, lifted his arms and waited while Yevchenko frisked him.

'Get in.'

Bucharensky immediately bent down to obey. Not even the sight of the Stechkin in Stanov's gloved hands caused him to hesitate.

'Good morning, comrade Marshal', he said carefully. He sat rigidly, staring straight ahead, trying to look as though he were at attention.

'You have been shopping, Captain?' said Stanov, his voice testy.

'Yes, comrade Marshal. It is my free day. I have been saving up . . .'

His voice tailed off.

'Show me what you have bought, please.'

Bucharensky undid his parcels one by one, careful to pre- serve the paper for future use. A borodinski loaf, pickled cu- cumber, herring, a very small bottle of vodka. Stanov raised his eyes from these modest purchases and said,

'You have to save up for such things, Captain?'

For the first time Bucharensky turned his head towards Stanov. 'Yes, Comrade Marshal.'

Stanov nodded. 'Today', he said, after a short pause, 'we are going on a picnic. Don't worry, we have brought our own food. There are many things I have to say to you.'

Yevchenko took the road to Usovo. In less than an hour they were deep in the wooded hills of the countryside. The car pulled up at the bottom of a steep, muddy track and the three men got out.

'Now', said Stanov, pulling his overcoat more squarely on to his shoulders, 'we climb.'

Even with the basket which he was ordered to carry Bu- charensky found the going easy. For the two old men, however, it was a different story; they puffed and struggled up the gentle incline until by the time the trio reached the top Bucharensky was having to support the combined weights of his elderly companions as well as the hamper.

At the end of the climb they emerged on to a grassy saucer of land set into the hillside, well-protected from the wind by fir trees on three sides, with a dramatic view over the plain across which they had recently driven. This was not a place you would find by accident.

Yevchenko took a thick blanket from the basket and spread it over the nadir of the saucer before sitting down and dispensing tea. Seated on the blanket Bucharensky did not feel cold. At first he found it mildly amusing to watch the two old men bicker over the jars and containers in the huge basket, but once they began to unpack Beluga caviar, and salmon, and fresh river trout and venison his amusement was forgotten and he was conscious only of ravenous hunger. He looked away.

'Eat, Captain. You can't listen on an empty stomach.'

Bucharensky could hardly believe his ears. After a moment's hesitation he took a morsel of trout and began to chew it slowly, restraining an urge to stuff his mouth as full as possible. But even while he ate his mind was alert. Why, he asked himself, why this absurd expedition? Stick followed by carrot? He recognised the technique.

When Stanov judged the moment ripe he said: 'So as not to waste words, Captain, you may take it that your period of disgrace is over. In fact you were never in disgrace. We had to be sure of you, that's all.'

Bucharensky had found an earthenware pot full of apricot jam boiled in brandy syrup. He had cracked the wax seal and was now taking minute teaspoonfuls of the exotic preserve, leaving long, appreciative pauses between each. On hearing these words he nodded.

'I know, comrade Marshal.'

Stanov was enraged. 'How can you know it?'

Bucharensky looked up slowly and stared at Stanov. He spoke with quiet deliberation.

'Because although the KGB often makes serious and foolish mistakes it is too resourceful and too careful ever to make a mistake about the loyalty of one of its own officers, who has served it conscientiously and well.'

Bucharensky put down the spoon and folded his hands in his lap before quietly turning his head away from Stanov's scorching stare.

'I am sorry, comrade Marshal', he said humbly. 'But I resolved that I would speak those words on the day of my rehabilitation. I did not dream, of course, that I would have to speak them to you.'

Yevchenko broke the ensuing silence by asking curiously, 'Do you really mean that, in spite of all that happened to you, you never doubted that your position was, well . . . secure? Not once?'

'Often, comrade Colonel, but I knew I had done nothing wrong.'

Stanov eyed him malevolently over his glass of tea.

'So the KGB makes mistakes, does it?'

'Yes, comrade Marshal.'

Yevchenko started to laugh. 'You chose well, old man' he said. Then Stanov too began to laugh, and after a moment Bucharensky joined in, happy for the first time in twelve weary months.

When they were all serious again Stanov commenced the briefing.

'Tell me, Ivan Yevseevich, tell me how you would defect to the West.'

This question rang coldly in Bucharensky's ears. The more he focused his mind on it the less he liked it. Was there a trap? Should he tell the exact truth? He decided on a middle course.

'I would try to reach a European city with which I was familiar. There I would approach the American embassy. Clandestinely, of course.'

'Of course . . . I suppose in your case Athens might be an appropriate starting point—you were stationed there for five years.'

'Or Brussels. Brussels for choice, although it is true I have spent time in both places.'

'London perhaps?'

Bucharensky looked up sharply. What did they know about London? But the faces of the two old men showed nothing.

'Certainly. Although London is not as close to Moscow as the other two places.'

'Think about this. We know where you were stationed, it's in your dossier. We would guess where you were probably making for. We would try to stop you.'

Bucharensky nodded unwillingly. The thought had occurred to him, but he was still wary.

'Would you keep to your original plan?'

Bucharensky saw that they were smiling at him. He was not sure how to formulate his reply. Stanov continued: 'I think you would. Because in those foreign cities you, like everyone else who has ever worked abroad, have money, a new personality perhaps, even a safe house. Insurance. Which we don't—officially—know about. Am I not right, Ivan Yevseevich?'

Bucharensky nodded again. There was no hostility in these questions.

'A moment ago we mentioned Brussels. Why is Brussels so important to us, and our finances in particular?'

'The money-route, do you mean?'

'Precisely. What do you know of that?'

'Outgoing money is laundered in Brussels via the Skaldia-Volga factory payroll. Some of it is paid out there, to the Red Brigades and so on. When I was in Belgium, Baader-Meinhof used to benefit, as did ETA. Arms are paid for in Brussels—I remember the panic in '71 when the Dutch seized Ominipol guns at Schipol because it could all have been traced back to the money-route. Then whatever is left goes on to London, Dublin and Belfast where some of it is used to arm and train the Provisional IRA, and then the rest goes to America.' He shook his head. 'That's all I know.'

'Very good. But tell me this—why is it that you, who worked in Europe for 20 years, know so little about the money-route?'

'It was not my business to know. I had no need to know.'

'Precisely. Everything in compartments. Share nothing beyond what you have to. Trust no one.' Stanov paused. 'The KGB is centralised, is it not?'

'So they taught us at spy school.'

'And the consequence is that only a handful of people at its head, six or seven at most, can ever hope to know most of what goes on.'

'Right.'

'So that below this supreme level people can see the most extraordinary things happen without being surprised, because they assume it's no business of theirs.'

'Certainly. I have been in just that position myself, many times.'

'And unless the people at the top are vigilant beyond the norm these extraordinary things may escape their lofty notice?'

This time Bucharensky did not reply. His mind began to race ahead, looking for bolt-holes. Stanov continued.

'Let me now pull together these strands, Ivan Yevseevich, so that you may see the point of all this. Somewhere in the KGB the British Secret Intelligence Service has managed to install a traitor. Putting it at its simplest, we would like you to find him for us. In order to do so you are going to defect to the West, apparently taking with you information of vital importance concerning our money-route and our project-plans. That, at least, is the story for your colleagues.' He paused. 'But some of those colleagues—your superiors, you understand—and the British will be told that you carry in your head the name of the traitor.'

Bucharensky blinked. The alarm bells had been sounding for some time now. He chose his next words as carefully as if his life depended on them, sensing that it might.

'There are many local operatives, comrade Marshal, whose familiarity with the cities you mention and their *referenturas* . . .'

Behind him Yevchenko methodically started to stack plates. When he had done that he began to toss cutlery into the hamper. The jangling got on Bucharensky's nerves.

'The leak is not in the *referenturas*, Ivan Yevseevich. Those are merely the local offices of the KGB.'

Stanov allowed the silence to develop. For Bucharensky the day had suddenly become cold again.

'Has it ever occurred to you to ask why we are squatting in this isolated spot, having come here in a beaten-up old car, armed, when we might have been sitting comfortably in my office, comrade Captain?'

Bucharensky said nothing. The question had never been far from his mind since the expedition started. Stanov turned to look him full in the face.

'It is because I, Voldemar Pavlovich Stanov, Marshal of the Soviet Union and Chairman of the KGB am, on the express orders of the Politburo, being followed by my own Seventh Directorate!'

Bucharensky looked away and said nothing.

'And they could be right. It could be me. It isn't, but our problem—yours too, now—is that it could be. And on the other side it is just the same. I am convinced that one man, and one man alone, has dealings with this traitor, and that is the Head of the British Secret Intelligence Service himself. You will be flying very near the sun, Ivan Yevseevich.'

He allowed the words to sink in. Yevchenko had finished packing the basket and was listening quietly.

'I will not burden you with the hours of work I have done in order to find this truth; suffice it to say they have been *long*. It is necessary for someone to spread out the whole picture on the table in front of him and go back years; that is the first thing. Only the Chairman can do it. My predecessors either did not bother or were too stupid to understand the results. Perhaps they wilfully refused to credit something terrible, I do not know. But once you have done the groundwork the truth becomes terribly simple, Ivan Yevseevich. It is, in effect, that for the past fifteen years and more we in the KGB,' he waved his hand to embrace everyone, 'all of us, have been missing the point.'

If he expected a reaction from Bucharensky he was disappointed.

'It is all to do with *dezinformatsiya*. For years now we have successfully been feeding false information to the West. On half a dozen important occasions, however, they have either not been completely taken in or have somehow been able to retrieve their position without difficulty. And on three, precisely three and only three occasions of consummate, vital, desperate urgency, they have rejected the information altogether.'

He paused. A cold wind was blowing up from the southeast, strong enough to penetrate even this sheltered spot. Soon it would snow.

'It does not sound much, does it? Nine occasions in all. But Ivan Yevseevich, if you were in my position and could see the Russian lives lost as a result, the man-hours wasted, the advantages thrown away . . . if you could add up the total damage over the years, you would mourn. And you would want to know who was responsible.'

His face darkened.

'The first two times of vital importance it was made to look as though the information never got through, thwarted by forces of nature beyond the control of the intelligence services concerned. But the last time, a matter of months ago, I was already suspicious and so was able to inspect the scene at once. The message was borne by a man, a man so important to us that only Yevchenko and I knew his name, we thought. But the man died, a week before he was due to attend the OPEC conference and deliver such a blow to the western world as you could not dream of. When I *think*...'

Bucharensky looked at the old man's clenched fists and closed eyes, fascinated. Such things were not meant for his ears.

'There was an avalanche. He was skiing. Eighteen other people died. It was not a natural occurrence. I know it. The members of the Politburo know it. Nothing has been said openly. But we require answers.'

Bucharensky broke silence at last.

'How soon?'

'The beginning of July.'

Bucharensky nodded. Nearly 6 months. Here was something practical at last, something within his province.

'If by then the answer is not known I shall be replaced. I tell you this because I want you to be under no illusions: the Politburo has spelled out the consequences of failure very clearly.'

He lowered his voice, so that Bucharensky was not sure whether he was supposed to hear, or if the old man was talking to himself.

'Believe me, you are the last, the very last chance. I have tried everything. For months at a time I have concentrated on each of these six or seven candidates for the role of traitor. Nothing! I have kept them under constant surveillance: they can't shit without me knowing the colour and consistency. I have laid false trails. I have fed them lies. I have sent each of them abroad and had them watched. Let me show you...' He snapped his fingers and Yevchenko handed him a file. 'This is the record of what I have done. Look at it!'

Bucharensky took the thick file. He read it quickly, skimming whenever possible, astounded at the extent of the oper-

ation, the time, the thoroughness, the lengths to which Stanov
had gone not only to prevent the subjects from knowing that
they were being watched, but also to keep this same information
from the men detailed to do the watching. Can this be happening, he asked himself over and over again, here in the
headquarters of the KGB? The whole machine turned in upon
itself . . . it was unreal. When he had finished he stood up and
walked to the edge of the clearing to stand with his back to it,
staring into the forest.

Eventually Stanov called to him.

'Nothing has worked. And every time I fail I go back to
the Politburo and they say: what now, Voldemar Pavlovich?'

The old man raised his eyes to Bucharensky's face.

'How long have I been Chairman of the KGB, Ivan Yevseevich?'

'Eight years, comrade Marshal.'

'And in that time, how many sleepers do you think I have
put to bed, in how many countries? How many plans? How
many networks laid? How many long, slow fuses have I lit?'
He laughed suddenly. 'Why don't I just retire? Why don't I
go away and let someone else sort it out? I could, you know.
That's what my *friends* in the Politburo say! Well, I shall tell
you, Ivan Yevseevich, I am not about to see a lifetime's
achievements thrown into the garbage pit. Albania!' He clapped
his fists to his forehead and closed his eyes. 'When I think of
the plans I have prepared for that benighted little country! How
near we are!' His eyes opened. 'Do you think I am going to
leave that *now?* Give it to some buffoon who instead of gently
prising the fruit from the tree would wait for it to rot on the
bough and then trample on it when it fell? No! On July 1st I
shall still be here, Chairman or dead.'

His voice became a whisper. Bucharensky leaned forward,
hypnotised.

'It will be my last duty to the Soviet Union. To root out
this traitor. And to save the KGB from . . . Kazin.'

At the sound of the name everything fell into place for
Bucharensky. Kazin, the Party theoretician and member of the
Politburo, a civilian without either knowledge or experience of
the KGB, a man thirsty for blood and the purification of another
purge, or so it was rumoured in Dzerzhinsky Square.

Other memories, other rumours came flooding back. 'Stalin's baby', that is what they used to call Kazin, and for years he had wondered why. Was it because when late at night they came to take the Monster to bed they would find him sitting beside the fire, Kazin kneeling at his feet? Or did some deeper, less savoury mystery lie concealed beneath the ironic phrase? Whatever the answer, the primal influence on Kazin's character was not in doubt. He was Stalin's man, would be to the last . . . and he was one of Nature's survivors.

For years he had been Stanov's sternest critic, baying for reforms and a more flexible approach to the modern techniques of espionage and internal security. Now the Politburo was dangling his opportunity in front of his eyes: either Stanov succeeded or the Chairmanship of the KGB would pass from his hands into Kazin's. Bucharensky shut his mind to it. It must not happen. No one could count himself safe under Kazin. It *would* not happen.

Stanov was speaking again.

'Someone near the top of one of the departments, here in Moscow. Someone who has been so careful for so long, someone with the nerve, the insolence and the rank to say to the West: I will not help you every time, I will not be your lackey, but when it is a matter beyond life or death, a matter of your survival, *then* I will help you. No matter what it costs, I will be there . . .'

For a while the three of them sat in silence, each engrossed in his own thoughts. Stanov spoke again.

'Let me tell you about the two occasions when this man acted, Ivan Yevseevich. The first was in Mexico, in 1971. Perhaps you know the story . . . 'Nuthatch', the operation was called. The man Gomez who was controlled by Nechiporenko from the *referentura*, it was his job to proclaim the *Movimiento de Acción Revolucionaira*. Everything was ready after years of work: explosives, arms, money. It could have set South America alight. It was brilliant . . . and it failed. Gomez was arrested. Five of our best agents were expelled. Total humiliation, not a voice was raised to help us. Then there was London. September 24th, 1971, 105 Soviet agents expelled from the United Kingdom. Lyalin 'defected'. The whole of Department V in Europe, Asia and Africa devastated at a stroke.

Pavlov in Montreal, General Vladimirov in Helsinki, Yevdotev in Bonn . . . the list was endless.'

'I remember.' Bucharensky could not help himself. 'We were all called in. No one was left on the streets. For days we waited in the embassy cellar, crowded round the telex machine. It was like the end of the world. But what is this to do with a traitor in Moscow?'

'Lyalin did not defect. It was a blind. He was tortured until he had told all he knew and then he was killed by SIS. He was the only agent in Europe to carry the names of the others in his head. His visit to England was supposed to be a total secret. But they knew he was coming. And they knew what even Lyalin himself did not know: that he had been doctored in such a way as to be allergic to scopolamine derivatives. The first injection of a conventional truth-drug would have killed him. But they used a massive dose of Pentothal instead. Do you begin to see? On both occasions our oh-so carefully prepared disinformation was utterly without effect. The British knew the truth.'

Bucharensky nodded.

'It was then that I first began to concentrate my suspicions on England. Such a sensational coup did not occur in a vacuum. By jettisoning the other NATO-pact countries from the scope of the inquiry many things at once became clear. We are looking for a man with a peculiar affinity for England, perhaps someone who harbours a personal relationship with the Secret Intelligence Service. I need to provoke this man—and quickly—into betraying himself. For this I have chosen you, Captain Bucharensky.'

'I shall be honoured, comrade Marshal.'

His voice was vibrant, and as he heard it Stanov's hopes rose. The gamble had paid off. Here was a man he could trust, and it had not after all been necessary to reveal exactly how near 'Masked Shrike' was to fulfilment and for that reason how desperately Stanov needed to be back in complete control by 1st July. Perhaps it was not impossible after all . . .

'Good. Then suppose the following. An officer of the KGB has fallen out of favour. Let us call him . . . Kyril. Everyone recognises the smell and keeps well away from him. Then one day, without warning, he is promoted full colonel, taken from his lowly quarters and installed in an apartment in the Sivtsev

Vrazhek district, supplied with his own chauffeur-driven Chaika and assigned to Marshal Stanov as his personal assistant in charge of co-ordinating liaison between the Main Directorates.'

'Since for all practical purposes there is no liaison between the Main Directorates', Yevchenko broke in, 'everyone will be suspicious at once.'

'Now this Kyril is a taciturn man', Stanov continued, 'not given to gossip, and so his colleagues must speculate as best they can—and they do. Soon the news is all over Centre; soon it has reached London.

'Then one day Kyril simply disappears. The lure of the West has proved too strong. Money, a new life . . . and now that he is an important man he is worth something to the British and their precious DI6.'

His voice became sharp.

'And it is known that while in London on an earlier tour of duty this Kyril formed an attachment to a woman. A woman who never married after he left her, possibly a woman who waits . . .'

Bucharensky closed his eyes. He could see her face so clearly, hear her voice, feel her hands cupping his face.

Vera. *They knew*.

'Do you see now, Captain, why I have chosen you for this mission? Anyone with access to your dossier will at once assume that you are making for only one possible destination—London. So much for the first, "official" version of your defection. But there is another story, one so secret that it circulates only in the very highest echelons of Dzerzhinsky Square—that Kyril has managed to uncover the name of a traitor within the Organs. Can it be true? Apparently yes, because within the hour the Chairman of the KGB has personally given the order: find this man, find him at all costs, for here is no ordinary defector. Find him *alive* and bring him to me *alive;* the fate of our country depends on it, for as well as knowing this traitor's identity he has stolen one of our most sensitive plans. What will happen then, Ivan Yevseevich?'

Bucharensky thought for a moment.

'The traitor will alert the British.'

'Yes. And then?'

'Every KGB agent in the world has been detailed to find

the defector . . . DI6 will try desperately hard to get to him first, to protect their source from disclosure and to retrieve this mysterious plan.'

'I believe so. The "plan", of course, is nothing but an added bonus, a lure. But the important thing is that none of this can happen in isolation. The traitor must act. Yevchenko and I will be watching closely to see who jumps. As of that moment Kyril will become a priceless commodity to both sides.' Stanov smiled a wintery smile. 'He will have to be quick on his feet. Many people all over the world will urgently wish to talk to him.'

'But comrade Marshal, where is Kyril to go?'

'To Athens. At least at first. Then on to Brussels and London. You remember what you said earlier: if you were going to defect you would try for certain cities where you had . . . assets. All former fieldmen have such assets, it is well known. Kyril is no exception. He must show himself to both sides while at the same time evading them. A message will go from our embassy in Athens to Moscow, and the head of the Eighth Department of the First Main Directorate. I shall be watching, for I will know Kyril's movements to the nearest half-hour. I will give him a detailed itinerary, to which he must stick *without fail*. If anything goes wrong—if that vital message from the embassy is delayed, or distorted, or slanted —then I may have found the source of the leak.'

'I am sorry, comrade Marshal, I do not understand.'

'The leak in our organisation, the traitor, will, I believe, have a first loyalty to the British in a case of this importance. Besides, he will be anxious to protect himself, and there DI6 will be far better placed to help, for unlike the KGB they will not necessarily have orders to take Kyril alive. So the traitor will not pass on the alert to KGB Athens, even though it emanates from the Chairman himself, without first ensuring that England has a head start on his own men. And he will not pass on anything *from* Athens until he is sure that DI6 is there ahead of us. He is off-balance, his life is in danger, he may do irrational things. If he does, I shall see.'

Stanov leaned forward to place a hand on Bucharensky's shoulder.

'You are Kyril. I do not underestimate the danger, comrade Captain. You must make sure that you are seen but not captured, not once but three times.'

Bucharensky looked him in the eye and smiled.

'And the traitor', he said lightly. 'What will he do all this time, eh? Watch with a kindly eye while I slip across Europe, ready to expose him if I fall into the wrong hands?'

Stanov released his shoulder.

'You are right. It has to be said. At first he will be uncertain. That is when he will make mistakes and I hope to catch him out. But suppose he can survive the first dreadful 48 hours. He recovers his nerve. He begins to make survival plans. The British . . . want you alive or dead, but if the "project plan" which you are reputed to have stolen is attractive enough, better alive. The Russians, the traitor's own men . . . they certainly want you alive. But he, he needs you dead, and very quickly, for if DI6 are not quick enough, and Kyril falls into *my* hands, and talks, then for him there is only a bullet in the Lubianka cellars. So every time you escape, the traitor's confidence in DI6's ability to stop you will weaken and the chances increase that he will panic and send an executioner after you, to kill you before you can be unmasked. But if he does try to kill you we shall hear of it, and that in itself will help us in our task of pin-pointing the traitor.

'No back-up, no emergency stand-by?'

'Nothing. Every KGB officer in the world will have orders to hunt you down. So will every SIS agent. One of them, maybe more than one, will have orders to kill you.' He hesitated. 'There may come a time when SIS decide to liquidate you before you are captured by us, purely in order to maintain the secrecy which protects the traitor. I hope not. I hope that if I can convince the British that you are carrying one of our most cherished project-plans, they will delay for as long as possible in the hope of interrogating you alive. But . . . well.'

'And if I get to London?'

Stanov sat back. Bucharensky could hear him sucking his teeth. The seemingly innocent question appeared to have cast a blight over the briefing.

'Ivan Yevseevich, I am going to tell you a secret. I do not want to. But it is necessary.' Stanov paused. Bucharensky could not begin to imagine what was coming.

'Scattered throughout the world there are a handful of men

who report only to me. They are not members of the KGB at all, not as you know it. They owe only one loyalty: to the Chairman. To me. They are in touch with no embassy, no *referentura* holds their files. But in their own way they are more powerful than even the KGB residents.'

Bucharensky saw that Stanov was watching him out of the corner of his eye. He was at a loss to know what to say. Such irregular agents went entirely against the whole underlying philosophy of the bureaucratic machine. To employ them was to open oneself to a charge of treason.

'A valuable weapon', Bucharensky ventured cautiously. 'As long as things go well.'

Stanov nodded. 'You come very quickly to the point, Captain. One of these agents in England is called Loshkevoi.' He smiled wryly. 'Kazin says I play it too much by the book. I don't. In fact if he knew about Loshkevoi, and others like him, who are nothing to do with any book, he would be screaming for my head even louder than he is at present. And in a way he'd be right, because I can no longer trust Loshkevoi. He has been . . . diverted. There is interference. Subtle, but noticeable.'

Bucharensky raised troubled eyes to Stanov's face. The Chief had gone out on a limb, and as a result who knew how many lives were in danger. Stanov read his thoughts.

'As you say, Captain, a valuable weapon when things go well.' He grunted, then—'Find Loshkevoi', he said abruptly. 'He poses as a descendant of White Russian emigrés, running a garage in South London. The address will be in the phone book. Find him and make him talk. Be careful, because he's a powerful man. No one knows more about the money-route than Loshkevoi. He's supposed to be my direct liaison with the Provisional IRA: banker and adviser in one. So he has both money and thugs at his back; look out for yourself. But you *must* get him to talk, for either he knows who the traitor is or he can give you clues to his identity. I'm sure of it.'

'But how can you be sure?'

'The pattern is there. All signs point to England as being the traitor's first loyalty. The life has gone out of my most gifted, trusted agent in England. That by itself would suggest that the one we seek is using Loshkevoi as a pawn. But there is more.'

Stanov hesitated, as if trying to recall some long lost detail, to pierce an invisible veil.

'You remember the events of 1971 in London? The September Massacre, we called it then. I was still a Deputy Chairman only, but already Loshkevoi was established. He was to attend a secret meeting with Lyalin. But he never attended that meeting. Instead the British were at the appointed place. Oh, Loshkevoi had a good enough alibi at the time. He was supposed to have been involved in a car accident. I had the records looked up, and it was true, so I thanked my stars that Loshkevoi himself was not ambushed and taken. But suppose the traitor had arranged for the records of the accident to be faked? You see? Make no mistake, Captain: the ultimate goal and purpose of your mission is to find a way into Loshkevoi's head. Oh, I don't play down the importance of your race across Europe . . .' Stanov gazed into the distance and his voice fell. 'I see you as a rapidly moving, highly-charged magnet, sometimes attracting others to you, sometimes repelling them, but always, always, always forcing them to *move* and be *seen* to move. It is inconceivable that the British will not seek to open new channels of communication with their precious source when they learn that you are carrying his name, and once they do I can hardly fail to detect them. All that . . .'

Stanov flicked his fingers dismissively.

'But if you can find Loshkevoi and make him talk . . .'

Stanov paused and nodded with heavy emphasis.

' . . . We shall have the name, comrade Captain. I am convinced of it. I know it. All that matters. *The name!*'

The long speech was over.

Bucharensky thought about his instructions. As far as he could see they led to inglorious and inevitable death. As an experienced field officer he reckoned his chances of reaching London at less than ten per cent. But . . . it was somehow attractive. Anything was better than the crippling desk-work in Moscow, the loneliness, the deprivations; after the year he had just endured Hell itself could not be worse. He would see he drank some good wine, smoked a few packs of decent cigarettes before the end. Perhaps he could spin it out a bit; after all, he had spent most of his adult life evading the Americans and the British; also the French, the West Germans, the Dutch . . . and he knew his brothers in the KGB so well, oh so very well: how they thought, and acted, and reacted. Perhaps it was not impossible. Perhaps he would get to Brussels at least. And there was Vera, always Vera . . .

Besides, he had no choice. Better make the best of it.

'When do we start?'

Stanov exhaled a long breath.

'Tomorrow. Report first thing to the Voyentorg—they have a colonel's uniform ready for you. Then move into the new apartment, we will see you have everything you need. Take the rest of the day off. Dine somewhere expensive. Book a seat at the ballet. Kick a few arses. Make enemies. Don't worry, I'll back you. Act as a new member of the *nomenklatura* should.' Stanov nodded to Yevchenko. 'Give him the stuff.'

Yevchenko pulled a thick leather wallet from his overcoat.

'We are giving you this now so that you will be able to leave at a moment's notice if you have to. Guard it carefully. Four American Express cards, each in a different name. Travellers' cheques, $10,000. Letters of credit in Athens, Brussels and London. Four passports, all with valid visas. Back in the car, 200 rounds of ammunition.'

'Gun?'

'This . . . Stanov thrust the Stechkin into Bucharensky's hand and smiled. 'Why do you think we brought it?'

'Credit limit?'

'None. Although we want you also to use money and arms you have left for yourself in Greece, Belgium and London. Everything must look as far as possible as though you are genuinely defecting.'

Bucharensky took a deep breath and nodded.

'We anticipate that if you reach London you may have to buy a house. It is the only way you can hope to protect yourself, and you will need a secure base in order to interrogate Loshkevoi effectively. Pay cash if you can, or next best thing, banker's draft or whatever. Don't rent; buy.'

Bucharensky was still in the grip of astonishment.

'But comrade Marshal . . . I could simply disappear with all this.'

'You could', observed Stanov drily. 'In some ways you would be no worse off: evading the Intelligence services of East and West. Only then it would be for the rest of your life. We would never forget you . . . Kyril.'

Bucharensky laughed. 'I can assure you I had no intention . . .'

'I did not think you had. Next. No ciphers, no drops. Your isolation from Centre will be absolute and immediate from day one. You will be beyond our reach until the operation is brought to an end. Understood?'

'Understood.'

'One way or the other, matters should be settled by July 1st.' He hesitated. 'If Colonel Yevchenko and I should then be dead, papers will automatically be sent to the First Secretary of the Communist Party of the Soviet Union, informing him of all we know and commending you to him as a brave and loyal officer. He may believe it, he may not; that is a chance you must take.'

Stanov rose awkwardly to his feet, waving aside Bucharensky's offered arm.

'There is much more to tell you in the way of detail. Your briefing will be long and thorough, but all that can wait. I'm tired and it's getting cold out here. Any more questions?'

Bucharensky stood deep in thought for several moments.

'One thing. You are going to put it about that I have stolen a valuable project-plan. If you're going to make that stick it'll have to be one I'm in direct contact with in my new job, and something attractive to the West, a plan the loss of which would scare the hell out of the Politburo as well as my colleagues. And . . . well.' He hesitated, suddenly aware of his thought's true destination. 'It would increase the chances of SIS's deciding to capture me alive if that plan were important, really big.'

Stanov laughed.

'In my safe is supposed to be the only extant copy of Operation "Sociable Plover".' Noting Bucharensky's startled expression he added, 'It is the name of a bird, comrade Cap-

tain . . . or Colonel, as I must call you now. The file consists
of about 500 single-spaced pages and has attained "blue status",
which, as you know, means that only one copy can be in
circulation at any time. When you go, that file goes too.'

'And what is this . . . "Social Plover"?'

'Nothing. It does not exist. But your colleagues—yes, and
the British too—will be told that it is something we have been
working on since the War, that it sets out in precise and minute
detail the connection between the KGB and organised, worldwide terrorism: the history, the financing, including the money-
route, the co-operation, proposed joint operations, everything,
including the names of key agents, the numbers of secret bank
accounts, the locations of Soviet-financed and run training
centres, and much more. Can you imagine what the loss of
such a file, if it existed, would mean?'

Bucharensky gaped at him. For a hostile intelligence agency
the prospects would be irresistible. Mossad, for example, could
use the information to wipe out the PLO as an effective Middle
East force. The CIA could expose the KGB to the world as an
utterly unscrupulous, manipulative gang of thugs, no better
than the murderers they financed. Soviet foreign policy would
be set back years. Countless trusted officers of the KGB would
at best be rendered useless and at worst be exterminated as a
result of such a file falling into the wrong hands.

If Stanov could make his officers, and SIS, believe that
Kyril was carrying such a priceless weapon, they would turn
the world upside down in their search for him.

Stanov and Yevchenko were starting off down the path.
Bucharensky picked up the hamper and followed them, his
mind still reeling under the impact of what he had been told.

'The possessor of "Sociable Plover"', said Stanov over his
shoulder, 'could either dominate or effectively eradicate world
terrorism, as he pleased. Its "loss" will make those vultures in
the Kremlin shit their pants.'

2

The telephone made a noise like a clock about to strike the hour. Royston's hand lifted the receiver before the bell could ring while the rest of him was still struggling up to the surface of a deep sleep.

'Do you recognise the voice?'

Royston fought for bearings in his personal history. His sick daughter had cried in her sleep. Night ops., and the enemy were coming. The burglar downstairs making off with the silver. Special Branch at the door...

'I said, do you recognise...?'

'Yes, I know who you are.'

Royston was awake in the bedroom of the house in Sheen, his wife beside him, still asleep, his children grown up, the past dead. Cold sweat on his back and a less than steady hand were now the only links between him and the unquiet world beneath the surface.

'For God's sake, man, do you know what time it is?'

'Later than you think.'

Royston held his watch up to his eyes before realising that the caller intended this for a warning.

'What is it?'

He was fully awake now.

'Meet me in exactly 25 minutes at the junction with the South Circular. My car, not yours. Don't be seen if you can help it.'

A click heralded the purr of the free line. Royston swung his legs out of bed and went to stand by the window, partly out of professional instinct to see if there were watchers in the street, but mainly because he wanted to know what the weather was doing. In the glare of the white street-lamps the pavements glistened with drizzle. He sighed and quietly began to put on his clothes, while Jenny, his wife, slept on.

As well as being wet it was cold outside, typical March weather, and as Royston hurried along with his head down he prayed that Bonham wouldn't be late for the rendezvous. About half a mile from his house a phone-booth stood at the junction of the South Circular Road with a side-street. It took him eight minutes to reach it, allowing for an elementary detour to shake off any tails. From the shadow of the booth he had an uninterrupted view of the main road and of the street down which he had come. Both were empty. In the few minutes he had to wait he saw only two cars, both travelling west. Royston's dark mac and brown suede shoes, shrouded in the angle where the phone-booth met the wall, made no impression on their headlights.

Bonham was late. To divert himself Royston tried to devise stories that would satisfy the curiosity of an hypothetical policeman on the beat who chanced to find him leaning against the wall, wrapped up in a shabby old gardening mac. The ideas wouldn't come. Royston looked at his watch. Bonham was three minutes overdue. 'Exactly', he had said, when appointing the rendezvous.

Something was wrong.

For the first time Royston felt a stab of real curiosity about Bonham's mysterious phone call. It wasn't like him to use the telephone. It wasn't like him to be late, either.

Royston wanted to walk up and down, a process which helped him think, but resisted the impulse. Somewhere in London, something which affected Royston was happening without him. And it had gone wrong.

He was about to step from the shadows and damn the risk of being detected when he saw the lights of the car. The driver was coming up the long arm of the 'T' to the South Circular Road, the engine labouring in second. As Royston raised his head the front nearside indicator began to flash. The car idled to the junction and he saw it was Bonham's. Two steps took him across the pavement and in through the passenger door, already ajar; as he pulled it shut after him the driver revved the engine to drown the noise of the slam and engaged gear. A hidden observer might have seen Royston enter the car, provided he hadn't blinked at the crucial moment.

Bonham went gently through the gears, travelling east, and for a while there was silence.

'Whatever it is that keeps Five awake at nights', said Royston eventually, 'it had better be bloody important.'

Without waiting for a reply he took a portable electric razor from his mac pocket and began to shave, tracing progress with his fingertips. Royston's pointed, angular face was not well suited to electric shaving. As a young man his skin had been too sensitive; now, in his early fifties, the skin had slackened, making it hard for the rounded shaving-head to cut close inside the folds of the worry-lines.

'There's some after-shave in the dash', said Bonham, and Royston wrinkled his nose. 'Yes', he said. 'I can smell it. Is that why you're late? Been shaving, had you?'

'Another phone call. Sorry.'

'Exactly, you said. Twenty-five minutes exactly.'

Bonham moved his hand and the indicator warning-light glowed. As the car swung right Royston saw the locality sign reflected in the beam of the headlamps. Battersea, Clapham, Balham. He suddenly realised that Bonham was driving very carefully, well within the statutory limit. The tingle of apprehension which Royston had first experienced outside the phone booth was refining itself into a state of permanent unease.

He put the razor back in his pocket. 'Where's the fire?'

For a moment Bonham said nothing, but continued to concentrate on the road ahead. Then he turned to look at his passenger, just for a second, and in the reflected glow of the orange standards Royston saw that Bonham seemed older than his 45 years.

'Does the name Loshkevoi mean anything to you? No? We rather thought not. A couple of years ago the Special Branch raised a query on him. For the owner of a used-car-cum-garage business in Balham he was taking some pretty funny trips abroad. They ran the usual checks. Seems the Revenue weren't too happy about some of his trading accounts, but nothing else showed up. They put a note in the file and let it pass, you know how it is. Interested?'

Royston grunted. He had pushed back the passenger-seat and was now sprawled out as far as the Rover's limits would allow, his eyes level with the glove compartment. He was finding it hard to stay awake, or so Bonham must have thought, because now he raised his voice.

'Earlier tonight we took a look at Loshkevoi's business premises. There was some evidence of handling stolen cars . . .'

'Some evidence . . . ?'

The irony sounded through the drowsiness in Royston's voice, and Bonham smiled.

'The police said "some". I didn't press it.'

Another grunt from Royston.

'I went round myself. We had all night. Loshkevoi is currently assisting the police with their inquiries, and likely to be so for at least another eight hours. No one else lives over the shop, so we didn't have any worries. What fun. An armoury, for a start. Automatic weapons. Grenades. Hand guns. And rifles.'

'So Loshkevoi's a terrorist.' Royston sounded bored. This wasn't his line.

'With Kalashnikov AK-47s? American FC-180s? A pretty well-equipped terrorist, wouldn't you think? But you haven't heard it all yet. We found approximately £50,000 in hard currencies. Passport blanks. Secret compartments in some of the cars, large enough to hold a man. And a radio set, tuned to a short-wave band which we've been monitoring off and on for the past ten years. Without any great success, I may say. A band where the messages are invariably in code and the code-pattern is unmistakably Russian.'

Royston pulled his chair forward again and struggled upright.

'You're telling me', he said softly, 'that you've uncovered

a KGB treasurer . . . an armourer . . .'

'Yes.'

' . . . Who's been lying low, undetected, for . . . how many years?'

'He came here in 1944, when he was still in his teens, claiming to be a refugee from north Italy. Son of White Russians fleeing the glorious revolution by a neck, drifting from place to place, you know the sort of thing. He had papers that fitted, then. We're checking it out.'

'More than 30 years late', mused Royston. His unspoken conclusion hovered between the two men like an accusation.

'We're unlikely to find very much', agreed Bonham. 'I know. That's where you come in. Here we are.'

He swung the car on to the forecourt of a large garage: Royston got out and looked around. Some dozen cars were stationed to one side of the pumps, each with a fluorescent orange price-sticker on the windscreen. Above his head and all down either side of the forecourt tiny red and white flags fluttered and flapped in the breeze. By the light of the nearest street-lamp he read this week's Special Offer plastered across a fluorescent green board: half a dozen 'tumbler type' glasses. Royston had seen a hundred places just like it and never turned his head.

'Come on.'

With an uncomfortable start Royston realised that Bonham had silently materialised beside him and was hissing in his ear. The garage looked shut up and deserted. Bonham took him by the forearm and guided him through the darkness until Royston sensed an obstacle across their path. Bonham knocked quietly, using what was obviously a prearranged tattoo. A thin line of light appeared in front of the two men, turned into a rectangle, became an open door. Bonham hustled Royston through and an unseen hand closed it behind them.

The interior of what Royston now realised was a large workshop had a dreamlike quality about it. The only lighting was provided by a muted red glow from lamps strung round the walls at head level. Royston could hear muffled hammering in the far corner, and quite close to where they were standing a steady stream of white sparks illuminated the masked face of a welder.

'They're clearing up', explained Bonham. 'All nice and tidy for the morning. He had this knack of building the stuff into cars, you see.'

'He's never going to fall for that', muttered Royston. 'He'll know.'

'Of course he will.' Bonham's voice was tired but patient. 'That's the point. We're going to sweat him, aren't we?'

Royston frowned. 'You mean . . . you're going to leave the stuff lying around?'

'Of course. Then perhaps we might find out what chummy's up to.'

Royston had not hitherto credited DI5 with such imagination. The idea appealed to him, despite the risk.

'You'd better just hope that the Minister doesn't find out', he said grudgingly.

'That's why I was late', Bonham replied casually. 'That other phone call I mentioned, remember? Ever tried to get the Home Secretary in the middle of the night? Don't. That's my advice to you.'

'He actually wore it?' Royston sounded incredulous. Bonham did not answer. Instead — 'Come over here', he said. 'I told them to leave this one open for you.'

He led the way down the steps of an inspection pit. As Royston's foot touched bottom a torch flashed in his eyes.

'Who's this?'

'This is the guest I told you about, Superintendent. I'll even sign him in the club book, if you like.'

There was a moment of uneasy silence. Royston stood perfectly still and did not try to hide his eyes from the glare of the torch.

'It'll have to go in my report, Mr Bonham.'

'No it won't, Superintendent.' The torch was suddenly extinguished, and Royston was aware of whispering close by. Bonham must have sounded convincing, for when the torch came on again a few seconds later the beam was directed to the side of the pit.

'The brickwork looks new', said Royston.

'We're waiting to hear from Forensic on that.' The Superintendent's voice was a shade less hostile. 'Six months is my guess.'

'Look at this', said Bonham. The beam of the torch centred on a large cavity in the side of the inspection pit. Bonham put in his hand and withdrew it holding something heavy. Royston took it from him and with a tremor of excitement recognised an FC-180. The barrel felt cold and slightly damp. His fingers played with the trigger while his thumb, guided by instinct, found the switch to the laser sight. A thin red beam of light darted along the barrel. Royston turned the gun on end and looked up at the ceiling of the workshop. Thirty feet above their heads the red beam flickered across the corrugated iron, its focus still no bigger than a fivepenny-piece.

'Amazing.' Royston was slightly shocked to hear the awe in his own voice. 'Amazing.' Almost reverently he handed the automatic rifle back to the Superintendent, who wiped it with a handkerchief before replacing it in its hiding place beyond the wall.

'You say there are more of them?'

'Forty in all. Another forty Kalashnikovs. British SLRs. Mr Loshkevoi appears to do business internationally.'

'And you're just going to leave it all here ...'

Royston shook his head, dumbfounded by the audacity of it. Suddenly he had had enough of the suffocating, oily darkness. He wanted to breathe fresh air. 'Let's go up', he said.

Back on the workshop floor he took a last look round, while the Superintendent gave orders for bricking up the cavity in the pit wall. The operation seemed to be winding down; the welder had finished and somebody was starting to unsling the first of the several ropes of red light-bulbs which adorned the walls.

'Come outside', said Bonham, and Royston steeled himself for the pitch. Publicly the secret services enjoyed an unparalleled degree of mutual trust, co-operation and brotherly love. That was the official version. On the ground, in the undergrowth, it was different.

'Smoke?'

They were sitting in the Rover again. Royston accepted the proffered cigarette and inhaled gratefully, holding the smoke deep in his lungs.

'I suppose you're wondering why I brought you here.'

Royston said nothing.

'I wanted to convince you. I wanted you to see for yourself that we're not joking. Think about that. If you merely saw the photographs, heard about it in a briefing, would you believe it?'

Royston was forced to shake his head.

'We badly need someone on the inside, Michael. Someone who can get close to Loshkevoi, what is it you call it? "Befriending", isn't it? We want to borrow a P.4. A lawyer. The best.'

As Bonham said 'best' Royston launched into his prepared speech.

'You are well aware that P.4 is attached to DI6, furthermore that it operates solely and exclusively beyond the seas, beyond the jurisdiction of Five.'

'And you know that's a load of shit.'

Bonham's quiet voice was as controlled as ever but Royston could hardly mistake the anger in it. He registered, not for the first time, that heads were going to roll over Loshkevoi. In the operational files of the domestic security service tonight's find must represent a failure of monumental proportions. For Royston it was a seller's market.

Bonham paused, as if conscious that his self-control was less than perfect. When he resumed his voice was still tired but all emotion had been shaded out of it.

'I could name you every occasion on which P.4 has worked in England over the past 18 months. There are seven of them. All illicit. All without ministerial knowledge or sanction. The psychiatrist who treated a certain Member of Parliament for the two months immediately before he shot himself, that was one of yours. Not very good at his job, it seems. The architect who designed the security chambers in the basement of Sheikh Ab' A' Man's house in Cumbria. Are you telling me a copy of those plans isn't sitting in the safe at Vauxhall Bridge Road? Shall I go on? What about a certain highly respected venerealogist' in Wimpole Street . . .'

'My, my' said Royston. 'You have been working hard.'

'Hard enough. Well? Do we get our lawyer? Or do I go back to my office and prepare a regretful report stating that certain irregularities have come to light in DI6's conduct of one of its key sectors?'

Royston stubbed out his cigarette and said nothing for a moment, reasoning that it would do Bonham no harm to sweat a little.

'What's in it for me, then? Apart, of course, from avoiding the consequences of your burn.'

'What do you want?'

'A lift back to Vauxhall Bridge Road, for a start. By the way', he continued, as Bonham turned the ignition key, 'congratulations on finding out where DI6 has its London HQ. I always knew you people in Five were bright.'

Bonham braked hard to avoid a police Scimitar manoeuvring off the forecourt without lights, and swore.

'I want to know everything you know. Same day, same *hour*. Got it?'

'Yes.'

'Say "agreed".'

'Agreed.'

'That's better.'

'So long as it works both ways.'

'What?'

'Somewhere out there in your world, the world beyond the seas, there's a man listening for that transmitter. You'll be looking for him. If I know anything about the way you work, and I do, before 9.00 a.m. this morning there won't be a single out-station from Seville to Sydney which hasn't been set to work on Loshkevoi's name. I want to know what you find out. I have a *need* to know.'

Royston thought about it. 'All right', he said at last. 'I buy that. Now listen. There's rules, see? One. My man has to be protected at all times. Two. He reports only through me, right? You go near him and two things will happen very quickly: he'll shut up like an oyster and I'll post him to Katmandu on the next flight. Three. It's your job to get Loshkevoi to pick my lawyer out of the hat. If he wants another solicitor, that's tough.'

'All agreed.'

'Good.'

Traffic was beginning to pick up. Bonham passed several cars and cut in front of a lorry in order to make a left on to Vauxhall Bridge. Royston smiled to see how the standard of driving had declined since leaving Balham.

'Where's chummy being held?'

'Lavender Hill nick.'

'Right. This is the name. Sculby. S-c-u-l-b-y, Laurence. Got it? He'll be in the Law List.'

'Sculby', muttered Bonham, and Royston knew relief when he heard it. The car drew up outside London Station. Royston got out and stood on the pavement, a hand on the car's roof, his head bent to Bonham's level. Bonham wound down the window a fraction.

'Thanks', said Royston. 'Be in touch.'

As Station Chief Royston was able to go through the fandangle of electronic alarms without assistance, the only man who could. He went first to the cellars to reassure the Duty Officer, then to the first floor where they kept the Personnel files. Equipped with Sculby's bulky dossier he made his way upstairs to his office on the second storey.

It was an undistinguished room, hardly a fit place in which to enjoy the summit of a career. The wiring had originally been installed when the building was erected in the '20s; the light-switch was a nipple set in a round twat, easy to find with the fingers in the dark. Royston momentarily closed his eyes against the flashing white neon (which at least was new), waiting for the noisy hum which meant the strip-lighting had settled down. When he opened his eyes nothing had changed since yesterday. All was as it should be. The yellow net curtains, in need not just of a wash but of outright replacement; the bulbous, old-fashioned radiator under the stone window-sill; leather-covered dining-room chairs strategically positioned to cover holes in the threadbare grey carpet; upturned tin-lids still full of dog-ends. But the desk was brand new Ryman's, as was the swivel-chair behind it, and the green press-button telephone stood out brightly against the heavy black scrambler. Give it another year or two, thought Royston to himself, as he always did on coming in first thing, and I'll have renewed everything.

If they haven't renewed me first.

Royston dumped the file on to the desk and sat down in his swivel-chair, thinking that he was not often presented with a tailor-made opportunity for disposing of a subordinate as troublesome as Sculby. It was an ill wind...He opened the dossier's cover, read a few words; then the events of the night overtook him; he rested his elbows on the desk and placed his head in his hands.

They had caught up with Loshkevoi at last, then. For the past ten years not a day, not an hour had gone by without Royston wondering whether somewhere, out there in the London suburbs, a man was walking up to Loshkevoi with a warrant card in his left hand while he kept his right firmly closed over the gun in his pocket. He had evisaged the scene over and over again. The variations were infinite. Now at last it had happened. From where he was sitting Royston bleakly reviewed the possibilities, starting with merely inconvenient and going methodically through to bloody catastrophic; although if he had been sitting in the club to which his superiors had, after years of baulking at his polytechnic education, finally elected him, sipping port and watching his vowels, he would doubtless have described the worst in more prosaic terms. A bit of a bore, perhaps. Or: a singularly unattractive prospect.

But whatever the language, Royston didn't mean to spend the twenty declining years of his life in prison if he could help it.

3

To Bucharensky's astonishment, Stanov's office was locked on the outside. He struggled to get his breath back while Yevchenko fumbled with the keys. At last the double doors burst open.

Bucharensky thought the old man was dead. He sat slumped in The Chair, eyes closed, one arm flung awkwardly across his chest, and the room smelled terrible. At the sound of Yevchenko closing the doors, however, Stanov stirred and mumbled as if in pain.

On the desk in front of him lay a sheet of paper. Green stripe on blue flimsy. Flash signal. Urgent.

'What . . . time?'

Stanov's speech was slurred. He seemed to have trouble in recognising Bucharensky. Yevchenko looked at his watch.

'Seven.'

Bucharensky was trying to read the upside-down signal. Something about 'arrest' . . .

'Were . . . you . . . sleep', colonel. A . . . pologise.'

'It's nothing, comrade Marshal.'

Stanov indicated the signal with a slight movement of his

head. His voice echoed with plaintive surprise, the voice of a man faced with some outrageous breach of the rules.

'It's happened 'gain. Sure of it. Betrayed.'

The race through the darkened streets, the motorcycle escort, the howling sirens, Yevchenko's grim silence . . . everything fell into place. The smell Bucharensky had noticed earlier when he first came in. Human sweat. Terror. But only here, in this room. Outside, no one knew. Yet.

'It's time for you to go.'

The old man seemed to be only half in this world. His wide-eyed stare missed Bucharensky's eyes by inches. Kyril's heart contracted as he read the signs. A stroke. Not serious, perhaps, certainly not fatal, but a stroke nonetheless. The security-empire which was all he had ever known since he was a boy was teetering on the brink of the abyss. Outside, somewhere in the city, Kazin was waiting. Had he heard?

An icy hand seemed to clutch Bucharensky's heart. He knew the KGB. Kazin had heard.

'We are not ready.'

'I know.' The arm draped across the old man's chest shuddered in a feeble gesture of despair. 'Nothing . . . prepared. Your detailed schedule . . .'

He tried to rise, sank back, made his greatest effort yet:

'You must leave . . . today. Mus' talk . . . soon. Not now . . . tired . . . sleep . . .'

Yevchenko took Bucharensky roughly by the arm and hustled him out before closing the double doors behind them. Bucharensky opened his mouth to speak but Yevchenko laid a forefinger to his lips.

'He is right. You must go. Leave everything to me. But for the moment you have seen nothing. You know nothing. You have just arrived. Keep in character. Run a lightning check. Give out a few weeks' detention all round for inefficiency. Make them hate you more than ever before. Go.'

Bucharensky swung on his heel and made for the lift. After only a few steps, however, he was arrested by a croak from Yevchenko.

'The diary!'

Bucharensky froze. The old colonel came quickly to his side.

'Is it up to date?'

'Yes. I finished it last night. A piece of luck, that.'

They spoke in rapid whispers, their faces close to the wall, but even so Bucharensky looked nervously around. This diary was the linchpin of Stanov's plan. It lay concealed in a drain in the grounds of Bucharensky's new apartment-block, not so well hidden but that the KGB would find it when they ransacked the place after his 'defection'. It purported to be the daily record of Kyril's slow awakening to the presence of a traitor in KGB headquarters in Dzerzhinsky Square. On the third floor. The generals' floor . . .

It was the record of someone identified only as *'Lisa'*—the Fox. Bucharensky and Stanov between them had devised this pseudonym for the traitor, and it was through the pages of the diary that the KGB must be made to hunt.

'It is in its proper hiding-place?'

'Yes. I always replaced it myself, it was never kept in the flat.' Bucharensky could not keep the anxiety from his voice. 'Will it work, d'you think?'

'How could it not?' Yevchenko sounded surer than he felt. 'You stood at Stanov's elbow all this time. Closer even than I did. He is old and sick. Your sharp eyes would see many things that escaped his, that is what they will assume. And you would not be the first to keep a written record, evidence for later. "Who is Lisa?" they will ask. All except one. The one who knows who "Lisa" is . . .'

Bucharensky was unconsciously clutching the lapels of Yevchenko's tunic, almost pleading for his reassurance.

'The traitor will see through it . . . He will realise that it is a trap, we do not know his real name . . .'

'No! Did the old man and I not help you write that diary? Did we not dictate every sentence, every word? It has our blood in it, that book! There is more than enough to convince the traitor that you really know. Listen to me . . .'

Yevchenko took Bucharensky's arms and shook them free of his coat. Their suppressed tension was beginning to find expression in raised voices.

'You were almost certain of the identity of the traitor. Then you were sure but you lacked final proof. All this is plain to anyone reading the diary. *It will work!*'

In the silence that followed they could hear only their own laboured breathing. Bucharensky gave Yevchenko one last, imploring look, straightened his uniform and, without another word, marched off down the corridor.

The old colonel was right: he must act true to form. It was the start of the morning shift and to the great misfortune of those who were yawning their way on duty in KGB headquarters, Colonel Ivan Yevseevich Bucharensky had unexpectedly arrived.

In the office of the Chairman, Stanov remained slumped helplessly before the cable which lay on his desk. 'ORIOLE' ARRESTED, it read. NEST SEARCHED + PRODUCT FOUND + ASSIST AGAIN ASSIST + URGENT URGENT URGENT

'I, Victor Gregory Loshkevoi, wish to make a statement . . .'

The Russian sat at the rickety table which took up most of the floorspace in the tiny cell, forehead resting on his hands. The black writing at the head of the ruled A4 sheet coiled before his tired eyes. He desperately wanted to sleep but knew that he must keep awake. A statement. The one thing he did not wish to make. He had proved it by saying nothing at all for six hours while they worked on him in shifts, always going over the same ground, again and again, until at last they had left him alone with his exhausted, over-stimulated thoughts, and a sheet of paper on which someone had already written the words, 'I, Victor Gregory Loshkevoi, wish to make a statement . . .'

Keys jangled down the corridor and stopped outside his cell. Loshkevoi spread his fingers and through the gap saw the grille swing open to admit a pair of official-looking dark blue legs.

'This is what you asked for earlier.'

A second sheet of paper landed on top of the first. Loshkevoi screwed up his eyes in concentration. A list. Names.

'Solicitors. They all do Legal Aid work if you're short.'

Loshkevoi slowly raised his head. The voice was young. He saw it belonged to a fresh-faced constable in shirt-sleeves. Seeing him look up, the boy—to Loshkevoi he was a mere boy—smiled. Loshkevoi immediately lowered his gaze in the only defence he had against the insidious psychological warfare of love—and—hate.

'Cuppa tea?'

A cracked mug of reddish-brown liquid was deposited at Loshkevoi's elbow. He ignored it.

'That one's pretty good.' The young constable jabbed a thumb at the last name on the list. Loshkevoi said nothing.

'They're all okay. Except him.'

Again the jab. Through half-closed eyelids Loshkevoi read the name. Sculby.

'Claims he's never lost a case in this court. Way he operates, I'm not surprised, meself.'

With more jangling of keys the constable let himself out. He was about to clang the grille to when he seemed to hesitate.

'Seriously', he said. 'Do yourself a bit of good. You have that Mr Roberts. He's all right, he is. One of the boys. Know what I mean?'

As the keys clanked back down the corridor Loshkevoi nervously fingered the list while he strove to concentrate. The police obviously wanted to see Roberts on the case. The other names meant nothing to Loshkevoi. His head was going round and round with sheer fatigue. I, Victor Gregory Loshkevoi, wish to make a statement . . .

Never lost a case . . . not surprised . . .

'Sculby', he said aloud.

4

When the phone rang shortly after six, Laurence Sculby had already been up for an hour. From his chair at the desk the double-bed was visible through the half-open bedroom door, and in it the sleeping form of Judy, his current. Some men would have found that a distraction. Not Sculby.

At ten o'clock he was due to attend the West London Coroner's Court for the start of what promised to be a very long inquest. Most of Sculby's time over the past few months had been spent preparing for this case. He was deeply committed to it. A naked girl in his bed did not even begin to compete.

David Sanson had been a card-carrying member of the Communist Party and fully paid-up member of the TGWU. He was employed as a driver by a medium-sized firm of hauliers. Shortly before Christmas the drivers at the firm's Acton depot went on strike over threatened redundancies. Sanson did not work at the Acton depot but that did not prevent him from joining the picket line. At 7.30 a.m. on the first day of the strike there was trouble. Sanson died, his head staved in by a violent blow which a number of witnesses might (or might not) have seen delivered by the baton of a mounted policeman. The baton could not now be found. The dead man's fiancée had retained Sculby to attend the inquest.

It was right up his street, but even by his standards it was a plum. At 28 Sculby already had a reputation for being a 'difficult' lawyer with an impeccable pedigree of left-wing activism going back to his years as an undergraduate at the London School of Economics. On two occasions the Police had lodged formal complaints with the Law Society's Professional Purposes Committee in connection with his conduct of criminal litigation. Neither complaint had been upheld, but relations between Sculby and the Police were strained to breaking-point. No one on the inside was surprised when Sculby's name began to be mentioned in the same breath as Sanson's. No one doubted that Sculby would do the case as vitriolically as if his own brother lay buried in the cemetery, and several times more efficiently.

So when the phone rang shortly after six and Sculby lifted the receiver to hear Royston say, 'I'm having the Sanson case adjourned', he knew a moment of black, uncontrolled rage so powerful that he couldn't speak. The sheer bloody-minded effrontery of it struck him dumb.

'Oh you have to be joking' was all he could say, at first.

'I'm sorry, Laurie. I know how much it means to you.'

Judy, roused by the sound of Sculby's voice, was getting up. She stood naked in front of the dressing-table, combing the long blonde hair which cascaded almost to the cleft of her buttocks, and Sculby didn't even notice.

'*Meant* to me. That's a laugh. *You* said when I told you I'd got the Sanson papers, *you* said it was the best fucking thing that we'd had in years. Run it for all it's worth, you said. Do it so as they'll never forget you, in Fleet Street or anywhere else, and now all of a sudden it's pious bleat about what it meant to *me*. Jesus Christ, Michael, who the hell do you think I am?'

'I've said I'm sorry...'

'Well fuck that for a laugh. What about that woman out there who thought she was going to a wedding and ended up going to a bloody funeral? She's *paying* me, do you realise that?'

'We pay you...'

'That's different. That is totally different. That is so irrelevant...'

Judy came out of the bedroom, fully clothed, and picked up her handbag from the floor. She tried to catch Sculby's eye, failed, shrugged and went out to the kitchen.

'I'm adjourning it', Royston was saying. 'I'm not sacking you, am I, for Christ's sake? I'm not taking you off the case.'

'Well I won't adjourn it.'

'But the Police have already said they'll ask for an adjournment anyway.'

'And I'll oppose it.'

'Coroner won't, though.'

And Royston sniggered, a loathsome sound which echoed in Sculby's ears long after the call was over. The lawyer was aware of the coffee grinder going and Terry Wogan in the background. The snigger made him feel suddenly futile.

'I see', he said dully. 'Well, if that's how it is.'

In his anger he had stood up. Now he sat at the desk and tried to think productively. Judy put her head round the door, saw him slumped over his papers, shrugged again and disappeared. A moment later the front door slammed loudly. Sculby, a connoisseur of early-morning door slams, was not unduly worried.

'That's how it is', confirmed Royston. 'So ring up the office and get somebody sent down to agree to an adjournment, all right? And believe me, I wouldn't ask you if it wasn't important.'

'Sanson was important', said Sculby. He was no longer using the harsh, hectoring tone employed by trades union leaders to state the terms on which 'the lads' would settle. 'His fiancée was important. To themselves. And me.'

There was a short silence. When Royston spoke again his voice, too, had changed.

'But that's what it's all about, isn't it, Laurie? Giving up when it matters most...'

Sculby swallowed. 'You promise this is only a delay.'

'Yes. But something's come up and I need you. Now do I have you, Laurie?'

'Yes.'

'Good. It may come to nothing, I can't tell. All I want you

to do for the moment is be available. Just that. You may get a phone-call about a character called Loshkevoi. I'll spell that...'

Sculby picked up the pencil he had dropped on the floor in his earlier rage and wrote down the name.

'He's being done for handling stolen cars. I've arranged for your name to be fed to him. He may bite, he may not. If he does, stick with him. Do your level best for him, no holds barred. I want that man to love you, Laurie. I want him to see in you the dead father, long-lost brother and innocent child he never had, all rolled up in one. Okay?'

'And if there's no phone-call?'

'Then forget it. You don't try to contact him. I'll be in touch.'

Royston hung up. Sculby replaced the receiver on its cradle. He realised he was hungry.

Judy had left a note for him propped against the coffee-grinder: something about the Albert Hall and two tickets. He screwed it up and threw it in the trash without trying to decipher it further, then made himself some toast and black coffee, which he carried back to the living-room and proceeded to bolt. While he was still chewing the last mouthful of toast he dialled the home number of one of his partners and tersely explained that on account of an overnight development he wouldn't be in a position to fight the Sanson case after all, and he wasn't going to be in before lunchtime. The partner promised to arrange for an adjournment by consent.

No sooner had Sculby replaced the receiver than the phone rang.

'Is that Mr Sculby?'

'Speaking.'

'Mr Laurence Sculby, the solicitor?'

'Yes.'

'Detective-Sgt. Fitzgerald, Lavender Hill police station here. I am telephoning on behalf of one Victor Gregory Loshkevoi. He has been charged with handling stolen property, contrary to section 22 subsection...'

'Yes, I'm familiar with it, Sergeant. Go on.'

'He wishes to retain you as his solicitor to act for him in preparing his defence.'

It amused Sculby to hear the undisguised hostility in Fitzgerald's voice. 'When's he coming up?'

'Ten o'clock this morning at Lavender Hill Magistrates' Court.'

'I'll be there. You're not going to try to attach any stupid conditions to bail, I suppose?'

'We shall oppose bail.'

'You'll do what?' scoffed Sculby, but the line was dead. He stared at the receiver as if seeking confirmation that he had heard correctly, and shook his head. The filth never ceased to amaze him.

He took a cab all the way from Kilburn to Clapham, knowing that Royston would pay. He spent the journey sunk in depression, staring vacantly out of the window. This was his daily grind. Most of his time-sheets recorded visits to obscure magistrates' courts on the outer fringes of London in buildings never designed for the purpose, where he would trade cigarettes and sometimes larger favours with bored policemen while together they engaged in the most common of legal practices— waiting for something to happen. Today should have been different.

He was at Clapham by half-past nine. For Sculby, the worst moment always came on entering the cell. Each one looked alike: brick walls painted dark green to chest height and pale green thereafter; a dark stripe round the room at the level where a man's head would leave a grease-mark if he sat long enough; a table and a chair. Through the narrow doorway Sculby saw these familiar things and unconsciously squared his shoulders.

Loshkevoi was sitting at the table, head in hands. At the sound of Sculby's entry he rose to his feet and retreated until he was standing with his back to the far wall.

'Mr Loshkevoi?' breezed Sculby. 'I'm a solicitor, my name's Sculby, and I'm here to see what I can do for you. As an arrested person charged with an indictable offence you have certain rights, one of which is to apply for bail...'

Sculby continued with his easy-going, reassuring speech, reminding Loshkevoi of his rights, outlining the cash limits for Legal Aid, inquiring about his client's means. But underneath he was troubled. Loshkevoi had a bad smell to him. He was tall and thick-set and fit-looking, obviously a man to have on your side in a fight if at all possible, and his neatly-trimmed black beard gave him the appearance of one who has secrets to hide. Fatigue would account partly for his haggard look, but there was more to it than that. Someone had got to Loshkevoi. He was running scared.

Sculby paused, so as to give his latest client a chance to speak. Loshkevoi muttered something incomprehensible. He seemed dazed.

'I'm sorry?'

'I said I'm ... I have committed no offence. I do not ...'Loshkevoi shook his head from side to side. 'I do not know what is happening to me. I am in your hands, Mr Sculby.'

The deep bass voice was hoarse with strain.

'Let's take it a step at a time, shall we? Bail, that's the first thing. Let me explain about court procedure ...'

Loshkevoi's case was called on first. A Detective-Sergeant outlined the charges and asked for an adjournment pending further enquiries. Sculby formally stated that his client would plead not guilty and reserve his defence; he had no objection to a remand, provided it was on bail.

'Sergeant?'

'I oppose bail, Sir. We have reason to believe that further offences may be committed and evidence destroyed if bail is granted.'

'I protest!'

Sculby was on his feet. The Stipendary Magistrate raised his hand. 'All in good time. Anything else from the police?'

'No, Sir.'

'Now, Mr Sculby ...'

'Sir, I would respectfully remind you of the provisions of the Bail Act. My client has no previous convictions. He is prima facie entitled ...'

The magistrate listened stoney-faced for five minutes while Sculby said everything he could think of on Loshkevoi's behalf. Then—

'The prisoner is remanded in custody for seven days.'

Behind Sculby there was a sudden commotion. Loshkevoi was standing in the dock, his hands grasping the rail in front of him, while two policemen struggled to restrain him. He had hurled himself forward with such violence that his body was bent almost double over the bar of the dock. The subdued man whom Sculby had interviewed in the cells was gone; in his place was a frenzied, white-faced maniac.

'Get me out!'

Sculby's jaw dropped. He looked helplessly from the bench to the dock, and back again. 'Be quiet', he hissed. 'You'll do yourself no good.'

'Sculby, I'm telling you...'Loshkevoi's voice was a bare croak. '*Get me out.*'

'Take him down', said the magistrate.

5

While Sculby was shaving that morning, the government communications centre at Cheltenham finally cracked the runaway code.

They called it the runaway code because transmissions invariably disintegrated into repetitions of the same group of letters, then of one letter, then silence. It was only two weeks old, and for most of that time it had been sitting in the SIS computer, subjected to millions and millions of electronic operations designed to analyse its mysteries.

The print-out of the latest message together with a copy of the key were finally delivered at about 8 o'clock on the morning after Loshkevoi's arrest. Shortly after nine, Telecommunications reported a worldwide transmission emanating from Moscow, destination all embassies and consulates. The monitors sat up. This was unusual. They were using the runaway code. Fingers began to tingle. The message was sent to Computer Operations under a red flag. Less than an hour after the transmission had ceased 'C' was being dragged from a meeting to inspect the product.

He arrived back in his office to find it unusually crowded.

The head of the Inquisition was there, together with the Director of Planning and the Chief of Staff. Sir Richard Bryant put on his gold-rimmed half-spectacles and read the cable lying on his desk.

'REDFIRE + COL IVAN YEVSEEVICH BUCHARENSKY DESERTED MC 03 MARCH + CASENAME KYRIL + BELIEVED SEEKING BRITISH CONTACT VIEW DEFECTION + POSSESSION TOPMOST SECRET DOCUMENTS + POSSESSION IDENTITY SIS CONTACT MC + ALL STEPS NEUTRALISE SHORT SHUTDOWN + SECURE PRIMEMOST + REDFIRE END + +'

'Redfire' was the most urgent classification a Soviet transmission could carry. Two of the men present in C's office had never seen one.

'I don't understand this', said C. 'What is the meaning of "shutdown"?'

'Execution', explained the head of the Inquisition. 'They want him alive.'

'I see.' Bryant pondered the explanation. 'Hardly surprising, in the circumstances. What do you have on this . . . Bucharensky?'

'The file is coming across from Registry. Meanwhile we have a photograph for you.'

The Director of Planning turned to the IBM console that was built into the side of C's desk and tapped out some figures, while the Chief of Staff drew the curtains. A picture was flashed on the far wall. They all turned to look at the face of the one the Russians called 'Kyril'; sad but friendly, the kind of man your child could safely talk to in the park. From the darkness C spoke.

'Find out the Colonel's movements. Seize him alive by any means possible.' He paused, so as to give his next words greater emphasis. 'You are to regard this as a major emergency. I am prepared, if absolutely necessary, to risk a diplomatic incident. But bring him to me, alive, here, in one piece. If you all manage to achieve nothing else for the next twelve months, at least do this and do it *soon*.'

6

Sculby was surprised to find his secretary still in the office. She ought to have gone to lunch long before.

'You shouldn't have waited', he said.

Betty eyed him over the sheet of paper which she was feeding into her typewriter.

'I had to. Guess who's in there.'

Sculby did not need to guess. Royston was the only 'client' who regularly came in at lunchtime without an appointment. It upset the routine when he called because the office in Milward Street was small; only Sculby and his secretary worked there, so that one of them always had to be around if a stranger was present. The other seven partners in the firm of Sculby O'Connor & Co worked in plush City offices with a pretty receptionist to protect them from the outside world. Sculby preferred Whitechapel, though. He liked being the boss.

'What is it this time?'

'Says it's the kids. She's threatening to take them with her and go off with that karate instructor.'

Sculby nodded morosely. The advantage of his secretary was that she pried.

'Rough morning?'

He nodded again.

'Want a quickie before you go in?'

'No. I've had a couple.'

'Yes, I thought so.'

This time Sculby smiled. 'Shows, does it?'

Betty grinned at him and started to type. Sculby removed his macintosh and hung it on one of the cheap metal hooks provided for the use of clients. The only other garment on the rack was a faded, thin overcoat, the pockets of which overflowed with soiled kid gloves and an old scarf.

'Don't wait any longer. See you at 2.30. Oh, leave me a line through, will you?'

'Okay then. 'Bye.'

As Betty picked up her bag and made ready to lock up she heard the beginning of Sculby's usual opening remarks before the office door closed behind him.

'Now then, Mr Royston, what can I do for you? Cold day, isn't it, sorry to hear from my secretary . . .'

Royston stood up as Sculby entered. The two men shook hands formally.

'Good of you to see me without an appointment, Mr Sculby.'

'Not at all, some things won't wait, will they? If you'll just hang on a minute . . .'

Sculby began to shuffle papers across the untidy desk, trying to replace chaos with a semblance of order. When he was tired of that he sat back in his chair and gazed across the mess at Royston, as if expecting him to say something. Sensing this, Royston opened his mouth to speak, but Sculby held up a hand. For a moment they sat there, frozen, silent, until afar off they simultaneously heard the sound of the street door closing and the clink of keys.

Sculby loosened his tie, undid the top button of his shirt and pushed with his feet against the desk until he was able to rest his legs on the top and slump back in his chair. For a moment he did nothing except raise his hand to his forehead and massage it gently. It helped to ease the muzzy pain which the gin he had drunk earlier had done nothing to alleviate.

'My God, Michael, I don't want any more mornings like that one.'

Royston smiled. 'How'd you get on?'

'Oddly. It's all on tape. Which reminds me . . .'

Sculby stood up and went to fetch the briefcase which he had let drop to the floor on entering the office. 'Here.'

Royston picked up the tape. 'Anything to interest me?'

Sculby didn't answer at once; instead he took a long, cool look at the man sitting opposite him. On the whole he liked Royston. He was an excellent control, one who worked in full sympathy with his agents. But in six years of emphatic co-operation Royston had never learned that there were some questions which couldn't be answered, at least not in the same language as the questioner used.

'He's crazy. And he scares me witless.'

Royston sat back in his chair and thought about that. He knew that what Sculby had just told him might be exaggeration born of nerves. But it might be streetwise instinct. And you didn't ignore that.

Royston tossed the little cassette in the air, caught it and pocketed it.

'Tell me', he said softly.

Sculby quickly ran through the morning's events.

'When I found him in the cells afterwards the surgeon was about to stick a needle in him. I stopped that, of course. It seems he thought as long as he shut up and didn't incriminate himself he'd get bail. That's all he cares about, for the moment. When it didn't happen he couldn't take it. That's a hell of a frightened man you've got yourself there, Michael. Says he's innocent, it's a fit-up. Fair enough. I can't do any more until I've seen the police depositions. I suppose it's no use asking you what's going on?'

Royston was silent for a moment.

'What are you going to do now?'

'Go to the Judge in chambers.'

'Come again?'

'Get bail. You appeal against the magistrate's decision by going to a High Court Judge sitting in private, in chambers.'

'I'm only guessing', said Royston, 'but I think you may find the police don't oppose on appeal.' Noting Sculby's sour look he added quickly, 'It was nothing to do with me that Loshkevoi didn't get bail. Five are still clearing up, that's all.'

'Five are cunts', said Sculby. 'And you're another' hung
unspoken in the room between the two men. 'What happened
to my inquest, anyway?'

'Never mind that for a moment. I'm going to tell you all
you need to know, Laurie.' Royston drew his chair closer to
Sculby. 'And not a word more. That's for your own protection.
Last night, Five found a whole heap of arms and other stuff
on Loshkevoi's premises. We're leaving them there, pretending
we haven't noticed anything, in the hope he'll lead us up the
line. This handling charge is just to give us something on him
for now. You understand? All you've got to do is worm your
way into his confidence. When I give the word, you'll be the
one to make the pitch. Safety in exchange for hard information,
that'll be the name of the game. And for now that's all you
need to know.'

Royston stood up, and Sculby realised he wasn't going to
learn any more.

'You're all right for cash on this one?'

Sculby nodded. 'Loshkevoi's loaded.'

'Then I'll be off.'

Sculby was overtaken by a burning desire to score over
Royston, something, anything...

'Just one thing, for when you next come, Michael. That
coat outside, the suit you're wearing...they're all great, no
one would think you weren't a client. But those shoes...'

In spite of himself Royston had to look down.

'...It's not that they're filthy. Quite a lot of my clients
have dirty shoes. But you don't see that much suede on Milward
Street, Michael. Hope you don't mind me mentioning it.'

While Royston was formulating a reply the phone rang.

'Hello...hold on, please.'

Sculby held his hand over the receiver and frowned across
at his companion. 'For Christ's sake, who knows you're
here...?'

Royston snatched the instrument from Sculby's hand.

'Hello...yes.'

Sculby watched curiously. Royston's mouth had developed
a tic. Suddenly he went very white.

'He did...*what?*'

7

Kyril stood frozen at the centre of a huge, intricate web. Silence and shadows had isolated him completely from the tangible world outside. Only tiny tingling sensations on the extremities of the strands which he had woven round himself revealed that he was still alive. First his hearing went, worn out with the strain of listening for sounds which did not happen. Now his sight was failing with the short winter twilight. Soon all the systems of his body would shut down, night would come, and he would be dead...

He shook himself angrily. *Think*.

From his vantage point on the bedside chair he could see the old-new skyline of Athens through the broad tunnel of his bedroom: a maze of aerials and high-tension cables linking the uneven roofs, beyond them a hill topped by stately ruined columns. Earlier in the afternoon the hillside had been the colour of washed sand; now it was ground ginger; soon it would become black, indistinguishable from the surrounding night.

By standing on the chair he was able to look down into Kaningos Square without approaching the window. The two men were still there, talking, every so often directing a swift glance towards the hotel. One of the men operated a souvlaki stall with some pretence to efficiency; Kyril acknowledged that the Athens *referentura* had improved its standards over the last nine years. In some ways.

The hotel had been unnaturally silent for more than an hour. None of the usual sounds rose from the kitchen, no porter whistled aimlessly as he carted crates of empty, rattling bottles through the hall. They were inside, then. Somewhere in the corridor, in the room next door, on the terrace above him, men were waiting patiently for the next move.

Kyril's heart beat faster than usual and his palms were sweating, but he could detect no signs of internal panic. The old training still held. It was not as though anything which had happened today was unexpected; Stanov had promised him all this. But Kyril had left it so very late. He had slipped up, once. Nothing in his impassive face or his quiet, controlled movements disclosed that he had been thrust willy-nilly into the most nerve-wracking crisis of his career.

Below him in the dusty square, one of the two men detached himself from the souvlaki stall and began to walk towards the hotel. A three-wheeler van hooted aggressively; the man faltered, advanced again, and was lost from Kyril's sight.

It was not the city he remembered. More cracked walls, dirt, empty building-sites. Fewer taxis. No quick 'deals' by virtue only of having the language. The smell, that was the same: hot oil, carbon monoxide, red dust, air-cured tobacco, wine. Salt, a dash of the sea. Everything else was changed.

The friendly lorry-driver had dropped him in Omonia Square and watched for a moment of amusement as the 'German teacher', doing Greece on the cheap off-season, withstood the first shock of downtown Athens. The hooting, hustling roar of the cars hurtling five abreast down the broad avenues, the vendors, the crowds . . . the first point of familiarity, of contact: a man dressed in a grey, short-sleeved shirt over black slacks, an attaché case under his arm, stopping to buy Papastratos cigarettes at the kiosk. Kyril's eyes began to focus. Suddenly he knew where he was.

• • •

He shifted his weight gingerly on the chair and stood still again, listening. Nothing disturbed the eerie quiet of the hotel. With the thumb of his right hand he eased the safety-catch of the Stechkin to 'off' while at the same time his forefinger curled round the trigger, testing the pressure. He forgot he had once had to learn that simple movement in far-off days when it still seemed clumsy and unnatural. Only his body and its well-trained muscles remembered.

By turning his head a fraction he could see part of the corridor through the skylight over the door. No awkward shadows. No diminution of light. No sounds. Nothing.

Through the window the far hillside had dissolved into a smoke-laden mist. Nightfall was minutes away. Neon lights flickered outside and a Greek boy shouted before gunning his motorbike and zooming down a side-street. Kyril could hear bazouki music coming from a nearby *taverna*. Athens was changing into its evening attire. The siesta was over. Soon there would be enough noise in the street to mask any unpleasantness which might occur on the upper floor of a small hotel.

He had selected this hotel from working files on possibly useful 'stations', buildings recognised by the KGB as having operational potential but not yet tested by them. The 'Silenus' occupied a narrow site in one corner of the triangular 'square', with its tiny patch of green in the centre and a mish-mash of cafés spilled on to the pavement. The hotel overlooked a busy intersection with excellent sightlines and ready access to neighbouring apartment-blocks at the rear. In March he was able to obtain a top-storey room at the front without difficulty, paying for a day's lodging in advance. He allowed himself one hour in the roof-top open bar, already balmy in the pre-Spring, drinking Hellas and smoking Benson & Hedges, before lunch and a short rest. Then work.

It was the first chance he had had to think since leaving Moscow. He discovered he quite enjoyed his role—for the moment. It could not last, of course: sooner or later he would find an executioner on his tail, someone determined to see he did not fall into the hands of his own side alive, and then the fun would be over, but for the present he could cope. A magnet,

that was what Stanov had called him, and the image appealed
to Kyril. Everything depended on him. If he snapped his fingers
on the street somebody, somewhere, perhaps thousands of miles
away, knew about it and acted accordingly. Kyril liked that.
In its way it represented more power than he had ever known.

He wondered whether they had found the diary yet. They
should have done. Would it fool anyone? Kyril shook his head,
the old doubts returning. Would the traitor fall into the trap of
believing that a comparatively junior officer like Ivan Bucharensky had discovered his secret when all others had failed? He
might. Kyril appreciated the possibility. If his nerves were
already on edge, if he were sufficiently near the brink, then
the diary might just instil a doubt . . . and it would have served
its purpose.

After lunch he lay on his bed for an hour, but could not
sleep. The weather was mild and overcast. He took a taxi to
the intersection of the two main arteries, Leoforas Alexandras
and Vassilissis Sofias, then walked slowly south along the latter
until he had passed the American embassy. He kept going.
After a while Vassilissis Sofias became Vassileos Konstan-
tinou, and he turned right into Stisikhorou, which took him
behind the Russian embassy before pointing the way back towards his hotel. One last call, the Odos Stadiou branch of the
National Bank of Greece, there to collect his nest-egg from the
deposit-box where it had languished for the past nine years,
and he was ready to go home. It was a long route but Kyril
did not hurry; he wasn't used to walking and his feet ached.
Even at the end, when he realised with a stab of unease that
the KGB were ahead of him and on either side, he did not
break his stride.

For the next half hour he enjoyed himself, glad to be back
in the old game again. Stores with rear exits, taxis stuck in
traffic-jams, entrances to the subway; all the techniques came
flooding back. As he entered his hotel he was smiling at the
ease with which he had shaken off the tail. The rest of the
schedule was easy: collect his things, make for the station,
double-check for tails, hitch a lift, change cars every three
miles for the first leg of the journey, then . . . disappear. He
was still smiling when he took a final glance out of the window
of his bedroom, and saw the two men outside, waiting.

Kyril held his luminous-faced watch up to his eyes. He could hear nothing, but his instincts now told him that between his room and the stairs someone waited: unseen, soundless, but there.

He padded across to the telephone and lifted the receiver. A room-waiter would disrupt anyone loitering, or at least identify his precise location. Becoming impatient he jiggled the cradle up and down. Nothing. They weren't answering.

Kyril took a fold of skin from his forefinger between his teeth and bit, not so hard that the pain distracted him but enough to pump the blood a little faster, sharpen his reflexes. Now he was ready.

He felt along the bottom seam of his rucksack. Tucked into a fold of the lining, as if to save it from a casual thief, was a thin platinum cigarette-lighter. He unscrewed the fuel cap and extracted an inch-long bullet-like tube from the lighter. He placed it carefully on the bed. Then he began to pile things over it: his German passport, detected by the feel of its cover and the embossed lettering; the American Express card with a notch in the left-hand corner; a letter of credit also with a notch in the left-hand corner, all now expendable. He pulled the bedspread over the little pile. As an afterthought he placed on top of that a newspaper which he had bought that morning, and his room key.

He shouldered the rucksack, tightening the straps until they would go no further. He did not need light to tell him that he had forgotten nothing; his memory was as sharp as ever.

For the moment all was still in the corridor. Kyril padded over to the sash window and eased it up, silently cursing the noise made by the heavy counter-weight chains. Other ears must have heard it too, for suddenly a shadow flitted across the strip of light from the oriel. Kyril didn't wait to investigate.

Once on the narrow ledge outside his room he turned to face the wall and scrabbled upwards with crooked fingers. Sure enough, there was the parapet, above it the open-air terrace bar where he had sat drinking earlier in the day. He hauled himself quickly upwards. The two men in the square might see but he didn't care any longer; it could even be turned to his advantage.

Below him he could hear voices in the bedroom he had just

left. He glanced quickly around. The bar was unlit and deserted; nobody wanted to drink out in the open on a March night in Athens. Kyril grinned. Two men at least in the bedroom, talking increasingly loudly in Russian. Very careless. He would advise Stanov to shake out the Greek Resident on his return . . .

Kyril held up the slim platinum lighter and flicked the lever. The impulse leapt forth. There was a muffled boom as the silver nitrate and potassium bomb exploded on the bed in the room below, a scream and a sudden waft of hot air over the parapet. Kyril smiled and pocketed the lighter. Suddenly he froze. A hand was coming over the edge, garishly illuminated by a flashing neon sign above. Before he could move a man was up on the ledge of the bar, crouched low in order to minimise the target. His other hand was coming up level. Kyril knew what was in it.

For a split second he deliberated. The assassin's hold was precarious; if Kyril could only get close enough he could push him over the edge. But that meant running into range. In the dark, with a hand gun, the chances were that the man would miss a target moving away from him. Before the split second was up Kyril was pivoting on his toes and racing for the far end of the terrace.

Earlier that day he had stood on this very spot, calculating distances, some professional part of him alive to potential danger. Kyril knew that five metres separated the terrace from the roof-top of the adjacent building and there was a drop of one and a half metres to allow for as well. His stride never faltered. Using every scrap of momentum he could gather he sped along the patio until, at the far end, he hopped on to the low ledge and propelled himself into the darkness. A whirl of light far below him, a sick feeling in his stomach and then his right knee and left forearm crashed into concrete, the breath went out of him and he lay there, winded but alive.

The 'ping' of the bullet roused him. He rolled rapidly to one side, seeking desperately for cover. Another 'ping'—the gunman was using a silencer, bad for accuracy but still dangerously close. A third 'ping' spattered concrete chips over his head; at the same moment he saw the skylight and launched his way towards it, praying for a soft landing. A second before impact he punched forward with both hands, letting them take

the brunt of the broken glass and protect his head. Another
sickening fall into darkness, then a soft bump and scream, this
time a woman's. A dim bedside light went on. He had landed
on top of a girl, very beautiful he noticed—and not alone.
Details began to penetrate: bare breasts, a hairy chest . . . surely
not the girl's, no *not* the girl's . . .

'*Lipomai, kyrie. Kalinikta sas.*'

Kyril fled. One or two curious heads peered out of partly
opened doors as he emerged on to the landing. He ran uncaring
until he was down the stairs and out the back door among the
dustbins, a passageway ahead of him, and escape.

He was in a side-street, dimly lit and deserted. Nothing
moved. He did a swift damage-check. It was bad. Blood everywhere, crystals of splintered glass, a knee that was beginning
to seize up in spasms of pain. Hide? No . . . He had to get out
of town while the evening crowds still thronged the streets,
then he could rest.

It was a long, painful night. Several times he nearly blun-
dered into the bright lights of a busy avenue, and once he
thought he was being followed. It was an illusion, but after the
scare he put on more speed. Dawn found him on the road to
Aharne, well away from any route he could be expected to
take, bruised and shaken but alert. His wounds had been bathed
in cold spring water; a clean shirt and a new identity from the
rucksack had done wonders.

He consulted his map. Athens Station had tried to stop him,
but he had got away. There was no doubt in his mind that they
had not intended him to escape completely. From now on the
schedule would be tight. If he was to arrive in Brussels in
accordance with Stanov's carefully-timed plan he would have
to cut corners, take chances.

He looked up sharply. Far off to the south he could see a
cloud of reddish dust rising from the road. It was a local delivery
van.

Kyril hesitated for only a moment, then folded the map,
shouldered his burden, stepped on to the highway and lifted
his thumb.

As the cloud of dust grew closer his tired brain began to
register details. An old van coated with layers of grease and

grime, its gear-box crunching . . . typically Greek. No, not typical. Something was different.

Kyril lowered his thumb. He had to make a quick decision.
The van was okay, he told himself, desperate to believe it;
nothing was wrong.

The windscreen was just a black rectangle. Soon he would
be able to see the driver.

The windscreen . . .

Suddenly he knew what was wrong. Every Greek driver
plasters the inside of his windscreen with brightly-coloured
post-cards, slogans, trinkets . . . this van had none of them.

Kyril flung himself off the road and began to run.

'Stand still!'

The van had drawn up by the side of the road. Kyril did
not look back. Not even the sound of an English voice made
him falter.

'I'm warning you . . .'

Kyril began to weave right and left. Already some part of
him knew it was hopeless. He was miles from the nearest cover.
When the first spray of bullets hit the ground within inches of
his racing feet he stumbled, fell and lay perfectly still.

8

On the first floor of the Royal Courts of Justice in the Strand there is an area called the Bear Garden. Anyone who needs to ask his way to it will probably never get there, for, as with members' clubs, newcomers normally arrive only in the company of old hands. The Bear Garden consists of two large, high-ceiling'd rooms connected by a short corridor, and in some ways it resembles not only an exclusive club but also a medieval palace ante-room. The setting is much the same: heavy wooden tables with carved chairs and benches along the walls, dusty portraits of old men clad in flowing, scarlet robes, even a gallery at one end; and the rooms are thronged with gossiping, conniving courtiers ready to present their petitions, make their requests. But there the resemblance ends. The carpet is twin to that in Royston's office, the air is heavy with cigarette-smoke and the twentieth century princelings who occupy the seats of power wear dark grey suits.

Leading off the short corridor which connects the two main rooms is an office known as 'Room 98'. Here a Judge of the Queen's Bench Division of the High Court sits daily to hear matters within his jurisdiction, including applications for bail, and it was from Room 98 that Laurence Sculby emerged at 4 o'clock on the day after his meeting with Royston.

'Wasted brief fee', murmured the young barrister who followed him.

'Nah', said Sculby. 'Worth every penny.'

The barrister laughed uneasily.

'"I've read the affidavit, Mr Gyddon, I don't see the police, order as asked, two sureties in the sum of £500." I wasn't exactly overworked, was I?'

'Beautiful bit of advocacy', said Sculby. 'Lovely touch, Spence. I'll just have a word with the Judge's clerk and we'll get that order down to Brixton tonight. Then first thing tomorrow, he's out.'

'That's fast', said Spencer Gyddon. 'I'm surprised you got in front of the Judge so quickly, Laurie. How do you do these things?'

Sculby winked. 'Trust me', he said.

'I do', said Gyddon as Sculby turned away from him and started towards the stairs. 'I think', he added under his breath.

At 11 o'clock next morning, formalities complete, Sculby met Loshkevoi at Brixton jail. To the lawyer's surprise his client looked in better health, and he remarked on the fact. 'Sleep', replied Loshkevoi. 'Fourteen hours at a stretch, Mr. Sculby. I needed it. Nothing else to do, anyway.'

'Please call me Laurie', murmured Sculby. 'Everyone does.'

'Victor.' Loshkevoi held out his hand and grasped Sculby's in a painful squeeze. 'You do a fine job, Laurie. What next?'

'I expect you want to get home, see to things . . .'

'For that I have a manager. He's been in charge two days, another couple of hours won't break him. All I want right now is to beat that fucking charge. You excuse my language, please.'

Sculby's grin widened. 'S'long as you'll excuse mine. Tell you what. There's a nice little Eye-tie place up the hill. I'll buy you lunch.'

'It's on me.'

Sculby put a friendly arm round Loshkevoi's shoulders. 'Argue about it over the coffee', he said.

Loshkevoi made a good lunch. Sculby wondered if he always ate that much or if prison had sharpened his appetite. Only when the coffee came, and they were well into the second litre of Soave, did the two men begin to talk seriously.

'I come from Italy, you know. Years back. The food travels well, even here it's good.'

'What part of Italy?'

Loshkevoi raised suspicious eyes to Sculby's face and evidently decided the question was innocent, for he replied 'Bergamo'.

'Why'd you leave?'

'The war.'

Loshkevoi swilled down half a glass of wine and wiped his beard with his napkin.

'I was a boy then. My father was killed, my mother went missing. There were plenty like me, wanted in Russia by the Bolsheviks. I made friends with the right Captain, he took care of everything.' Seeing Sculby's look of puzzlement he added, 'Sure I slept with him. I'm not bent, you understand. But rather that than a bullet in the neck. Illegal, too: it gave me a hold over him. Too late to do anything about that now, eh?'

'I hope so', said Sculby thoughtfully. 'Why do you think they'd have sent you to Russia?'

'It's where we came from. My parents, I mean. They drifted from place to place. In Bergamo my father was mechanic. He taught me. So, I come here with a trade.'

Sculby reached for his briefcase and pulled out a notebook. 'Tell me a bit about yourself. Married?'

'No. You get yourself a wife, you got overheads. I select the company I want, when I want.'

Sculby grinned. 'Me too.'

'I'm starting to like you, Laurie.' Loshkevoi lit a thin, black cigar and offered the pack to Sculby. 'Smoke?'

Sculby hesitated only a second. He was trying to give up, but Royston said to make an effort. All in the line of duty . . .

'How long have you had your own business?'

'Ten years. I bought it off my boss when he retired, did it up a little. Jaguars, that's my speciality. The occasional Daimler, maybe. Your Fords and Vauxhalls . . .'

Loshkevoi made a heavy gesture of dismissal with the cigar. Sculby found his diction curiously irritating. A mixture of styles, it sounded put on, but the lawyer was coming to realise that it wasn't.

'You haven't got a regular solicitor?'

'Never needed one. Except when I took over the business, but that was years ago and I didn't like him anyway.'

'No previous? Convictions, I mean . . . ever been in trouble with the police before?'

'No.'

'Straight up.'

Loshkevoi's head was sunk on to his chest. At Sculby's question he lifted his eyes and subjected the solicitor to a long stare.

'Straight up?'

'Sorry. But I have to know. You'd be surprised the number of people who tell you they've no form when they have.'

'Laurie, I deal in used cars. *Nothing* surprises me.'

They haggled amicably over the bill. Loshkevoi overrode his lawyer, and paid. Outside the restaurant Sculby said, 'I'll give you a lift. My car's just round the corner.'

It took less than 15 minutes to drive to Loshkevoi's garage. Sculby watched him scuttle inside the workshop, waving a hand to the man in the cashier's booth. Nobody seemed surprised to see him. Sculby hung around as long as he decently could but in the end had to drive away without being any the wiser about his client's affairs.

Loshkevoi closed the sliding-doors of the workshop.

'Sammy!'

A bald, fat man emerged from behind an XJ6 wiping his hands on an oily rag.

'Vic . . . Didn't expect to see you. The Old Bill was here yesterday, give the place a right going-over.'

Loshkevoi brushed him aside.

'Half day. Come on lads, I'm shutting up.'

The man called Sammy stared at the gaffer in puzzlement.

'Yer wot?'

'We're closed until eight tomorrow morning.'

'How'd you get on, boss?'

A young mechanic had slid from under a jacked van and was grinning up at Loshkevoi from the floor.

'Button it, Kelly. Go home.'

Other men in overalls began to appear from the hidden recesses of the shop. No one tried to argue. Within minutes

Loshkevoi had the place to himself.

For a while he did nothing but stand with hands on hips, treating every inch of the walls and ceiling to a minute scrutiny. He started with the bottom left-hand corner of the rear wall and worked horizontally along the line of bricks before, at the end of the row, lifting his gaze a fraction and working back over the second line of bricks the way he had come. It took a long time for him to be convinced that nothing had apparently changed. But of course, the ferrets would have taken photographs before they began, and replaced everything in order afterwards.

Only after he had satisfied himself by this superficial visual inspection did Loshkevoi go in search of a crowbar and a torch.

Once inside the inspection pit he peered closely at the wall. It all looked the same. He began to hack at the bricks. Inside the cavity the light-sensitive cell attached to the ultra fast camera concealed by DI5 picked up the first flash of Loshkevoi's torch. At once the shutter began to operate, 90 times in the first minute, then a pause of a minute, followed by a further 90 exposures. As the last frame of infra-red film passed the shutter the camera automatically switched itself off. When the film was retrieved and developed Loshkevoi would be identifiable on approximately two-thirds of the shots, which was more than the makers of the camera claimed for it.

9

It had been a week of frenetic activity in Dzerzhinsky Square. By the time the weekend came all the heads of the First Main Directorate wanted to do was get away. The two Generals drove down to Zhukovka on Friday afternoon, before the traffic built up. Because he was going with Michaelov, Povin had dismissed his own driver until Monday morning with orders to report to the dacha at 8 a.m., ready for work. The man was pleased but not surprised. Most senior KGB officers who were also bachelors (there were not many) insisted on staffing their holiday retreats with chauffeurs, cooks and bottle-washers, but Colonel-General Stepan Ilyich Povin was not among them. He preferred the simple life: books, records, a little vodka and his own company were all he wanted.

Unfortunately, however, it was the first week-end of the month, so he was bound by convention to dine with his superior Michaelov and his wife Nadia. Privately Povin thought little of Nadia, who was a bore, and would have liked to break this convention if he could, but he was a good-natured man and he sensed that his visits helped the Michaelovs, in a funny sort of way. So month in and month out he did his duty on the first

Friday, always vainly hoping that illness or the exigences of the service might intervene to save him.

But nothing that happened in Dzerzhinsky Square, not even the defection of a traitor like Bucharensky, ever seemed sufficiently serious in Michaelov's eyes to warrant the breaking of a social engagement.

On arrival in Zhukovka Povin managed to dredge up a smile and the hug which was the very least required by such a long-standing friendship as theirs, before delivering himself of his presents.

'Stepan Ilyich, you really should not do this...'

'It is nothing, nothing. My contribution to the feast, eh?'

Michaelov caught Povin's eye and surreptitiously tapped his throat—the Russian way of saying 'Drink?' Povin smiled and nodded. Once he was closeted with his chief in the study, and Nadia was safely ensconced in her culinary domain, he could relax.

'The usual?'

'Please.'

Povin watched while Michaelov poured a generous tot of petrovka, the brown vodka which goes so well with milk mushrooms. He had been addicted to it ever since officers' school at Ryazan.

'Still nothing for you?'

Michaelov shook his head dolefully.

'The doctor...aah! Sometimes I'm tempted, but then Nadia always reminds me of what happened last time.'

Povin nodded sympathetically. His chief suffered from ulcers. Alcohol was forbidden. The last time Michaelov broke the embargo and drank cognac, the surgeons only just managed to save his life. Nadia, thought Povin, would be unlikely to forget.

'But to go back to what I was saying in the car...' Michaelov sat down opposite his deputy and lit a 'papirosy', a vile, sweetly-scented cigarette consisting of a cardboard tube half-filled with tobacco. They were manufactured for him specially by the makers of 'Novostj', a popular brand obtainable in Moscow. It was a joke in Dzerzhinsky Square that you always knew where old Michaelov was by the smell.

'...Stanov was a fool to have compiled "Sociable Plover"

in the first place. All that information collected together in one place . . .'

'Maybe.'

'You're still not convinced?'

'I just wish I could be sure he'd ever compiled it in the first place, that's all.'

'What do you mean?'

'Oh, nothing really. But if it's gone, why hasn't it surfaced by now? How explain the fiasco in Athens? And the trick he played on the British—what do you make of that?'

Michaelov shrugged. 'Don't talk to me about Athens. What a ball-up. But Bucharensky's another idiot, thank goodness.'

'Not such an idiot as Stanov for trusting him in the first place.'

'You're right, Stepan. So much for double-oh-seven-eight.'

Povin downed the last of his vodka and made a face.

'That one was a born loser. I've always said so. The Administrative Organs Department of the Politburo was never going to release its hold on our appointments, I don't give a damn what Kazin's supposed to have said. It's all a myth.'

'Well if it wasn't before, it is now,' Michaelov assented. 'They'll never let Stanov forget it was he who recommended Bucharensky for promotion. Chairman's Order 0078 won't be promulgated in our lifetimes. Here, give me your glass.'

'Make it a tumbler', said Povin gloomily. 'I tell you, Valery, if we don't catch up with Bucharensky soon, we're going through The Door, you and I. Is there anything new on the diary?'

These innocent-sounding words seemed to lower the temperature in the room by several degrees. 'The Diary' was a sensitive subject among KGB officers of general rank; this was the first time since its discovery that Povin had summoned up the courage to talk to his Chief about it, and on reflection he realised that it might have been more tactful to avoid the subject so soon after mentioning The Door.

'Forensic say it's genuine.'

Michaelov addressed the wall, busying himself with drinks.

'The paper and ink were official issue, but the pen was Bucharensky's own. His handwriting. Stanov's enjoying this, you know. He likes having us all on a plate. There are times I almost think he wrote that bloody diary up himself . . .'

As Michaelov handed Povin a fresh drink the door behind them burst open and he turned round, startled, the glass in his hand forgotten. In the doorway stood a lanky, long-haired blonde girl. Povin blinked. She was wearing thigh-tight faded jeans, obviously from the West, and a denim jacket. It took him a second to recognise Olga, the Michaelov's eldest daughter. She nodded carelessly in his direction, then said:

'Where are the car keys, father?'

Michaelov straightened his shoulders and barked: 'Olga! More to the point, where are your manners? Come here at once, say hello to General Povin.'

From the mulish look which crept across the girl's face Povin judged that she would refuse outright, and was mildly surprised when she obeyed. She approached the sofa where he was sitting and said, 'Good evening, Stepan Ilyich. It's good to see you. How are things?'

'Very well, thank you, Olga. You?'

'Yes, well. Father . . . the keys. Please.'

Michaelov felt in the pockets of his uniform. 'Here. But remember, don't be back late.'

'Yes, yes. G'night, Stepan.'

The girl bounced out of the room without acknowledging her father. Povin turned an inquiring eye towards Michaelov in time to catch the baffled look on his face.

'A concert. It all started with this Elton Jahn . . . John?'

'John', confirmed Povin.

'Now it's every Friday. Underground, of course. I've asked Stupar to tell his boys to be damn careful who they pull in tonight.'

Povin nodded approvingly. What father would not do as much for his daughter?

'All the same, I don't mind telling you . . . it's tough, being a parent these days. They get harder to control. What can I do?'

Michaelov pulled a gun-metal cigarette case from the pocket of his coat and lit up. Povin's nose wrinkled; after years of working with this man he still couldn't help it. Despite his doctor's warnings Michaelov had proved unable to cure himself of the nicotine habit, and continued to smoke his revolting cigarettes.

Povin smiled at Michaelov, who commanded the First Main Directorate of the KGB and was responsible for the Soviet Union's entire foreign intelligence system.

'The young are so difficult to manage, Valery. Don't let it worry you. She'll grow up soon.'

Before Michaelov could reply Nadia summoned them to table, and the subject was closed. Povin knew from hard experience that you did not discuss the children in front of Michaelov's wife.

The evening passed off quietly, as usual. Povin declined a lift home and set out through the pine woods shortly before midnight. It was very cold; the snow squeaked under his feet. Above him a white moon sailed in a cloudless sky devoid of any threat; tomorrow would be fine.

As he trudged homewards his thoughts kept returning to the dacha he had just left—what would become of Olga, he wondered? In five years, say: a brilliant scientist devoted to the service of the State...or a dissident, in exile, or worse...on the archipelago. Povin let himself in through the back gate of his own house and began to trot up the path.

The empty house, solitude, had never worried him. The woman who came twice a week to look after his dacha in winter had left the stove piled high with wood, so that his place was warmer than the Michaelov's. He poured himself a last glass of his favourite petrovka and switched out the lights. From his chair by the window he could look out across the Moscow river, winding like a snake through the snow-laden pine trees that fringed his spacious property. In the moonlight everything looked still and peaceful.

But Povin's inner mood was rapidly losing touch with the tranquil surroundings. It had been an effort to appear calm in front of the Michaelovs. Now he was a desperately worried man. For the past few days he had pushed everything to the outer fringes of consciousness while he strove to concentrate on the immediate problems of office. Once the pressure was off, however, he could no longer delay facing the harsh realities of his situation. The truth was appalling. But he had to keep calm. Panic was a short cut to the grave.

Something had to be done to stop Bucharensky. And the quicker the better.

Povin put down his glass on the table beside him and eased himself on to his knees. Praying was not as simple as it used to be.

He had started his career in the KGB by being assigned to what is now the Fifth Direction of the Fifth Main Directorate, which oversees the practice of religion within the Soviet Union. At first the prospect had bored him. Then he was instructed to infiltrate a Ukrainian sect of the Russian Orthodox Church, and overnight his life had changed. He came away from the first meeting, held in a darkened cellar with someone on the door to listen for the guards, shaken out of his old complacency. To run such risks, merely in order to join with a few others in a demonstration of faith . . . there had been a Red Army officer there, his head bowed with the rest of them, also a local Peace Committee leader. Something kept Povin from reporting their presence. A few days later his superior, Major Oblensky, called him into his office. When Povin faced him across the table the Major's eyes were cold.

'The other night you attended a meeting of the Krinsky Square sect. Captain Mitkov of the 16th Airborne Division was there. So was Rudolf Maximov, from the Peace Committee. Yet you did not report these matters. Why not?'

Povin stammered. 'I did not recognise them, comrade Major.'

'Don't make it sound worse than it is already', said Oblensky coldly. 'You're in deep.'

Even at that moment Povin had no regrets. He looked stubbornly at the floor.

'Lesser men might have been finished by this.' Oblensky was speaking again. 'Fortunately for you, Povin, your family is too well connected for me to take the steps I originally had in mind. I'm transferring you to other duties.'

He nodded curtly. The interview was at an end. As Povin laid his hand on the door handle Oblensky fired his parting shot.

'Stay away from religion, Povin.'

It was advice he had persistently ignored ever since. He sometimes wondered what had happened to Major Oblensky who one day, like so many other people, simply wasn't around any more. Shortly after that he had met Michaelov and struck up a friendship with him; ever afterwards Povin had advanced smoothly under the benign influence of his own highly-placed Party family and the man who was destined to become Russia's chief foreign spymaster. It was all God's work, Povin had no doubt of it. With growing power and rank he had more time to read and think, greater freedom of movement and expression. It was no secret that the elite frequently discussed among themselves subjects which were officially taboo and Povin was soon in a position to talk over his innermost doubts and convictions with others of like mind. There were more of these than he had ever suspected. When one day Povin simply began to think of himself as a Christian, he was acknowledging something which had in fact occurred long before.

So that night Povin stayed on his knees for a few minutes, praying for Oblensky, as always, and for Michaelov and his family and all the nameless others in general who impinged on his consciousness: the prisoners in the camps, the poor, the helpless ... the words of the ancient Orthodox prayer came readily to his lips: ' ... for those under trial, or condemned to the mines or bitter labour in exile ... '

There were so many to pray for. But chief among them tonight was Povin himself.

Next day he was up early, ready for his expedition to the Khruschev Store.

Most people did their shopping in Zhukovka at the large, single-storey complex which was the nearest thing the Soviet Union had to a supermarket. If your face didn't fit you didn't get in, but most of the high-ranking officers, ministers, scientists and artists who were allowed to live in the region were well-known there. Even though Khruschev had officially ceased to exist, his name lingered on with this shop, the Khruschev Store. Inside, the white hygienic shelves were always well-stocked with fresh dairy products, meat and fish; to the left, as you entered, were racks of men's and women's clothes shipped from France and Italy, while at the far end, by the

check-out, stood rows and rows of fine French and German
wines. Everything sold cheaply; this was a state-subsidised
store. It was an almost classic demonstration of the theory that
all are equal but some are more equal than others; the poor and
unconnected weren't allowed in, but one afternoon Solzhen-
itsyn and Rostropovich had stood in line to buy tomatoes while
behind them Molotov waited patiently to pay for Scotch and
cigarettes.

The stores are presided over by a woman known to her
customers only as Mother Kerenina. She has survived every
purge, every change at the top, every reversal of policy; she
knows all her customers by their patronymics; her stock of
good-humour is boundless. This morning as Povin entered the
store Mother Kerenina was dusting down a huge stack of tins
piled up by the door.

'Ah Stepan Ilyich', she cried, her eyes lighting up at the
sight of him. 'How are you?'

The hug he gave her was warmer than the one he had given
Nadia the night before.

'Very well. Good to be back.'

'You like my latest line?'

She waved a proud hand in the direction of the tins. Povin
peered closer.

'Gravlaks! Is it any good?'

She shrugged. 'As good as tinned stuff ever can be. I suppose you'll want herring, Stepan Ilyich.'

'Please.'

'Over there, in the ice cabinet. Deep frozen, I'm afraid, but
good quality.'

He wandered over to inspect the recently delivered 'catch'.
Suddenly he became aware of someone standing by his side.

'If you pick that stuff over any more, Stepan Ilyich, it will
be unfit for human consumption.'

He looked up to find the laughing face of Stolyinovich close
to his own. Povin grinned.

'Capitalist. You'll be wanting me to cook it for you next.'

They embraced affectionately. Povin was very fond of the
pianist and had all his records in his Moscow apartment. Since
Stolyinovich had been granted his own dacha the two men
spent much time together—Povin had shyly sought the other

man out to declare his admiration and respect, stayed for a drink, then for dinner and overnight. They had even gone into a kind of partnership: on his frequent trips to play in the West Stolyinovich bought up as many Deutsche Gramaphon records as he could, the aim being to equip and maintain a jointly-financed music library.

'Anyway, why aren't you in some western paradise, you idle wretch. Not sunning yourself in the south of France, eh?'

'Not yet. But I go tonight. So here I am, getting in my herring for the journey.'

'It will go off. Besides, you can buy herring anywhere.'

'Ah, but not like this. And I have a freezer pack; it is filled with some kind of chemical, don't ask me what, but it stays cold until I can get it into my hotel fridge.'

Povin shook his head indulgently. 'One of these days, Pyotr, I shall get the boys to work you over at the airport.'

Stolyinovich flicked a contemptuous finger. 'I go through Vnukovo now. Your boys don't get a look in.'

Povin chuckled. He knew that the distinguished pianist had recently won the right to use the V.I.P. airport on the other side of Moscow. 'Still', he said, 'you'd be surprised at what the hidden x-ray cameras show up at Vnukovo.'

He made no secret of his job to Stolyinovich, had told him long ago that he was the Deputy Director of the First Main Directorate. His friend even knew his speciality: England and Ireland.

'I can guess. Pornography and state secrets.'

'More or less.'

'And in my case, herring. Now tell me, Stepan, which should I choose. What about that fellow, eh? He looks nice and plump.'

Povin studied the freezer-shelf where he had himself been rummaging a moment before. 'I should take . . . *that* one.'

'You are sure?'

Povin nodded and moved away, as if uninterested. Stolyinovich followed him on his round of the shop, talking excitedly about his coming trip to Stockholm. When at last their bags were full they stood for a minute in the slush outside the store, reluctant to part.

'Come to lunch.'

'I can't old friend. I have an early flight. I must practise. Then I must sleep.'

Povin nodded resignedly. 'Go safely, then.'

Stolyinovich smiled and nodded. Povin stood on the steps and watched him until he was out of sight, carrying the frozen herring which was addressed to the head of the Secret Intelligence Service, London.

10

Kyril rolled over very slowly and lay on his side. He could hear footsteps approaching over the stony soil of the roadside waste. Suddenly they stopped, and Kyril raised his head to see a very young man, scarcely more than a boy. He was flushed and breathing heavily: more from nerves than exertion, Kyril guessed. The machine-pistol looked awkward in his hands, and Kyril noted that his captor was unused to firearms.

'You're English', he said.

The boy jumped at being addressed in his own language. He was standing about four feet away, as if not sure what to do next. His lips were dry and he continually flicked a stray lock of hair out of his eyes. His patent nervousness alarmed Kyril.

'And you're Colonel Bucharensky', the boy replied. 'Get up. Keep your hands where I can see them, nice and easy.'

If he meant to sound confident he failed. This boy puzzled Kyril greatly. He was hardly twenty and his inexperience showed in everything he did. His obvious lack of control over the situation made the Russian feel faintly ridiculous. He stood up slowly and dusted off his clothes.

'But I was looking for you. The KGB ran me out of Athens...'

'Yes, yes, we know all about that.'

By now it was fully light. If the boy dithered much longer a bus full of school-children would come along, with everyone ooh-ing and aah-ing. The image brought a smile to Kyril's lips.

'Here...put these on.'

Kyril's smile faded. The boy had produced a pair of handcuffs.

'Look. I'm on your side, see? I'm looking for SIS. Don't you understand? I'll come quietly, because I want to.'

'Shut up. Now listen. Put on the right bracelet and snap it shut.'

Kyril stared at him. This was going wrong.

'Do it!'

Kyril hesitated no longer. The gap between them was too great for heroics and he didn't like the way the boy's finger kept tightening and loosening on the trigger. His throat was dry. With every second that passed his options narrowed.

He snapped the bracelet shut.

'Now...get in the other side. Move!'

Keeping a healthy distance between them, the boy covered Kyril while he walked round the front of the van and sat sideways on the passenger seat, leaving the door ajar.

'Put the other cuff through the handle.'

On the inside of the door was a metal grip attached to the frame by two screws. As he fitted the cuff through the narrow gap Kyril cautiously tested the handle's strength. The screws were firm.

'Now put on the other bracelet and close it.'

Kyril tried to swallow and failed. His throat had a dry, wooden feel to it. This couldn't be happening. He had evaded the might of the KGB and now this boy...

'Get in!'

This hysterical boy. Kyril swung his legs off the road, ignoring the fiery pain which radiated through his injured knee, and sat in the passenger seat.

'Close the door.'

Kyril obeyed numbly, hearing another chance disappear with

the click of the closing lock. Now he was squeezed up against the door, his hands incapacitated. The boy went round to the driver's side, got in, and tucked the machine pistol away between him and the door.

Kyril began to calculate. They could not be more than ten kilometres from the centre of Athens. At this time of day the roads were still quiet: during the time it took for the boy to pick him up and immobilise him not a single car had passed in either direction. Assuming no breakdowns or hold-ups, they should make good speed. He had a quarter of an hour in which to act. Maybe less.

Think.

The boy started the car, reversed in a three-point turn, and started off towards the south. The engine sounded rough but was obviously still a long way from total collapse.

Make friends. No . . . Rattle him.

'I don't have to tell you that I could kill you now', he said quietly. The boy's hands tightened on the wheel and he shifted angrily in his seat. The van swerved.

'Shut up.'

Kyril let the silence develop. The gear-lever was a stalk on the steering-column. The floor of the van between him and the driver was flat.

'I don't want to hurt you. You're just a kid. Forget what they told you at Gosport. We don't murder kids.'

The front seat was a single bench. The boy had to sit close to his prisoner. Kyril began to gauge distances, rearranging his body slightly so that he was facing more to the front.

The boy took his left hand off the wheel and let it stray to the gun by his side.

'And if I want you to be silent, I can make you be silent.'

It sounded childish. It wasn't. Kyril knew he had pushed the boy to the limit. He turned still further and stared at the youthful profile. The driver's skin was greasy and pocked with acne; he had nicked himself while shaving and cut off the head of a spot, which still oozed. And suddenly it clicked, the solution to the mystery which had eluded him since he first heard the boy speak. An adventure. Fresh from England, he had read the telex and decided to come out alone, on the off chance. The great game. Kudos, promotion, the love of pretty women . . . Kyril saw it all, and cursed himself for not realising before. It was so many years since he had had to deal with this phenomenon, he thought it was extinct. The amateur in a world long ago grown professional. The maverick attempting the impossible feat, unaided, when only iron discipline and subjugation of self enabled a man to stay alive at all. And with this poignant recognition there came for Kyril a second of unspeakable sadness.

He was still looking at the boy. By lowering his eyes a fraction he was able to see a long jack-handle thrust under the driver's seat. It was the one thing he had been seeking, the one thing he still lacked: a lever.

'Stop looking at me like that.'

Kyril stole a glance at the road. It was flat and a sturdy-looking hard shoulder gave directly on to unfenced fields. Say 40 kph. A bend coming up . . .

'It's your day off, today', said Kyril gently. 'Isn't it?'

As the boy turned to snap at him he swung his legs up, clenched the ankles together and, catapaulting backwards against the door to give himself every last available ounce of force, he pounded his feet into the boy's trunk above the spleen.

The breath went out of the driver's body in a long groan and he slumped over the wheel, his face hidden from view. The van slowed as the boy's foot came off the accelerator. Kyril shut his eyes and prayed for a soft landing. The van lurched off the road, bumped over stony ground for what seemed a long time and finally stalled. The horn was sounding continuously.

Kyril opened his eyes. He was in one piece. His shoulders ached where they had thudded against the door but that was nothing. His first thought was for the boy. His arms were hanging down on either side of the wheel; Kyril was glad he couldn't see the face. He kicked again at the body, managing to dislodge the head from the horn-button, and it fell to one side.

Kyril raised himself up and cautiously peered out. They had come to rest about 20 metres from the road on rocky, untilled ground. Anybody seeing the van from the road would assume an accident had occurred and come to investigate. He must work fast.

He sat upright and wrenched the door handle. No result.
He tried again, throwing the whole weight of his body away
from the door, towards the boy. Still no good. Kyril took a
deep breath and exhaled it while counting to ten. Steady pressure, maybe that would do it.

After a couple of minutes he gave up. The muscles of his
forearms ached beyond endurance and the metal cuffs were
starting to chafe his skin. A tag of skin had already flaked
away from his right wrist, leaving a rough square of red flesh
in contact with the metal.

The jack.

Kyril twisted his body round so that he was half lying on
the front seat, his feet on the floor beneath the steering wheel.
By scrabbling with his heels he was able to shift the handle a
little. Another kick and the handle was out from under the seat.

Kyril paused to get his breath. He must stay calm. Don't
look out of the window to see who's coming. Don't waste
energy. Concentrate on that handle, nothing else.

Kyril squeezed his feet together, the handle between them,
and lifted his legs. At once the handle clashed with the steering
wheel and fell. He tried again, straining to see what he was
doing. This time he managed to negotiate the handle round the
wheel. The sweat was running down his face. His injured leg
throbbed with pain and his body had begun to tremble with
muscular effort.

Kyril twisted until he was lying on the seat, his knees pulled
up to his chest, the jack handle dangling between his clenched
heels. To his horror he saw that the handle was slipping. He
squeezed his feet more tightly together and commenced the
most difficult phase of the whole operation.

The chain connecting the handcuffs was about three inches
long, allowing him some play but not much. Somehow, using
only his feet and, in the last second, his manacled hands, he
had to lodge the shaft of the jack handle between the metal
grip and the door to which it was fastened.

Kyril pulled his knees up even further into his chest and
spread them slowly while keeping his feet clenched together.
The van's roof was low but by twisting his body he could just
manoeuvre the handle until it was above his head. A loud gasp
was forced from him as the crippling effort began to tell. Let

him not get cramp, for the love of Lenin. He stretched up his hands to the very limit of the chain. It was now or never. He would have to flick the handle with his feet and pray that it dropped close enough to his hands for him to catch it as it fell. There would be only one chance. If he fluffed it the handle would drop to the floor, permanently out of reach.

Kyril relaxed his legs slightly, took a deep breath, and jerked violently backwards, separating his heels as he did so. The handle grazed his shoulder, fell to one side, out of reach of his left hand and came to rest in his right.

Kyril closed his eyes and did nothing for a while. Relief had drained him of oxygen, he had trouble breathing. When his body was more or less back to normal he entered on the final stage.

With short, jerky movements he was able to insert his newly-acquired lever between the door and the metal grip. By sliding his right hand up the shaft as far as it would go he gained the necessary purchase. The second heave wrenched the handle from its screws, and he was free.

Kyril sat up and looked around. There was some traffic on the road but so far no one had stopped. Kyril turned his attention to the boy. The key to the handcuffs must be somewhere. He searched rapidly and found it in the top pocket of the driver's shirt. Now he had no option but to examine the face.

As he pushed the body aside the boy groaned. He was still alive!

Kyril sat back in amazement. The kick had been meant to kill. Maybe the awkward angle had robbed his effort of some of its efficacy . . . ? He shook his head. Perhaps he had spoken the literal truth. There were more important things to do than murder children.

Kyril shouldered his rucksack and struck out for the road. Someone would rescue the boy before too long. Now the important thing was to hitch a lift.

He had lost valuable time when every second was precious. Somehow he would have to catch up on schedule, only now SIS would have a score to settle and he could no longer hope for an easy ride to England.

He needed time in which to rest and heal, and that in turn

meant he needed a secure base. He would somehow have to get to London...and Vera...

For the second time that day Kyril stood on the road to Aharne and lifted his thumb.

11

Royston's car swung into the filling-station at the foot of the 20-storey glass and concrete office block which houses the international headquarters of the British Secret Intelligence Service. A ramp led downwards to a steel shutter which rose at his approach. Royston parked neatly and extinguished his lights. He walked to the lift, inserted a thin plastic wafer into a slot, and pressed the 'call' button. After a short wait the doors opened to reveal two hefty young men in shirtsleeves, pistols tightly holstered to their thighs.

They went all the way to the top floor. Once out of the lift it looked like any other big modern office; the clatter of typewriters mingled with the sound of people talking on the phone and the distant clang of filing-cabinets. C's personal assistant was a pot-plant enthusiast, and there was a long-running office scandal about the Personnel Director's relationship with one of the typists.

Today, however, Royston was not in tune with his surroundings. He never looked forward to his weekly meeting with 'the chief,' and this morning his nerves were on edge from lack of sleep. One topic of conversation was going to

dominate the discussion: Bucharensky. Royston had problems
enough at the moment. Kyril was a subject he would have liked
to avoid.

The first thing he noticed was a dead fish lying on a wooden
board which took up the place of honour in the middle of C's
desk.

As he advanced slowly into the huge room familiar details
began to impinge on him: the thick curtains at the windows,
threaded with fine-spun lead wire, the lush carpet, the smooth
air of affluence which pervaded the place like a perfume. Above
C's head was the usual picture of the Queen. And in front of
him was the fish. C raised his eyes from it when Royston had
almost reached the outer edge of the desk and treated him to
a long, appraising look before returning his attention to the
platter in front of him. For several moments no one spoke.

'In Russia they have a saying...'

C's voice, addressed to the fish rather than to Royston, was
quiet and cold. Royston could not imagine it ever being raised
for any purpose whatsoever, a voice devoid of passion, love
or anger.

'..."A fish rots from the head".'

C picked up a knife which Royston had not noticed before
and delicately prised away the upturned eye of the fish. Royston
watched as if hypnotised. With the sharp point of the knife C
eased a tiny black spot from the eye and held it aloft. A man
standing behind his left shoulder bent down and took the knife
from C's hand, the black spot still impaled on its tip, before
quickly leaving the room. C raised his eyes to Royston's face.

'The pupil. A microdot.'

C turned his head slightly.

'Take it away.'

Another man standing behind C's right shoulder removed
the board and the remains of the fish, leaving Royston alone
in the room with C.

'I want to talk to you about that microdot. But not now.
Let them decode it. Deal first with the routine material.'

Royston spoke from memory. In the next half-hour the two
men covered a lot of ground without taking notes or referring
to files. At last there came a break in the conversation and C
sat back.

'Bucharensky.'

Royston stiffened. 'Anything new?'

'You received the report from Head of Athens Station?'

Royston nodded. He could still recall the sense of crippling unreality which came over him as he took the phone from Sculby's hand and learned of Kyril's defection from Moscow Centre. That was days ago. A lot had happened since then, including Athens.

'What will they do with the boy?'

'We shall pay for his hospitalisation, then get rid of him.'

Royston shook his head. It scared him to think that other such 'heros' might lurk in the lower echelons of the Service, perhaps in his own Station. Trying to take Bucharensky alone was on a par with inviting a rattlesnake into bed with you.

'The Soviets would still have us believe that he is defecting, but if that is so a pretty mess he is making of it.'

'But if the boy scared him off . . .'

'Perhaps. Do you think he is coming here?'

Royston made a face. 'I haven't thought about it', he lied. 'I only know what I've read on the float, a Russian defector wants to make contact with us. But he doesn't have to come to London to do that.'

C sighed. 'I'm sorry about this', he said. 'But the remainder of this conversation is to be most secret. I'm going to have to ask you to sign a minute in blank.' Seeing Royston twist uncomfortably in his chair he added, 'If it's any consolation to you, I had to sign just such a minute myself in Number Ten last week. I know how it rankles.'

Royston nodded reluctantly.

'Of course.'

C was about to speak again when the door opened without a preparatory knock. Royston recognised the man who earlier had taken the knife from C's hand. He advanced to the desk and laid a single sheet of paper before C, who scanned it rapidly before once more raising his eyes to Royston's face. He waited until the messenger had left the room, then said:

'You are aware, I think, that some years ago we managed to install a certain source in Moscow Centre?'

Royston knew a moment of utter stillness, a second of silence and light.

'Source Nidus.'

'Correct. Nidus and I have certain common interests, the nature of which I need not trouble you with. As a result a contact was made of a . . . personal kind. No one else is aware of his true identity. We speak to each other quite outside the usual channels of communication. You follow me?'

Royston nodded.

'The microdot you saw earlier, of which this . . .' C tapped the sheet of paper, ' . . . is a translation, emanated with Nidus. His message puts beyond doubt certain matters of which I have felt reasonably sure for some time now.'

C sat forward and folded his hands on the desk in front of him.

'Bucharensky is going round all his old haunts. He's on the money-route. He is supposed to be carrying as bait a plan which is tied into world terrorism, including the IRA. In London, where he was once stationed, he formed an attachment with a girl called Vera Bradfield. And he's coming here. He's coming here *soon.*'

C hesitated.

'I have given instructions to Brussels station that if Kyril is indeed on the money-route, and turns up there, they are to leave him strictly alone. It would be a waste of time when he is so obviously coming to London. As head of London Station the principal burden of neutralising Bucharensky therefore now falls on you. I have to tell you—although I regret it greatly—that Bucharensky is, or may be, aware of Nidus's true identity.'

Royston swallowed. The silence unreeled itself like empty tape off a spool. It seemed to him that in a weird kind of way the whole of his life had hitherto been but a preparation, a training, for this moment and what was to follow.

C's cold eyes bored into Royston's own.

'You realise what the Planners will tell me.'

'Oh yes', Royston replied gloomily. 'If we can't catch him damned quickly we'll have to kill him, won't we. Otherwise we run the risk that the KGB might kidnap him, and then they'll know Nidus, too.'

'You had better make a start with the Bradfield woman. Bucharensky has another lead, however. Somebody called Loshkevoi is apparently . . .'

Royston looked up sharply.

'Say again?'

'Loshkevoi. The name is familiar to you?'

Royston felt like a traveller who desperately wants to reach some high ground in order to learn where he is.

'It's difficult. I don't want to burden you . . . We have an operation at the moment involving Loshkevoi.' Royston hesitated, conscious of C's narrow gaze. Both men were well aware that C could not compel Royston to disclose operational details against his will. The 'need to know' convention had long ago become an inflexible rule.

'Five are receiving unofficial assistance . . .'

C held up his hand and Royston was inwardly relieved; almost by accident he had found the right words to curb the chief's curiosity.

'Tell me only this. Does the operation involve keeping this Loshkevoi under constant saturation surveillance?'

'It does.'

'So that if Bucharensky comes into close proximity with him we may reasonably suppose that we shall know it?'

'Beyond doubt.'

C nodded curtly. 'Good. Because I tell you this, Royston. The KGB have as their number one priority the arrest of Bucharensky. If he should fall into their hands no explanation or apology will be acceptable in the place where I was recently required to sign my own minute in blank.'

C stood up and moved away from his desk, the interview at an end. As Royston went through the door he heard his chief say,

'We are too old to live on social security, you and I.'

Royston's face set hard. It was a true thought. Roubles, perhaps, but not the dole.

12

It tool Kyril two days to reach Brussels. In western Europe it is easy to cross frontiers undetected and he did not have to show a passport once. On the evening of the second day he lay up in Mont-St-Jean, just below Waterloo, keeping out of sight and catching up on his sleep. His plan looked good, because it was simple. He had learned from his experiences in Athens. Skip the famous 'hidden assets', for a start; the KGB would be watching the banks. Instead take the bus to the centre of Brussels, an anonymous face in the morning rush. A quick walk to the Boulevard du Regent, home of the American Consul-General, where the KGB would not expect to see him but where they would be maintaining their usual skeleton watch. Tram to the Gare du Midi, as if to take the Ostende train, shake any tail at the station, with a fallback along the route at some local stop before heading north to Holland, and Breskens, where Kyril could make his own, very private, arrangements for a passage to England. Speed was the essence of success: once he stepped off the bus in the morning rush hour he would not stop moving until he reached the coast at nightfall. As a kind of insurance policy he had started to

grow a beard and altered his hairstyle; the reports flowing back
to Centre from Athens would bear little resemblance to his
present appearance.

But it did not work out like that.

He stepped off the bus in the Gran' Place, another tourist
doing Belgium in the low season, a stranger wrestling to get
his bearings in a foreign city. He slowly unshouldered his pack
and rummaged for a street-map, his eyes darting hither and
thither in search of watchers. There were none, but he did not
expect them. The regulars would be monitoring the places they
always monitored, every day, without imagination or flair. And
on the boulevards, in the squares, along the bustling
streets . . . there would be one irregular killer, the man sent to
assassinate Kyril before he could put a finger on the traitor . . .

He pushed the thought out of his mind. He had to make a
move. Innocent tourists did not spend the whole day in the
Gran' Place, they saw sights. He folded his map like a man
who has made up his mind and moved off in the direction of
the Rue Royale.

The killer was not there, not yet. That would come later,
in England.

Keep moving. Never present the same profile twice. Hug
crowds. Stay away from the edge of the road . . . Extracts from
his training lectures, years old. 'If you are lucky you will hear
the very high-pitched song of the bullet, somewhere between
a whine and a hum. You must learn to identify it. There is no
sensation to equal it. Your life will change . . .'

Stay with people. No alleys, no side-streets, no short-cuts
down deserted passages. Do everything lawfully. No jay-walk-
ing, nothing to justify an 'arrest' by someone who might be a
genuine policeman but probably was not.

He took it slowly, changing direction every few blocks and
varying his pace to suit the flow of pedestrians on either side.
After a while he knew he had company.

He frowned. That was bad luck. For the next ten minutes
or so he studied the pattern while ostensibly continuing to drift
aimlessly along the boulevard. There were two of them; a young
girl with a dog and a man in soldier's uniform. They were
good at the job but to Kyril's experienced eye it stood out a
mile that they had been programmed by KGB instructors. He

shrugged. Better them than the British.

Something about the tail pattern told Kyril that they were not sure of his identity, not yet. For a second he agonised, longing to pack it in and break for the coast but knowing it was wrong. Moscow Centre—and Stanov—had to be certain that he had arrived in Brussels.

He was nearing the Boulevard du Regent.

'Pardon me, can I ask you something...?'

The lilting, unmistakably American drawl caused Kyril to look up sharply and see a woman planted squarely in his path, street-plan fluttering in her hand. Mid-West, middle-aged; bespectacled; lost... harmless.

As he prepared a few words of French with which to give her the brush-off he felt a tap on the shoulder and instinctively wheeled round before his conscious mind could stop him. In the same second the 'lost' American tourist clamped herself to his side, suddenly developing a grip of steel; the second agent took up an identical stance on Kyril's right; a car screeched to a halt and all four doors burst open. He had a sudden confused vision of the crankshaft case rushing towards him, his chin jarred on the floor and for a second he passed out. Then a blanket was thrown over his head and he was suffocating. He screamed, but the noise was stifled in the heavy folds of material enveloping his head. He panicked and began to struggle, but strong hands held him down. His heart was pounding in his chest and a terrible roaring filled his ears. The more he struggled the worse it became.

Kyril knew the first seconds of the rough disengagement of death. Then he was pulled upright and the blanket was snatched from his head. He gasped for breath. He could see nothing, his eyes were blurred. His heart-beat began to lessen. Slowly his head cleared. The car was racing along a broad avenue, the sun was shining, the radio was playing pop music. Kyril swayed, grabbed the front seat to steady himself and was sick. Someone exclaimed and opened the window to let out the smell. Another man tossed him the blanket and indicated that he should wipe up the mess.

'Sorry about that, fella', he said. 'But you were looking kinda lost back there. Guess I'd better introduce myself. Nat McQueen, CIA.' He grinned. 'You made it, buddy.'

For a few moments Kyril covered his confusion by bundling up the pile of vomit in the blanket. He did not speak until he was quite ready.

'Am I glad I found you. The KGB had me staked out back there.'

The man called McQueen laughed. He sounded pleased with himself.

'That soldier guy was so excited when he saw you he almost wet his pants. But you were O.K. We'd look after you.'

Kyril inspected his face. The man seemed honest enough. He turned to look at the passenger on the other side of him and recognised the 'tourist'. When she smiled at him he smiled back, and settled down in his seat, feeling the other two relax as he did so. The tension was fast draining out of the situation. He was supposed to be defecting to the West with precious documents, and he had made it . . .

Inside, however, he was seething. In all their calculations he and Stanov had completely overlooked the CIA. With benefit of hindsight Kyril couldn't understand how they could have made such an incredible mistake. The British worked on a shoe-string, their resources abroad were minimal. What could be more natural than for them to ask the CIA to lend a hand, with their superior technology and limitless manpower? Or perhaps . . . no, surely not, *surely* the CIA wouldn't decide to take a hand anyway, without consulting SIS? Kyril closed his eyes and tried to see through the countless possible permutations.

But not for long. Escape: that was the important thing. Progress was fast; with every second his chances of making a break diminished. Soon they would be in open country and then he was finished.

Kyril stole a glance out of the window. The car was travelling north-west along the Avenue de la Reine, towards Laeken. Soon they must cross over the Bassin Vergote. There was a chance . . . but a mortally dangerous one. Kyril quietly ground his teeth.

Make friends. Put them off their guard.

'Where are you taking me, please?'

'One of our airbases. There's a plane coming for you. This time tomorrow you'll be in Washington.'

Kyril allowed a look of anxiety to play over his face.

'You say a plane is coming. Can't we leave at once, please? How long must we wait?'

'Not long. We didn't know where you were going to show up, see? Planes have to be cleared in advance; this is some of the most crowded airspace in the world. Don't worry, fella. We'll take good care of you.'

'Please, you do not understand. My life is in danger. They have orders to kill me.'

'Don't worry.' McQueen's voice was reassuring. 'No one's out to kill you, buddy-boy. They just want your hide back in Moscow. Once we get to where we're going they haven't a chance in hell.'

'Where are we going?'

McQueen smiled but did not reply. By now Kyril was almost fawning on him.

'Please ... when we get there, let's stay in the open. Guard me as much as you like, but don't coop me up, eh?'

'Okay, fella. Why'ncha just relax and enjoy the ride?'

Kyril sat back slowly. His lips were dry. They had almost reached the long, low bridge over the neck of the Bassin Vergote. Every agent is taught how to throw himself from a rapidly moving vehicle. No agent ever does it willingly.

There was the bridge.

Kyril shut his eyes and drew a deep breath.

'Are we being followed?'

The driver glanced in his rear-view mirror and shook his head.

Kyril swivelled in his seat and pretended to stare out of the back window.

'That red Fiat ... I've seen it before today. The registration's the same.'

McQueen and the woman turned to look. In the same instant Kyril hurled himself at the nearside door and flung it open, pitching forward with all his might. He had a glimpse of the road coming up at an ugly angle, a tremendous shock ran the length of his spine, then he was rolling in the dust, over and over ... Through a red haze he made out the steel bridge wall. Somehow he was on his feet, not only upright but running. Confused noises behind him ... toot of a barge's siren below... let, oh let there be clear water...

After the shock of the initial icy plunge he seemed to go
down and down for ever. He couldn't move. For an eternity
of time he hung suspended in a cold, thick, muddy-brown
mixture of sewage and oil; then he was rising, very slowly,
the sky above lightened, and suddenly his head broke water
and he could no longer put off the increasingly painful business
of struggling to stay alive.

He heard McQueen shout 'Get him!', and knew he had been
spotted. Kyril trod water, desperately looking round for help.
His rucksack was weighing him down, his strength was de-
serting him. He had drifted about 50 metres from the bridge.
Opposite him a long line of barges was slowly travelling north
on the way to Antwerp; the leading tug's siren was the last
sound he had heard before hitting the water. The end barge
was almost past him now. Attached to it by a painter was a
small dinghy, scarcely big enough to hold a man. Kyril struck
out for it.

At first he seemed to make no impression at all on the water.
Invisible ropes attached to his pack were pulling him down,
down... He began to panic. The last barge was well past him
now, and he was still several metres from the dinghy. He
thrashed hard and was rewarded with a mouthful of wash from
the tug. Choking and spluttering he fought to keep his head
above water. Surely he must be moving. No one could struggle
as hard as that and not move...

His fingers scraped on something solid. The boat... It was
passing him, going away out of his reach. *No!* He scrabbled
desperately for a hold, got it... and next second almost let go
as the momentum of the convoy picked him up and swept him
onwards towards Antwerp, towards the sea.

He dragged himself out of the water with slow, laborious
movements, and looked back. A small crowd of people had
gathered on the bridge, among them McQueen and the anonymous American woman. They made no move to follow him.
It would have been hopeless in any case. Kyril was passing
through a Gehenna of bleak, dock badlands, where such few
roads as there were ended in cul-de-sacs, crumbling warehouse
walls, railway sidings... he turned to face the front and saw

no signs aboard the tug that anyone had noticed him.

As the convoy chugged onwards beneath a cold, stony sky Kyril lay down on the bottom of the dinghy and fell into an exhausted sleep.

13

From his rocking-chair in the little conservatory beyond the kitchen Povin could see across the Moscow River to the pine-clad slopes of the hills opposite. The sun had gone half an hour ago and it was nearly dark. The General, hovering between wakefulness and sleep, could just hear the strains of the B flat minor sonata quietly played by Stolyinovich.

The music stopped. A moment later the pianist's hand descended on to Povin's shoulder and he opened his eyes.

'That was very nice, Pyotr. Thank you.'

Stolyinovich drew up a chair and sat by Povin's side.

'Thank God for Chopin.'

Povin raised his eyebrows. 'God, Pyotr Ivanovich?', he said, with mild reproof. Stolyinovich was about to protest when Povin held up his forearms, crossed, and spread them with a sudden chopping movement, his lips set in a tight line. Stolyinovich was appalled.

'Here?'

Povin nodded and placed a finger on his friend's lips. 'In

the office, too', he whispered gently. 'Things are bad. I'll tell you sometime. Not now.'

Stolyinovich stood up and moved restlessly to the window. Povin's words disturbed him. When generals were under suspicion, who was safe?

'You've done it well', he said to the glass. 'Champagne, caviar, fresh strawberries even. You must be broke.'

'No. It comes from the club.'

'What! You mean the KGB pays for all this at subsidised rates?'

Povin shrugged. 'Of course. We all do it. Tonight it's my turn. Did you see the oysters?'

Stolyinovich laughed. 'Stepan, I congratulate you on your sagacity and resource. Look, your first guest is coming. Lights on the hill . . . let's have some music.'

As Stolyinovich went back to the day-room Povin hauled himself out of his rocking-chair and stretched. He knew without seeing it that the car coming up his drive belonged to Michaelov. Nadia was ill, and her husband had promised to look in on Povin's party for a short while on his way home from the office. Michaelov did not know this, but it was Nadia's illness that had prompted Povin to give a party in the first place.

As Povin passed through the day-room Stolyinovich was beginning some Mendelssohn. Povin's driver was doubling up as doorman this evening; the General went across the hall to find him helping Michaelov off with his greatcoat. The two officers greeted each other warmly. As they entered the day-room Povin, to his horror, heard Stolyinovich weave a phrase from the Khovantschina March into the melody of the Albumblatt. But if Michaelov noticed, he said nothing about it. Instead, he offered the pianist the kind of perfunctory bow which their difference in social function and standing required, and Stolyinovich gravely reciprocated.

'Stepan, a quick word . . .'

Povin ushered his chief through into the little conservatory, closing the glass-panelled door behind them.

'News?'

Michaelov shook his head despondently.

'No. We've missed him, Stepan. I've got Belgium crawling

with men, they couldn't have failed to find him if he was still there. Kyril's given us the slip.'

'So it's London', mused Povin. 'And "Sociable Plover" . . . ?'

'Not a ripple.'

Povin smiled. 'I'm really beginning to think it never left Stanov's safe.'

'You said that before and I laughed. Now I'm not so sure. But why, Stepan? Why go to all that trouble to fake a theft?'

Povin bit his lip. He seemed on the point of telling Michaelov something, then changed his mind.

'Let me at least offer you some tea.'

They went back through the kitchen and into Povin's dining-room. Two large tables laden with food were set against the far wall, and at the sight of them Michaelov's eyes widened.

'When you said a small party I didn't realise you meant a feast.'

'Look at this.' Povin beckoned to one of the servants, supplied by the KGB along with the food. The man came up smiling, a dark green bottle in his hand. Povin took it from him and passed it to Michaelov.

'See what Pyotr Ivanovich brought me back from France.'

Michaelov looked at the marc. He looked at the year. And he sighed.

'Just a little drop in the tea', murmured Povin. 'What d'you say?'

'In the *tea!*' Michaelov was outraged. Povin saw him hesitate and held his breath. 'A thimbleful in a glass. Just to taste, you understand.'

'Of course. A glass at once for General Michaelov!'

His chief took a cautious sip. 'Magnificent', he said. 'The best brandy I ever tasted.' He knocked back the tiny glassful of spirit and wiped his moustache with the back of his hand. 'Well', he said reluctantly, 'I must be getting back to Nadia.'

'Of course. How is she, by the way? I should've asked earlier.'

'On the mend.'

'I think I'll have a glass of this myself, Valery, since you say it's so good. I won't offer you another, I know how it is with your health.'

'I've been feeling much better lately, as a matter of fact.'

'I'm glad to hear that, Valery.'

There was an embarrassed silence. Povin appeared suddenly to realise the consequences of what his chief had said.

'Oh, but then why not have another little glass? For the road. I'll join you.' Povin waved away his chauffeur, who was standing nearby with Michaelov's coat in his hands. 'Sit down, do.'

'Thank you, Stepan. I won't stay long but it does a man good to get out of the house now and then.'

'I've always said so. Pyotr...' Povin leaned over the back of his chair and called through the doorway. 'Play us something cheerful, something jolly.'

'There's this little song they taught me in France, comrade General. But it's blue, does that matter?'

Michaelov slapped his leg. 'The bluer the better!'

Stolyinovich launched into an obscene ditty about some French soldiers who come home on week-end leave and discover that all the girls in their village have signed on at a nunnery. As Michaelov leaned forward, straining to catch the words, Povin used the opportunity to top up his glass unobserved.

'Lights in the drive, comrade General.'

'Thank you. Stay here, Valery, and listen. I've got to see to new arrivals. There's quite a crowd coming tonight, you know most of them. Excuse me...'

On his way to the front door Povin beckoned his driver. 'Tell General Michaelov's chauffeur to go home and come back later', he said. 'Much later.'

By midnight Povin had reduced Michaelov to the precise state of intoxication he intended. It was no easy task. A slight miscalculation and his chief would either have fallen asleep or, worse, had another seizure and been carted off to the nearest hospital.

He had deliberately invited a lot of people to this party, most of them drawn from Moscow's artistic sub-culture. By the time he lent Michaelov his shoulder in order to help him into the conservatory the mood of the evening was maudlin. Stolyinovich, who for some reason was now minus his shirt, poured out love songs in a tear-laden baritone to an admiring audience, mostly women, one of whom was sobbing her heart out. Three quarters of the food had disappeared and the champagne had given out in favour of neat vodka. Only with great effort had Povin managed to keep Michaelov on brandy.

He closed the door and slipped the lock before turning round to find Michaelov already slumped in the rocking-chair, his eyes closed. Povin took the brandy bottle from his chief's fingers and swilled down a large tot. He was sweating profusely.

'Listen, Valery...'

'Wassup? Wassermatter?'

Michaelov's head tilted backwards and he began to rock to and fro, a look of astonished delight on his face. ''S moving, Stepan, y'room's moving. Dja know?'

'Are you feeling all right?' Oh Christ, Povin was thinking, don't let him pass out on me, not yet. 'Valery, old friend, I have to tell you something. I should've told you earlier, I nearly did, only I lost my nerve. Kazin...'

'Warrer 'bout him?'

'He was here. This afternoon.'

Michaelov stopped rocking. Povin watched anxiously as the first stages of cerebral activity manifested themselves on his coarse features.

'Wha'... why?'

'To see if I knew what was going on. What Stanov is up to. And he wants to get his hands on a copy of Bucharensky's diary.'

Michaelov raised his hands to his temples. 'What 'ja tellim?'

'I said that the diary was impossible, out of the question, and as for anything else I had to ask you. He won't talk to you directly because he knows Stanov is having you watched.'

'What!'

'Valery, we're in deep trouble, you and I.' Povin squeezed his hands together and went to kneel by Michaelov's side. His chief's face was flushed with drink but his eyes were no longer vacant. He looked like a survivor again.

'Kazin says Stanov is on the way out... well, we always knew that. But he's plotting something and using Bucharensky to see it through.'

Michaelov's eyes widened in sudden comprehension.

'"Sociable Plover" . . . it always was a fake, just like you said.'

'But not in the way I originally thought. At first I couldn't believe that Stanov was such a fool as to compile the plan. But he did. It exists. It's the theft that's a fake.'

Michaelov was rocking to and fro, his head still in his hands.

'And this traitor, the British source in the KGB the diary talks of . . .'

'It's *our* source in London that Kyril knows. He's carrying *Royston's* name. And he's going to use it to buy Stanov a place in the sun!'

Michaelov staggered up from the chair and started to blunder about the room, hands still clapped to his forehead.

'Fools', he cried. 'Why didn't we see it?'

'Ssh, *please*, Valery. It's only a theory. But we have *got* to act. Do you realise what the loss of Royston would mean to us. *Do you?*'

Michaelov stopped in mid-stride and turned very slowly to face his deputy.

'What?'

Povin chose his next words with care, infusing them with every ounce of sincerity he could command.

'For us, it would finish England for the next ten years.'

There was a pause. The sentence seemed to percolate very slowly into Michaelov's deeper consciousness. When at last he was quite satisfied he understood his deputy he raised his head and stared into Povin's eyes.

'An executioner. We must liquidate Bucharensky before he can do any more damage. An executioner, it's the only way . . .'

Povin gnawed his lip. 'It's a hell of a risk.'

'Yes, but . . . hey, wait a minute.' Michaelov's mind was by now functioning almost normally. 'This is all rumour. Why can't Kazin come out with it in the open? Why talk to you?' His voice had a sudden edge of suspicion in it. 'Why not come to see me? I'm the First Deputy Chairman of the KGB.'

'I've explained all that. Kazin's anxious not to endanger you by being seen in your company. We all know what Stanov thinks about Kazin, and if he thought you were associated with him in any way . . .'

'But what proof do we have? Kazin is asking us to disobey

a Chairman's personal order and he won't even put it in writing...'

'He gave me...this.' Povin slowly held up a key. Michaelov squinted at it. 'What's that?'

'An earnest of the Politburo's good faith. It's a key to Stanov's blue safe.'

Michaelov's eyes bulged. 'You're kidding! That's impossible. Not even the First Secretary of the Party has the right to ask Stanov to open the blue safe.'

'Who said anyone had asked?'

Michaelov seemed about to retort, then fell silent. He was overwhelmed.

'Kazin says that inside the safe we'll find "Sociable Plover." He's seen it. He's seen it *since* Kyril defected.'

Some of the colour drained out of Michaelov's face.

'It'll mean trouble if we're caught.'

'I know. In effect we'd have to burgle the Chairman's office. But Valery...think what it would mean if Kazin is on the level. We know that there is only one copy of "Sociable Plover!" According to Stanov—the only person officially in a position to know—Bucharensky has taken it. If it really is in the blue safe, all the time...'

Two murderous sparks burned at the back of Michaelov's eyes.

'Then we'll know Kazin's telling the truth...and if he's telling the truth, Stanov is himself...a...'

'We've been on the wrong track with Bucharensky, all along. He's just a pawn. He doesn't know anything important, Stanov lied to him, told him any old thing...The famous diary. A fake. Stanov's doing. He told Bucharensky what to write.'

'But why?'

'To divert suspicion from where it belongs—with him!'

There was silence while the two generals sombrely contemplated the significance of Povin's revelation.

'You work late at night, Valery, everyone knows it. You won't cause any suspicion. Take a look one week-end, when it's quiet. And if it's there...'

'Kyril's a dead man.'

Povin played his last card.

'Perhaps we should wait, Valery. Maybe we ought to try

to take Kyril alive, like Stanov says...'

'And risk blowing the whole KGB operation in England sky-high! Are you out of your mind?'

'But there's no proof...'

Michaelov's face set into a mask of angry malice. He knocked aside Povin's hand and stomped out to the kitchen.

'Proof! No time like the present... Where's my car?'

Povin signalled through the doorway and his chauffeur nodded.

'It's coming, Valery. Can you manage alone? You've got the key?'

He helped his chief on with his coat. From the dayroom he could hear the strains of a lugubrious cossack song with Stolyinovich leading a ragged chorus. 'Go safely', he murmured.

As if struck by this farewell Michaelov paused in mid-stride and turned to face Povin, who was surprised to see how serious his chief's face had suddenly become.

'And you Stepan... you go safely also. This Kazin...'

He seemed to falter over his next words.

'...He's dangerous. A killer. He'd slit your throat, or mine, with his own hands and never think twice. Watch your back.'

Michaelov was many bad things but no coward. Povin looked uneasily away, and it was not until the First Deputy Chairman of the KGB was seated in the back of his official car that he began to relax.

This slight chill apart, he reckoned he had judged it perfectly. Michaelov was now sufficiently sober to run rings round the night watch at Dzerzhinsky Square while at the same time operating in the grip of a manic obsession. Povin stood on the steps and watched his car wind down the hill towards the river, and the road to Moscow, until the tail-lights were lost from view.

Back in the day-room the party was all but over. Most of the guests were asleep. Seeing Povin in the doorway, Stolyinovich stood up abruptly, leaving the music in the middle of a bar, and came over to him. A woman protested before consoling herself with a swig of vodka from the bottle in her hand.

'It's hot in here', murmured Povin, loosening his collar. The room was oppressive with smoke and the heat of many human bodies. 'Let's go for a walk. Bring that...'

He indicated an unopened bottle of petrovka standing on a nearby table. Stolyinovich obeyed, laughing. Outside in the hall they pulled on their boots and Stolyinovich donned his outrageous heavy mink coat, the gift of a besotted admirer high up in the Kremlin. The pianist stuffed Povin's bottle of petrovka in one of its huge pockets and a bottle of brandy for himself in the other, and the two men set off.

Stolyinovich was hard-pressed to keep up with Povin, who strode vigorously up the hill behind the dacha as if he was on a route-march. Before long Stolyinovich found himself well away from the beaten track, almost up to his knees in snow, with Povin so far ahead that he was scarcely visible in the white moonlight. 'Stepan', he panted. 'For God's sake...'

At the sound of his voice Povin stopped and waited for his companion to catch up. Stolyinovich found him resting with his back against a tree, hands held to his eyes. He reached out to touch him but Povin sensed the movement and shied away.

'No', he cried hoarsely, and Stolyinovich checked himself. Were they tears that he heard rattle in Povin's throat? Surely not.

'Stepan', he said cautiously. There was no reply. 'Stepan, what's the matter?'

Povin turned to face the tree, resting his head on his arms crossed against the bark, and Stolyinovich heard him take half a dozen slow, deep breaths. The pianist was by now thoroughly alarmed. He looked around. He had no idea where they were or what the time was. Povin was acting entirely out of character. This could take some explaining if they were found.

'I ... I'm all right now.'

'Stepan, what is it?'

Stolyinovich could not keep the fear out of his voice. If Povin cracked now ... he forced the thought quickly out of his mind. What could have happened to reduce him to this miserable state?

Povin raised his head and moved away from the tree.

'Vodka.'

Silently Stolyinovich handed him the petrovka bottle, and Povin drank. When next he spoke his voice was firmer.

'You remember what I told you earlier ... Things are none too easy just now.'

'What . . . tell me?'

There was a long silence while Povin wrestled with the temptation to make a clean breast of everything to his friend.

'Remember always, Pyotr, that what you don't know you can't tell them. I don't feel I'm trusted any more, that's all. And I . . . well, I've been used.'

'Used?'

'Stanov used me to pass on a . . . a certain message, last week. As if I were a dirty *schpick* learning the ropes in some God-forsaken embassy in the Third World. He did it to see how I reacted.'

'To see if I was loyal', he added, under his breath.

Stolyinovich chuckled and Povin gave him a hurt look. 'You think that's funny.'

'I'm sorry. It's just that I and, well, you know, the people I talk to . . . we assume that kind of thing happens all the time in your job.'

There was silence while Povin thought about that. 'Yes. It's true. In a way. Oh Pyotr . . .' Povin suddenly came close to Stolyinovich and laid his hands on the pianist's coat. ' . . . Pyotr, am I going mad, do you think?'

This time Stolyinovich laughed out loud. He was beginning to feel reassured. To him the question was itself a proof of sanity.

'Sometimes I wonder if I am', Povin went on. 'I look around me at what goes on, at the people who give the orders and the others who carry them out and I ask myself, what am I *doing* here?'

'But Stepan, we've been through all this before.' Stolyinovich's voice was gentle. 'You know that God places some of us in a position where we can only do good by stealth. It's His will for us. He knows what it costs.'

'Does he? Is there not to be an accounting, Pyotr Ivanovich? And when it comes, what am I to say?'

Povin moved away from his friend and spread his arms in a hapless gesture of appeal.

'How many Jews have I . . . *I*, Pyotr Ivanovich . . . exiled to starve? Look out there!' Povin flung his arms wide. 'What do you see?'

Stolyinovich hesitated. 'I see . . . darkness. The forest . . .'

'And I see barbed wire. Hundreds and hundreds of miles of it. Watch-towers. Dogs. Kalashnikov machine-guns. *Camps*, Pyotr. How many godly souls rot on the archipelago tonight because of me?'

Again that strange wet rattle in Povin's throat.

'Stepan, *Stepan*.' Stolyinovich shook Povin roughly, his former fears returning. 'For the love of Christ! Pull yourself together. You're over-reacting. You forget yourself.' He glanced uneasily about him. 'Even here . . . you forget yourself, who you are.'

Povin's head lolled forward on to his chest and for several moments there was silence.

'I am sorry, Pyotr. You should not have had to put up with that.'

Povin's voice was calm, unnaturally so. Once more the lid was on and screwed down tight. Stolyinovich felt awkward.

'No, it's good to let loose once in a while. I'm sorry, Stepan, I should have listened, I . . .'

Povin dusted some snow off his friend's coat.

'It's nothing. Let's go back.'

He moved away; then, sensing Stolyinovich's reluctance to leave it there, he stopped.

'Don't worry, Pyotr. I really am all right.' He paused. When he spoke again his voice was sad, almost reproachful. 'You're not in any danger. You never were.'

Hearing these words Stolyinovich looked away, ashamed.

They went down the hill more slowly than they had come up, Povin seemingly reluctant to go home. When they were in sight of the house, almost at the boundary fence, Povin stopped.

'Do you ever wonder . . . ?'

'Eh?' Stolyinovich's thoughts were far away and he was confused by this unexpected arrest of their steady progress down the hill.

'Do you ever ask . . . how far you would . . . how far you *could* go . . . to save yourself? Do you?'

Stolyinovich, failing to plumb the depths of this question, said nothing.

'Would you kill, Pyotr?'

'I don't know, Stepan.'

'But . . . *could* you?'

There was a long silence.

'Yes. I believe so. If it meant . . . no pain.'

For a while this seemed to content Povin, for he said nothing. But he had not quite finished with Stolyinovich.

'Do you ever feel that . . . we could do more?'

'More?'

'For the things we believe in.'

Stolyinovich fought to stifle his impatience. Although, like Povin, he was a Christian he was content to accept his lot in life without questioning overmuch. God had done well by him. He showed his thanks by rising early and practising for eight hours a day to perfect his divine gift. He was very tired, and the events of the last half-hour had drained him of resilience.

'Stepan, we've been through that before. Remember how it goes? "God has plans for you, plans for good and not for evil"? You do His will in your daily life as far as you can. Sometimes I help you, I'm your secret messenger, and that's my part. We get by.'

'I wonder . . . You don't know what I've had to contend with over the years, Pyotr. No one does. And sometimes I think to myself: you'd suffer less if just once in your life you came off the fence and did the whole of what you believed in . . .'

'You'd suffer for less time', agreed Stolyinovich wearily. 'They'd take you down to the Lubianka cellars and shoot you within the week.'

Povin shook his head and remained silent. But as he turned in at the gate of his house some troubled instinct warned Stolyinovich that the General was taking the first steps towards conscience, towards choice, an instinct so strong, and with consequences so terrible, that the pianist was seized with a sudden irresistible urge to reach out and stop him.

14

Sculby pulled on to the forecourt of Losh-kevoi's garage and switched off the engine. He had been expecting to find at least the pumps still open, it was only eight o'clock, but everywhere was shut up and deserted.

'We can't figure it out', Royston had said to him earlier that day. 'Chummy seems to have gone to pieces.'

He's not the only one, thought Sculby. The Sanson inquest was in a mess, he had an intolerable backlog of paperwork and to cap it all he had spent the day arguing at Marylebone County Court in an unsuccessful attempt to save a client from being committed to prison for contempt of court. Royston was the last straw. His face was drawn and there were dark rings under his eyes. Sculby thought he looked tired and ill. So when Royston told him that Loshkevoi had gone to pieces, Sculby thought that that made three of them.

'He shuts up the garage at five or six and goes on the bottle. But that's not all. He keeps futzing up to this road in Clapham and hanging around, as if he's supposed to be meeting someone, then loses his nerve and goes home again. We've got a pretty good idea who it is, too. Woman name of Bradfield, Vera Bradfield.'

'Who's she?' inquired Sculby.

'Never mind. But we're interested in that, Laurie. *Very* interested. Go and see him. Try to find out what's going on, will you.'

Sculby rifled through his 'In' tray. 'You might be in luck, at that. I seem to remember the depositions coming in a while back . . . oh yes, here we are. Regina v. Victor Gregory Loshkevoi. I suppose I could always make an appointment to go and see him.'

'You do that.'

Royston stood up and Sculby walked with him to the door. 'You look all in', he remarked cheerfully, and Royston made a face.

'I've not been sleeping too well.'

'Early night, then.'

'Fat chance. It's my wedding anniversary today.'

'Congratulations.'

Royston grunted. 'She's expecting to be taken out to dinner. That's thirty quid down the drain for a start. Then there's the taxi . . .'

Sculby grinned. 'Think of all the years you've been coming here for a "divorce", Michael. Just say the word and I'll make it for real.'

But now, sitting in his car on Loshkevoi's forecourt, he didn't feel like laughing. It was bitterly cold, and he pulled up the collar of his overcoat even for the short walk from the car to the entrance to Loshkevoi's flat. He pushed the bell-button and waited for the whine of the entry-phone. Nothing happened. Sculby began to feel uneasy. Loshkevoi had sounded strange on the telephone when he had rung earlier to make the appointment; as if he'd been drinking, perhaps. Sculby tried again. This time the buzzer sounded and the latch of the door clicked back. Loshkevoi obviously didn't care to find out who was calling.

Inside the door some narrow stairs led straight up to the first floor. Sculby found himself in one of the most depressing living-rooms he had ever seen. The only lighting was provided by a single table-lamp half obscured by a dark brown shade. The predominant colour of the wall-paper and the furnishings was deep, dark red; the materials struck the eye as heavy and substantial.

'Hi, Laurie.'

Loshkevoi was lying across the sofa, apparently watching a portable television. Sculby looked again and saw that the picture was of the forecourt where he had stood a moment ago. It seemed a lot of expensive trouble to go to over a tiny flat in one of the poorer quarters of London.

Loshkevoi was holding a remote-control unit; he flicked a switch and the picture dissolved into darkness.

'That's neat.'

'Thank you. I like gadgets . . . mechanical things. You wanna drink?'

Sculby examined his client carefully. It was impossible to say how much Loshkevoi had drunk before his arrival, but the lawyer sensed that it was a good deal. The effects showed only in the slow, ponderous movements of Loshkevoi's body, and speech that was faintly slurred. To Sculby, it was rather like encountering the real Loshkevoi in a dream: everything was fuzzy at the edges.

'Thanks. Gin.'

'Help yourself. Over there . . .'

A large, heavy mahogany table carried a wide selection of bottles. Sculby poured himself a drink and looked in vain for tonic.

'Don't you have any mixers?'

'Never touch the stuff. Water in the tap if you want.'

Loshkevoi gestured vaguely in the direction of a door and Sculby went through to find himself in the kitchen. There everything was at sixes and sevens. Loshkevoi couldn't have washed up anything for at least a week. Sculby negotiated his glass round a pile of dirty dishes in the sink and added some water to the neat spirit, trying to avert his eyes from the globules of cold fat floating on the surface of the nearest plate.

'At least we know what the Police are going to say now,' he called. 'It doesn't add up to much. I reckon we're going to win this one without too much trouble, Victor.'

Loshkevoi seemed not to be paying attention. Sculby went

back into the living-room and poured a couple of drops of
Angostura into his glass. He looked around for a chair. There
was only one, opposite the sofa, and he flopped down into it.
A spring had broken, allowing him to sink down further than
he expected, and causing him to spill his drink.

'I've got the depositions here. We can go through them if
you like.'

Loshkevoi waved a hand. 'Later. Cheers.'

They drank.

'Would you mind passing me the bottle, Laurie. Vodka.'

Sculby obliged. Loshkevoi poured himself a generous treble
and then appeared to forget about it.

'These charges', he said. 'A joke. A fraud. What's that
expression? To do with cards...' He rubbed a hand across his
face. 'Trumped up.'

'Could be. It's pretty flimsy stuff. It's there, but only just.
But why would anybody do that to you?'

Loshkevoi rested his glass on the floor and sat up, placing
his head in his hands and his elbows on his knees. Sculby heard
him sigh.

'Oh... all kinds of reasons. You get to make enemies. There's
a lot of trouble I could make for a lot of high-up people in this
city, you know?'

Sculby sipped his drink and said nothing. It was a sentiment
which most of his clients expressed at one time or another, but
if Royston was involved it just might be true.

'Sometimes I think I'd trade it all for a little peace and quiet.
You know what I mean? Another name.' Loshkevoi paused
and sighed again. 'Somewhere warm, where it don't rain too
often. A little money as well, maybe.'

Sculby raised his eyebrows. 'You'd have trouble finding a
buyer if that's your price.'

'No.' Loshkevoi seemed to talk to himself rather than to
Sculby. 'There's plenty of people in this country who'd pay
my price, Laurie. Aach...'

He stood up, putting out a hand to steady himself on the
arm of a chair.

'Life used to be simple. Y'know? Uncomplicated. There
can only ever be one boss, Laurie. S'right, isn't it? One boss...'

Sculby shifted uneasily in his seat.

'Forget it. Just forget I said anything, will you?'

Loshkevoi was standing by the window. Sculby saw him pull the edge of the curtain aside a fraction and peer out.

'I tell you what I need ... I need a woman.' He giggled. 'I fancy a night out. Coming, Laurie? It's on me. There's a massage joint round the corner. Anything you want. Hand job. French. Even a screw. Nice girls, they are. Cheap.'

He was swaying slightly, his back still turned to Sculby.

'... Or maybe we could go and see Vera ... sweet little, pretty little Vera B.'

Sculby stood up, not quite sure whether he had heard correctly. 'Who?'

'Vera, Vera, Vera B.'

Then Loshkevoi did the most extraordinary thing. With slow, elephantine movements he knelt down in front of the window, as if about to pray: first one leg, then the other. Having done that he paused, as if not sure what to do next. Sculby moved forward uncertainly.

'Victor ...?'

As if in response to some unspoken command reflected in Sculby's voice, Loshkevoi keeled over to the left and began to snore.

At first Sculby was so taken aback that he couldn't do anything. When he recovered from his initial surprise he went over to where Loshkevoi was lying and arranged him more comfortably, placing a cushion from the sofa under his head and loosening his collar. Then he stood up, wondering what to do next. He realised that there was nothing he could do.

He took his glass out to the kitchen and left it on the dresser. Then he let himself out quickly, pausing for a second at the top of the stairs for a last look at this curious room the colour of blood, before descending to the forecourt and getting into his car.

French, Loshkevoi had said. Even a screw. Maybe Judy would be free tonight ...

Sculby drove away in search of a phone-box.

15

Stanov stood in his favoured position by the tall windows, looking out over the square. From the other side of the room Colonel Yevchenko watched him curiously. For once the Chief was unsure. Yevchenko could tell from the way he twisted his steel-rimmed spectacles this way and that, unconscious of what he was doing.

The office was hermetically sealed against the outside world. Somewhere in the same building men monitored transmissions, typed reports, kept the machinery grinding away. They might have been on another planet. In the office of the Chairman of the KGB no word had been spoken for twenty minutes.

'Where is he? Where *is* he?'

Yevchenko kept silence. Stanov had asked the same question with a variety of emphases many times that day. Kyril had been kidnapped by SIS in Athens and given them the slip, so much was certain. Stanov's contacts in the KYP, the Greek Intelligence Service, could help no further. After that the veil came down until Bucharensky showed up in Belgium.

'If he ever got out of Brussels, where the hell did he go?'

Stanov continued to stare out into the darkness while Yev-

chenko pulled a heavy, cork-covered flask from his inside pocket
and poured two generous tots of vodka. The heating was turned
low in the evenings now; one of many spending-cuts ordered
by the Politburo. He tossed down his drink and poured another.

'Vodka.'

Stanov turned away from the window and absentmindedly
collected his drink. After a moment's indecision he wandered
across to 'The Chair' and sat down so that he could face Yevchenko over the desk.

'It's going wrong, Nicolai', he said abruptly. 'None of our
people put a foot wrong over Athens. The Eighth Department's
completely in the clear. I was watching every move they made.
It's the same with Brussels. The Fifth Department's clean, too.
The traitor *has* to be elsewhere.'

Yevchenko shrugged. He had had enough of this. He wanted
to go home.

'One thing is sure, old man. There is nothing you . . . any
of us . . . can do.'

Stanov nodded glumly. 'I agree. But things are very tight
now. Today . . .'

He compressed his lips and for a while said no more. Yevchenko knew that the Politburo had met that morning. For
Stanov life was becoming progressively more tense.

'They took some convincing over "Sociable Plover." At first
they flatly refused to believe it ever existed, but I had to tell
them it did, of course. Then they wouldn't accept that Bucharensky hadn't got it with him—or at the very least, a copy.
I had to show them the original—I ask you, Nikolai, a blue
file leaving this office!—and explain about the paper, how it
shows up if it's so much as touched by human skin, but even
then they weren't really convinced. Kazin said . . .'

Stanov tailed off, got a grip on himself again.

' . . . That man is a trial to me, Nicolai.'

Yevchenko grunted but said nothing. Stanov mused, his
sunken eyes glittering dully in the poor light. Since the day of
his stroke the illness was fast increasing its hold on him. Privately Yevchenko doubted whether he would ever see July 1st,
and for the hundredth time reminded himself that if he did not
make plans soon it would be too late.

'Suppose, Nicolai . . .' Stanov's voice rose barely above a

whisper. Yevchenko had to strain to hear the words that followed. 'Suppose we find this . . . this one we are looking for.' He looked up slowly. 'What should we do with him?'

'Kill him. Torture him until we're sure he's told us all he knows, then . . .'

Yevchenko drew his finger across his throat. Stanov nodded slowly, like a man who wants to convince himself.

'Perhaps. But suppose we could persuade him to work for us again, just for a little while, eh, Nikolai? Perhaps he has a wife, a child?'

'Turn him, you mean. A dangerous game, that.'

'Dangerous . . . But deadly, if properly used. Does it not appeal to you, the thought that we might be able to undo some of what this traitor has done? Think of the store of trust he has built up over the years.'

But Yevchenko was still doubtful. He signified as much by raising from his seat and saying, 'Time to go. Tomorrow I'll tell you what I think. Now, we go home.'

Stanov placed his hands on the desk-top and used them to lever himself painfully upright.

'Sometimes Nikolai, I even wonder if you weren't right about Bucharensky. If I'd told him a little more of the truth . . .'

Yevchenko shrugged with obvious annoyance.

'It seemed so pointless, that's all. I thought you were being devious for the sake of it. We both know that Loshkevoi isn't the answer. The traitor won't have revealed himself to a slug like that. If Kyril ever does manage to interrogate him, he'll be wasting his time.'

'But I had to give him a goal, Nikolai. Something for Bucharensky to work towards, take his mind off the knowledge that he was really only a moving target, put up for the sole purpose of drawing fire. Surely you can see that? And you're wrong about Loshkevoi. Have you seen his latest report?'

Stanov began to rummage about on his desk. Suddenly his hand fell on what he was looking for and he held it up to the light, eyes squinting.

'It's crap. Loshkevoi's gone adrift. Why, he was drunk when he wrote this, he had to be. He knows something. I feel it in my bones. He may not know it all, but *something* . . .'

'You could be right.'

Yevchenko hated dithering. He wanted to go home to his warm appartment and have dinner, preceded by a drink, several drinks. His flask was empty.

'What's happening in A2?'

Yevchenko ground his teeth.

'Every one of our executioners was still accounted for as of 5 o'clock this evening. Nothing suspicious. If '*Lisa*' means to send somebody after Bucharensky . . .'

'If!'

To Yevchenko's horror Stanov sat down again.

'Put yourself in *Lisa*'s position. What facts does he know?'

Yevchenko said nothing.

'First. Because of the diary it is possible that Kyril knows, or may know, his true indentity. Second. He knows that I have issued a personal order; return Kyril to me alive. Third. He knows that down in the cellars here they can be very persuasive. If Kyril is caught the traitor must reckon that he will talk. So, Nikolai . . . knowing all these facts, what would *you* do, eh?'

'Then why hasn't he done it already?'

Stanov lowered his eyes.

'I don't know', he said after a pause. 'Perhaps because he's clever. Perhaps . . . because like us he doesn't yet know where Kyril is going to end up.'

He rose, and Yevchenko helped him on with his overcoat, now several sizes too large for him. As the Colonel stepped aside for his chief to pass through the double-doors he heard the old man mutter,

'But where is he? *Where?*'

16

One o'clock in the morning. Sculby floated
on the surface of sleep, half-conscious of the wind that drove
down the street outside while scattered images from the day
competed for attention behind his sore eyelids. He was distantly
aware of being cold; that same night Judy had broken off
relations for the third time, calling him (among other things)
a self-opinionated pseudo-Marxist, and the wind's sough made
the lawyer doubly conscious of the empty space by his side.

He tugged the crumpled duvet over his shoulders, tried yet
another position and pretended that he was at the beginning of
a dreamless night's sleep.

The undersheet was saturated with sweat from his naked
body. He threw himself across to the other side of the bed and
in desperation began deep-breathing exercises . . . one, two, three,
in, one two, three, four, five, out; one, two, three . . .

He started to go under. Judy was waiting for him, long
blond hair unleashed from its tight bun to cascade around her
waist. She was so real that Sculby could see the little scar
which fascinated him, a thin, blue line on the slant across her
left breast . . . she turned her back to him and bent forward

slowly, soft buttocks parting. Now she was on her knees. With one hand she reached back to caress the long strands of hair away from her supple back and over her neck.

Sculby moved in his sleep and awoke, sharp pain in his bladder causing him to lose the erection at once. He stumbled, cursing, to the bathroom. Everything in his familiar flat had suddenly grown a point or a sharp edge.

As he slumped back on the bed he fought to stifle his thoughts, but it was no good. That afternoon he had been wrestling with a point of Social Security law. Sculby was one of the very few people who knew anything about it, though that wasn't saying much. The client had been denied a benefit to which she was entitled but there was a time limit for an appeal, he couldn't remember how long. Sections, subsections and paragraphs floated before his tired eyes. He felt sick, nauseous with lack of sleep. The answer to his problem was there, in the regulations . . . it had to be there . . .

Time passed. Slowly, very slowly, Sculby's hyperactive brain released its hold and he sank into a proper sleep.

The telephone rang five times before he could bring his jolting heart back under control. As he lifted the receiver his imagination supplied the illusory clicks and hums which signalled that in the telephone-tapping centre at Ebury Bridge Road tape-recorders had automatically switched on, activating the voice analysers which would determine whether the caller was known to DI5 or the Special Branch. Until lately he had resignedly tolerated surveillance as part of the price he had to pay for his cover as a standard-bearer for the Left. But recently he was becoming increasingly resentful of the all-seeing, all-hearing eyes and ears of The State.

Sculby struggled upright in bed and strove to concentrate.

'Laurie . . . you know who this is, don't you?'

Sculby was about to acknowledge his awareness of Royston's identity when the latter said, 'Don't bother to confirm. Don't say anything. Just listen. I have to see you within the hour. Drive to Shepherds Bush tube station. Park under the bridge leading to the shopping-centre and wait.'

'Hang on . . . Where will you be? For God's sake . . .'

But the line was dead.

Sculby replaced the receiver and swung his legs off the bed,

annoyed and vaguely ill at ease. Royston had hardly ever contacted him at home before in all the years of their association.
Now this call came out of the blue in the middle of a winter's
night . . . Sculby checked the time. Two a.m.

Afterwards he found it odd that he had never thought to
deny Royston's request, roll over and go back to sleep.

Royston was waiting for him in the shadows of the foot-
bridge over the road. As he saw the white Ford Mexico with
its distinctive broad red stripe he stepped to the edge of the
pavement and waved. Sculby squelched to a halt, and for a
second Royston listened, hearing only the rain and the scrape
of the car's noisy wipers across the windscreen. There was no
tail. All was well.

'Do me a favour, Michael,' said Sculby as he got in. 'Take
this and give it a wipe.'

Royston accepted the duster and removed the accumulated
condensation from the inside of the windows.

'Which way, squire?'

'The Goldhawk Road. Make for the M4: plenty of traffic
going the same way, even at this time of night, and keep to
30. At least you weren't followed.'

Sculby's vague feeling of uneasiness increased. Something
about Royston's clipped instructions conveyed urgency and
more than that . . . a kind of warning.

'Followed? Why on earth should I be?'

Royston did not reply at once. When he spoke again it was
with a question of his own.

'How long have we known each other, Laurie?'

'Six years.'

For the next mile or so there was silence in the car while
the two men recalled their memories of that time.

'Somewhere in England', Sculby's tutor had written, 'a
tailor is even now perfecting a three-piece suit in clerical grey
which will fit this young man to a "T". All you have to do is
wait outside the shop until he's ready to buy it—which will
be soon.'

Royston had believed it, then. From the very first moment
he met Sculby he disliked him, but he never doubted that he
would be good at the job. The tutor was right: Sculby was
ready for conversion to High Toryism and faith in the Estab-

lishment. What Royston had failed to bargain for was Sculby's delighted attachment to his chosen cover as a left-winger. It was, as the lawyer never hesitated to point out, the perfect logical choice: a simple extension of his wayward youth lived in a world where no one really believed that the leopard changed its spots. But when his 'cover' began to take the form of moving against the Special Branch, stirring up feeling against the Police, that kind of thing, Royston's assessment abruptly changed. It irked a man who had fought his way up the post-Philby ladder the hard way, to see this arrogant coxcomb having it all so easy at the expense of the sovereign state. His dislike of Sculby deepened in direct proportion to the lawyer's increasing store of experience and consequent usefulness.

Sculby, on the other hand, admired and quite liked Royston. The role of secret agent appealed to him more than to most people; that was his nature. Whenever he passed on to Royston some piece of information which a client had confided in him, it never failed to send a delicious thrill down Sculby's spine. For him, the rules of conduct and etiquette imposed by his profession did not begin to compete with the well-being and future safety of his country. And it was Royston who had shown him how best he could serve, Royston his control, mentor, perhaps even friend. Certainly they were on the best of terms. If only he wouldn't insist on being quite so smug about his lower-middle class upbringing, it wasn't as if we were all still living in the sixties . . .

'I ask', said Royston, 'because I'm afraid I've unwittingly got you into something, Laurie. Something messy. And we've never done that with you before. So you see, we've got to find out how to play it from now on.'

In the silence which followed, Sculby was uncomfortably aware of his heart beating faster than usual.

'Messy . . .'

He tried to make it sound neutral but the little stab of fear must have showed in his voice, for at once Royston said by way of confirmation, 'Dangerous, yes.'

Sculby concentrated on making a left turn. Only when he had completed the manoeuvre successfully did he say, 'You mean . . . professionally? It could affect my career?'

'It could affect your life. Danger of death.'

Sculby was startled into a new awareness of his surroundings. He suddenly realised that he was exceeding the speed limit and applied the brakes, using too much pressure. Royston swore.

'Careful. I don't want us attracting any attention. Nice and easy, now.'

'Sorry.'

They had reached the start of the M4. At a sign from Royston Sculby took the inner carriageway.

'Keep your speed down to a steady fifty.'

It had stopped raining. Sculby switched off the wipers.

'While you drive I'm going to tell you where we're at, Laurie. But before I do I've got to say this. I can't force you to do anything against your will. Equally, I can't promise you anything fancy if you decide to stay in the game. So what we've really got to decide tonight, you and I, is whether you're the same man who joined up with me six years ago, or whether things are different now. D'you follow?'

Sculby's mouth was dry. He opened his mouth to say 'Yes', but only a squeak came out and he had to clear his throat quickly, hoping that Royston hadn't noticed.

'Mind if I smoke, by the way?'

'Give me one, will you', Sculby muttered.

Royston lit two, keeping one for himself and placing the other between Sculby's lips. Then he took a deep drag and began.

'I'll tell you only what you need to know. When I've finished, if you don't want to go on with this, you simply forget it. Understand?'

Royston stole a look at Sculby. In the orange glow of the sodium lamps which lit the centre divide of the motorway it was impossible to see the colour of his face, but the lawyer's eyes were staring fixedly at the road ahead and Royston had a feeling he was white.

'Yes.'

'Then there's a high-ranking defector on the run from the KGB. A colonel, no less. Everyone knows him simply as Kyril. That's not his real name, it's what the Russians call a casename. Kyril is coming to London. He used to work here, years ago. He's probably got money put away somewhere, and in any case he may want to do a deal with SIS. Now this Kyril used to have a girl-friend in London.'

Royston took a deep drag on his cigarette and exhaled it slowly, relishing the momentary uplift.

'She's called Vera Bradfield.'

Sculby said nothing. Royston allowed the information to work in him for about a mile, then continued.

'Something else we know about Kyril is that he urgently wants to talk to Loshkevoi.'

The car swerved slightly and Royston grimaced.

'Take it easy, Laurie. We don't know why he wants to, and we'd dearly like to. Now you know why we're all so interested in your client.'

London Airport dropped away to the left, lurid oasis in a desert of darkness. Sculby kept the car going at a steady 50, navigating by reference to the chain of orange lamps which stretched away from him to the horizon.

'We would like nothing better than to talk to the Bradfield woman. But we can't. The chances are that she is sympathetic to Kyril and the last thing we want to do is put the wind up the people he's due to visit. On the other hand, by leaving her alone we run the risk of passing up valuable information about Kyril's time of arrival in this country and what his plans are. We can't afford to talk to her. And we can't afford not to.'

Royston allowed Sculby a long pause in which to digest this latest chunk of information. He was not an angler, but he understood the angler's need for patience.

'Why not just concentrate on Loshkevoi?' Sculby asked. 'Pull him in. Give him a right going over.'

'Because Loshkevoi is sensitive. We're holding our breath with you in there as it is. And in any case, Kyril is unlikely to give Loshkevoi advance warning of his plans: quite the contrary. Whereas the same can't be said of Vera Bradfield.'

Royston waited until he was sure that Sculby wasn't going to speak again.

'This is the pitch, Laurie. We'd like you to make an appointment with this woman, go to visit her. Say that you have a client who's mentioned her name. From what you told me about the other night, that's virtually true anyway. See how she reacts when you name Loshkevoi. Pretend to be doing your best for an uncooperative client. Loshkevoi's coy about her and won't talk, but in the exercise of your professional duty you feel obliged to follow up every possible lead, that kind of thing. Try to see if the spare bed's made up. Find out whether she's expecting visitors. Whether she's nervous, afraid even. While you're in the house, plant a bug, something we can monitor. You're a solicitor, she'll never suspect you.'

'You've thought it all out, haven't you,' said Sculby. 'Have DI5 gone on strike, or something? I thought they employed lads dressed up as telephone engineers to do that kind of thing. You don't need me.'

Royston could hear the anxiety in the lawyer's voice. Was he nerving himself up to a refusal?

'Kyril is DI6 material. You know the rules, Laurie: no inter-service poaching. Five have no need to know about Kyril, so they're out. This is strictly London Station territory. P.4 is the only executive arm we have which isn't obliged to operate exclusively beyond the seas. So it's you or nobody, I'm afraid. You see, Laurie, you're uniquely placed. That's the trouble.'

It had begun to rain again. Sculby switched on the wipers. One of them was sticking badly: zink-zonk, zink-zonk . . .

'You said it was dangerous.'

'If Kyril does visit the Bradfield woman he's going to find out about your appearance on the scene. And it isn't going to take him long to discover that you're connected with the only other person he wants to see: Loshkevoi. That's going to make you a very interesting proposition to Kyril. He's going to want to know where you stand.'

The noise of the wiper was getting on Royston's nerves. Zink-zonk, zink-zonk.

'The chances are that he'll pay you a visit. And if he does, well, then you're going to carry the standard, Laurie. You'll have to play him for all you're worth, using your wits. No one can help you. I can't back you up. I've just got to trust you to do the best you can for us. Because we want Kyril. We want him more than we've ever wanted anyone in the six years I've known you. But he has to come willingly, of his own accord, if he's to be the slightest use.'

The car breasted a slight rise and Sculby saw that there was less than a mile of sodium lighting left. After that came darkness.

'What do you want me to do?'

'Make friends. Play him along. With your lefty leanings that shouldn't be too difficult...' Royston checked himself, wondering if he had gone too far. Sculby said nothing.

Zink-zonk, zink-zonk.

Ahead of them the darkness was coming up with terrifying speed.

'But whatever you do, however it goes, you must say one thing. You must work a phrase into the conversation. "For love of the motherland." Just that. It has a special meaning, has done for years. It enables sleepers who've been adrift from Moscow Centre for a long time to identify themselves as members of the KGB. That's what you've got to do, Laurie, if you're to make Kyril swallow it. Nothing less will do. Make him believe you're on his side. Make him talk to you. Find out what the hell is going on...'

Zinz-zonk, zink-zonk.

'...But take care. I said it was dangerous and I meant it. Kyril has killed. Not once, but many times.'

The last link in the chain of orange sodium which had lit the car's progress from London loomed up, flashed by, was gone.

17

As soon as he saw the house Kyril knew that he had found exactly what he was looking for. The short, grey-brown terrace was over-shadowed by a high railway embankment at a point where Queenstown Road veered round to the left, the gap between the frontage of the end house and the soil being blocked off by a brick wall twice the height of a man. That was the first thing to strike him as he stood in the shelter of the broad railway bridge, listening to the hollow roar of the trains overhead. There was no back entrance, so anyone who wanted to approach otherwise than by the street would have to brave either the wall or the trains and the live rail above. The location was as near perfect as he could hope for. Apart from providing him with a secure base, the house was within easy reach of the people he wanted to see. This had to be the place.

Kyril curbed his mounting excitement. No over-hasty decisions, no false starts. For now he was living by one golden rule: he would be seen only when he wanted to be seen, and for the rest of the time he was invisible.

Kyril had been doing a lot of thinking since he left Athens.

The more he considered Stanov's briefing the less he liked it. What had seemed clear-cut and straightforward in Moscow appeared rather more nebulous under a watery, slate-grey London sky. For the moment he was concerned only with self-preservation.

Kyril opened a flap in the side of his rucksack and rummaged through the wadge of agents' particulars. Early inspection was recommended. Kyril agreed.

He looked up sharply, distracted by a sudden movement. The board advertising a long lease of the first floor maisonette was fixed to the wall of the end-of-terrace house. From the adjoining front gate a young woman and a child were emerging: the next-door neighbours. Kyril weighed them up from the shadows of the bridge. One reason why he chose this area was that he knew it well from his spell of duty in 1974 as part of the London team, and the woman gave Kyril a familiar, 'good' feeling. She was running to fat and looked neglected; possibly a single parent making do on too little money. Friendly but not nosy. Typical Battersea.

The kind of woman who would hear a scream in the night and roll over with a shrug, reasoning that it was none of her business, and anyway, she had enough problems of her own . . .

Kyril nodded slowly. He was not going to find anything better.

At first, Mr Williams thought it was just another routine legal transaction. His very good friend Mr Simmons, partner in a well-known firm of Estate Agents, rang up to say he was passing along a client who wanted to buy No 703 Queenstown Road, Battersea. Mr Williams raised his eyebrows. The property had been on the market at £15,000 for months, but no one wanted to buy. It was a Victorian house, nestling in the shadow of a railway embankment, which had long ago been divided into two flats, one up and one down. The freehold was owned by the upper tenant, who had died in the spring. The executors were anxious to dispose of the whole house but money was tight and no one was interested in a rundown end-of-terrace dwellinghouse subject to a controlled tenancy of the downstairs part. Mr Williams's draft contract had lain in a file, unopened, for most of the summer and autumn. The prospect of a purchaser pleased him no end. It would be a simple transaction, for title was registered, and then he could wrap up the estate of the deceased owner once and for all.

Something in the estate agent's voice led Mr Williams to ask a few more questions.

'Well, it's just that the client's very . . . odd.'

'Odd?'

'Yes. Scruffy. Not the sort of person who usually pays cash.'

'Cash?'

'Yes. Banker's draft, already made out to bearer. But he's not the sort of chap to have a banker, if you know what I mean.'

'Is he a foreigner?'

'Don't think so. Sounds frightfully British.'

Mr Williams grunted. 'Anyway. Plenty of time to sort things out. Local searches are taking four months at the moment, you know. Which solicitor is acting for him?'

At the other end of the line there was a chuckle. 'Don't think I'll say any more, old man. You'll meet him soon enough. You see, he's under the impression that you're acting for him. 'Bye now.'

Mr Williams replaced the receiver with a frown. It was most improper for the same solicitor to act for both parties in a conveyancing transaction. There were exceptions, but the Law Society held strong views on the matter. He would have to be very firm with Mr . . . (he consulted his notes) . . . Mr Webb.

Fifteen minutes later there was a commotion in the outer office, a disturbance which ended when Mr Williams's secretary flung open the door to admit the firm's latest client. Mr Williams shot upright, upsetting his swivel-chair. Advancing towards him was a tall, solid-looking man, his face half-obscured by a thin growth of beard. Mr Williams looked into his eyes and felt momentary reassurance. This did not look like an assailant. The face was genial and full of life, the look of a man of the world who had earned his experience the hard way but kept his humanity.

'Mr Webb?'

'Mr Williams. Such a pleasure to meet you, sir, the gentleman at Kelly Stimpson's said how well you looked after clients,

I'm afraid we've never met but I'm sure you'll find we get on like a house on fire. May I sit down? Thank you. Now this property.'

'703 Queenstown Road?'

'As you say, Mr Williams, the Queenstown Road house. Do you have a contract for me to sign? Only I'm very busy today and it's quite essential for me to have possession by this afternoon. I propose to pay by banker's draft made out to bearer, of course you'll want to telephone the bank. I don't mind waiting. Such a pleasant office.'

Mr Williams drew a deep breath. This was going to take time.

'The first thing I must tell you, Mr Webb, is that you'll obviously need your own solicitor.'

Kyril smiled bleakly. As far as he was concerned, this was not going to take any time at all.

'I appoint you', he said. 'I will pay your fees before I go.'

'But the professional impropriety . . .'

'Have your secretary type up a legal waiver. I'll sign it.'

'Local searches . . . inquiries of the local authority . . .'

'Forget it. I'm a gambling man. The upstairs is vacant, yes? That's all I need to know.'

Mr Williams was flummoxed. In front of him he saw a man, a nice enough man he was sure, lounging in the best chair. He noticed one or two details. The man's clothes were shabby and travel-stained. By his side was a large rucksack, the kind of thing Mr Williams's children carried when they'd hitchhiked around Europe. The clothes had a foreign look about them, although the quality was there all right. Mr Webb wore no tie; evidently a habit, for Mr Williams could see a sunburned triangle of skin between the folds of his collar.

'I'm afraid I must ask you to wait a minute, Mr Webb.'

'Of course. Can I possibly have a cup of tea, d'you think?'

Once 'Mr Webb' had been dealt with by handing him over to the secretaries Mr Williams closed the door of his office and drew the telephone towards him.

Five minutes later he sat back, a look of puzzlement on his face. He had spoken personally to the manager of the bank at the branch whence Mr Webb's draft emanated. It was perfectly above board. For good measure Mr Williams had requested the manager to call him back, when he had again confirmed that there was nothing suspect about the draft. Then Mr Williams had phoned his contact in the Law Society, who had hummed and hawed and finally said that it should be all right as long as Mr Webb was prepared to sign a waiver, as he suggested.

Mr Williams took out the draft contract and studied it. Everything was in order. He had a power of attorney to sign it on behalf of the executors, who lived abroad. Vacant possession could be given that day. He sat in silent thought for a minute, before flicking down a switch on his intercom and asking his receptionist to show Mr Webb back in.

When he was through with Williams Kyril went down to Dawsons, the builders' merchants at Clapham Junction, and worked his way through a long and expensive shopping-list before returning to the house. Once he had let himself in he contented himself with making a thorough inspection while waiting for Dawsons to deliver.

It was a solid house with few signs of neglect or decay; the impression which he had formed on his quick walk-through with the agent was accurate.

The door-bell rang. Kyril clattered down the uncarpeted stairs to take delivery of his order, tipping the driver generously enough to prevent resentment but not so lavishly as to cause him to stick in the man's mind.

Kyril took his coat off and set to work. He had given himself plenty of time to get established before he need reveal himself on the streets of London. There was no particular hurry.

Kyril had never owned a house before. The thought that it was his to do as he liked with, that he was accountable to no one, quickened his interest and made the prospect of hours of physical labour somehow less daunting. As he bored the first hole in the wooden window-frame he began to whistle quietly to himself, a cheerful air which he had inherited from his father, who had learned it from his father before him.

First he dealt with the outer defences. All the windows were sealed with bonded adhesive and angle-brackets fastened to the frame. The single drain-pipe at the rear he treated with anti-burglar paint and a wrapping of barbed wire. The chimneys were already bricked up, so Kyril didn't waste time on them, but he secured the hatchway to the roof-space with double iron bars let into the woodwork.

Then he began to seal off the interior. The main front room he designated his headquarters, that and the tiny kitchen leading off. All the other rooms were fastened with the same bonded adhesive, double bolts on both sides of the frame, and padlocks. The front door at the foot of the stairs he fitted with a padlock, double bolts and a new Yale deadlock. When he had finished he bundled up all the keys to the various locks he had bought, with the single exception of the key to the front door, put them into a small canvas bag and slipped out for a quick trip to the nearby river, glad of the excuse for some fresh air. He waited only long enough to see the bag sink beneath the slimy water before returning to the house.

Next came the really heavy work. At the head of the stairs was a door leading into the main room. Kyril hadn't touched it. Now he knelt by the door, on the inside, testing the floorboards. A padsaw would do for the initial incision, and that he had, but for the main task he was going to save a lot of time by using a power-saw. That meant another shopping trip.

It was getting late, but Kyril didn't worry. That was one of the reasons why Battersea, attracted him, an aspect which reminded him of Moscow: he was living in a cash economy. On the street outside his house brand new Jaguars were parked side by side with cement-dusty builders' vans and the front halves of articulated lorries; men in dirty jeans came home at six o'clock and emerged half an hour later dressed in good quality suits, their equally well-dressed wives or girlfriends on their arms. Kyril liked that. He knew there were little shops open where normally you would not even expect to find trade premises, shops down quiet alleys, or in the basement of a terraced house. Within 20 minutes he had found what he wanted, a second-hand Black & Decker, haggled with the shopman, relishing the sound of his own voice again, struck a bargain and paid cash. On his way home Kyril stopped in a 'Mini-Mart' and bought bread and tea from the morose Asian proprietor, again enjoying the brief touch of human contact.

Darkness had fallen, but the street was noisy and Kyril had

no compunction about using the power saw. Let the neighbours complain, much he cared. Besides, it was necessary to make the downstairs tenant aware of him.

At nine o'clock Kyril broke off for a scratch meal and a smoke. He didn't eat much. The bread felt damp to the touch and tasted of nothing while at the same time coating his mouth with a faintly acidic, bilious substance. He thought with regret of a borodinski loaf, coarse and brown and liberally sprinkled with caraway seeds. Kyril sighed. There was nothing like that in England.

After he had eaten he lay down on an old mattress which he had picked up in the market earlier and looked through the black oblong of the window at the sky. Quite close to his house, though not so near as to be uncomfortable, a lamp-standard cast a garish orange glow into the room. Despite its softness this glow brought Kyril no comfort. It made him afraid. He propped himself up on one elbow and tried to analyse the feeling.

So far he was undetected; no one knew where he was. That was fine. Why, then, be afraid? Kyril drew deeply on his cigarette. It was something to do with the area... he had come to the end of his journey now, there was nowhere else to go. Except home. And Kyril felt exposed. He was at the centre of a web fringed with terraces of crumbling property, a tangled labyrinth of high streets and main streets and cross streets and side streets, all leading to him, in the centre, alone. Kyril remembered how as a boy his father would take him fishing on a Sunday afternoon, the sun glinting on the river as it wound down from the Urals, the sound of birdsong, the feel of a clean wind on the skin. He smiled. His father... there was a good man. But he had died, as had Kyril's mother; his wife left him, there were no children. He was in London, at the cold centre of a concrete maze where the sky was always grey and the rain never washed the grime from the stained, forbidding walls which hemmed him in.

The rain. A thin drizzle had begun to fall, coating the window-pane with a dirty mixture of lead, carbon-monoxide and filth. For a second Kyril thought of the stalactites in the caves in the mountains above his childhood home: there too, the moisture never washed anything away, never cleansed, never purified, it merely added stone to stone, drop by drop.

Somewhere out there was another world, in which Stanov plotted desperately, the Athens *referentura* fought to cover its tracks, the KGB combed Brussels, then Belgium, then all of western Europe. But it was not his world any longer. He had no means of knowing what went on there. How much did SIS know? Had Stanov succeeded in exposing the traitor? Precisely *how much* danger was Kyril in, and how immediate was that danger . . . ?

The last question was easy to answer. If the diary had any effect on the traitor at all he must try to eradicate Kyril. He could not afford to run the risk that Stanov might get to him first and make him talk. Now that Kyril was stationary, the peril was immediate. He put that question aside as answered and went on to something else.

Loshkevoi.

This aspect of his mission had begun to trouble Kyril greatly. Before, he could ignore it. Now, at the end of the road, it must be faced.

Stanov had lied about Loshkevoi.

A high-ranking traitor was not going to reveal himself to one of Stanov's irregular agents. It went against all the rules of the game. So what was the point of telling Kyril that Loshkevoi held the key? To divert him from something else, perhaps? But why do that? What was this mysterious something that Kyril ought not to know?

Should he try to see Loshkevoi anyway? Should he leave him strictly alone? Assuming he did meet Loshkevoi, what then?

Why had Stanov lied?

He extinguished his cigarette and stood up, shaking off these doleful thoughts. Action. He had been putting it off for long enough.

It was time to meet the neighbours.

He spent a few moments hanging the drapes at the window, all he would ever need in the way of curtains. Then he went out by the front door and immediately turned left, so that he was facing the entrance which belonged to the downstairs tenant. Halfway up the frame glowed an illuminated bell. Kyril peered closer. 'Trumper', that was all the sliver of cardboard said. It could mean anything. The estate agent had spoken of 'old Mr Trumper' and called him 'a nice old man', but there might be other occupants; Kyril didn't trust agents. Well, there was only one way to find out. Kyril pressed the bell.

For a long while nothing happened. At last Kyril heard the sound of shuffling movement on the other side of the door, together with a tapping noise he couldn't identify.

'Who's there?'

A male voice. Breathless. Frightened. Old.

'It's your neighbour from upstairs. Ian Webb. I've come to say sorry about all the noise.'

There was a long pause.

'What did you say your name was?'

'Webb. Ian Webb.'

There was an indistinguishable sound; the speaker could have been saying 'Go away', or 'Wait a mo', or any one of a number of things. Kyril gnawed his lip. The last thing he wanted was to have to break in. But suddenly the door opened, and Mr Trumper was revealed.

'You'd best come in, then. It's a wet night.' The voice had lost some of its terror. 'Sorry about you waiting, and that, but it's the kids, see? Rotten little buggers, some of them. I thought it was them.'

Kyril took in the white stick, the staring, vacant eyes. The old man was blind.

He stepped over the threshold, feeling and hearing the cold click of lino under his feet. The only light came from a single naked bulb halfway down the passage. As Kyril followed the stooped form of the old man towards the back of the draughty house he began to notice details, take measurements with his eyes. It ought to be possible, the layout was the same as in the flat above . . .

'Come in here, it's warmer.'

'Here' was a small scullery leading to the kitchen. Such warmth as there was came from a paraffin stove which gave off more stench than heat. Kyril wondered how the old man managed without setting the place alight. As if in answer to his thought Trumper said, 'Don't trouble about me, I can see a bit. Find yourself a chair and sit yourself down.'

Kyril looked round. The only vacant chair was a motheaten

pouffe with its stuffing beginning to come out of a tear in the side. He lowered himself onto it gingerly.

'I'm glad you came. I appreciate that. I wondered what all the banging was.'

The old man had awkwardly let himself down into his own chair, a few inches away from the stove. Presumably he was used to the poisonous atmosphere. The only light in the room came from the same bulb in the hall: a shaft of yellow fell through the open door between the two men, illuminating neither of them. Kyril blinked and struggled to get his bearings.

'Things were in a state upstairs. I only moved in today.'

'I'll bet they were. I'll bet they were.'

The old man spoke very slowly, and with obvious effort. Although Kyril could not see him he was gaining an increasingly powerful and detailed impression of Mr Trumper. In his late seventies, probably; breathing poor; partially-sighted; bronchitic . . . Kyril thought he could detect the dead smell of cheap pipe tobacco somewhere, strong and black, but doled out sparingly.

He was incredibly frail. Too frail to live long.

'The old couple upstairs, the Walkers . . . he died, then she died, you see. That's how it was.'

Kyril nodded sympathetically and said 'ah'.

'She was always untidy but when he died she went to pieces. It's been empty for ever so long.'

'Ah', said Kyril again. 'Cigarette?'

Trumper sighed and shook his head. 'No thanks. I used to but I've given it up. Doctor's orders. He's another bugger, an' all.'

'Does the doctor come often?'

'Does 'e hell. There's nobody comes now. My daughter and her husband, they live in Canada. They never write to me and I never write to them. Since my wife died there's nobody calls.'

'But . . . there must be somebody. The people from the Council, now, what about them?'

'What? Welfare, d'you mean? Social Security?' The old man cackled, caught his breath and choked. Kyril waited patiently for the fit to end. 'Don't make me laugh.'

Kyril had a sudden vision of himself, at the end of his life, like this. Alone, in a damp flat without light or heat. He leaned forward and peered at Trumper. He seemed to be wrapped up in layer upon layer of wool, like an advertisement for a jersey manufacturer.

'You shouldn't have to live in a place like this. Wait 'til I'm fixed upstairs. It shan't be long now. Then you must come and visit.'

'That's good of you, that is. Kind, I call that. I don't mind about the noise. It's your home now. You've got to get it fixed. Don't worry about me, the noise tells me you're up there, and I like that. It's been lonely since the Walkers. You'll like it here, you will really. You can't beat south of the river, that's what I say.'

Kyril sat back slowly. He hadn't meant it to be like this.

'I wanted to ask you a favour.'

'Ask away.'

'I keep a bit of money in the flat. I'm worried about thieves. I've bought some of that non-dry paint and barbed wire and I've treated the drainpipe outside. Would you mind if I did the downstairs half of the pipe as well?'

Trumper seemed not to grasp what he was saying.

'It's to stop them climbing up', Kyril explained. 'Burglars.'

The old man cogitated awhile, then chuckled.

'You do what you like', he said. 'Suit yourself. Want a cup of tea?'

Kyril swallowed. To his annoyance his hands had begun to shake, not so as to be noticeable to anyone else, but *he* knew.

'Thanks', he said. 'Thanks a lot.'

The old man prodded the floor with his white stick, as if to check that the wood was still safe, then levered himself up from his chair. Kyril was halfway off the pouffe in order to help him but the old man waved him back. 'No.' His voice was very firm. Kyril knew pride when he heard it. In a sudden fit of disgust he clenched his hands together and squeezed hard.

Trumper awkwardly changed his stick from one hand to the other, and Kyril realised that he relied on it for support as well as to warn people of his infirmity. The vision of his own life's end came back to Kyril. For a moment he lacked the energy to push it away, and instead he stared at it, appalled.

'D'you take sugar?'

With a start he realised that Trumper had gone into the kitchen.

'No, thank you. And no milk either', he added mechanically.

'No milk?' Normally the old man's querulous voice would have brought a smile to Kyril's lips, but now they remained set in a dead straight line.

'The only other person I ever knew who didn't take milk in his . . .'

Trumper looked up from the stove, surprised to find Kyril by his side. His visitor made no more noise than a shadow on the wall.

'Can I help?'

Kyril was thinking, it would be an easy thing to dispose of the body: two dustbin-liner bags over the feet, two more over the head, and all these houses had cellars. Why, then, not do it now?

No. Trumper's death would be unnecessary. He was worrying needlessly. When the time for action came the old man must take his chance, but for the moment he presented no threat.

Kyril fished out a cigarette, saying 'Do you mind?'

'You suit yourself.'

Kyril held the cigarette to the gas flame. Why was it necessary, all of a sudden, to use both hands? To check the trembling which he had noticed earlier?

Kyril observed his body's latest phenomenon with detached interest. Tension. That was all. His body and brain had been aligned for the kill; now the order was rescinded it took both a little while to adjust.

The old man had finished making the tea. Kyril accepted a cup and sipped the strong, black liquid. It was good: not as good as in Moscow but unmistakably restorative and refreshing. He felt the tension of the kill begin to drain away.

'Come and sit yourself down', said Trumper.

But suddenly Kyril couldn't face any more. He put his cup on the sideboard and said, 'I must go. Really. It's been a long day for me.'

Trumper seemed to understand his abrupt change of mood for he said, 'Right you are. I won't keep you. But I hope you'll come down again.'

'I will. Soon.'

He wearily climbed the stairs to his own part of the house, remembering to bolt the front door behind him. Tomorrow, he said to himself, I shall finish. The hole in the floorboards will be completed and then concealed, leaving only a thin float of plaster between me and the flat below.

I will begin my preparations for entertaining Loshkevoi. And I shall see Vera again.

He was standing in the middle of the main upstairs room, the mattress in front of him. His mind couldn't function any more.

Tomorrow, said Kyril to himself...

Tomorrow, I shall...

His head was spinning round and round. The wall opposite rippled up and down, backwards and forwards.

Tomorrow I shall conquer the world.

Kyril knelt on the mattress, lay down, and slept.

18

Sculby was having a dream.

On this, the first occasion, the details of the dream were unclear, although it was destined to recur, night after night, until at last everything was plain.

Sculby knew he was in Russia, in the middle of Red Square, exposed and alone. All around him men were marching, rank upon rank of goose-stepping soldiers, passing before him from right to left, from left to right, sometimes away from him, at others towards him. A great ceremonial occasion, May Day perhaps. The sun was shining brightly, throwing the scene into sharp relief, but it was very cold in Red Square, cold enough to make the cheeks burn.

A solitary figure detached itself from the marching men. An officer, identifiable by his drawn sword. He began to cross Sculby's field of vision from right to left, the white blade swinging in the crook of his arm. Details started to emerge: highly-polished cavalry boots, an immaculate uniform ...suddenly the officer executed a left turn towards Sculby, who looked for his face and found only shadow cast by the officer's stiff, peaked cap. He came closer; soon Sculby would be able to see clearly, and he knew he would recognise this man as someone he had known for many years past, someone he was anxious to avoid, an enemy. Sculby wanted to run and found he couldn't move a muscle, not even to raise a hand against the oncoming threat. But when the officer was only a few feet away and the shadow cast by his cap was starting to lift, all the bells of the Cathedral suddenly tolled so that Sculby looked away, startled . . .

Sculby picked up the alarm clock and threw it across the room. It went on ringing. He staggered out of bed, cursing his failure to switch it off first. His head was throbbing: too much Chianti the night before. A heavy grey feeling of dread, its source as yet unidentifiable, pervaded the flat.

Sculby sat down by the window and put his head in his hands.

The night before, he had arranged to take Judy out to dinner in an attempt at reconciliation. But the Registrar of the Haywards Heath County Court sat after hours at Sculby's request, so he was late at the restaurant, and thereafter the evening went from bad to worse. The double bed remained in single occupation.

Sculby picked up the newspaper from the mat and inspected his post. Recognising his mother's handwriting he made a face and thrust the letter, still unopened, into the pocket of his dressing-gown.

Well why *don't* you go to see them more often? he asked his face in the shaving-mirror. Is that *such* an unreasonable question to ask? His mother was fond of underlining key words.

Then Sculby remembered why the day was bleak. He had an appointment to see Vera Bradfield at 9.30.

She went to the front door with the solicitor's letter in her hand, as if that short, courteously-phrased missive could somehow guarantee protection from the hand that had written it.

'Miss Bradfield?'

'Mr Sculby?'

They spoke simultaneously and smiled the same half-rueful, half-resentful smile.

'Come in.'

She decided not to turn her back but stood aside to let him pass, recoiling a little. She did not much like Mr Sculby, with his pebble-lensed glasses and cynical mouth. There seemed to be a lot of him in her tiny hallway: obviously the kind of man who liked to fill all the available space.

'In here?'

'No.'

She had to reach across Sculby to pull shut the door of the spare bedroom, recognising in him the sort of person who deliberately chooses the wrong room in order to make his presence felt. Something in the way he refused to budge while she dealt with the door suggested that the mistake was her fault.

'I'm very busy this morning. In here, please . . .'

She ushered him into the workroom and pointed to the typewriter.

'. . . I've got a deadline to meet. For a manuscript. Can you make it fast?'

She had been looking forward to his visit. It should have made an interesting break in an otherwise dull routine. But already she wanted him to go.

Sculby took a note-book out of his briefcase and opened it at a blank page. He looked everywhere but at what he was supposed to be doing. Vera sat down at the typewriter, keeping the wooden screen of the table between her and the lawyer's roving eyes.

'You must think this is very odd, Miss Bradfield. I'm most grateful to you for agreeing to see me at all.'

He had a nice voice; she conceded that. But he wasn't really grateful.

'One of my clients is a Mr Victor Loshkevoi. Does that name mean anything to you?'

She shook her head. 'I've been racking my brains ever since I got your letter, Mr Sculby, but I've never met anyone of that name.'

For a while he said nothing but merely looked at her, so that she was reminded of the Social Security inspector who called to see if she was living with a man. She pushed the memory hastily away.

'It means nothing to me. Really.'

After another short pause Sculby began to tell her about

Loshkevoi, keeping to the truth as far as possible and trying to make it sound convincing. Vera's attention wandered; it didn't seem a very interesting story that he was telling her. She decided that Sculby was unlikely to be married: any woman worth her salt would have tried to do something about the ragged tie, grimy cuffs, and unkempt, overlong hair. But perhaps he had a wife, and she was meek and ineffectual? It seemed improbable. His type nearly always married a forceful, strong-willed woman and then proceeded to row with her in public. Vera knew. She had seen such men often, even gone out with one or two.

'So there it is, Miss Bradfield . . .'

Suddenly she wished he wouldn't call her that, and knew it was time to get rid of him.

'I'm sorry', she said abruptly. 'You've been wasting your time. I can't imagine where your client picked up my name. I do freelance typing work and I advertise in the South London Press, he may have seen it there. But apart from that, I can't help you. And quite frankly, I think you should confine your inquiries to him.'

Sculby smiled and put away his notebook. He seemed as relieved as she was that the interview was over, and not at all disappointed at the outcome. She rose to her feet with him and waited while he placed his briefcase on the table in order to close it properly. The latch seemed to be sticking.

'Well, goodbye then. I'm sorry to have taken up your time.'

Now he really was sorry, she decided. In the hall he looked around.

'Nice flat you've got. Best part of Clapham, this. Quiet.'

'I think so.'

'It makes a difference having the other room. I do a lot of conveyancing, you know. Space. That's what people want these days.'

'It's too much for me, really. I never have anyone to stay . . .'

Vera checked herself. Careful.

He walked to his car and she watched at the front door until he had driven away. As she closed the door she noticed that the same man who had been there yesterday was sitting in a car opposite, reading a newspaper. Was it really the same man? The car was different, surely . . . Vera hesitated. Could it be burglars, seeing who lived where and what was worth taking? You read a lot about that kind of thing these days . . .

She sat down at the typewriter and rattled a sheet of paper into the carriage with unnecessary violence. 'Honestly, Vera', she said to herself. 'You'll be seeing Reds under the bed next.'

19

The KGB 'year' runs from 1st July, and every spring the controllers of the Main Directorates meet the Chairman to prepare a work plan for the coming twelve months. This meeting, known as the Collegium, is a formal showpiece. All the real work is done beforehand and behind the scenes. Stanov had vainly been trying to improve the process for the last eight years.

'Every time it is the same', he snapped. 'What I need is hard intelligence: not wishful thinking, not obsequious flummery, not lies, but genuine intelligence. Yet you insist on trying to deceive me. Why?'

The six Deputy Chairmen of the KGB stared up the long table, their expressions varying from abashed to annoyed. The first annual planning session was always like this. It ran to a precise pattern. Stanov gave everyone a bollocking for rigging the statistics, then went meekly along to the Politburo and lied with the best of them. Everyone knew the KGB was inefficient. Nobody seriously believed that each year the number of recruits went up by 12.67 per cent, or that each year Counter-Intelligence arrested 14.74 per cent more foreign infiltrators than the year before. But it was necessary to give the Supreme Soviet delegates something to applaud before they dispersed to Georgia, and the Ukraine, and Byelorussia, and who knows where. It had always gone on like this. Why try to change it?

Michaelov leaned forward and opened his mouth to speak. As First Deputy Chairman he carried more clout than the rest of his colleagues.

'You wish to speak, General?'

Michaelov froze with his mouth open, temporarily distracted by Stanov's acerbic intervention.

'Nothing suggests, comrade Marshal, that the statistics are any less reliable this year than last.'

'I know that,' yapped Stanov. 'That's what I mean!'

Michaelov sat back gloomily. The old man was at his unspeakable worst today. All the Deputy Chairmen had been working for months to try to get Stanov to sign Chairman's Order Number 0078, an instrument which, if promulgated, would alter the delicate balance of power which subsisted between the KGB and the Administrative Organs Department of the Politburo. It was now or never, the ramifications of the affair ran deep, and Stanov, who knew perfectly well how important this Order was, still refused to sign it. The last thing anybody wanted was a row.

Stanov had other things on his mind. The fake defection on which so much depended was entering its final phase. Kyril was due to show his face on the streets of London this afternoon. It was hard to concentrate, knowing that if things went wrong the next meeting of the Collegium, for which the men round this table were supposed to be planning, would be his last.

The morning wore on. Stanov turned his attention from false statistics to the increasing number of 'exceptional incidents' which had occurred in the past year: drunkenness, unnruly public behaviour, even rape. Concentration wavered. The Deputy Chairmen knew of these matters, just as they knew the complaints were important and reprehensible. They did not need to be reminded.

Coffee was served at 11.30, and with its arrival flasks were pulled from deep pockets. The meeting resumed in better humour after a twenty-minute break, some progress was made.

When the adjournment was announced at half-past one there was a general consensus that time had not been altogether wasted, although Chairman's Order No. 0078 still remained unsigned.

Stanov returned to his office on the third floor to find Major Krubykov of the Kremlin Kommandant awaiting him. Stanov tensed. The Kremlin he could do without at present.

'The First Secretary of the Communist Party of the Soviet Union presents his compliments to comrade Marshal Voldemar Stanov, and asks him to attend the meeting of the Politburo which is now in progress.'

Stanov mechanically signalled Yevchenko to bring his overcoat. However courteously couched the language might be, it was unmistakably an order. Normally Stanov had a month's warning of Politburo meetings which he would be expected to attend. This meant trouble.

'Look after things, Yevchenko', he said, nodding his head to emphasise his true meaning. Yevchenko's job this afternoon was to monitor Kyril, nothing else. But Major Krubykov had another, greater surprise for him.

'Colonel Yevchenko is also requested to attend.'

For a second Stanov could not grasp the enormity of what was happening. Someone was at the back of it, an enemy. Someone who knew the importance of this afternoon to the Chairman of the KGB, a man with a motive for keeping his superiors out of the way while he dealt with a message from London.

Someone who could command the Kremlin? No, it was impossible. However high the traitor, he could not simply snap his fingers at the Politburo, say 'Get rid of Stanov for the afternoon, will you?' Stanov struggled to keep a foothold while the ice cracked and creaked around him. There had to be another explanation, something he had missed . . .

'Major, it is necessary to make certain arrangements. Perhaps we could join you in the car?'

As the door closed behind Krubykov Stanov swung round to face Yevchenko. 'Quick', he hissed, 'ring up Sulitsky in the Seventh Directorate. Tell him I want an urgent "time and motion" on cipher traffic between Moscow and London. Don't tell him what it's for, just get him to fix it up by this afternoon.'

'Hopeless. Everyone will know at once, you can't keep that sort of check secret.'

'I know, but it's the best we can do. If they detain us— and oh, my friend, but they will detain us—we must have someone here to watch. What else can we do?'

Yevchenko discreetly watched his chief's face from under thick eyebrows, reading distress and indecision. He was right. What else could they do at such short notice? He lifted the receiver and spoke into it urgently.

A black Zil was waiting in the courtyard to take them on the short journey to the Kremlin. Ensconced in its soft, luxurious interior Stanov spent the drive looking blankly out of the tinted window at the crowded streets. He was at a loss. Yevchenko never went with him to the Politburo. Who was interfering? They would have to try to cut the visit short, make some excuse and leave before three, when, allowing for the time difference, Kyril should be on the streets.

Krubykov rode in front with the driver. Yevchenko leaned across to Stanov and whispered in his ear.

'Does anyone in the Politburo know it's today Kyril is due in London?'

'I've told nobody. *Nobody!*'

'Nor I. Hold on to that. However much the traitor knows, he can't know when and where Kyril is next going to surface. This has to be a coincidence, nothing more.'

Stanov pounded a gloved fist into the palm of his other hand.

'It's a conspiracy', he hissed. 'You know what this is about as well as I do. They're going to try and separate us. It's come at last, Nikolai, the day we've always dreaded. Look out for yourself, that's my advice.'

'Well . . . here we go.'

'Good luck!'

The car drew up in another courtyard and the two old men climbed out between saluting sentries. Inside the Kremlin it was warm. Officers came forward to relieve them of their overcoats and gloves. Stanov followed the well-trodden route, knowing that as they rounded the last corner the huge double-doors at the end of the corridor would be opened to permit them to enter without so much as breaking step.

But this did not happen. The doors remained firmly closed. Major Krubykov, who had never left their sides, was apologetic.

'I was warned there might be a short delay. Forgive me for not mentioning it before, comrade Marshal. Please be seated.'

Yevchenko was looking around him curiously. He had never set foot in the Kremlin before. They were in a wide, parquet-floored corridor down the centre of which ran a strip of dark blue carpet. The colour scheme was easy on the eye: pale blue walls picked out in white rising to rococo ceilings embossed in gold leaf. Opposite the double doors leading to the Politburo's chamber stood a bust of Lenin perched on top of a column which tapered downwards to the floor. It looked precarious. For the first time in his life Yevchenko felt he had something in common with the founder of modern Communism.

Time passed. Stanov paced up and down the corridor, muttering to himself and looking at his watch. Yevchenko shared his chief's anxiety. If they did not get their business over with soon they would inevitably miss Kyril's appearance in London.

Something else was troubling Stanov. With every minute that passed, the personal snub to him grew greater. Not even the Politburo had the right to keep the Chairman of the KGB and a Marshal of the Soviet Union waiting indefinitely. His thoughts became positively murderous. Didn't they know what dirt he had on them, back at Dzerzhinsky Square? Didn't they realise?

The double-doors opened. Stanov stopped in mid-stride and rounded furiously—only to find himself face-to-face with Kazin.

For a few seconds the two men looked each other up and down, neutral smiles on their faces. Whatever their personal history may have been, it was necessary to preserve a dignified public record. Behind Kazin the other members of the Politburo were dispersing in opposite directions down the long corridor, some of them darting curious glances at the two men, standing face-to-face, about whom so many strange stories were told.

'Voldemar.'

'Oleg.'

They held each other by the elbows, briefly, before separating. Stanov thought: no, you have not changed. A little
balder, perhaps, the thick spectacles stronger than ever, but it
is you, Oleg Kazin, still you. Still the same.

'We must get together, sometime. Sometime soon.'

Deep in Stanov's guts a rising spasm of anger caught him
off guard, nearly gave the game away: I'll see you in the last
circle of Hell first . . .

Kazin stood back, fitting a cigarette into a little cane holder,
a genial smile on his face. 'He wants to talk to you, Voldemar.
Alone.' A slight twist of the shoulders and an eyebrow raised
in the direction of the double-doors indicated that Kazin was
referring to the First Secretary. 'He doesn't trust us, you see.
For your ears only, eh?' He laughed good-humouredly. 'But I
asked if I might borrow Colonel Yevchenko. Well, as I knew
you were coming I thought it wouldn't do any harm if I killed
two birds with the same stone. There's a sub-committee being
formed . . .'

'Comrade Marshal!'

Major Krubykov stood in the doorway, one hand raised in
summons.

'The First Secretary asks if you will take lunch with him.'

Stanov had time for one last furious glance at Yevchenko
over his shoulder before Krubykov had ushered him through
the double-doors and he saw no more.

Kazin turned back to Yevchenko to find the old Colonel's
curious eyes full on his face. He smiled. Yevchenko's expression did not change.

'Colonel, I have been asked to chair a sub-committee of the
Politburo. If we are to do our job properly we shall need a lot
of very high-quality technical expertise, people close to the top
in the KGB who know what really goes on there. Naturally,
you were our first choice. I'm sure Marshal Stanov can spare
you an afternoon each week, eh? Come, we'll meet the other
members of the committee, have some lunch maybe. And we
can discuss this Chairman's Order No. 0078—the whole question of the KGB's involvement with the Administrative Organs
Department interests us tremendously.' He put his arm round
Yevchenko's shoulders and began to walk down the corridor.
'Those two will yak all day. I believe the First Secretary has

a number of questions to raise in connection with Bucharensky's famous diary.' He paused in his stride, so that he could look Yevchenko in the face. 'We have lots of time. In fact, we have all the time in the world.'

So it's come, Yevchenko was thinking as he walked down the corridor, conscious of the deadweight of Kazin's hand on his shoulder. It's come at last. Decision time for me, old man.

But why, oh why, he was thinking as they turned the corner together, did it have to happen today?

20

The morning passed too quickly for Kyril's liking. Every time he looked at his watch the hands seemed to have jumped an hour or so. He tried to make himself slow down, take things easily, but it was no good. He was going to visit a woman he hadn't seen for six years but who was as fresh in his mind, his body, as the solicitor's secretary he had spoken to yesterday.

He went shopping, then spent the morning constructing a chair, the sole piece of furniture he reckoned he would need during his stay in Battersea. He used oak, dear and hard to come by, but indispensible. When he had finished the basic structure he set about fixing it to the floor, using cast-iron clamps with holes sufficiently large to admit steel bolts. Then he nailed thick leather belts to the arms and legs and made holes in the leather in such a way that the belts could be used to restrain whoever was sitting in the chair from making the slightest movement, however small.

He cut a round hole in the seat part, so that it looked like a crude lavatory. Behind the chair he embedded a large, closed-eye screw in the window-sill, and to this he attached a length of wire which he had unwound from the clay rod of an electric fire, purchased in a junk shop. In the same junk shop Kyril had picked up the last component he needed in order to complete his remarkable chair. Now everything was ready.

At last he stood up, well satisfied. The house would fall down before anyone escaped from that chair.

The chair was for Loshkevoi. Kyril had made up his mind.

Next Kyril turned his attention to the gas. The result of an hour's work was that he could flood the lower floor with mains gas, making it uninhabitable, or divert the stream to its proper use upstairs. His preparations were complete.

He needed a break. For a few minutes he stood back from the window, smoking, while he inspected the street. No one was watching the house, he was sure of it. Apart from the evidence of his own eyes he did not feel watched, and that was the acid test. The nerves of his body did not register surveillance. The house opposite his own was occupied by the same family each day and there were few visitors anywhere along the road. The same cars stood on the street but their positions were different each day, and that was normal. No one made a pretext to come to the door.

Kyril likened the street to a busy river which threw up no sediment, formed no visible sandbanks, but continued to flow uninterruptedly past his door. If one day there was a sandbank, he would notice it.

Kyril ate some more of the insipid loaf and threw the rest away. 'You need a meal', he said aloud. 'Something to keep you alive. Do you realise you haven't eaten properly for...'

He shut up, suddenly conscious of the folly of talking to himself. But the idea was good: he did not want to faint when she opened the door and he saw her for the first time, did not want to betray anything which might be construed as weakness.

At last he was ready. He went down the stairs to the front door, put his hand on the night-latch and turned it. A shaft of sunlight flooded into the dingy hall, causing Kyril to blink. The street was empty. He looked to right and left. Nobody came. No curtain moved.

He stepped into the small area of concrete which separated the house from the pavement and pulled the door to behind him. A car cruised slowly up the street. The black youth behind the wheel took no notice of Kyril. Somewhere close by he heard the noise of milk bottles smashing, followed by the miaow of a cat.

Now he was on the pavement.

Before he had gone more than a few paces he heard a door open and slam. The noise came from behind him, on the same side of the road. The door must belong to the house next to his own. Kyril's breathing quickened. That's where they'd be, the enemy . . . no, of course not, it was too soon. Surely it was too soon.

Footsteps behind him now, quick and young-sounding. A woman.

'Hal-*lo*. Lovely day, innit?'

Kyril reluctantly stopped and turned. His next door neighbour was young and blonde, her hair trailing down to tiny breasts. On her hand hung the same silent child, thumb stuck firmly into mouth, as he had seen earlier. The child stared up at Kyril with unblinking curiosity.

He smiled and nodded. The girl's eyes never quite fastened on his, as is the way of those who talk to strangers. Nothing about his appearance seemed to strike her as odd or worthy of comment. He began to breathe more easily.

'Is that you making all the noise next door?'

Kyril wrestled with indecision. For a second he had thought she meant to move on but now she seemed rooted to the spot, ready to chat all day. He looked at the fourth finger of her left hand and found no ring. His first reaction had been the right one. A single mother; bored, lonely, slave to the voracious little monster by her side.

He pretended to be afflicted with a violent bout of coughing and banged his chest.

'You all right?'

The girl's eyes widened in concern. *Why didn't she go?*

'Me chest', he croaked. 'Very bad lately.'

'You ought to see someone about that. My movver died of it. Yeah. Bronchal, it was. 'Aven't seen you since you come in. 'Ow you getting on then, all right?'

Kyril nodded again. The muscles of his lower abdomen were tight with nerves. He could stand only so much more of this.

'You don't half make a row. I dunno 'ow I put up wivit.

An' you don't look at all well, honest.'

'Feelin' all right. Sorry about the noise. All done now.'

Kyril smiled and turned his back on her. He could feel the girl's eyes boring into him. She did not move. He took a step. And another.

She was by his side.

'Look, why don't you come in for a cuppa tea or somefink? One day soon.'

Kyril nodded and coughed again.

'Yeah, well, look after yourself. I gotta be going now. Playgroup.'

As if to emphasise this last point she gave the child a good shake. It—Kyril couldn't tell the sex—extracted its thumb from its mouth and gave the girl a long, hard look that might have meant pain or just simple hate. Then they were going down the hill away from him, the child half-walking, half being dragged along by its mother, who said nothing but marched straight ahead, not turning back, until they reached the corner and disappeared.

Kyril was certain that the girl did not come from any of the major intelligence services. She was not, in any sense of the term, a 'watcher'. Children were sometimes used as cover, but not children as young as that, and certainly not one parent children who might suddenly require attention at an inconvenient moment.

Stanov? No. He would not as yet be aware even that Kyril had made it to London unscathed. But there was something of Stanov in the set-up, nonetheless: a baby-sitter next door, just in case.

Kyril shook his head. He was imagining things in his search for reassurance. She was just a girl, a girl with a bastard child, someone so tied up in her own affairs that she would be unlikely to remember even that she had invited him for tea.

He spent the next half-hour checking for tails. There were none. Once he was sure of that he ceased wandering aimlessly and began to walk with a purpose. He took a snack in a sandwich-bar, scanning the pavement as he munched his roll and drank his milk. When he left the traffic had grown busier, the streets more crowded. At last he was negotiating the busy junction at the end of St Johns Road.

A little shop on the corner caught his eye, and he realised he was getting low on cigarettes. He went in, and for the umpteenth time marvelled at the glittering array of packages and jars which confronted him. Every kind of chocolate, sweet, cigarette, even cigars were on prominent display here, in this tiny south London corner shop. Yet the people he passed on his way to the counter looked dour and dissatisfied, as if all this meant nothing. Kyril dithered for a moment between several brands of expensive king-size filters, enjoying the embarrassment of choice. The shopman took his money without a smile. 'We will bury you', that is what Kruschev had said, and he was right. That is what you did to dead people, people who were long ago rendered incapable of appreciating that they were alive at all.

He looked at his watch. The timing was perfect. A few more steps and he was in Vera's road. Immediately it was like Athens all over again. The criss-cross rays of surveillance meshed to entrap him in their web. Now, however, Kyril did not falter in his stride. He was expecting watchers here; their absence would have spelled danger. He had orders to be seen at this time, in this place.

A car...no, two cars, on opposite sides of the road. Very obvious—the arm on the door, that was poor craft. If it had been up to Kyril he would have had the windows tightly closed and used a mirror from a concealed position on the floor. They must feel very confident.

If they were taking the game seriously, as Stanov predicted, SIS would have requisitioned the houses on either side of Vera's and the one directly across the street from it. As he approached, Kyril vainly strove to see behind the net curtains. Nothing differentiated these houses from all the rest.

He turned into the gateway of Number 48 and walked up the path.

'They sacked her, of course', Stanov had said, peering closely at him to see how he took it. 'Even the British Foreign Office retains some pragmatism. But she's still living in the old house. She works at home, typing mostly. So she'll be in when you call.'

As his finger hovered over the bell Kyril hoped desperately

that she was away, on holiday, in hospital, anything. Like his own house, No 48 Turpin Road was divided into two flats, only in this part of Clapham they were called maisonettes. Kyril didn't have to look for the right bell. His finger found it as if by instinct.

Behind him in the street a car engine fired. Kyril did not turn his head. He became aware that within the house there was suddenly silence, and he realised that a typewriter had been clacking away in his subconscious ever since he reached the door.

The car drove slowly up the street. As Kyril resisted the nagging voice in his head which told him to look back, the door opened.

She had changed, of course she had changed, but Kyril knew her instantly. The eyes could not alter. The same shy, diffident eyes with the same light in them, the look of surprise he remembered from years ago.

She stood with one hand on the doorframe, her lips slightly parted in the first shock of surprise at seeing a stranger and realising that he was not quite a stranger, after all. Then knowledge came; her mouth fell open, the hand dropped away from the frame, and she was retreating into the hall, her head moving from side to side in slow, disbelieving sweeps.

Kyril came over the threshold very quickly and shut the door.

'Hello, Vera.'

She said nothing at first. Kyril wondered whether she had heard.

'If you don't mind,' she said weakly, 'I'm going to sit down.'

He followed her into the sitting-room. That had changed. The bare walls were now covered with a pretty paper, full of light and space, with neat watercolours carefully chosen to complement the pattern. In place of the old trestle, much stained with the rings left by hot dishes and mugs, was a fine piece of solid pine with carver chairs to match. The carpet looked new, as did the wing-chair in the window and the sofa, both covered with a loose version of the wallpaper.

In the window, beside the chair, stood a Chinese vase containing a spider-plant. That or a similar plant had stood in the same vase six years ago. It was as if someone had dismantled the room Kyril remembered and very carefully constructed a new one round the plant and its vase, so as not to disturb them.

Kyril looked again at Vera, for the first time noticing things other than her eyes. She looked tired but well. Her face was tanned, as if from lying in the sun, but the skin showed few signs of aging. Only the neck, where the first indications come, was slightly mottled. Her hair was different; she used to wear it long but now it was cut short, curling inwards round her neck. It suited her. She was neither fatter nor taller than he remembered. The features were the same. Why was it, then, that she was no longer pretty?

He struggled for something to say, anything to break the silence. 'This is . . . wonderful. You've done well.'

She looked around in response to his gesture, a look of puzzlement on her face.

'The flat?'

'Yes.'

She studied him, as if unsure whether he was playing a joke on her.

'It's all very cheap. It's all I can afford.'

He stared at her. 'But . . . in Moscow there is nothing like this. Only for wealthy people.'

She shook her head, the beginnings of a smile on her lips.

'You never learn, do you? In England you have to be very poor now not to have a room like this. You and your Moscow. Oh Ivan.'

Her voice was a mixture of tired amusement and hopelessness. There was a new, inner calm about her which Kyril found unsettling, he couldn't fathom why.

Her clothes were different, too. She was wearing a pair of faded denim jeans, the sort of thing which fetched a good price on the black market at home, and a thick, chunky sweater. With a little start of surprise he realised that almost everyone in London seemed able to afford clothes like that.

'Oh Ivan, why did you go?'

She was sitting on one of the carver chairs, hands folded in her lap. He stood up abruptly and went to the window, taking care not to disturb the net curtains. One of the two cars was still there, the other had disappeared. The house opposite showed no sign of life.

'Still the same Ivan. Who's following you this time?'

Keeping his back to her he said, 'Do you have a radio?'

For an answer she got up and went to a cabinet by the far wall. A second later loud pop music spilled into the room.

'Nothing changes, does it Ivan?'

He moved about restlessly. Her probing annoyed him.

'Some things do. For instance, I'm not sure, but I think they have a laser beam directed at this window. Whatever we say gets ferried along the beam to their receiver in the house over the way. Have you had any unusual visitors lately?'

She thought. 'No.'

'Telephone repairmen, gas inspectors, that sort of thing?'

Vera shook her head. 'Nobody. Unless...'

'Yes?'

'Well, unless you count the solicitor.'

Kyril moved close to her. 'Where did he stand? Did he sit?'

She showed him by acting out Sculby's movements as far as she could remember them. Kyril watched her intently.

'Wait... what was he doing over there?'

'His case wouldn't shut properly... he rested it on the table.'

There were a number of possibilities, but the first guess turned out to be correct. His fingers slid along the edge of the table and almost as once found a tiny plastic box on a spike, the size of a drawing pin's. He held it up between his fingertips for her to see before throwing it on the floor and jumping on it.

'Come.'

He beckoned her over to the sofa. She followed slowly, her wide eyes darting this way and that, the first signs of fear apparent on her face. As she sat down beside him he pulled her close and left his arm around her shoulder. She stiffened but did not pull away. After a while she relaxed a little and unconsciously nestled into the crook of his arm.

'Whisper. Who was this solicitor? Tell me about him.'

'He made an appointment to see me. He thought I might be able to help one of his clients by being a witness, I think...'

'Name?'

'Sculby. I've got his letter somewhere.'

She went across to the mantelpiece and felt behind the clock. 'Here.'

Kyril read it quickly. Vera saw him crumple the paper at one point, as if something in the message had moved him. Then he held it up against the light. The letter seemed innocent enough. He handed it back to her with a frown on his face.

'You can keep it if you like.'

He shook his head. 'I'll remember. What else did he say to you about this...Loshkevoi?'

Vera told him the morning's events. Kyril sat with his head in his hands and his eyes closed, as if recording every word. When she had finished he said nothing. After a while she subdued the nervousness which his silence inspired in her enough to ask a question.

'What are you doing?'

Kyril opened his eyes and licked his lips.

'Defecting.'

Her eyes widened still further and for a moment she did not speak.

'Who's out there?'

'Everyone. The KGB. They have to stop me, you see. And the British.'

'Can't they protect you? The British, I mean. If you're going over to them...'

He shook his head sadly. 'It's not as simple as that. I have to choose my own time, Vera. They think I'm a plant, in any case. They're just as likely to shoot me as the KGB.'

At the word 'shoot' her hand tightened on his arm, and immediately relaxed.

'Then why have you come here? You must know they'd be watching me if they're waiting for you...'

'I had to see you. Don't worry, Vera, I want nothing from you, not shelter, not money, nothing. But...can you understand this? I'm in the middle of making a decision, the biggest decision of my whole life. And if I get it wrong...'

He pulled her closer, and she gave without resistance. 'But how can I help?'

'By talking. About the past. About...us. You never married after I left.'

'No, I never married.' Her voice was suddenly cold. She allowed her head to loll back on the sofa so that she could stare at the ceiling without meeting Kyril's eyes. 'I told myself to forget you. I *did* forget you, in a way.'

'In a way...?'

'Yes. There never was a day went by without my thinking of you, seeing your face. The memories are blurred now.'

She slowly raised her head and turned to face him.

'Not like they'll be tomorrow. When you're gone. Because you are going, aren't you?'

He hesitated for a second before nodding.

She shook her head sadly. 'Then why did you have to come back, Ivan? I could live without you. I have done for six years. Why come back and spoil it all. Wasn't it enough, what you did to me?'

For several minutes the music from the radio was the only sound to be heard in the sunlit room. Vera pulled herself up abruptly and went to stand by the window, her arms folded, hands caressing forearms in a remote, despondent gesture.

'Stay away from the window', warned Kyril. Vera shook her head violently.

'I said...' Kyril jumped up and reached out to jerk her back. Vera pulled away from him, keeping her head turned, and he realised that she was crying.

Inside Kyril something snapped. All his roughness died away. When he reached out it was to take her in his arms and hold her tightly, clutching her body to him while his hands began to stroke her hair, the glorious raven-black hair. It was as if his hands were reliving a memory. They had done this before, so many times. Vera's body was shaking, the sobs communicating her distress straight into him, while they stood, locked together, uncaring, before the bright white window.

When he picked her up Vera did not protest. She lay quiescent in his arms, looking at him like a trusting child. As he laid her on the bed she raised her hands to help him remove the sweater, and when his own hands fumbled with the strap of her bra she showed him how it went. Only when he lay down beside her did she hold him away for a moment while looking up and down his body, as if in wonder. Her hand went to hold his erect penis, stroking it gently upwards in a way he remembered; Kyril lay there, passive, striving to keep his body under control while she renewed her acquaintance with his body. At last she raised her hand to his lips and he kissed the fingers one by one, tasting the faint musk of his own genitals, before folding her in his arms. The second before penetration, just as he was gently lowering his weight on to her, she pushed at his chest with her hands, in a moment of rebellion; then the same hands slipped round to his back and as her flesh closed round his he felt the sudden reflexive rending of her nails.

For Kyril everything was old and familiar and new and exciting. They made love twice, very quickly, and then, after an interval, a third time, more slowly. It was as though they were trying to compare the memory with the reality, unable to decide which was best. When they were tired and the room was growing darker he made her put on the sweater, nothing else, and lie in his arms with her head on his chest. For the first time, they began to talk: talk as old friends, old lovers.

'What did they do to Stefanie?'

For a moment Vera wanted to pretend that the name meant nothing to her, but only for a moment. Poor, dear Stefanie, whose negative vetting did not disclose that she worked for the KGB, relaying information to the embassy through Ivan Bucharensky. First my boss, then my flat-mate, thought Vera. Friends. Until the day when, through a mixture of appallingly bad luck and Stefanie's negligence, Vera had met Ivan.

'Nothing, in the end. There wasn't quite enough evidence for a trial. She went abroad, wrote for a while.'

'And you?'

'Oh come on, you know what happened to me.'

It was not hostile. They continued to lie in the gathering gloom, still content.

'And you're really poor?'

She smiled. 'Not really. Not in the way you mean. It's just that . . . oh, I don't know. We always lived in different worlds, you and I. The stuff in this flat, the furniture, the clothes, the food even, they're *ordinary*, Ivan. Can't you understand that? They're the sort of thing we have in this country, that we're used to. It's funny, do you remember the famous weekend in Paris?'

His face crinkled in a frown. 'Paris. I can't . . .'

'I'd been saving for months, long before I met you, a little bit put by every week, for two days in Paris. Stefanie and I, just us. And when we told you, you were so angry. Don't you remember? You went on and on about extravagance, and decadence. When I learned the truth, later, about you and her . . . well, I thought perhaps Paris interfered with one of your plans, or something. But then I thought: no. It's because where Ivan comes from people don't go away at all. Because they can't. And even if they could, even if the authorities would let them, they don't have that kind of money. They don't have the freedom to blow everything on one glorious spree of pink champagne and smoked salmon. The Soviet state will save them from their folly.'

She wriggled out of his arms and went to the dressing-table. Kyril heard the scrape of a match and smelled smoke.

'Cigarettes? You?'

'Oh yes, me. People do change, you know. England's changing.'

'How do you mean?'

'We're getting like you.' She inhaled deeply and lay back in his arms, letting the smoke escape with her next words. 'The state is determined to save us all from ourselves. Look. Have you seen this? Oh damn, it's dark in here . . .'

She reached out to the bedside light, but he restrained her gently. 'Just tell me.'

'It says on the packet: Her Majesty's Government Health Warning. Smoking can be dangerous to your health.'

'Yes. I've seen it. But we don't have that in Russia.'

'No, but it's all the same thing. It's the low road, and we've started to tread it. Bit by bit, year by year. So slowly that we don't even notice it's happening any more.'

Kyril lay back, cradling his head in his arms, and looked at the ceiling. He didn't understand. What had a packet of cigarettes to do with travelling abroad? In Russia every citizen had to carry an internal passport containing the all-important 'propiska', which entitled the bearer to reside in a particular locality. In England it was different. In England everyone was free. The greenest new 'schpick' enduring his first day's training in the KGB knew that.

'Ivan.'

'Yes.'

But Vera did not respond at once. Instead she drew hard on her cigarette; Kyril watched the little point of red fire glow in the darkness of the bedroom before dying away.

'Ivan, have you come back to me? Have you? You said you were defecting...'

For a moment Kyril did nothing. Then he swung his legs off the bed and began to dress.

'Ivan, no, listen to me, please listen to me. I didn't want to interfere, it's just that you said...'

'I know what I said.' His voice was low and sad and somehow humble. 'Vera, I...I think I made a mistake to come here. I'm sorry.'

This time she managed to switch on the light without him sensing in advance what she was going to do. They blinked in the sudden flash. In a split second Kyril was by the window, drawing the curtains with a violence that surprised even him. As the anger drained away he let his head fall forward on to his hands where they met, holding the curtains tightly together.

'I see.'

Vera stood up and mechanically began to smooth down the crumpled bedclothes. When she had done that she started to dress, keeping her back to Kyril.

'Vera, listen.' Kyril swung her round to face him. Vera's eyes were cold, her expression closed against him. 'Everything's a mess at the moment. But if I manage to sort things out, if I can get through safely, then...then yes, I've come back to you. I promise.'

His hands dropped from her shoulders; she swayed a little, as if missing their support, but her eyes never left his face.

'I love you, Vanya', she said evenly. 'I've always loved you, right from the first. I'll always love you.'

For an answer he held out his hands, and she came to him.

'Tell me what to do', she said after a while.

'Let's get dressed first.'

When they were sitting in the front room again she brought him gin and supper. It was the first decent food Kyril had tasted since he arrived in England.

'No vodka I'm afraid. Too painful. Silly, isn't it?'

Kyril shook his head gently. 'Not silly.'

She tilted her glass at him, and they drank.

'The first thing is this. People are going to come and talk to you, lots of people. Tell them the truth and they won't hurt you. I came. I stayed a while. I didn't tell you anything except I'm defecting but I have problems. They know all that anyway. But most important, you don't know where I am.'

'Vanya, I . . .'

Kyril held up his hand. 'No, Vera. It has to be this way. When I leave you, you don't know where I'm going, and you can't tell them what you don't know. They'll see the sense of that. They don't seriously expect you to know.'

Her face seemed to have shrunk. He could see fear in her eyes, fear and the realisation, at last, of what it all meant.

'No one'll want to hurt you', he said reassuringly. 'But they'll ask you things and they'll be very insistent. Don't give in. And don't—Vera, this is so important—don't have anything to do with this solicitor who came to see you. Or his client. If Loshkevoi turns up here, don't let him in, just call the Police at once, you hear?'

She nodded numbly. For the second time her Vanya was turning the world upside down. She didn't want to face the future, not yet.

Kyril stroked the hair off her forehead.

'Be patient', he said. 'Don't believe anything you hear on the radio or television or read in the papers. Promise.'

She nodded again.

'And now you have to help me get out of here.'

She looked up sharply, tears glistening in her eyes. 'Now?'

'Yes, Vera. I'm sorry. Now.'

He put down the tray and helped her to her feet. She clung to him and they kissed, long and hard. Then she pushed him away to show that she was ready, and he pointed to the telephone.

'I want you to call a taxi. Choose a firm you haven't used before. If they ask where you want to go, give an address somewhere quite close, but Vera . . . make sure it's a real address. Ask them to say how long they'll be in coming.'

Vera started to flip through the Yellow Pages. Kyril stood by the window, pushing aside the curtain a fraction, enough to give him a restricted view of the road. Everything was quiet.

It took a while for Vera to find a company prepared to
answer the phone, let alone undertake the journey, but at last
she had discharged Kyril's instructions to the full.

'Get your coat. You're coming with me to the station.'

'The station . . .'

'I have a plan, Vera. But I need your help. Outside there
are at least two men waiting for me, maybe more. One of them
is British and he doesn't matter. DI6 are waiting for me to
make the first move. So long as they can see me they won't
worry. But the KGB are out there too, and they're a different
proposition. I'm wanted in Moscow—alive. Not even the KGB
are stupid enough to kidnap me here, especially with a DI6
agent watching what goes on. But it's doubly important for
them not to lose me. Their only chance is to tail me from here
back to my home-base.'

'But can you be sure? Mightn't they risk anything if they
want you enough?'

'They need to know where I'm staying. I'm supposed to
have stolen one of their project-plans and it's extremely unlikely
that I'd have it on me.' He smiled bleakly. 'Don't worry, Vera.
I'm only followed if I want to be followed. And this time, I
don't. But you've got to help me. Now listen . . .'

About a quarter of an hour later a minicab drew up outside
the house, and as the driver opened his door to get out he found
the fares already slipping quietly into the back seat.

'Clapham Junction', said Kyril, adding, as the driver was
on the point of complaining, 'We've changed our minds. Will
ten pounds cover it?'

The driver said nothing, but started the engine.

Kyril looked back through the rear window. The darkened
street was full of cars parked down both sides. Even as he
looked, one of them pulled out and started to follow.

The minicab reached the junction of Turpin Road with St
Johns Road, and stopped. The side-lights of the car behind
approached very slowly, halting perhaps ten yards behind the
cab. Beyond that Kyril could just make out a third car, its
indicator winking.

The cab-driver turned right and began to accelerate. Through
the rear windscreen Kyril saw both cars copy the manoeuvre,

and smiled. The convoy travelled at a steady 40 mph, 20 or 30 yards between each car.

'Your money's on the seat.'

The driver looked askance at the notes which fluttered on to the Draylon beside him.

'Ten for the firm. Ten for you. And you've never seen either of us.'

'Blind', said the driver. 'That's me.'

'It must make driving very difficult. Left here and stop *hard.*'

The driver obeyed, instinctively snapping to the command in Kyril's voice. He gave no previous warning and Kyril had a sudden view of the car behind sailing on through the traffic-lights, which obligingly changed to red.

'Out.'

Vera leapt out of the car and ran across the road to the footpath which led up to Clapham Junction station, Kyril at her heels. As he rounded the corner he caught a glimpse of the second car narrowly avoiding a collision with the stationary cab.

They were through the barrier and racing for the platform before the sleepy ticket-collector could do anything about it.

'Just pray we don't have to wait long.'

'Platform 12', panted Vera. 'I can hear it coming.'

They reached the top of the steps just as a Victoria-bound train was squealing and grinding its way to a halt. Kyril hustled Vera into a compartment of a carriage with no connecting corridor and stood at the window, like a lover who wants to discourage company on the ride.

'Stan' 'way!' yelled a porter.

The whistle blew. Kyril's fists clenched. What was the hold up? Why didn't they *go?*

He heard the hiss of the vacuum brake and relaxed. The train started to move. A man flung himself up the last two steps to the platform and dived for the nearest carriage-door, wrenching it open and scrabbling with his feet for the running-board. He made it, just, and Kyril swore.

'One', he said as he slammed up the window. 'Too bad. But . . . only one.'

He and Vera had the compartment to themselves. They sat holding hands for most of the short journey to Victoria. When the train halted for a signal outside the terminus they each stood at a window, staring out.

'D'you see anything?'

'It's dark this side . . . no, nothing.'

Again the hiss of the brake. The train began to roll forward. Kyril raised his window and turned to Vera.

'He stayed put, then. No movement my side. I half-expected him to crawl along the footway. He's biding his time. Maybe . . .'

He fell silent.

'Maybe what?'

'Nothing.'

He did not want to tell Vera the thought which had crossed his mind, that in the few seconds it had taken them to board the train the tail might have had time to radio his base and arrange for them to be met at Victoria.

Suddenly lights were everywhere; they were coming into the station. Kyril hurriedly took Vera in his arms and kissed her.

'Now look.'

She broke away from him and lowered the window on the platform side.

'About a dozen people scattered along the platform . . . I can see a door opening, I think it's him, he's only a couple of compartments down. There's a porter . . .'

The driver applied the brakes and the train shuddered.

'Only another 20 yards . . .'

They were going at little more than walking pace.

'Ten yards . . . oh Vanya, *Vanya*.'

The train halted. Doors opened. Vera got out and turned to face the compartment, smiling up as if to snatch a last kiss before saying goodbye. Out of the corner of her eye she could see a man. Unlike the other passengers he was not walking away from her, down the platform to the barrier. She had an impression of jeans and a wind-cheater but kept her face up-turned to the window, reaching for that final kiss. Her lips moved, as if talking to the unseen man inside. In fact, she was praying for the simple subterfuge to work.

A number of things happened very quickly.

The stranger reached across Vera to see that the compartment was empty, its far door open and a dark void on the other side. In the same instant he hurled himself forward into the compartment, thrusting Vera aside, only to fall flat on his face. Through bewilderment and pain he realised that Kyril had been concealed under the seat all along, and had reached out to grab his ankle.

Strong hands collared the stranger, he felt a knee in the small of his back and heard a voice cry, 'Get in!'

It took a moment for Vera to realise that Kyril meant her. She scrambled back into the train and slammed the door, shutting off the melee from any curious passengers who might come along the platform, and stood looking out as Kyril had done earlier.

Behind her she could hear the muffled grunts and thumps of a fight. She clenched her fists to the glass and stared out as if her life depended on it. She was talking to herself: please finish it, finish it . . .

Through the open door on the other side of the compartment came another sound, that of a train drawing into the station along the adjacent track. It grew rapidly louder and was suddenly punctuated by the howl of the windhorn: its driver must have seen the open door and sounded a warning. The approaching train was almost level with Vera's compartment, its horn moaning continuously. Suddenly she could bear it no longer, and swung round crying 'Vanya!'

But Kyril had gone. The compartment was empty.

With a piercing squeal of brakes the oncoming train ground to a halt outside the door opposite Vera, its horn still sounding a single note.

Her mouth fell open. For a second the carriage went round and round, somebody seemed to be twisting a band of steel into her forehead . . .

Vera Bradfield clutched her stomach and was violently sick.

Kyril lay between the rails, fighting to get his breath back. His brain had temporarily seized up. All he could think of was stories of men who suffered terrible amputations and could feel nothing, numbed by shock into the belief that they had miraculously come through unscathed.

He moved his right leg, then his left. He was alive. He could feel all his limbs.

And he could hear. A horn, the sound of many voices. It was time to go.

Carefully avoiding the live rails he flipped from under the train across to the track nearest the platform where he had arrived with Vera a few moments ago. He wanted to look back to see what had happened to his attacker but his brain, active once more, forbade it. Better not. You've got enough to cope with. So has Vera...

Using the monkey crawl he edged his way along the tracks beneath the first train, making for the end farthest from the barrier. There, all was peaceful. He poked his head out cautiously. Anyone who had been standing at this point a moment before would understandably have been attracted back along the platform where all the commotion was. He climbed from under the train and stood upright between the rails. There was nobody about. No one looked in his direction.

Kyril vaulted up on to the platform. A few metres away he could see an iron stairway leading to a gantry which spanned the platform. He ran up it three steps at a time, coming to rest in the shadow of the overhead air-terminal which the gantry was designed to serve. He peered round the corner to find that he had a bird's eye view of the scene for which he was responsible.

Vera stood in the middle of a crowd of people, her face white. She was crying. A policeman was standing next to her, notebook in hand. An ambulance advanced slowly down the platform towards them.

On the other side he could see where the incoming train had stopped well short of the buffers, and there the crowd was smaller, more professional. A second ambulance was already parked close up to the train, its open doors flanked by policemen who every so often waved back a curious passerby. But for the most part the casual watchers had gone, repelled by their glimpse of what lay under the wheels of the train.

A necessity of the mission, Kyril told himself as he walked casually along the gantry, making for the platform farthest from the scene of the 'accident'. For Vera he had no worries, once the initial shock had worn off: before leaving the house he had primed her with things to say if it went wrong, and he never doubted her ability to stay cool in a crisis.

For a moment he allowed his heart to go to her in a spasm of sympathy and remorse; then he was himself again. He had to go on. No matter what, he must succeed.

He took his seat in a 'local' which was going to Battersea Park. From there it would be a short walk to the house in Queenstown Road. Then a long, long sleep.

As the train accelerated out of the station Kyril allowed himself the brief luxury of visualising a scene in Moscow Centre. Against all the odds the moving, highly-charged magnet conjured up by Stanov had reached London. Stanov was talking, perhaps even now . . .

'There was a telex this afternoon . . . it came in at 1548 Greenwich Mean Time . . . it came to you . . . why did it come to you, comrade . . . ?' Comrade what, Kyril wondered. Colonel, probably, but a General was not out of the question. Anyway. 'Why did you not report this?', Stanov would go on. 'Why did you hold back?' Or perhaps . . . 'Why did you at once order an executioner from the A2 Institute to go to England?'

Kyril blanked out his thoughts. Hour by hour, minute by minute. That was how he had to live. Let the next minute come, that was all.

Above the clatter of the Battersea train crossing the points outside the terminus, Kyril's sensitive ears detected the first high screech of a siren.

21

The news of Kyril's sighting came through to Centre shortly after three. The head of the First Main Directorate consulted with Col. Gen. Povin and gave certain orders. Since then General Michaelov, rather unusually for him, had been reading a dossier. When he had finished it he remained lost in thought for a moment before lifting the telephone.

'Is he here?'

'Yes, comrade General. Shall I show him in?'

Michaelov hesitated. 'Very well.'

Two sentries delivered Sikarov to the door of the First Deputy Chairman's office. Michaelov impatiently signed the chit which acknowledged his receipt of Employee No. ZPQ 09458, Dept. V, A2 Institute, and dismissed the escort.

His visitor remained standing rigidly to attention. As Michaelov turned back from the door he caught a glimpse of Sikarov's upturned chin and was reminded irresistibly of a human skull; the skin was stretched so tightly over the jaw that the line of his cheekbones seemed to dominate the whole face, making of it a death's head.

'Sit down, Sikarov.'

As he resumed his chair behind the desk Michaelov was aware of an acrid, unpleasant smell radiating from Sikarov's clothes. His nose wrinkled in distaste. Michaelov did not hold with all this pansy deodorant nonsense, which seemed to be gaining a suspiciously firm hold in Dzerzhinsky Square, but he liked his men to wash and he preferred them not to wear clothes which stank of death.

'I have a job for you. In England. You are ready to move at once?'

'Certainly, comrade General.'

Sikarov continued to stare ahead of him, his gaze just missing Michaelov's eyes.

'It will be very quick; you go in, you come out, in less than 48 hours. Absolute secrecy is essential. If at all possible you must make the job look like an accident, but the important thing is to secure a quick death. Understand?'

Sikarov nodded abruptly. 'Who is the target?'

'Colonel Ivan Yevseevich Bucharensky. Casename "Kyril".'

For the first time Sikarov looked directly at Michaelov and his eyes came into focus. Michaelov regarded him curiously, trying to assess the effect of his former colleague's name on this crude assassin. What memories did he have of that single occasion when they had worked in tandem?

'Excuse me, comrade General, but according to the Chairman's personal order Colonel Bucharensky is to be brought back alive.'

Michaelov smiled. 'Don't trouble your head about that, Sikarov. It's not your concern. But to reassure you, let me say this. Some orders are to be obeyed. Some are to be lost in the pipe. You follow?'

Sikarov's tense face relaxed into a grin. 'Yes.'

'Some orders get back to the enemy in the West. They are meant to get back, no? And when they do, the information contained in those orders serves its purpose.'

Sikarov nodded. 'I quite understand, comrade General.' Then he frowned. 'You are, with respect, sure that the target is in England. There was some doubt . . .'

'He was observed on the street in south London less than one hour ago. We do not know where he is based, not yet. That is for you to find out.'

Sikarov waited to be dismissed. His body had begun to tingle with suppressed excitement, his eyes burned with nervous tension. He had been desk-bound for too long. But Michaelov seemed dissatisfied about something.

'The reason why I am briefing you myself, Sikarov, is that you are not to talk to anyone about this. Not to anyone at all. Do you understand?'

Sikarov nodded again.

'If you get into trouble in London you are to call on *me*—you will report your presence in the UK to the London Resident but after that you will leave the embassy right out of it. You may even get a little opposition from that quarter. You're not the only one going around parroting Chairman's Orders, let me tell you. Ignore it. Ignore everything except what I tell you. This is a matter of high policy. If it later emerged that you had disregarded my instructions, Sikarov...'

Michaelov allowed his sentence to taper off in a smile.

'I shall say nothing, comrade General. Believe me, the embassies are nothing but trouble. I am honoured to have been selected for this mission. Traitors... well, traitors are special, no?'

Now it was Michaelov's turn to nod curtly.

'And I want no funny business, Sikarov; no police involvement. Understand *that* also.'

Two points of colour burned in Sikarov's gaunt cheeks. 'That is in the past.' There was a trace of sulkiness in his tone. 'A regrettable lapse.'

'Lapses, Sikarov. Plural. First Berlin, then Paris. Innocent people dead, and women in each case. I quote from the report of Colonel—then Captain—Ivan Yevseevich Bucharensky: "It brings too much attention." What an understatement!'

Sikarov scowled at Michaelov, who saw his fists suddenly clench. He banged the desk-top. 'You come highly recommended to me, Sikarov. They tell me you're cured of all that. I've read your file very carefully. I'm going to trust you. But if you fail...' Michaelov lolled back in his chair, his lower lip jutting. 'You won't be coming back to Moscow. Now listen. There's not much to go on. London is arranging to have Kyril followed but I shouldn't place too much reliance on that if I were you. Kyril is good. Better than we thought, in fact.'

Michaelov grunted, stung by the memory of Athens.

'But we have two other leads. Kyril is reported to be hunting a man called Loshkevoi, Victor Gregory Loshkevoi, don't ask me why. Also, he used to have a girl in London. It's all in the case-file, but find those two and Kyril won't be far away. Understand?'

'Yes, comrade General.'

'Good. One other thing. If you get a chance to interrogate Bucharensky, do so. See what he's carrying in the way of papers. But don't expect miracles. You'll be on your own in a foreign country. The death's the main thing. That's all. On your way.'

A faint smell hung in the room long after Sikarov had been delivered back into the care of the sentries. Michaelov stood up and went to throw open the window, braving the cold March air for the sake of a clear head. He remained there for a long time, looking down into the Square, wondering if he had done the right thing. It was a gamble, he knew that. After a while he decided to take advice and comfort.

Povin's office was but a step down the corridor. As he entered Povin himself was sitting beside the coal fire, one leg draped over the arm of his chair, a book in his hands. On seeing Michaelov he stood up with a smile, straightening his uniform. Michaelov laid a hand on his shoulder and pushed him gently down, conscious of a sudden feeling of warmth for Povin, who after all these years still rose automatically when his chief entered the room. That mattered to Michaelov.

'Has Sikarov been to see you?' Povin asked.

'Yes, a moment ago.'

Michaelov was not surprised to hear his deputy speak these unguarded words, in other times an unforgivable breach of security. Ever since the night of Povin's party, when he had gone back to Dzerzhinsky Square and found 'Sociable Plover' in the blue safe, Michaelov had had their offices electronically 'swept' twice a day. So far he had not uncovered any evidence of surveillance. But since that night he had suffered from an irrepressible need to talk to Povin at regular intervals, almost careless of the possible consequences.

Michaelov sat down, his face gloomy. 'If we're wrong about Stanov . . .'

'Now Valery, we've been through all that. It's a policy decision. Either we can afford to lose Royston or we can't. We both know that we can't. By the way, remember I told you I'd heard a rumour that the Second Main Directorate were trying to foul things up? It's true.' He leaned forward, offering his cigarette-case to Michaelov as he did so. 'You know old Yatsyna in counter-intelligence? We were at training-school together, we still go drinking now and then. He's told me, in confidence of course, that Veber is trying to use A2, but the Institute won't play.'

'Veber!' exploded Michaelov. 'The deputy head of the Second Main Directorate! Why, I'll kill him. A2 is ours!'

'I know, Valery, I know, but that's how things are right now. Everyone's angling for position. We all know the old man can't last . . .' Povin shrugged a dismissive shoulder in the direction of Stanov's office. 'Who's going to come out on top, that's what everyone wants to know. Veber thought he'd steal a march by sending an A2 raiding party to Brussels, but they turned him down flat, or so Yatsyna told me. Asked to see an order signed by the First Deputy Chairman personally, and threatened to report to Yevchenko when Veber couldn't produce it. They all know about the diary now, that's the trouble. But do me a favour, Valery, don't mention this to anyone. Yatsyna's a good man, even if he is with Second.'

Michaelov chewed his lips, and for a while there was silence.

'All right', he said eventually. 'The last thing I want to do is cut out your contact in Second. But I'm telling you, Stepan, A2's ours.'

'Of course, Valery, but you see the point. If they're trying to muscle in on the Institute, the word's gone out. The old man's finished.'

Michaelov nodded. 'And if anyone's going to terminate that poisonous little rat Kyril . . .'

'It's going to be us. Quite.' Povin smiled and extinguished his cigarette, as if to end the meeting, but Michaelov remained deep in thought.

'Stepan . . . why did you recommend Sikarov?'

Povin frowned. 'Did I?'

'Well, you said you thought he was fully rehabilitated.'

Povin's frown relaxed. 'Oh yes, I did say that.'

'We were talking about Bucharensky, you remember...'

Povin nodded slowly. 'It was about the same time, yes, you're quite right, Valery. He was very good, in the old days. Before the trouble. When I was under Golunov we always used him, there were never any complaints. And of course, as you know, he once worked with Bucharensky. Perhaps I thought he might recall some of Kyril's style, that it would give him a head start over the rest. Why do you mention it?'

'He's a funny bastard. Even Bucharensky said so after that time in Paris.'

'They all are. Do you realise, Valery, we are now one of the only three major intelligence services in the world that still has an execution squad? I mean, a squad on day and night call, year in and year out? All the full-time Institute boys are odd.'

Michaelov still wasn't satisfied. 'He's not worked for a long time, you know. In fact, he's worked very little since ...Moiseyev.'

Michaelov seemed to have trouble over pronouncing that name. For a while neither man spoke. Moiseyev could still silence his murderers.

'Ah yes', said Povin at last. 'I had forgotten that.' He gave a sudden laugh, humourless and short. 'It always stuck in my mind', he said. 'That report. "He was forcibly drowned in the Black Sea at a depth of 156 cm..." Why 156 cm, Valery? Why not 160 or even 150 cm, for the sake of a round number?'

Michaelov grunted but did not reply.

'"Mechanical asphyxiation as a result of drowning", that's what the death certificate said. Of course it was Sikarov, yes, I had forgotten that.'

'Did you ever see Malsin?' Michaelov interrupted gruffly.

'Malsin?'

'Moiseyev's commanding officer. A Lieutenant-Colonel. He really hated all those Christians, and as for the Reform Baptists...well, they were the worst. When Moiseyev started to have visions and disrupt the unit he threw a fit. He had high connections in the old man's office, no wonder the Institute were called in. I saw him a few months after it all happened. He'd just lost his only child and his wife was having a nervous breakdown...'

'It's coming back to me.' Povin sounded doubtful. 'I recall something of the kind. Didn't he get invalided out? Delusions, something about delusions...'

'He thought he was being pursued by the judgment of God', said Michaelov sombrely. 'And it finished him.'

Povin nodded slowly. 'Well', he said at last. 'Sikarov's done some good work since then, Valery. I don't think you need have any worries.'

'But he's never done anything big, not since 1972 when Moiseyev died. He smells.' He stopped, suddenly conscious that he had said something funny, and both men laughed.

'Cleanliness is not his strong point, that I grant you. But he's a good man, I'm sure of it. I don't actually remember recommending him, Valery, but he should do all right. He's a natural-born killer, through and through. If anyone can liquidate Bucharensky it'll be that little swine, right enough.'

Michaelov stayed sunk in thought for several moments, still only half-convinced.

'They hate each other, you know.'

'Mm?'

'After that time in Paris. Bucharensky and Sikarov. They hate each other.'

Povin frowned. 'I'm not sure that's such a bad thing, Valery.'

Michaelov stood up, his fears somewhat allayed by Povin's unshakeable calm. 'I'm sorry to have taken up your time, old friend.'

Povin smiled. 'I was glad to be interrupted.' He held up the book which had lain in his hands since his chief's arrival. 'I'm trying to see why the Dublin *referentura* is so excited about this rubbish.'

Michaelov peered closer, and saw that the book was entitled 'A History of Christian Philosophy'.

'The author's one of ours', explained Povin. 'In Dublin University—what's it called, Trinity? The Resident is worried he's turning subversive.'

Michaelov shook his head, laughing. 'The things we have to do for the Motherland. I'll let you get on.'

But at the door he turned.

'Loshkevoi.'

Povin looked up, surprised. 'What about him?'

'Had you ever heard the name before this?'

'No.'

'Nothing on file?'

'No, I've looked and checked with London.'

Michaelov shook his head. 'Then where the hell did the old man get the name from?'

Povin's face set in a guarded look. 'He's playing a very deep game. I'm scared out of my wits, I don't mind telling you. Always plotting away and never telling anyone. Take "Sociable Plover", a good example. I've been thinking about that . . .'

Povin stood up and threw the book on to his chair.

'Look, what have we got? You went to find out what was in the blue safe and you found "Sociable Plover". We know that Kyril hasn't got it. For some reason Stanov's using Kyril as disinformation. I've been thinking what I'd do in his place. I'd have told Kyril that "Sociable Plover" doesn't really exist. I'd lie to him, in fact. Then if he's caught, SIS are going to be confused: does it exist or doesn't it? In other words, I think we can forget about "Sociable Plover". It's a blind.'

'But why go to so much trouble?' Michaelov shook his head in exasperation. 'He seems to be hell-bent on stirring us up, not the British. If anyone's being fed disinformation, it's us here in Dzerzhinsky Square. What *is* the point of it all?'

Povin lowered his eyes. 'I told you what Kazin thinks.'

'Aah, that's a load of shit. I'll believe a lot of things, Stepan, but not that the Chairman of the KGB is on the point of defecting to the West. Not *this* Chairman.'

'Then . . . what?'

'I don't know. But I'm damn well going to find out. One thing at a time. First we liquidate Bucharensky and protect Royston. *Then* we go to work at this end. And no sleep for us until we know all the answers.'

Michaelov banged the door-jamb with his fist.

'You've never been followed, Stepan. You don't know what it's like. It's getting so I can't sleep nights. I'll never forgive him. Never!'

On leaving Povin's office Michaelov looked at his watch. Five o'clock. As he walked back to his own room he became aware of a commotion at the end of the corridor. Stanov swept past the sentries, closely followed by Yevchenko, their faces black as thunder. The Chairman of the KGB seemed excited about something; his voice was raised and despite the distance which separated them Michaelov could distinctly hear the sound of a fist pounding wood. He ducked quickly into his own suite of offices and closed the door firmly behind him.

'No calls', he growled to the young lieutenant who guarded the inner sanctum. 'If the Chairman asks for me, I've gone for the night.'

Once inside his own room he relaxed a little. Sikarov was already forgotten. Most of the afternoon had been wasted and waste put General Michaelov out of sorts. There was a lot to do. He reached for the phone.

'Get my wife... Hello? Nadia? Look, I'll be working late tonight. Don't wait up.'

For several minutes after his boss had left the office Povin remained motionless before the fire, the book forgotten. He stared into the middle distance, a half-smile on his lips. Then, like a man who has done with a daydream, he put down the book and walked over to the cupboard under the window. Inside was a bottle of petrovka. He uncorked it and poured himself a generous measure, which he downed in one before pouring another and drinking it more slowly. After he had put away the bottle and the glass he swept a strand of hair from his forehead. His hand was shaking so badly that he had to do it twice.

22

'We always thought Kyril was only a moderate performer. But he's good. He's very good indeed.'

C stood at the window looking out over the Thames, his spectacles dangling loosely in his hands. He seemed distracted. Royston bit his tongue and refrained from snapping at his chief. 'I know that', he wanted to shriek. 'I don't need an old fool like you to tell me that we've lost him, perhaps forever...'

Royston had not been sleeping well. His doctor prescribed a course of Tuinol, and at first the tablets helped. Now Royston was almost back to where he started: a period of sleep between midnight and two, followed by a long drift into wakefulness and uneasy dreams. Jenny was concerned. So was Royston.

'You could step up surveillance on the Bradfield woman', said the Head of the Inquisition. 'She'll be out of hospital tomorrow.'

Royston turned smouldering eyes on him, but remained silent. In the good old days, if the London Station-Chief had a good idea he'd go along for a chat with Maurice Oldfield, who'd be as likely to talk about cricket as anything else and make him feel in ten minutes that it was worth £2700 a year.

Christ, thought Royston savagely, to think we used to live on
that. No London weighting then . . . and no bloody kitchen cab-
inets, either; no interminable discussions, always ending with
a reference back to Accounts and Audit . . .

'And this other man, Loshkevoi', put in the Senior Planner.
'If Nidus is right in supposing that Kyril wants to see him, for
whatever reason, I was wondering whether it might not be a
good idea to propose a joint venture to someone with superior
capacity . . . the CIA, now . . .'

Royston twisted sharply in his chair and the Head of the
Inquisition tut-tutted. Only Sir Richard Bryant did not move
or say anything, but continued to stare out of the window.

'I think that Edward's well-known preference for liaising at
every level with the Cousins should not be allowed to cloud
the fact that this is, ah, essentially a domestic matter.'

'I agree', said Royston, mildly surprised to find himself
supporting the Head of the Inquisition for once.

'And so do I.'

C's voice was very gentle.

'There's been far too much noise as it is. Soviet agents
under trains . . . Once we invoke the Cousins we'll find them
wanting participation rights. It's happened before.'

He turned to face the room and Royston saw that his face
was dark with trouble.

'You probably do not know—there is no reason why you
should—the terms on which Nidus is reimbursed. He is a man
of some principle. At his own request, his monthly stipend is
paid directly into a numbered UNICEF bank account in Geneva.
For reasons into which I have never inquired, dollars, in any
shape or form . . .'

C's voice was at its most austerely chill.

'. . . are not acceptable. No, gentlemen: leave the Americans
out of this.'

C resumed his seat behind the desk.

'Bradfield and Loshkevoi: they are your immediate targets.
Watch them and eventually Kyril will cross your line of sight.'
He smiled briefly. 'Damn the expense; take what you need.'

He nodded to indicate that the meeting was over, and two
of the other men present at once stood up. Royston remained

stubbornly rooted to his chair. C raised an inquiring eyebrow and tilted his head slightly.

'I need a few moments with you alone, please.'

Royston felt that in his present exhausted state he would have had to submit to anything C said or did. The relief he experienced when Bryant waved the other two out found tangible expression through all the taut muscles of his aching body.

'If we're going to get him . . . I mean, get him properly, nail him down . . . I need a nugget.'

'Yes. I thought it might be that.'

'Nugget' was a Service euphemism for a lure. It could take many forms: a woman, money, political asylum.

'Kyril was very high', Royston continued, keeping his eyes fixed on C's face. 'Stanov's man. I need something he can identify with—a piece of information only the Chairman or his assistant would be likely to know. Something . . . rare.'

'Rare in the sense of precious. Quite so. A shibboleth.'

Royston's eyes widened. He had not expected such a sympathetic hearing. 'Yes, that's it. Something to show we're two of a kind.'

C said nothing. That look of trouble had returned to his normally placid face. Royston became conscious of a hollow, faintly nauseous feeling in the pit of his stomach. He couldn't face breakfast these days, not since it first crossed his mind that during his recent spell in Dzerzhinsky Square Kyril might have learned a lot more about a man called Royston than C ever knew.

'Did you have anything specific in mind?'

'I did, as a matter of fact. There used to be an executive arm of the Kremlin on which we could never get any hard information. Maybe things have changed since my Moscow-watching days, I don't know. Some kind of inspectorate. The members had to swear a special oath of alliegance to a plenary session of the Politburo. Strictly for officers only. It went under several names. The one I remember was Kremlin Kommandant.'

'Used to be . . . ?'

This response puzzled Royston. Why was C prevaricating?

'Still is, I'm sure. If my contact-man could persuade Kyril

that he's a member of the Kommandant...'

C stood up and turned his back on Royston. The air of
restless trouble had now overlaid his entire manner. Royston's
puzzlement grew. What was wrong? *For Christ's sake, what
did they know? What did Kyril know?*

'The Kremlin Kommandant still exists, yes; nothing has
changed. Brezhnev's personal inspectorate: the spies who watch
the spies. Their powers are almost unfettered. But you're asking
a lot. There is only one source for a secret of that magnitude.
If it became known that a Western intelligence agency had
penetrated it, well...'

Royston leaned forward.

'But if that source you mention was himself in danger... if
the Chairman of the KGB was on the point of capturing a man
who could unmask him...'

C wheeled round.

'You underestimate Nidus', he said curtly. 'We cannot dictate to him. He helps me in fits and starts, at his own pleasure,
and usually only in the gravest of emergencies. I doubt very
much whether personal considerations would play any part in
his decision to give or withhold the information you seek.'

'You seem very sure of that...'

Royston made no attempt to keep the cynicism out of his
voice. The two hard points of C's gaze dissolved, went hazy
and out of focus.

'Yes', he said. Then, after a long pause—'I am very sure.'

Royston stood up too quickly and suffered a momentary
penalty of giddiness. For a scintilla of time he wanted to say,
'By the way, just who is Nidus?'; then sanity returned. If he
ever chose to ruin everything he could do it in much finer style
than that.

'I will do my very best for you', said C. 'I understand your
point of view. I regard it as having validity.'

He nodded dismissively. On his way out Royston heard him
say, 'This is not a time for illness. I need fit men. Try to take
a day's leave.'

A holiday, thought Royston as he rode down in the lift.
That's what I need. Twenty years in which to think things
over...

23

Sikarov timed his arrival to coincide with the middle of the trans-Atlantic rush-hour. Four Jumbos had disgorged their human cargos in the last 30 minutes and the Russian had no difficulty in finding a package-party to join. Passengers and immigration officers all looked equally haggard.

As he approached the high, sloping desk a man in a dark grey suit materialised beside the immigration clerk for no apparent reason. While Sikarov's passport was checked this man stood behind the clerk's shoulder, his impassive stare never leaving Sikarov's face. The Russian gazed stonily back at him. As the clerk stretched out to give him back his passport the man in the grey suit took it and examined the open page. Sikarov felt no qualms. It had been made in East Germany and was of the first quality. It proclaimed him to be Pietr Gablenz, an Austrian businessman on his way from Paris to London, and the visas were authentic.

The man in the dark grey suit handed Sikarov back his passport with a smile.

Once in the taxi Sikarov used its darkened rear window to observe the traffic without himself being seen. Before they reached the end of the motorway spur he knew that he was being followed and had identified the vehicle.

He frowned. He had crossed enough frontiers in his time to know the power of coincidence, but this looked suspiciously like a prearranged tail. The DI5 officer at the immigration desk had a reason for being there at the precise moment when Sikarov presented his passport. But it was unlikely that Five were having him followed on mere suspicion.

Someone had talked, then. In Moscow or, more probably, here in the London *referentura*. Sikarov's lips curled back from his prominent teeth in the snarl that passed, with him, for a smile. Well, he would have a bit of fun. A short holiday before getting down to business.

He directed the cab driver to Piccadilly, and Fortnum & Masons. A large tip secured a promise to wait while the fare picked up some parcels. As he went inside Sikarov glanced to right and left. The tail vehicle, a brown Capri, was stuck behind a bus in the slow lane. Sikarov had a fleeting impression of an irate driver straining over his shoulder to find a gap in the impenetrable traffic. Excellent.

For the next five minutes the staff of Fortnums were kept very busy. Box after box was handed out to the street, there to be piled into the back of the cab by an obliging doorman. After a while there were so many parcels in the taxi that the driver had to get out and start rearranging them, putting some in the front compartment, and some in the boot. Just as everyone was starting to wonder where the fare was going to sit a number of things happened simultaneously. A policeman came up and demanded to know where the hell the cabbie thought he was, in the garage at home? The driver realised that he had not yet been paid for the trip from the airport. The shop-girl who had been kept busy taking Sikarov's order woke up to the fact that he had not, as promised, left his American Express card with her while he went out to supervise the loading. The driver of the brown Capri collected a ticket. But Sikarov went clean into London—and disappeared.

After his initial and unexpected brush with DI5 Sikarov was

forced to rethink his strategy. He felt isolated. It was time to invest in a little insurance.

When he reached the embassy later in the day it was to find everything at sixes and sevens. He learned that Kyril had been seen at the house of Vera Bradfield, but then there had been a ball-up which resulted in the death of a *schpick* and the target escaping surveillance. A full-scale cover-up was in progress. Sikarov grunted. He was too used to this kind of error for it to worry him. As long as he had the girl's address he would manage somehow.

On the pretext that his gun was jamming he visited the armoury on the third floor and handed it in for a quick service. While the armourer was working on it Sikarov leaned over the counter and with a gloved hand picked up the Luger that was lying on the shelf.

'What's wrong with this?'

'Faulty trigger-setting. It's mended now.'

Sikarov weighed it thoughtfully. The armourer was coming over.

'Should be all right. There was some dirt caked round the pin.'

Sikarov nodded. He had put it there.

'Want to try?'

'Sure.'

'We'll have to go down to the cellars, then. That's where the range is.'

Sikarov pretended to hesitate. 'All right. But it'll have to be quick. Can I try the Luger?'

'Sure, why not.'

A few minutes on the range revealed that Sikarov's gun was now in perfect working order. Then he loosed off six shots from the Luger. It felt fine.

'Thank you. I still prefer my own though.'

The armourer shrugged. 'We don't use them much now. That belongs to someone in Department V. He won't part with it.'

Sikarov's body was between the armourer and the table on which the guns lay. It was the easiest thing in the world for him to switch holsters.

'I left my bag upstairs. I'll carry these up for you.'

While the armourer turned off the lights Sikarov buttoned down both holsters firmly. Now it was impossible to tell which was which, unless you knew.

On his way out Sikarov wondered whose fingerprints would be on the Luger with which he killed Colonel Ivan Yevseevich Bucharensky. Not that it mattered. Nothing was going to mar his enjoyment of this mission, not while Kyril still owed him for what happened in Paris. And anyway, the boys in A2 enjoyed a joke.

24

Povin nearly always woke up early, even at week-ends. This Sunday he opened his eyes to find a bar of sunlight lying across his face and he blinked, surprised; did that mean Spring would be early this year?

He slid out of bed and went to stand at the window whence he could look out over his neighbours' roof-tops. Povin had long ago become entitled to occupy a larger flat on the second floor but he preferred the tiny suite of rooms tucked under the eaves for what in any case he regarded merely as a pied-à-terre. The sky was a bright, cloudless blue. He opened the window and took a deep breath of fresh air, cold as ether.

Somewhere, far away, a church bell was ringing.

He closed the windows reluctantly. That was an illegal, if frequent occurrence, and the outcome was always the same. Soon the bell would stop, the arrests and interrogations begin. Povin didn't want to think about that.

He was used to this flat. 'My penthouse' he called it, with a rueful smile, but the accommodation, which was cramped and tiny, belied such a grand description. A bedroom just large enough to hold the single bed, a living-room too small to do his Grundig stereo justice, kitchen fitted out with a microwave oven and precious little else; bathroom with no bath, only a shower. It was enough for the nights during the week. When he entertained he used the dacha in Zhukovka, which he regarded as 'home', and it was on the dacha that he spent his money.

He went across to the record-player and put on the Bruch No 1 violin concerto, played by Perlman, one of Povin's few HMV recordings. A rare exception to his normal collecting policy, he preferred it to the Deutsche Gramaphon version by Oistrakh.

In the kitchen he made himself tea and examined the interior of the small, old fashioned refrigerator. He ate only a biscuit smothered with *tvorog*, the stodgy cottage cheese of the peasants. Povin was due to lunch at the Armed Forces Officers Club with a colleague and he found that nowadays he couldn't manage too much food early if he was going to eat a big meal later. The Club was worth saving up your appetite for: it served the best '*zakuski*' in Moscow. Povin loved hors d'oeuvres, and rarely bothered with a second course if they were good, especially when the milk-mushrooms were in season.

He went back to the living-room with a second glass of tea, still wearing only his dressing-gown and slippers, and sat down to listen to the music. He missed being in the country at weekends. Yesterday, however, he had been lucky enough to obtain a ticket for the ballet, and today there was an offer of a free lunch, a commodity as difficult to come by in the East as in the West, so Povin had decided to break his routine. He was not altogether sorry. In Zhukovka someone was always giving a party or dropping by for a chat, and what he wanted most of all was time to be alone and think.

For reasons which he could not explain to himself he felt strangely relaxed. Perhaps it was the false calm at the eye of the hurricane, but that did not matter; for the moment at least he was sure he was safe.

It was a feeling hard to justify in rational terms, he reflected as he stirred his tea. The picture was fairly straightforward now. Stanov knew there was a traitor and, broadly, where to look for him. Bucharensky might or might not figure in Stanov's scheme of things, Povin wasn't certain. He was probably just a pawn, used by Stanov in an attempt to provoke his suspects into panic. Povin long ago decided to discount the diary. If Kyril was really in a position to unmask a traitor he would have stayed and earned his promotion accordingly, not run halfway across Europe to the very people who were supposed to control their agent in Dherzhinsky Square. Unless... Povin frowned. Unless, of course, he was looking for final proof. But in any case, as long as he could be sure of neutralising Kyril there was no particular need to worry; all he had to do was lie low and demonstrate his continuing loyalty to the Politburo with every passing day. And whatever Bucharensky's function, he would shortly cease to be a factor in the equation. Povin had great faith in Sikarov. If anyone asked questions later, well, it was Michaelov's decision to send Sikarov to England, not Povin's.

From his comfortable armchair high above the Moscow roof-tops, things were looking, if not good, at least not so bad. What could he do to make them even better? The question gave Povin a momentary sense of frustration. All that power at his fingertips, power over life and death, and yet so little effect...

Loshkevoi.

Povin put down his empty glass and went to turn the record over.

It would be better if Bucharensky and Loshkevoi did not meet. Loshkevoi could not identify Povin directly, he certainly did not realise that the General was a double-agent, but still he represented a risk. He must be put out of circulation for a while... yes, maybe that was the answer. Somewhere in Dzerzhinsky Square there was a legal department—of sorts. Povin made a mental note for action on Monday morning. 'English legal system.'

The word 'English' spoken quietly in his own mind sent Povin off at a tangent. Suddenly the day seemed less sunny, less relaxed. New problems all the time...

He went to the bathroom, leaving the door ajar for the sake of the music, and began to shave. What was he going to do about Bryant's request?

When Povin first read the message he almost laughed aloud, would have done if he were not so astonished at being presented with a request for aid which had not been volunteered. But then he had thought—well, and why not?

It was that 'why not' which troubled him as he lathered his face. To respond to Bryant's request would be dangerous folly at the best of times. But now, with Kyril on the loose and Stanov perhaps watching his generals' every move, it would be nothing short of suicidal.

, Why, then, did the memory of his talk with Stolyinovich on the night of the party haunt him so? 'Do you ever feel that we could do more?'—those had been his own words. 'No', said the pianist, flatly rejecting the philosophical tangle behind the apparently simple question. And yet . . . and yet . . .

There was so much that Povin might do if he had a mind. Royston, for example: strategically by far and away the most important 'gain' the KGB had ever made within the United Kingdom. Povin had not underestimated his importance when he told Michaelov that the destruction of Royston would devastate their British operation for at least ten years. All it needed was one word from Povin to Bryant . . . No, these were foolish, wayward thoughts. Why should he jeopardise himself by making such a revelation? The same applied to Bryant's request for information about the Kommandant.

Povin patted his face dry with a towel and considered his reflection in the mirror. Not bad for 55, he decided: the skin had kept most of its tension and his complexion was clear. But that melancholy gaze . . . where had it come from, and when? Povin shrugged and smiled a faint smile, knowing that it had been there since his early days in the Komsomol, when he first became conscious of a sense of loss, of not quite having found the answer. But at least the pale grey eyes were fearless; they stared back at him without flinching from their knowledge of what lay behind the facade.

Povin went back to the bedroom and stood for a few moments with his head bent in prayer. He never felt quite able to kneel down, here in Moscow, the hub of the KGB's massive wheel of power. With the passing of the years he paid less and less attention to the outward flummeries. Throughout the centuries soldiers had always stood to pray, and Povin was a soldier. He wore a uniform. And he stood on guard. Always.

He dressed quickly, keeping an anxious eye on the weather. The sky was still blue, and when he looked out of the window again the air actually felt warmer. He craned down to survey the little corner of Kutuzovsky Prospekt which was visible from 'the penthouse'. It was only eight o'clock and there were few pedestrians on the street at that hour. Good. He fancied a walk, a long walk. He decided to strike out in the direction of Izmailovo Park and see how far he could get before 10.30, when he would turn back in order to keep his lunch appointment.

There were no watchers, as far as he could see. He wasn't sure whether Stanov had actually got as far as to have the KGB generals followed; in the past year he had sometimes thought one thing, sometimes another, and on balance had written off his fears as groundless. But if there had been surveillance in the past, he was almost sure that it prevailed no longer. Now the only danger was Stanov himself and his beastly dog.

As Povin rode down in the lift he was making contingency plans for evasive action. When Stanov's wife died two years ago the old man bought himself a dog for company, a mongrel of scruffy appearance and uncertain temper. Sometimes when Povin went out early he ran into Stanov exercising the brute along Kutuzovsky Prospekt, and this invariably resulted in an invitation to breakfast with the lonely Marshal. Povin disliked pets. They interfered with his fastidious standards of personal hygiene and comfort. To sit in Stanov's overheated first-floor apartment sniffing old man and stale dog through the rich flavour of freshly ground coffee was almost more than he could stomach, but he knew it would be impolitic to refuse.

Povin stepped cautiously into the street and looked to right and left. All clear. He strode away from the discreet entrance of the block of flats, pulling on his gloves. He would think about Sir Richard Bryant's request on his walk. Eight-thirty. Allowing for the time difference, the Englishman would soon be getting up, ready for early mass. As a devotee of the Tridentine rite he was finding it harder and harder to satisfy the spiritual yearnings which were his major point of contact with Povin. So much for religious freedom. In Dzherzhinsky Square they knew of this difficulty, just as they knew most other things about the private and public lives of the head of the British Secret Intelligence Service. Povin smiled to himself. Poor Sir Richard. Yes, he would definitely give his request for information about the Kommandant the most serious attention.

Povin had reached the end of the Prospekt, and there was still no sign of either Stanov or his wretched cur. It was going to be all right, thought Povin as he strode off across the road. If by the grace of God he could only manage to keep his head, everything was going to be just fine.

25

As Vera awoke for a second she thought herself back in the hospital; it was the middle of the night, her room was in darkness, and the events of the past few days had so confused her that even during the day she sometimes suffered a sense of disorientation, of loss of Self. Then she sat up in bed and remembered. She was in her own bed in Clapham, home and safe.

She put on the light.

Sitting in her bedside chair was a squat young man dressed in black from head to foot. Every muscle, every nerve in Vera's body instinctively combined to force her back against the head-board, knees drawn up to her chin, arms folded across her breasts, mouth open to scream . . . But suddenly there was an impediment, a ghastly, suffocating gag which took the pent-up fear and smothered it unborn.

Seeing the terror on the woman's face Sikarov grinned. Everything was going well. Lazily he bent down to untie his shoes, which had begun to pinch. A sour, sweaty smell rose to Vera Bradfield's nostrils, making her stomach churn. This was her nightmare. A burglar. A raid on an empty house while

she was safely away, that she could just about contemplate.
But this was different. This was a man, and he was here, in
front of her. A man who stank and had an evil look about him.
Oh God, oh God, oh God...

'Get back into the bed. It's cold. I don't want you to be
cold.'

A foreigner. One of the semi-vagrants she saw so many of
these days. Christ, just let him not want *her*. Vera snuggled
back under the bedclothes, pulling the blanket up to her chin.
She was shivering and he noticed it; she felt him notice.

'You cannot make a noise, I am going to give you paper
and pencil. Here.' Sikarov rolled up his sleeve to reveal a roll
of paper around his forearm, together with a pencil. 'Now you
are going to write on it the address of the man you call Vanya
or Bucharensky.'

A tiny part of Vera relaxed. So it wasn't rape, not even
theft. Then the fear closed down again, numbing and total.
They were on the track of Vanya at last. And from the look
of the intruder it was obvious that they meant to kill him. The
man in the bedroom reeked of death.

Vera shook her head and turned to face the wall.

Sikarov's eyes gleamed with lascivious anticipation of pleasure. They had warned him that she would not be easy.

'You will tell me', he said. 'I give you one more chance
to do it with dignity. Where is Bucharensky?'

Again the shake of the head, but Sikarov could see the
trembling bedclothes which told their own story.

'What nonsense has he told you? That he is in danger? That
we want to hurt him? What rubbish. You are old enough to
see through that kind of tale. We want to help him. He is sick.
He needs medical help. Surely you realised that when he came
here? Wasn't it obvious?'

The bedclothes had stopped shaking.

'But he doesn't understand that. Won't you help him by
telling me where he is?'

Vera turned away from the wall and violently shook her
head. Sikarov sighed, and reached out for her. She fought him
off until, in a fit of rage, he stunned her with his fist. When
she came to her hands and feet were bound to the four corners
of the bed.

'For you', murmured Sikarov, 'the night is only just beginning. Nod your head when you are tired.'

She proved tougher than anticipated. Several times she fainted and he had to revive her with douches of cold water. He became steadily more impatient, his methods cruder. Still she would not break. Sikarov wiped the sweat from his forehead. There were limits to what he could do in a London bedroom, it was not as if the resources of the Lubianka cellars were at his disposal. Blood began to mingle with water and urine on the sodden sheets. Somewhere deep inside Sikarov a tide of sexual desire was beginning to draw inwards, concentrating all his energies. Again and again he fought it down, only to feel it rise again within him.

'Don't come back to Moscow.' Michaelov's words echoed in his brain. *Concentrate!*

It was all right, she had nodded. Sikarov ripped away the gag. For several minutes all she could do was pant and gasp. Saliva was running down her chin, and for one terrible second Sikarov wondered if he had driven her over the edge.

'I don't know where he is. If I did . . . I would tell you. But I don't.'

Sikarov breathed deeply, trying to instill a degree of control. 'Tell me.' His voice sounded murderous. *'Tell me.'*

'I don't *know*.'

Sikarov watched with interest as a figure detached itself from his body. This figure carried a pistol by the barrel. It walked across to the bed where the naked woman lay, legs apart, and with slow, leisurely swings of its arm began to club her about the head until eventually she stopped groaning, her head no longer tried to evade the pistol, her legs twitched once in a muscular convulsion, and she lay still. Sikarov saw it all as if in a dream, until the figure climbed back into his body and made it whole again. Then he awoke. The room, the gun, the soaking bed, they had all disappeared. There was only the woman. She filled the whole of his consciousness, he could see nothing else. But he could feel. There's no point in hanging on, a voice was saying, no point because it's too late, isn't it. It's too late.

Sikarov climbed on to the bed and knelt between the woman's bloodsoaked thighs. His hand went to the zip and when the gun got in the way he dropped it on the floor. Then his trousers were round his knees, the erection sprang free, and Sikarov's lips curled back into the familiar snarl as his hand set to work.

The two-seater van was indistinguishable from many others parked on the south London streets that night, except perhaps in the care which the driver had taken to ensure that he did not breach any of the numerous regulations and bye-laws concerning stationary vehicles. The interior of this particular van, however, was unusual. Down one side was arranged a truncated mattress on which a man was uncomfortably dozing, his legs pulled up almost to the low roof. On the other side a second man wearing a pair of headphones crouched with his back to the first. Every so often he reached out to twiddle knobs on the radio-receiver in front of him. For the past half-hour he had been showing signs of increasing restlessness.

'Better wake up, Ted.'

'Wha'? Wassup? Oh fuck.'

The man on the mattress struggled upright, only to bang his head on the van's metal ceiling.

'I can't figure it out. There's been some weird noises in there for about half an hour now. Like . . . struggling. You know what I mean?'

Ted was unscrewing the top of a vacuum flask.

'No.'

'As if she was having a fight with someone.'

'Lover, maybe.'

'Well he didn't go in the front door, did he? We'd have seen.'

Ted took a sip from the plastic cup while he thought about that.

'Dream. Could be having a nightmare.'

'What? For all that time and never waking up? Do us a favour, will you. I shouldn't . . .'

The radio-operator's hand moved to the set, his face suddenly tense.

'Listen, Ted, where did they put that transmitter when she was in hospital? In which room?'

'Lounge.'

'The telephone's ringing. If she doesn't come out of the bedroom to answer it, she's in trouble.'

Ted swallowed the last of his cup of tea and, pulling aside a piece of sacking, looked out of the tiny rear window.

'Raining, sod it. I'd better get my coat on.'

'Right. Hallo. The phone's stopped. Seven rings. No answer.'

Ted came to kneel by his colleague, shouldering his mac as he did so.

'Better ring up LS, Phil. We need a car.'

'You do it. I'm listening for a while.'

Ted picked up the radiophone and spoke urgently to London Station. Phil was vaguely aware of what he was saying while he strained to interpret the silence which had once again fallen in Vera's flat.

'Can't do a tail... yeah... two exits, he might go either way... 20 minutes, Christ, can't you do better than that...?'

Ted replaced the handset.

'They're on their way. Twenty bloody minutes, Christ...'

'The phone's ringing again.'

Sikarov was dressed and ready to leave. The Bradfield woman had been a bad mistake. He shook his head glumly, mindful of the old Russian proverb which said: 'A woman isn't a jug; she won't break if you hit her'. Well, Vera Bradfield had broken all right.

The important thing now was to do a first-class job on Bucharensky. That way Michaelov's wrath could perhaps be bought off.

Then the phone rang. Seven times.

Sikarov looked at his watch. Nobody rang at that time of night. Wrong number. Unless...

He paused. He ought to leave. But suppose that nocturnal caller was someone who had to be very careful how he contacted Vera Bradfield. Someone who phoned in the small hours and let the phone ring only seven times before cancelling the call, and moving to another phone-box in another area, as he, Sikarov, had done many times before.

Seven rings. The old code. Sikarov sat down on Vera's bedside chair. There was an easy way to test his theory. Sometime in the next 20 minutes Bucharensky—if it was Bucharensky—would call again. This time the phone would ring five times. And then, when nobody answered, he would know that his contact had been blown and fade away into the night...

Sikarov shook his head. Not Bucharensky. Not with this contact. When there was no answer to the second call he would come to see what was wrong. Sikarov knew how Bucharensky's mind worked. He always disobeyed the rules in one vital respect... he telephoned from a box which was too close to the contact. That was what had gone wrong in Paris. Sikarov grinned. He wouldn't make that mistake again. This time he knew that if Bucharensky rang a second time, he would be at the house within minutes after replacing the receiver.

Time passed very slowly while Sikarov waited for that second call. Something told him that it was bound to come, almost as if the five rings were already programmed into the wires which separated Bucharensky from the house. He withdrew the Luger from the waistband of his trousers and checked the mechanism. All was well. There would be no chance for a second shot.

When the phone rang again Sikarov took a sharp intake of breath and held it. Ring-ring. One. Ring-ring. Two. Ring-ring...Ring-ring...Ring-ring...*Five*...and no more.

Sikarov stood up and moved quickly into the hall, leaving the bedside light on to guide him. The living-room? No, too obvious. The kitchen? Bucharensky would come that way.

The cellar.

The door at the back of the hall gave directly on to a steep flight of steps. Sikarov went down a little way and pulled the door to, leaving a small gap through which he could hear whatever went on above.

The minutes dragged by. Every so often Sikarov hummed gently to himself, to keep his hearing alert. He knew that unless you did that you began to hear imaginary noises and the last thing he wanted was to emerge from his hiding-place too soon.

When nothing had happened after 20 minutes Sikarov began to worry. This wasn't the Bucharensky he remembered. Perhaps he had been wrong about the phone call. But then, who else would use the Leningrad Response in the middle of the night, in order to make contact with a woman called Vera Bradfield? Sikarov forced himself to remain silent and tried to shore up his rapidly slipping patience.

Occasionally his thoughts strayed to what Bucharensky would find upstairs and his lips parted in a wet smile. Traitors were special, that was what he had told Michaelov. They were singled out for special treatment.

Then at last he heard the click of the latch on the kitchen door, and he knew the waiting was over.

In his mind Sikarov began to follow Bucharensky's cautious movements. First he would discover the circle which Sikarov had cut into the glass-panelled door, and use it to insert a hand and make his own entry. Then he would stand for a while in the kitchen, taking the flat's pulse, as the instructors called it. Next...ah yes! Sikarov's ears had not deceived him. Bucharensky was moving out of the kitchen, passing within inches of the cellar-door, to the threshold of the bedroom. Any minute now...

The quiet footsteps overhead, audible only to someone with Sikarov's superfine hearing, stopped. There was a moment of silence during which he stared up at the ceiling of the tiny cellar, lips faintly parted. Then the man upstairs turned and broke into a run. Sikarov heard him pound through the kitchen and out the way he had come, reckless as to whether he made a noise. Sikarov waited a few seconds, then vaulted up the stairs and out of the back door, into the yard.

Ahead of him he could hear Bucharensky noisily clearing a succession of garden walls in his progress towards the end of the terrace, and the road. Sikarov smiled. Good. That should be easy enough to follow. He set off in pursuit.

He had no intention of putting a quick end to the affair. Bucharenksy's nerve had broken, so much was obvious. He would run back to his 'secure' base and bolt the door behind him, seeking the illusory warmth and comfort of that unnatural womb in which to rest and recover. Sikarov would follow. It would be a simple matter to destroy the wretched Bucharensky in his present unmanned state, before ransacking his lair at leisure. The death was what mattered: those were Michaelov's express orders. But before leaving Moscow Sikarov had heard

rumours, some of them very interesting. There was talk of a
sensitive project-plan, and Michaelov himself had spoken of
papers. If Sikarov could find the project-plan which Bucharensky was supposed to have stolen, that would be an added
bonus—quite sufficient to neutralise any unpleasantness which
might otherwise have resulted from the woman's death.

Bucharensky had reached the last garden wall which bounded
the house at the end of the terrace from the street. For a second
his crouched figure was outlined against the orange glow of
the street-lamp; then he was gone. Sikarov raced after him. As
he cleared the final hurdle and landed on the pavement, a
shadow unmoulded itself from the darkness 50 yards away,
and joined the hunt. Ted was cold and tired and still half-
asleep, but from his position on the pavement between the end
of the terrace opposite Vera's and the monitoring van he had
seen Kyril jump the wall. When Sikarov followed and set off
in pursuit, Ted took a deep breath and broke into a trot.

Kyril was running as if to win the 100-metre sprint. The sound
of his own heart's blood throbbing in his ears kept him from
remembering. As he ran his footsteps rat-tatted the same grim
tune.

Sik-a-rov, Sik-a-rov, Sik-a-rov . . .

They were in Paris, working the old tandem game. The girl
was pretty, rich and damn near nymphomaniac; the prize, a
minister, was rare, almost unobtainable. Sikarov had been sent
along to add weight, do the heavy stuff at the end. He was
regarded as an expert, then, a top professional, and Gaczyna
had yet to produce a better marksman. Only later did Kyril
discover that there had been other occasions, other corpses . . .

Sik-a-rov, Sik-a-rov. Now there was grass beneath his feet.
The common.

A Leningrad Response had brought up nothing. Something
about the empty, hollow dialling-tone spelled danger. Kyril
had taken a taxi instead of following the rules and proceeding
on foot. He had opened the door of the 'nest' with his passkey.
And there was Sikarov, his trousers round his ankles, mastur-
bating over the bloody thing which lay on the bed, its head
unrecognisable as belonging to a human being.

Ve-ra, Ve-ra, Ve-ra.

The strange sound in Kyril's ears was the heartbroken moan of a man at the end of his tether, a child who cries to ease the pain, its rhythmic ululation keeping time with the throbbing hurt.

His last view of Sikarov had been from the glass-walled corridor of the terminal at Orly, three men walking out to the Aeroflot Ilyushin after all the other passengers had boarded, two of them a pace behind the third, hands in pockets, collars upturned. Goodbye, Sikarov, he had thought then. For you, this is the end of the line...

He had reached the foot of Queenstown Road. If he did not stop soon he felt his heart would burst. Perhaps it was better that way.

Sik-a-rov, Ve-ra, Sik-a-rov, Ve-ra...

The traitor had never meant much to Kyril, until now. Suddenly he was face to face with an enemy, and the deadly game had become personal. No longer was Kyril merely trying to do his duty to the Homeland. His enemy had chosen Sikarov deliberately, ordered him to destroy Vera as a warning, as the first instalment of punishment. Now at last his way forward was clear. He would butcher Sikarov, that was the first thing. And then he would seek out this traitor, as Stanov had commanded. He would exact vengeance.

Kyril opened his front door, slammed it behind him and fell on his knees, hands clasped to his forehead. He was sobbing.

The crisis quickly came and passed. He allowed himself the luxury of release for a moment, no more, before dragging himself upright and dusting off his clothes. His body was exhausted but his brain was functioning. Revenge. Never before had he contemplated such dangerous luxury, the poison asp concealed beneath the figs' sweetness. He must plan carefully if he were to combine it with Stanov's plan. Escape. That was the first thing. He must break away from the house, go underground...

Kyril lifted his head, straining to listen. Was that a noise he had heard in the street? Surely it was his overheated imagination? He breathed deeply. His heart was almost back to normal, the throbbing in his ears had reduced to a low murmur. He must think. *Think!*

Suddenly he was back in Athens, in the hotel room again, listening so hard and for so long that his hearing had begun to fail. Kyril shook himself angrily.

Suppose Sikarov had been in Vera's flat all the time, and had followed him; suppose that it was Sikarov out there...

Kyril held himself perfectly still. The thought struck him cold. For the past half-hour he had been in the grip of an emotion so terrible that he had ceased to take even the most elementary of precautions. If Sikarov was in the flat, or even nearby, it would have been a simple thing to follow the raging maniac who raced across the common to Queenstown Road, never once looking back.

But then... why was he still alive? Why had Sikarov not finished him with a single shot? Kyril leaned against the wall and closed his eyes.

Of course. The project-plan. 'Sociable Plover'. Sikarov had orders to retrieve it. That was only logical. If Sikarov was indeed outside... if, if, *if!*

Kyril went slowly up the stairs, feeling his way to the door of the living-room and round the crude trap-door which he had cut in the floor-boards, now supported by only a few millimetres of sawn-through wood.

After a moment's hesitation he decided to put on the light. That could not make matters any worse. As he lit a cigarette his eye lingered on the half-empty bottle of vodka which lay by his mattress. Yes. It was wrong, but he so desperately craved something to fill the void which Sikarov had created inside him.

A man kneeling... blood everywhere... *Vera*. Kyril upturned the bottle and swallowed greedily. The neat spirit had no immediate effect other than to kindle a weak, warm feeling in his guts. He took another swig and replaced the stopper. The red haze which separated him from the outside world was beginning to dissolve.

It was necessary to make plans. Sikarov had to be flushed out.

Kyril went over to the window and listened. Suddenly he was sure.

The killer was out there. He had come to the house like a moth drawn to a flame, and like a moth he would come closer and closer until at last the flame killed him. But Kyril had to sit and wait. He could not escape. He could not even go out. All he could do was sit here, in this upstairs room, alone, in the dark . . . and wait.

You will be utterly alone, that was what Stanov had told him at their last meeting. Until this moment Kyril had never understood the full depth of those words. Mention of Stanov reminded him that the Chairman of the KGB could not escape responsibility for Vera's death. Everything done by his agents was done in his name. Had Stanov foreseen this night, wondered Kyril? Did he realise the part which Vera was destined to play in unmasking the traitor? Was that one reason—perhaps the main reason—for choosing Ivan Yevseevich Bucharensky?

The time passed slowly. Kyril chain-smoked until he felt sick. Every so often he would go to stand by the window to listen and wonder if the tiny noise outside was real or a figment of his imagination. To keep himself awake he played mental games, always pushing to one side the dark thoughts which insisted on forcing their way into his tired brain, thoughts of a half-naked man kneeling over a dead woman . . .

At last he could stand it no longer. He stubbed out the cigarette which he had lighted only seconds before, and stood up. Sikarov's life was worth a few risks. He was going out.

As soon as Sikarov rounded the corner and saw the house sheltering under its high embankment he had a sudden premonition of danger. It was a loaded gun, that house. Someone had primed it and oiled it, spun the chambers, inserted the bullets, cocked it. Now it was pointing at Sikarov, ready to go off.

The first glance was enough to tell him to avoid a frontal approach. But the wall at the side was too high and too smooth for a man to scale without assistance, and Sikarov was alone. The embankment, perhaps? He returned to the other side of the bridge, where only a fence separated the road from the earth wall. That was better. It did not take him long to clamber over the fence and struggle up the embankment. Eight pairs of tracks lay between him and the far side of the permanent way, each with its sinister, gleaming third rail to carry the current.

If he could only cross those tracks he would be on top of the embankment on the other side, overlooking the house which he had seen Kyril enter.

Sikarov hesitated. It was very late; the current was probably off. He would be bound to hear a train long before it came close enough to harm him. But for some reason he could not make himself embark on the short journey which led to his target.

Kyril had been inside the house for some time now. He would have had a chance to recover his self-control, perhaps even to put two and two together. Kyril would remember the incident in Paris; was it not his report which had so nearly finished Sikarov's career? He would realise the danger he was in, and he most certainly was not the kind of man to under-estimate an adversary.

With every step that Sikarov took across those tracks, he would be advancing into danger. He was already regretting his decision not to finish off Kyril in Vera Bradfield's flat. But the longer he left it, the better prepared Kyril would be.

That decided him. He began his cautious journey, lifting his feet carefully over the third rail of the first set of tracks so that not so much as a trouser-leg would brush the dull grey steel.

He was about halfway across when he saw the figure sil-houetted against the sky, and dropped to a crouch.

About 20 metres away someone was standing on the lip of the embankment, motionless. While Sikarov was trying to iden-tify this apparition he heard a goods train start up somewhere close by. Clank-clank-clank . . . so the current wasn't off. Si-karov stared uneasily at the rail by his feet, only to look up sharply as the figure on the embankment moved. It was coming slowly towards him.

Sikarov drew his gun. At the feel of the metal on his skin he underwent a subtle change: his mind and body slotted to-gether in the first stage of an instinctive technique. It was like pulling on an old, comfortable glove.

With half his mind he registered that the approaching train was diesel-powered, after all: he could hear the harsh idling of its engine. From the left, nearby . . .

The figure opposite had crossed the first set of rails and now stood motionless again. Sikarov fancied that the man—by now he knew it was a man—was peering into the darkness, across the tracks, in his direction.

The train approached with a squeal of brakes. As Sikarov raised his gun the diesel crossed his aim and he swore out loud. The goods train had slowed almost to walking-pace for a signal.

He could no longer see the figure opposite. He lay down between a pair of rails and strove to see underneath the train, but the low-slung trucks effectively impeded his vision.

The train was picking up speed again, its badly connected couplings giving out a cacophony of metallic grunts. Sikarov raised his gun to the level of the third, live, rail and prepared to fire.

But the last truck passed across his sightline to reveal only empty space where the other man had been standing a moment ago. Sikarov lifted his head cautiously and looked to right and left. Nothing. The mysterious figure had completely vanished.

He raised himself on one knee, taking his time about it. Nothing moved. By now the goods train, travelling fast, was disappearing into the distance, its red tail-light no bigger than the glow from a cigarette-end. Sikarov waited until the sound of the trucks had died away to silence while he considered his next move.

There were several possibilities. The man on the embankment might have boarded the train and been wafted away on one of the trucks, but that seemed unlikely. Assuming the man to be Bucharensky, it meant he had left his base unguarded. Or, he might have used the train as a shield while he slipped down the embankment into the back garden of one of the houses adjoining his own. Sikarov didn't think so. The man had seen him, he was sure of that. The most likely thing for him to do was retreat down the embankment the way he had come . . . and wait.

Sikarov licked his lips. He had to make a move. Once the news of Bradfield's death filtered back to Dzerzhinsky Square his own future would hang by a thread. Everything depended on his finishing Bucharensky, and quickly. There was only one answer. He had to go forward.

Sikarov stood up very slowly. Everything was quiet. Quelling the first signs of noticeable panic he forced himself to cross the next pair of tracks.

It took him five minutes to reach the far edge of the embankment, every move a slow, painful mixture of doubts and fears.

Safely across at last, he dropped to one knee and took a long look at the back of No. 703. He was almost level with its roof, and from his vantage point he could see a number of possible entrances. A light showed in an upstairs room. That must be where Bucharensky was holed up. Sikarov had noted the separate front doors: obviously there were two flats, one up and one down. His lips jerked back in their customary snarl. That was another problem. Somebody underneath might hear. Perhaps Bucharensky wasn't such a fool, after all, burying himself in the middle of London, surrounded by people.

There was no sign of Bucharensky anywhere. Where *was* he?

The downstairs flat gave Sikarov another idea. There would be no special defences there. It would be easy to force a door, gain access to the building, and then ... yes, that was the plan. Get in downstairs, silence the occupants. Gain *possession*.

Sikarov lay down alongside the set of rails nearest to the house and thought about his plan for a long time. It wasn't perfect, but for the moment he couldn't think of anything better. He looked at the face of his luminous watch. Almost four, too much time wasted already.

He tested the Luger's mechanism and left the safety-catch off. Then he crawled along the tracks until he was almost at the bridge over the road, in the shadow of the high wall which bounded Kyril's back yard.

A long, last look revealed no movement, and he could hear nothing. Sikarov swallowed. His lips were dry and his heart had begun to beat much faster than usual. But there could be no going back now.

Using the wall for cover he slid down the embankment. At the bottom he forced himself to remain still while he counted up to a hundred, faintly marvelling at the discovery that he was still alive. Nothing moved, no one gave the alarm. His progress down the bank had been noiseless and by good luck he had landed in a flower-bed instead of on the concrete slab which began just a few inches away.

On the other side of the wall a car cruised slowly along Queenstown Road. Sikarov waited until it had passed and silence had descended once more. That car could have represented a golden opportunity for him to move up to the back of the house, but even so he wasn't going to hurry. In London there was always a covering noise, even at this time of night, if you only waited long enough. Sikarov lurked in the shadows at the foot of the earthbank, surveying the house inch by inch. Apart from the lighted window on the first floor its huge, black mass was indistinguishable from the night which surrounded it.

A quarter of an hour went by. Time to make a move. For several minutes Sikarov had been aware of a distant plane, beginning its long circle of the capital before the descent to glideslope. As it passed overhead Sikarov slipped into the shadows of the house itself.

Another ten minutes went by while the sound of the plane droned into the west. Nothing changed. Sikarov craned up, trying to see where he stood in relation to the lighted window on the first floor. But the light no longer burned. Someone had extinguished it. His hand touched the drainpipe; it came away wet. He frowned, and reached out to grasp the pipe more firmly. This time his fingers found a barb and he jerked his hand away. Something slimy coated his hand. Paint. Sikarov nodded slowly in grudging appreciation. So much for that idea. It would have to be the back door, then.

It was unlocked. Every nerve in Sikarov's body screamed danger. He pushed at the door and stood quickly aside, half-expecting a trap. The kitchen was dark and silent. Sikarov reached inside and gingerly felt his way round the frame. There was nothing unusual. He hesitated. Was this the way Kyril had come? Perhaps the owners were merely forgetful, after all it took a brave burglar to cross the railway tracks or scale the high wall.

He stepped over the threshold, sniffing as he did so. The house seemed safe, down here at least. He felt his way round the room to the internal door and through it, into the scullery. A smell of old tobacco, that was all.

Sikarov weighed his next move. Without light he was in continual danger of tripping over furniture, but he dare not risk the wall-switch. He pulled out a tiny torch and sent the thin beam dancing round the room. Empty. Ah, a door...where did that lead to?

Sikarov advanced slowly towards the hall, his head cocked to listen for the slightest noise. In the hall he paused. A sound, from the next room. Or was it above? He looked up sharply, directing the beam to the ceiling. No. In the next room.

The door was ajar. Sikarov pushed it open very gently. It made no noise. He was in the front room; he could tell without the light because the windows were a slightly paler shade of charcoal than the surrounding darkness. The noise was coming from here.

Sikarov froze. Breathing. Somewhere, close by, another person was breathing. He tensed his muscles, ready to fling himself in any direction, out of danger.

The breathing continued at the same, even rate. Sikarov moistened his lips. Then it came to him. He was in a bedroom. The breather was asleep.

Very gently, so as not to disturb the sleeper, Sikarov fitted the silencer on to the barrel of his gun. It would take only a second. A flash from the torch, to direct his fire, and the bullets would follow instantaneously. Sikarov turned until he sensed himself to be facing the unseen sleeper, and raised the gun in his right hand. In his left he carried the torch. He extended his arms in front of him and gently brought his hands together. Any second now...

In the room above, someone moved. Sikarov held his position. Even the slightest movement could give him away. The muscular strain began to tell. He could not hold out his arms for much longer. His hands had begun to shake.

Upstairs, all went quiet again. Sikarov lowered his arms, feeling the sudden ache as the blood flowed back to the wrists. He took a dozen slow, deep breaths, and raised his hands together for the second time. Now they were level. Inhale.

The beam of light lanced out to illuminate Trumper's sleeping form on the bed and in the same second Sikarov fired twice, the shots coming so close together that they sounded like one.

Instinctively Sikarov raised his eyes to the ceiling. Nothing happened. No one moved.

Sikarov lowered his arms. There must be another room somewhere, surely? He padded back into the hall, only to wheel round at the sound of other breathing. No, not breathing. Hissing. A low, even sound, not unlike the very distant sough of the sea. Ignore it, he told himself. Move.

He found the other room. It contained a bed but no one was in it. His nose twitched. There was a funny smell in here. He backed away, into the hall. The smell seemed to follow him.

Keeping his back to the wall, Sikarov retreated silently to the scullery. The smell did not diminish; rather it seemed to be growing stronger. The hissing, what was that?

Gas.

Involuntarily Sikarov shuddered. Somebody had turned on the gas-tap. All the while he had been in the house, someone else was there too, noislessly following him. And he had turned on the gas . . .

What kind of gas? Domestic gas? Coal . . . natural . . . ? Was the gas they used in England poisonous? Was it volatile? But wait a minute, who said it was mains gas? Suppose it came from a cylinder . . .

Sikarov, unwisely, opened his mouth, and at once started to cough. Stuffing a handkerchief into his mouth he headed blindly towards the kitchen, and safety. There was the door leading to the back yard. Another couple of paces and he would be out of this hellhole, another step . . .

He heard nothing until the last moment. Then someone took a blunt instrument and with neat, surgical precision applied it to the length of his skull; for a fleeting second Sikarov thought he could feel the skin unpeeling itself from his head; then he fell forward into the darkness and disconnected.

When he awoke and his eyes came into focus the first thing he saw was the gaping hole in the floor, and he understood. The man he had seen on the embankment was Bucharensky. He waited until he was sure Sikarov would follow before retreating back to the house and sealing off the upper flat, whence he could direct a stream of gas into the downstairs room. When Sikarov turned to run he dropped through the hole to follow him. That was clever.

Sikarov turned his head to one side and retched phlegm on to the bare floor.

The light was on. Bucharensky stood leaning against the far wall by the window, smoking. When he saw Sikarov vomit he picked up a basin from by his feet and came over. The douche of cold water hit Sikarov in the face. A lot of it went down inside his collar.

He began to register details. He was sitting in an uncomfortable chair constructed of solid wood. When he tried to move, straps restrained his arms and legs. They were very tight: bands of white flesh showed on either side of the leather.

He looked down. He was naked from below the waist. His genitals hung through a hole in the seat. Something was twisted round them, something that stung when he struggled . . .

'When I last saw you . . .'

Kyril spoke dreamily, like a man under the influence of drugs. To Sikarov it seemed as if he had passed on to an altogether different plane of existence, bloodless and remote.

' . . . you were walking out to a plane. In Paris. Do you remember Paris?'

Kyril took a long drag on the cigarette and held the smoke in his lungs. His eyes were closed. Sikarov said nothing.

'I remember Paris, Sikarov. Every detail.'

There was a long silence. Kyril's eyes remained closed, as if concentrating on some scene being played out behind his eyelids. Sikarov's tongue had gummed itself to the roof of his mouth.

'I thought to myself then: that's it. The finish. Siberia or the Lubianka cellars. We are not animals, I told myself. Within the ranks of the KGB there is no place for excrement like that.'

Kyril's eyes opened and Sikarov saw that the pupils were unnaturally dilated.

'But oh Sikarov . . .'

Kyril's head tilted so that at last his burning eyes rested on Sikarov's body.

' . . . how I underestimated our masters then.'

He moved away from the wall, arms folded across his chest,

and slowly advanced towards the chair. Sikarov tried to shrink away, found he couldn't move, and knew a second of black horror which almost threatened to shut down his conscious mind.

'. . . I had forgotten that for the true killer, for the psychopath . . . there is always a role. Nemesis. Sikarov. Someone has sent you to be my Nemesis.'

Kyril sat down on his mattress in front of the chair and brought his legs up like a Buddha. Now he was staring directly into Sikarov's eyes and the prisoner found he could not turn his face away: it was as though invisible steel bars ran between the two men, forcing them to endure each other's souls.

'You have this choice. You can die quickly, and painlessly, from a bullet. Or you can die from . . .'

Kyril lifted a hand, the movement slow and clumsy like a deep-sea diver's, and gestured vaguely at the chair.

'. . . that.'

There was another long silence. Sikarov knew that very soon now the contents of his bowels were going to flood all over the floor.

'Who sent you, Sikarov? That's all you have to do to buy yourself an easy death. Tell me the answer to just one question. Who . . . sent . . . you?'

Sikarov said nothing. A slow smile spread across Kyril's lips.

'Let me tell you about that . . . thing . . . you are sitting in . . .'

Kyril unfolded his legs and stretched them out in front of him, like a man who wants to make sure he is comfortable before embarking on a long story.

'It's oak. Fastened to the floor. As you realise, you can't move. Wrapped round your . . . equipment . . . is what we used to call "the adulterer's knot". You've heard of that, have you? I hadn't heard of it. When I was a boy . . .'

Kyril stood up to light another cigarette and moved away from Sikarov.

'. . . We lived in a village just west of the Urals. The oldest man in the village was a cossack . . . he must have been 90 if he was a day.'

Kyril halted and looked at the wall, his face set once more in its smooth, dreamy expression.

'Do you know anything about the cossacks? They're a strange crew. This old man, one day my friends and I were discussing the local harlot. Married, she was. I suppose we got a bit high-spirited, you know how boys do...'

Kyril was in no particular hurry now. The memory of his childhood was very close, very real.

'The old cossack, he said..."where I come from, they'd put you louts in an adulterer's knot". "Where do you come from, grandad?" we answered, although we knew. He'd come from western Siberia...Surgut. Do you know Surgut?'

As if mesmerised Sikarov very slowly shook his head.

'But then we got curious...and one of us, I forget who, asked him about this knot. And he showed us. It's for when one cossack finds that another has stolen his woman. You take thin wire...not so thin that it breaks when fire touches it...'

Sikarov flinched. Kyril saw, and allowed another long silence to develop.

'...And you tie it, so...if you look down you'll see...in such a way that, as it heats, the knot contracts upon itself, eating through anything that gets in its way...'

Sikarov's face had turned perfectly white, even to the lips.

'I've had to improvise a little. Do you know what this is? It's called a Bunsen burner. You fix it to a gas pipe, so...'

Kyril plugged the rubber tube over a gas-tap let into the skirting-board.

'Then you turn on the gas and...you see?'

Kyril flicked his lighter, and watched the flame reflected in Sikarov's dull eyes as it moved towards the burner. A wing of yellow leapt into the air; Kyril adjusted the stern until all the yellow had drained away, leaving in its place a thin, purple column of naked heat.

'Behind you, the wire is attached to a hook in the wall, like the one you see holding it in front of you. As the wire turns red it cuts first through the upper edge of the penis, while underneath it severs the little neck of skin which connects the scrotum...you understand the principle?'

Kyril put down the bunsen burner in front of Sikarov, where he could see it, and sat back on his haunches. For a moment there was silence. Then Sikarov moaned, and his bowels opened.

The stench which filled the room was indescribable, but Kyril betrayed no emotion.

'I ask you again. Who sent you?'

The pause seemed to go on for a very long time. Sikarov's fists clenched and unclenched, his eyes fluttered open and shut. Kyril tried to imagine what was going on in his brain, what loyalties were asserting themselves, or finally being put to rest. How would I react, he asked himself, what would I do?

Sikarov's eyes opened wide. 'No.'

Kyril reached for the burner, and applied it to the wire. Both men watched, fascinated, as it began to glow. Then the red started to travel along the wire towards the chair. Kyril placed the burner directly under the wire, and waited.

He had not known what to expect. But the reality was frightful.

If an impressionist artist wanted to illustrate the meaning, the concept, of 'Scream', he would have painted Sikarov. The man's body slammed forward against the straps, his spine arched, his head went back until the horrible, glazed eyes were staring at the ceiling. All ten fingers stuck out rigidly. The lips curled back in a terrible rictus, laying bare the gums.

The stench began, a new smell to add to the old. Burning flesh. Seared meat.

And the scream. Explosively loud, expelled from Sikarov's body as if by an overpowering force, a high-pitched wail that spoke of death and things beyond death, a scream that suddenly rippled with syllables . . .

'Meee-ay, Meee-ay . . .'

Kyril snatched away the burner. *'Michaelov?'*

Sikarov's scream faded to a low, background moan. His head lolled on his chest. Kyril dared not look down his body to see what the fire had done.

Was there a name buried in that awful scream? Mee . . . ? It could have been Michaelov, it had to be Michaelov . . .

Kyril went to kneel by Sikarov's body. The man was slipping into unconsciousness. Kyril took him by the chin and hauled him upright in the chair.

'Who sent you?'

Sikarov's head rolled backwards, the eyes staring and blank.

Somewhere, as from a great distance, Kyril heard Stanov's own words to him, weeks before. *You will be alone*. When the lessons stopped, in the place where there were no more lectures and trade-craft failed, every agent was alone. In a sense. But not like this. Officers of the KGB, even the professional killers of the A2 Institute, went with the support of their fellows, in the knowledge that they could call on them in need.

Only Kyril, only he had been truly alone.

He picked up the Luger which had fallen out of the assassin's pocket when Kyril stripped him and used it to blow away the side of Sikarov's ugly head.

26

The car stank of smoke. Ted Jacques sat in the front with the driver, wondering what the hell was going on, while the man in the back seat alternately chewed on a nail and smoked his cigarette. Ted wanted to turn round and look at him but didn't like to. He had no idea what was happening but he realised that for the London Station Chief to come and sit in the back of a car under a bridge in Battersea at 7 o'clock in the morning it must be something pretty big. Especially when the London Station Chief in question was a quivering wreck.

'Let's have it once again.'

Ted screwed up his mouth but did not protest.

'I followed two men from the house in Turpin Road. The leader was in a great hurry and the other one was following him. Neither of them looked back. The car got here about 40 minutes later. Everything was quiet. Then we saw a movement...'

'What time was this?'

'About ten to four.'

'Go on.'

'We saw something move on the embankment. A man. He stood on the top with his back to the house, we could see him outlined against the skyline...'

'Yes, yes, go on.'

'He came down in a rush and a while after that this second man followed over the edge. He must have come over the tracks.'

'And then?'

'Nothing until about half-past five. Then we heard a scream, very long and very loud. Even for round here. Nothing since then.'

'The scream came from No. 703?'

'Yes, we think so.'

'Any reactions? Lights on along the street, doors opening, that sort of thing?'

The driver of the car laughed. 'Here? You've heard of the wrong side of the tracks? Well...' He jerked his thumb upwards, to the bridge. 'Those are the tracks.'

'And you haven't made a move yet, you've done nothing to alarm the occupants?'

'No sir. You said to wait and we waited.'

Royston lit another cigarette from the butt of the old one. Ted continued to face the front, maintaining a watch on the street. The night was thinning out, it was possible to distinguish the houses one from another. Suddenly he leaned forward.

'Movement', he said softly.

Royston's head materialised beside him.

'Where?'

Ted pointed. 'See that flash of white... some kind of... stick, I think. Yes, that's it. A blind chap. Coming out of the downstairs flat.'

Royston was puzzled. 'How do you know it's the downstairs flat?'

'Well, there are two front doors, you see. Next to each other. I didn't see the first man enter the house, but the second man did, because he was there ahead of me, and he spent a lot of time just nosing round the door on the left. There've been lights on upstairs, so I reckon the door on the left leads to the upper flat...'

'And the blind man came out of the door on the right . . . yes, I understand now.'

Royston lowered himself back into his seat.

'He's reached the gate. Shall I go and take a look?'

'No, don't do that . . .'

But Royston was too late. The tense, polluted atmosphere inside the car had become too much for Ted. He stood on the pavement, drawing in gulps of fresh air, then strode off towards the house under the embankment. Royston's hands tightened on the seat in front of him, but he said nothing.

As Ted approached the house another door opened further along the terrace and a shaft of light illuminated the pavement. A young woman emerged, holding in her arms a child who seemed to be asleep. She reached her front gate just as the blind man with the stick stepped on to the pavement.

''Allo, there, Mr. Trumper', said the girl. ''Ow are you, then?'

As Ted sauntered past in the grey half-light he was vaguely aware of a shabby mac and dark glasses obscuring the upper part of an elderly face. The old man muttered something that Ted couldn't catch.

'Oh dear, your chest bad again, is it?'

The man nodded and coughed bronchially. Ted was almost past now.

''Ere, what was all that racket upstairs, then? Screamin' and that.'

'Din' 'ear nuffin'.'

'Coo, wish I could sleep like that. Well, look after y'self. Cheers, then.'

Ted walked on a few paces, crossed the road and began to retrace his steps. The girl hurried off down the hill, still carrying the child, while the old man shuffled slowly in the opposite direction. Ted walked back to the car and reported. At first Royston said nothing, his face creased in thought.

'This man', he said suddenly. 'The one with the stick. You're sure the girl knew him?'

'Oh yes, no question. She spoke to him like an old friend.'

'He wasn't one of the men you followed?'

Ted suppressed a desire to laugh. 'No sir.'

'Even in disguise?'

'Different build, different . . . everything.'

Royston remained in thought a few moments longer.

'Right', he said at last. 'Check with the second car on the other side of the embankment. See if anybody's gone out that way, over the railway lines.'

The driver's hand moved to the radiophone.

'Then we'll go and get a warrant. Or rather, the Special Branch will. It sounds from what the girl said as if you're right about the upstairs flat, then. I want to take a look in there.'

The driver turned to Royston. 'No one's been out that way.'

Royston nodded. 'Get going, then.'

27

Sculby drifted into sleep to catch the first gleam of the silver blade in the crook of the officer's swinging arm as he stormed across Red Square in search of him. Throughout the night the dream intermittently returned, and this was typical. The most he could achieve was a light doze, interspersed with periods of wakefulness whenever the officer with his flashing sword came too close for comfort. All the details in the dream were clear by now. Only the face was still missing. Every time Sculby dropped off the sword gleamed brighter in the piercing sunlight, until it almost blinded him. An inner reserve of fatigue was building up inside him much as other men acquire reserves of courage or moral strength.

He woke to find Judy's letter still beneath his hand where it lay on the quilt. He had come home the night before to find it pushed through the letter-box, unstamped. The long scrawl was rambling and difficult to read but its general message was clear enough. We are not suited. Goodbye.

Sculby screwed up the letter and tossed it down the loo. He had to flush it three times before the heavy, water-logged paper disappeared round the bend, taking Judy out of his life.

That morning he was too tired to be conscious of any particular emotion, other than a mild annoyance at one of the phrases she had used in her letter. 'I don't mind trendy lefties', she had written. 'God knows, I've had enough of them, and they're OK as long as you don't take baby seriously. But pseudo-trendies, playing at playing at it, no darling . . .'

Playing at playing at it; that's what got up Sculby's nose. He wanted to believe that Judy would someday find out about the work of national importance he'd been doing for Royston over the last six years, would come grovelling to him in abject, humiliated apology, 'Laurie, I never realised . . .'

He saw where his thoughts were leading and angrily brushed them aside. Fantasies could be damaging. Pathos crippled. What he needed was breakfast.

While he made the toast Sculby forced himself to concentrate on Loshkevoi.

Today the magistrates would finally decide whether to commit him for trial by jury at Inner London Crown Court. Sculby had consulted Spencer Gyddon and together they had decided to allow the case to go through on the nod, without challenging the written statements provided by the Police. This was called a 'Section One' committal.

'They've got just enough there to open the case to the jury', said Gyddon. 'Don't worry, Laurie, I'll get it knocked out at half time.'

On the whole Sculby agreed with that assessment, but in the taxi to Lavender Hill he couldn't help wondering whether they oughtn't to have been submitting today that there was no case to answer. Spencer Gyddon was unavailable, however, and Sculby neither wanted to take in another barrister at this late stage nor to risk doing the case himself, so a Section One committal it was.

He met Loshkevoi in the foyer and took him to an interview room. The first thing his client said was: 'I tried to call you last night, Laurie. I didn't want you to come. It's all off.'

Sculby sat down and said nothing for a moment. He took out a cigarette, lit it and enjoyed a long drag while he thought about his next move.

Royston had never so much as hinted that this might be in the pipeline. Sculby had no instructions to drop the case.

'What's up, Victor?' he asked gently.

'I don't need you any more, Laurie. I've decided to go it alone. I'm pleading guilty.'

'What?'

'I did it, you see.'

Loshkevoi darted a sharp look at Sculby as he spoke these words, and the solicitor had a sudden hunch that his client knew perfectly well what the effect would be. No lawyer who was advised of his client's guilt in that way could thereafter put forward a positive case of innocence to the court.

'But why, Victor? Why save it up for now?'

Sculby was genuinely astonished. He had known clients do all kinds of crazy things, but nothing as outlandish as this.

'Have they threatened you? Have they promised you a deal?'

Loshkevoi merely shrugged and looked away.

'I can't just take this lying down, you know. In your own interests, I've got to try to talk you out of it.'

'You'll be wasting your breath. Leave it out, please Laurie. You can't do any more to help me now.'

Sculby considered his client. Loshkevoi seemed preoccupied, distraught; something far outside this courtroom was preying on his mind. The lawyer was conscious of a barrier between them, a wilful refusal on Loshkevoi's part to meet his situation face to face. Yet underneath it all he was scared out of his wits. Somewhere very near the surface was the jerky madman who had screamed from the dock on the day of the first hearing. If only Sculby could get through to him...

'You could go inside, you realise that, don't you?' Sculby's voice was suddenly hard. 'Doing bird is no fun, Victor. You don't want to get involved with that. Remand in Brixton, that was nothing, that's a doddle. Have you ever *really* been in prison before? Three men to a cell, and they all shit?'

'Laurie, I...'

'The smell at night, have you thought about that?'

Loshkevoi stood up and banged his clenched fists on the table in front of him.

'Get out!'

'Now look...'

'You're sacked, you hear me? Sacked!'

Sculby gave him a long, cool look, then packed up his

briefcase and made for the door.

'I'll be in court', he said just before he went out. 'If you change your mind, all you've got to do is say.'

Once outside Sculby thought about phoning Royston, actually went as far as the phone-booth, before deciding he couldn't go through with it. He had a 'life or death' contact number but somehow he couldn't bring himself to use it. Three months was the most Loshkevoi could expect, even if the worst came to the worst, and besides it was P.4's function to watch, not manipulate. Its members were 'spies' rather than 'agents', their powers limited.

Sculby reluctantly put the change back into his trouser-pocket and entered the court.

Today there were a number of matters to be dealt with before Loshkevoi's case was called on. Sculby sat in the solicitor's row and doodled in the margin of his notebook. At last he heard his ex-client's name and turned to see him in the dock, hands resting on the bar in front of him. The clerk to the justices ran through the formalities like an announcer reeling off stations. Loshkevoi declined to apply for Legal Aid, opted for summary trial, waived any claim to trial by jury. At a sign from the chairman of the magistrates Loshkevoi sat down.

'Sergeant?'

Detective-Sergeant Fitzgerald rose to his feet.

'Sir, normally there would be no objection from the Police to summary trial on these charges. But there has been a slight complication . . .'

Sculby looked up from his note-book to see that Fitzgerald was suffering from an advanced case of policeman's smirk.

'Owing to information very helpfully supplied by the accused himself, and I want to say now that the Police have received the very fullest co-operation, certain other offences have come to light.'

Sculby turned to the dock, willing Loshkevoi to look him in the eye, without success. His former client was alert but relaxed, and again Sculby was conscious of a feeling that he knew what he was up to, almost as if acting under advice.

Fitzgerald handed a typewritten list to the bench. The chairman looked up from reading it and said sharply, 'Two of these offences were allegedly committed while the accused was on bail pending these present charges, the ones with which we are concerned today.'

'Yes, sir.'

The chairman's lips puckered. To Sculby he seemed mildly embarrassed at finding himself in such low company for the discharge of a public duty. 'Well-meaning' was the phrase the Divisional Court would use when quashing his decisions.

'Er . . . Mr Loshkevoi, perhaps you'd like to reconsider your position. You're not legally represented . . .'

'It's okay.' Loshkevoi was standing again. Sculby, who had long ago ceased to write, sat with his mouth open.

'. . . I just want to get it over with. Finish. You understand?'

The bench went into a huddle. Sculby knew what would happen and it did.

'Put these further charges', said the chairman. The clerk ran through the same rigmarole all over again and Loshkevoi renewed his guilty plea.

'Anything known?'

Fitzgerald stood up.

'No sir. The accused is a person of hitherto good character. There are no antecedents.'

Again the chairman's lips puckered.

'Mr Loshkevoi, do you wish to call character evidence or say anything on your own behalf?'

Sculby half rose to his feet, thought better of it, and subsided.

'Not really. It's the temptation, you see. I mentioned this to the Sergeant there and he agrees. Very easy in the used car trade.'

The chairman looked incredulous. 'Is that all you want to say?'

Loshkevoi shrugged. 'Sure. Why not?'

'Do you regret having committed these offences?'

'Oh sure. Pity I got found out, eh?'

And Loshkevoi laughed, a hearty, booming sound which caused everyone in court to stop whatever he was doing and look at the prisoner in the dock, amazed.

Sculby put away his notebook and reached for his coat. The

proceedings were now drawing to a close which he regarded as inevitable. The bench went into its usual huddle; then the chairman was speaking again.

'We do not think we have adequate powers to deal with you. We therefore propose to commit you to the Crown Court for sentence, in accordance with the warning which the clerk read to you earlier.'

As Sculby left the courtroom the last thing he heard was the magistrate refusing Loshkevoi bail for which he had not actually applied.

28

The crypt was exactly as Kyril remembered it. Plain, whitewashed walls, tatty strips of carpet, red lights glowing outside closed doors. The central room, what was it called? 'Grocer's Gift'. Kyril had never understood that name. Nursing a cup of sweet tea he looked around with a tinge of nostalgia. The people here were so nice, so kind. The lady in reception had asked him if he minded waiting until someone was free. No, said Kyril, he didn't mind. He had all the time in the world.

The Samaritans were a unique find. Every agent has his personal trade secrets, things which he never reports back to Centre or shares with others. The Wallbrook headquarters of the Samaritans was one of Kyril's little personal treasures. He had used it only once before but he had great faith in it. You went down the steps and immediately became anonymous. You didn't have to give a name or an address, although one usually did in order not to be conspicuous; Kyril had told them his name was Ian, just that. Then after a decent interval one disappeared through the man-sized ventilator at the back of the

centre corridor, the only fire escape on the premises . . . and
that was that.

But not today. Today was different.

Kyril pulled Trumper's macintosh a little more snugly over
his shoulders. Getting the right build had been the most difficult
thing; that and trying to emulate a stooping walk which he had
never actually seen in life. The first problem he had solved by
wrapping himself in several of the old man's woollies. The
walk he had left to chance.

After disposing of Sikarov he had dropped down into the
flat below through his trap-door. The old man lived in conditions of extreme poverty; it was not much of a life to leave,
thought Kyril. He concentrated on clothing. When he had removed all that was wearable from the bedroom he began to
rummage through drawers, jackdaw-like, in search of anything
useful. There was a pair of dark glasses in a newish case,
perhaps prescribed by that bugger of a doctor, but not worn,
out of pride. Kyril pocketed them. The white stick was also
useful. In height he and the old man were not dissimilar; cotton
wool and hair dye would go a long way towards perfecting the
substitution. He knew the power of 'type': a watcher would
see only a white stick and dark glasses, say the word 'blind'
to himself, and look elsewhere for the elusive Russian agent
he was supposed to be seeking.

From the depths of his rucksack Kyril extracted a small,
lightweight box containing his make-up. He had brought nothing special, just the most basic kit for emergencies, but it was
enough. By inserting pads of cotton-wool into his cheeks and
moving them around with his fingers he was soon able to
fashion a face the same shape as the dead man's. Kyril shared
Trumper's weather-beaten complexion so he did nothing with
that, trusting the dark glasses, scarf and hat to cut down to a
minimum the area of skin that could be used for comparative
purposes. Thereafter it was a simple matter of high-lighting
and ageing, with particular attention to the corners of the eyes,
the neck and, last but most important, the hands.

Next came the difficult bit. He had to assume Trumper's
walk, but he had almost no idea what it looked like. The thick
cane was the only real indication he had to go on: it was used
to support the bearer as well as warn others that he was blind.

So it would pay to go slowly, rather than risk going too fast. Kyril had 'played blind' before, he knew all the business with the stick, but the rest he was going to have to chance.

The worst part had been waiting for the noises next door which would indicate that the girl was on her way out. Kyril used the time to ensure that he had forgotten nothing. His rucksack was stripped of its contents and discarded, everything of value now being secreted on Kyril's person. Then he stood in the hall, listening with all his might. At last he heard the tell-tale sounds: a door slammed in the adjoining house and footsteps thudded down the stairs. The girl pulled the front door to behind her and turned to see old Mr Trumper almost on the pavement.

From then on it had been easy. In a different frame of mind Kyril would have enjoyed the casual, dismissive glance which was all the DI6 agent in the street could afford. But today what mattered was escape. He discarded the white stick and the glasses behind some bushes on the common, then made his way to Bank by tube. Now here he was, safe for a time. They would never think of looking for him here.

He looked around. For some reason things looked different. Kyril couldn't think what it was. Then he remembered.

'Excuse me . . .' A young woman was passing his chair.

'Yes?'

'The cats, are they still here? You called them Push and Pull, I remember them so well.'

'Oh they died, I'm afraid.'

Kyril's face fell. 'I'm sorry.'

'That was a long time ago.'

'I've been away, you see.'

'Can I help you?'

Kyril looked up to see that a young man had come to stand by his chair. The woman used the opportunity to slip away while Kyril studied the man's face and his badge. 'John 1696', they never told you the surname. The security here was excellent, they would have made good spies.

'I'd like to talk to somebody.'

'Please. Come this way. We'll go into "Godfrey".'

Kyril followed the young man into the cubicle, sat down in an old armchair from which the stuffing had mostly escaped, and folded his hands in his lap. He was conscious of the young man's eyes upon him, and behind those eyes he knew that John 1696 was busily attaching labels. Shabby clothes. Old tramp. Query drunk, or just here for the hand-out.

'I don't really know how to begin.' He tailed off. The young man leaned forward.

'Take your time', he said. 'There's absolutely no hurry.'

Kyril pretended to study his hands. 'You see, the trouble is . . . it all seems so implausible.'

The young man shook his head and smiled. 'We're used to hearing all kinds of things here. It never goes any further.'

After a further period of reflection Kyril began his story.

'I must tell you first that I am a spy. I am a Colonel in the KGB, attached to the staff of its Chairman. I have been sent to England on a very delicate mission—to expose a traitor in our ranks. What I think you call a "mole", no?'

The young man sat back, his smile intact. 'Goodness', he said. 'I've never met a real spy before.'

'There aren't many of us. Now you see, my problem is this. The mole has sent an executioner after me. He's outside there now, in the street. He's armed, of course. And the question is, what am I to do?'

The young man appeared to be lost in thought. After a while he spoke. 'There's somebody here who I think could help you more than I can. Somebody who's, er, used to this kind of thing.'

'Really? You mean, he's a spy too?'

'Not exactly. He's a . . . well, a doctor, actually.'

Kyril nodded. 'Perhaps I could talk to him, then.'

The young man stood up.

'Please wait here. I shan't be a moment.'

He went out, closing the door behind him very firmly. Kyril smiled. It would take John 1696 quite a while to brief the resident psychiatrist on the latest nutter and there was a good chance that he would warn everyone else to stay away from 'Godfrey' until 'Ian' had been dealt with. He could spin this out for a while yet. First there would be the long, circuitous questioning designed to establish what the real problem was; then, later in the day, he would persuade them to find him a hostel for the night. Meanwhile there was time to think . . .

Stanov's moving magnet had come to the very end of the road. Either the traitor stood revealed by now or the plan had failed: Kyril had no means of knowing. Three times he had shown himself on schedule; three times he had evaded capture. *'Lisa's'* executioner . . . executed. That left only Loshkevoi. The biggest question-mark of all . . .

Other images crowded into Kyril's tired brain.

An old man locked into a stuffy office overlooking Dzerzhinsky Square, who lied to his own men and spun fine webs from the ruthlessly mangled lives of people he despised . . .

A younger man on a bed, half-concealing a bloody corpse . . .

An anonymous traitor who must be destroyed so that his very name was blotted out . . .

Kyril closed his eyes and sat back in the old, tattered chair. His head had begun to ache. It was going to be a long, long day.

29

At first Michaelov paid scant attention to the news of Loshkevoi's imprisonment, marking it down as just another mystery in the Bucharensky saga which would one day find an explanation. Then in the course of the afternoon Yevchenko came along the corridor to give him a tiny insight into what Loshkevoi had been really doing for the last few years and the picture changed. Now Povin and his boss were up before Stanov to learn the worst.

Michaelov noted with grudging approval that the old man looked suitably contrite. As soon as he saw the First Deputy Chairman he spread his hands wide and said ruefully, 'Valery Vasilevich, what can I say? Every rogue gets found out in the end, no?'

With difficulty Michaelov restrained himself from asking whether 'Lisa' had been found out yet, and said, 'If you had felt able to confide in me just a little, comrade Chairman.'

Stanov found it hard to resent the censorious tone of Michaelov's voice. For years he had, in effect, been running the show behind his deputy's back. As Kyril observed weeks before, it was a system which worked only when things went well. Today things were going very badly indeed.

'Have you heard anything?'

'He is in Wandsworth Prison. He was taken there at 1430 local time after a short period in Police custody. Since then he has been held incommunicado.'

'Is that usual in England?'

'Very unusual.'

It was Povin who spoke. His voice betrayed no hint of criticism, merely a desire to press on with whatever might be necessary. Stanov had a lot of time for Povin just then.

'Do we have anyone inside Wandsworth Prison?'

'Unfortunately not.' They were on Povin's home ground and he spoke with authority. 'Six months ago, DI5 took over a cell block at Wandsworth and turned it into a top security holding centre. We think not even the governor is allowed to know exactly what goes on in there. It stinks of anti-terrorism. I've been trying desperately to get a pair of eyes in there, but these things take time, and...'

Stanov waved a hand. 'No matter, comrade Colonel-General. You've done well. But... it could not have happened at a worse time. First Bucharensky, now this.'

He stood up and walked over to the window. Behind his back he could sense the other three weighing up his reactions. Yevchenko, loyal to the end but allowing personal concern for the chief to get the better of his judgement. Michaelov, unimaginative, concerned only to watch his step while he built bridges towards Stanov's as yet unknown successor. And Povin...

Stanov turned back to face the room. 'He must be brought out, Colonel-General', he said quietly. 'Brought out or otherwise dealt with.'

Povin nodded curtly. 'I'm working on it, comrade Marshal. My own inclination is to liquidate him fast, and not waste time on trying to spring him.'

Stanov nodded thoughtfully. 'I agree.'

'It should not be difficult.' Michaelov, impatient at being left out of the colloquy developing between his chief and his deputy, was determined to make a contribution. 'I have recently dispatched an A2 to London, comrade Marshal. It's not a problem.'

Stanov nodded. He seemed absent-minded, as though his attention was on other things. Through half-closed eyes he watched the two Generals. Michaelov wore an expression of pompous self-esteem. Povin's face was impassive. Did Stanov detect a trace of surprise at Michaelov's last words? Had Povin known that an executioner had been ordered to his territory? Stanov fancied not. But Povin was always loyal. If there was one thing Stanov valued in a senior officer it was loyalty. Loyalty was like oxygen. The higher you rose, the scarcer it became.

'Keep me informed, comrades. I want to hear of progress within the next 24 hours. Povin, I take it there is no news of Bucharensky, or you would have told me?'

'There is no news, comrade Marshal. I regret...'

Stanov waved him away. The debacle in Victoria Station had been no fault of Povin's. The two Generals saluted and withdrew, Povin standing respectfully aside for his superior.

'That Michaelov is a condescending, fat-arsed pig...' Yevchenko began, but Stanov stopped him by raising his hand. For a while there was silence. Yevchenko was about to resume when Stanov said, 'Nikolai, you remember the day we went to the Kremlin?'

Yevchenko felt his cheek-muscles tense. They had spoken little of that day. Despite Stanov's assurances, Yevchenko could never be quite certain that the Chief accepted his version of what had occurred over lunch with Kazin. The more Yevchenko protested that he had kept Kazin at bay, the more cynical Stanov's sideways glance became, as if the old man were quietly saying to himself, 'I'll bet'.

Yevchenko found this galling, not least because Stanov's suspicions were eminently justified. It had been a difficult lunch. He was a tough old man who had seen much, but when there was a pause in the conversation and he looked up to find those pebble lenses glinting at him over the table he had known fear. 'Stalin's baby'... such pink, well-preserved skin on one so evil, it was an unfair anachronism. It was as if he had found a way of channelling some of the fresh young blood he had spilled into his own veins. And the voice... that melodious, silken voice with its promises and blandishments still echoed in Yevchenko's ears.

He quelled the thoughts of treachery which rose to the surface whenever that day was mentioned and tried to concentrate on the present crisis.

'Of course. We came back and there was nothing, nothing at all. Every message in its appointed place, no tampering, no delays. Povin dealt with the matter as one of top priority. Surely you don't think...'

Stanov shook his head impatiently. 'No, it's the date that concerns me. It was on that day that Kyril first showed himself in London. You remember how I issued an order for his return to Moscow *alive?*'

'Of course.'

'Nikolai!' His old eyes were bright with excitement. 'It's going to work! He's panicked. Kyril arrives... an A2 is despatched to London... Loshkevoi is arrested...'

'You're going too fast. What's the connection?'

'Why, don't you see? Loshkevoi's been taken out of circulation. He's been put away. *Somewhere Kyril can't reach him.*'

Yevchenko pursed his lips.

'You're assuming a lot.'

'Am I? It can't be coincidence, it can't be. *First* the executioner, *then* this business with Loshkevoi. And Loshkevoi is in touch with the traitor!' He checked himself. 'But you're right, Nikolai. It has to be gone over very carefully. You must do it yourself. Discreetly. I want to know what Povin has on in London at the moment which would require an operative from A2. And if, as I suspect, the answer is "nothing"...' Stanov shot a glance at Yevchenko and saw the beginnings of a reluctant conversion in his face. '... You can come back here and tell me, Nikolai, precisely when and why General Michaelov took it upon himself to order an executioner to the United Kingdom.'

30

Looking back on it afterwards Sculby was never quite sure how it happened. He had gone to the outer office to say goodnight to Betty and watched while she bundled up the last batch of post. As he went back to his own room he heard the outer door close and the night-latch click. He sat down at his desk and was collating the sheets of an affidavit when he heard the voice.

'Don't move.'

Something in the tone compelled obedience. A sheet of paper slipped from Sculby's fingers; he sat rigidly, his head still bent downwards to the desk.

'Place both hands on top of your desk . . . that's right.'

Sculby noticed that his hands were shaking and pressed them firmly down on to the leather, deliberately tensing all his muscles. He had been wondering for a long time how he would react when this moment came. Now, looking at his hands, he knew.

The Soviet officer did not wear a uniform and the flashing silver-white sword had been replaced by a small gun. The face, so long concealed, had dark circles round the eyes, sunken

cheeks, tousled, unkempt hair and at least a day's growth of
stubble. Kyril's eyes were hard and flat, two bright shiny but-
tons sewn into the dark circles. Sculby knew that Royston had
told him only the truth: from now on he was fighting for his
life. And he was terrified.

Kyril walked across to the window and drew the curtains.
To Sculby it was as though his office halved in size. It became
very claustrophobic, very hot. The slightest movement by the
Russian seemed to come within inches of Sculby's face.

'I've put off visiting you for too long, Sculby. I should have
realised a long time ago that you weren't just a meddler.'

The clipped, too-perfect English sounded coldly in the solicitor's ears. Something was at work deep inside Kyril, a hard
core of fission which bordered always on the critical. Sculby
made himself concentrate on the man's face, keeping his eyes
off the gun.

'Last night a woman was killed. A woman who was important to me. Vera Bradfield.'

Seeing Sculby's involuntary start, Kyril raised the gun.

'You didn't know?'

Sculby shook his head.

'I wonder if that's true. You visited her two days ago. You
talked about Loshkevoi. I want to know why, Sculby. Who
put you up to it? Who are you working for, DI6?'

There was silence. Kyril slowly shook his head.

'Don't make me work for it. I'd enjoy it too much.'

'Yes, I work for DI6. Department P.4.'

Sculby's voice seemed to come from a great distance, perhaps deadened by the thick layer of fur which coated the inside
of his mouth.

'What is P.4? Be specific.'

'P stands for professional. Doctors, lawyers, accountants.
People who learn secrets about other people's lives. Their finances. Their habits. Their crucial needs.'

Kyril's eyes widened and narrowed again. 'That is clever',
he said softly. 'In Russia that would not work, but here, in
England . . . yes, I think I see the value of that.'

His face hardened once more.

'So you were told to find about Loshkevoi's secrets . . . and
Vera's.'

'Loshkevoi's, yes. I visited Vera Bradfield only because he mentioned her name.'

'Why should he do such a thing?'

'I don't know.'

Kyril strove to assimilate this latest piece of information. He did not doubt that Sculby was telling the truth: the lawyer was obviously scared out of his wits. But why should Loshkevoi ever know about Vera? Only Stanov understood her significance. *Stanov!*

'Tell me his exact words.'

Sculby did his best to remember. Kyril ran a hand over his face. As it brushed his mouth he became aware that his breath smelled terrible.

'Were you followed to the house?'

'I have no idea.'

Kyril bared his teeth in a snarl and restlessly took a few steps towards Sculby, who stayed motionless. The Russian wants information, he told himself, keep hold of that. As long as he thinks you have that information, he will not kill you.

'This P.4...' There was a sneer in Kyril's voice. 'Why do you do it, eh? You English lawyers, with your "ethics" and your "etiquette". You're not an agent, you're a solicitor. What have they promised you, eh? What do they pay you? Is it worth it?'

'I do it...'

Somewhere inside Sculby a great, billowing cloud of hot air was beginning to expand, buoying him up, making him heady with excitement.

'...I do it for love of the motherland.'

As he said it the balloon inside him collapsed. The absurd phrase made him sound like a brightly-coloured figure in the 'Boys' Own Paper'. But the effect on Kyril was remarkable.

He froze in the act of raising the gun in Sculby's direction and his lips parted. After a second of stillness he rubbed his hand across his face, as if trying to remove some tight, invisible mask, then repeated the gesture once, twice. He was sweating.

'You're lying.'

'I'm sorry?'

Sculby raised his eyebrows and subjected Kyril to a long, wooden stare.

'You're not a *schpick*. You're too . . . too . . .'

Kyril did not finish the sentence. Sculby was breathing more easily now. The intricate, precarious balance between the two men had shifted marginally in his favour.

'You can always check with Centre. Do you mind if I smoke?'

On the last word he slowly reached out for the box with his right hand. If Kyril noticed he gave no sign. Keeping his movements calm and smooth, Sculby lit a cigarette. The first gulp of smoke tasted bilious, and for a vile second he wanted to be sick, but the sensation passed.

'Tell me what to do', said Sculby. Kyril's eyes had never left his face, and behind them the lawyer read doubt. The odd sensation of buoyant floating was coming back, aided by the nicotine. The room no longer seemed so hot. Only the gun remained to convince Sculby that this was real, everything Royston predicted had come to pass, his life was no longer guaranteed. From trying to ignore the gun Sculby had now started to concentrate on it as a reminder that this was actually happening, he was no longer dreaming.

'Do . . . ? Oh yes, I'll tell you what to do.'

Kyril's voice had recaptured its former note of resolve. Now he spoke like a man who chooses his words with care.

'You're Loshkevoi's solicitor. You can get me an hour alone with him in prison.'

Sculby bit his lower lip. The initiative had shifted back again.

'Difficult. Loshkevoi's being held in Wandsworth jail. Some months back DI5 took over a cell block and transformed it into a top-security isolation centre. Loshkevoi's in there. I can't get in without a special pass. Besides, I'm no longer acting for Loshkevoi. Anyway, why do you want this?'

Kyril looked up furiously. 'Sculby, it would give me a good deal of pleasure to kill you, right now. You with your lawyer's questions . . . Just listen. Listen and do as I say.'

Sculby's fingers involuntarily pinched the cigarette, giving it an almost flat waist. Kyril's head was sunk on to his chest; he seemed to be lost in thought. When he spoke again Sculby had to strain to catch the words.

'Then you must get him out of prison, mustn't you?'

Sculby opened his mouth to protest but Kyril forestalled him. 'No, you can do it. Don't underestimate yourself. Tell whoever it is you tell these things that this is my price. I propose . . . a deal. On your side, one hour alone with Loshkevoi. On mine . . . I will come over to the British. Not the Americans . . . keep them out of my life, you hear!'

During this speech Sculby had been thinking furiously. Make friends, that's what Royston had said. Win his confidence. The prize is worth having: a defector from Moscow. But his use of the coded phrase had done little more than temporarily faze Kyril. What he needed was something concrete and constructive, something real.

'There might be a way', he began, almost reluctantly, and Kyril's lips creased in a humourless smile.

'What?'

Loshkevoi was booked on false charges. Five wanted to search his garage while he was out of the way. They found arms, grenades, all kinds of things. They decided to let it run, and turned him loose . . .'

'Like hell!' Kyril was almost spitting with rage. 'He's in prison, you told me so yourself. When I asked at the garage earlier they told me he could be gone months.'

'It was nothing to do with us. I had firm instructions to look after him and see he got off. He chose different, don't ask me why.'

'What do you mean, he chose different?'

'He sacked me and pleaded guilty. Threw in some other stuff as well, just to make sure he went inside. I told you earlier, I'm not acting for Loshkevoi anymore.'

'You mean . . . he *planned* this?'

'Yes. Or someone planned it for him.'

It was obvious to Sculby that for reasons he didn't understand this last remark stopped Kyril in his tracks. Every muscle in the man's restless body suddenly became still. During the long silence which followed Sculby stubbed out his cigarette and dusted the ash off his suit. Kyril did not object to this succession of unauthorised movements.

'What are you telling me? You said you had an idea . . .'

Sculby took his first tentative step across the abyss, teetering gingerly on a thin, taut wire of improvisation.

'It was going to be part of my job to go to him after a while and say, look, we have the goods on you. The arms, we know about them. Do you want to come clean or do you want to rot in jail for the rest of your life? That was the pitch. It was up to me to say when the time was ripe.' Sculby waited until he was sure that Kyril was looking at him directly before he spoke again. 'I think maybe the time just became ripe.'

There was a long silence, broken by Kyril sitting down in the nearest chair and saying, 'Give me a cigarette'.

Sculby obliged, remembering to keep all his movements nice and slow. Kyril smoked half of the cigarette in total silence, continually running the fingers which held the stub across the line of his lips. Sometimes he looked at Sculby, as if trying to gauge his sincerity; mostly he stared at the floor.

'But would your bosses buy that?' he said at last. 'After he sacked you . . . ?'

'They might. They don't know how he sacked me, remember. Or what was said. Then I throw you into the scale. You and he together add up to something pretty big, I'd say. Especially if they think you're connected in some way. They're bound to be curious, and that's all you'll need to persuade them to give you an hour alone with Loshkevoi.'

This time the silence seemed to go on for ever. Sculby was uncomfortably aware of smoke-induced nausea, coupled with a burning desire to urinate. Something must snap soon. The initial floating feeling had worn off, to be replaced by a grey, dead weight around his heart and stomach.

'All right.'

Kyril had finished the cigarette. He ground it into Sculby's carpet and looked up with a smile.

'This is one total agreement. SIS must assent to all or none, you understand?'

Sculby nodded.

'One. Time alone with Loshkevoi. Two. Immunity for all crimes I may have committed against English laws, ever. Three. A new identity and maximum protection. Four, I'll give everything I know except what would endanger agents working in the field at this moment.' His lips curled. 'That includes you, Sculby. You're part of this agreement. And you come in on a side-deal, too. It goes like this. You fix up the main trade and get SIS to agree to it. I won't betray you. And I won't kill you. But Sculby . . .'

Again the curl of the lips.

'. . . If you don't succeed in persuading your bosses to make the main trade, P.4 is going to need another solicitor. I mean it.'

'I know you do.' The words were wrung out of Sculby against his will. He couldn't help it. He knew that Kyril was sincere.

'Now listen. They will ask you many questions, probing to see what is in this agreement for SIS. I understand that. Do you know anything about the art of defecting, Sculby? What you are, you sell. I am carrying with me the plan which the Chairman of the KGB calls "Sociable Plover". It contains details of the KGB's contacts with world terrorism. In the right hands it could blow the KGB apart for years to come. It is my passport . . . my deposit. It guarantees that I am who I say I am. Have you got that?'

'Yes.'

'Repeat it then.'

Sculby did as he was told. When he had finished the Russian grunted.

'Tell them also that I will be on the main drive at Crowden at three o'clock in two days' time.'

'Crowden?'

'Never mind. The people you report to will understand. They have used this place for similar meetings before and I know it. Tell them that.'

Kyril stood up and Sculby resisted the urge to cry out. The room had shrunk again. The intruder seemed to fill every available square inch, blocking off any chance there might be of escape.

'I'll contact you after noon tomorrow. Stay here, by the phone. I won't have much time, so be quick. When I ring, say "Yes" or "No", that's all. This is strictly take-it-or-leave-it trade. You understand?'

Sculby nodded, and Kyril smiled. It did not extend to his eyes.

'Get them to tell you what happened to Vera Bradfield, Sculby. Read the pathologist's report. Then see what I did to the man who killed her. *Stay still.*'

As he moved round behind Sculby's chair the lawyer involuntarily squirmed away, raising his arms to protect his head in a primeval, instinctive gesture of defence.

'I'm not going to hurt you... not yet. But if you double-cross me... if you're not a genuine sleeper...'

Sculby waited in vain for the rest of the sentence. He did not hear the street door open and close. When he finally looked round, unable any longer to bear the sinister silence which followed Kyril's last words, he was alone.

Sculby held his hands to his eyes. He was shivering, his skin felt clammy. It was several minutes before the worst of the tension wore off. His vision was blurred: a curious medley of wheels and chains ground before his eyes until he shook his head roughly a couple of times and it cleared.

Kyril had come and gone unheard, unseen. That terrified Sculby. If the Russian called for him again there would be no warning, no chance of self-defence. Until this nightmare was over, Sculby would be alone. No matter where he was or what he was doing, irrespective of who was with him, he would be a target. An accessible target...

Running through his brain were the digits of a phone number. He had been warned never to use it except as a last resort, a matter of life and death.

'P.4 is going to need a new solicitor...'

Sculby dialled. There was a long wait while the 'hams' at London Station tracked down their quarry. Then—

'Royston', said Sculby. 'I want to see you. *Now.*'

31

For once the kitchen cabinet was not in attendance; Sir Richard Bryant and Royston were quite alone. C sat with his hands folded on the bare desk, never once removing his steady gaze from Royston's face. The London Station Chief could hardly lift his head from lack of sleep. They were nearly at the end of a long, wearisome conversation.

'Have you any idea of the damage that man can do, has already done?'

In view of what had gone before Royston correctly assumed this to be a rhetorical question.

'The woman Bradfield, dead. Why? Because Kyril, as he persists in calling himself, led an executioner straight to her. Why was there an executioner in the first place? Because Kyril is carrying one of the most dangerous secrets to run loose from the Kremlin since the last World War. The executioner, dead; mutilated to death in a particularly gruesome fashion. The suburbs of south London are being turned into a Mafia's playground and I am under pressure to frame proposals for dealing with the situation.'

If C waited for constructive suggestions from Royston, he

242

waited in vain. Certain aspects of 'the situation' Royston found highly attractive. Sikarov's death, for example. When first he learned of Sikarov's arrival in the UK he nearly panicked, reasoning that A2 had been ordered to liquidate him before Kyril could reveal his treachery to his employers. Even now that the picture was clearer the memory of Sikarov's gruesome mutilations did not appal.

'Also, I want from you a written appreciation of the events of the past two days. In a form fit for presentation . . .' C jerked his thumb to the north, in the vague direction of Whitehall.

'Appreciation?'

'It should not be difficult. The basics are reasonably clear, are they not? A defector on the run looks to a former mistress for shelter. A KGB killer, sent to destroy the defector before he talks, murders the mistress and is himself killed, doubtless as an act of revenge. That's all you need say. Nothing about who sent the killer, or why. No mention of Nidus. No hint that the killer was sent to stop Kyril falling into *their* hands, rather than ours. But there is one thing you can say. You can make the point that if only Five had been good enough to let us know of Sikarov's arrival a little earlier, none of this need have happened. Use red ink and underline it. As for Kyril . . .'

C unclasped his hands and spread them wide.

'Get everyone out on the streets looking for him. I want his description circulated to every police station in the land. I want every known A2 operative's description put on the wire. I want you where I can contact you 24 hours a day. Above all, I want this matter cleared up and I want it *soon.*'

Royston raised his haggard face and looked across the desk at C.

'Anything else?'

'One thing. The CIA are proving tiresome.'

'What?'

'Somehow they have found out about what they are pleased to call our "temporary local difficulty" over Kyril. Apparently they tried to kidnap him in Brussels and if we're not careful they may try the same thing again over here. Try to find out how much they know about Kyril and why they tried to snatch him in Belgium. Go and see Gulland. Stall him. We need time and I don't want any solicitous offers or American help in finding Bucharensky, thank you.'

Suddenly Royston wanted a drink more than anything in the world. Joe Gulland kept a bottle of Glenlivet in his room at Grosvenor Square. He placed his hands on the lip of C's desk and levered himself out of his seat.

'Right', he said.

Less than an hour later he was sitting comfortably in a deep, leather-covered armchair, savouring the single-malt Scotch his host had just given him. A tiny pulse of life was beginning to beat inside him.

His feelings about Grosvenor Square were mixed, rather like those of poor relatives obliged to visit their better-off kin for a family reunion. It was on the whole pleasant to relish the good things of life while counting up the number of export licences the British government must have refused in order to furnish this room. The centre-piece was a large rosewood table. Royston had seen one very like it in a shop near his house in Sheen. It cost £3500.

His eyes returned to Joe Gulland, mixing himself a bourbon-and-branch at the drinks tray. Rather a well-stocked tray, thought Royston as he remembered his own, pitifully limited supply of Amontillado sherry.

'There you go.'

He raised his glass politely in response to the informal toast, and drank.

Gulland was his chief liaison with 'the Cousins' at their London office. That made him reasonably senior, though like Royston himself his precise ranking was never disclosed to allies. The two men had known each other for five years, had visited each other's homes and were, in so far as the term has meaning in this context, friends.

Gulland took off his jacket to reveal a couple of Oxford blue stains under the arms of his Cambridge blue shirt, and loosened his tie.

'I sure as hell am glad we were able to meet like this, Mike.' Gulland swung his legs over the arm of his chair and smiled to reveal several gold fillings. 'Tell you the truth, things have been a little difficult right now. This Russky they been burning up the wires over. Cigarette?'

'Please.'

Gulland went through the long process of selecting a Kent from the packet on the occasional table by his side, lighting it, inhaling, flicking some ash into the brass saucer, and sending a compact column of smoke on its way to the ceiling. If he had hoped to provoke Royston into making a hasty response, he was disappointed. He would dearly have liked to know what was going through the Englishman's mind at that moment. Royston was thinking that fat men shouldn't smoke, and they certainly oughtn't to drink as much as Gulland.

'We were kind of wondering whether you'd be interested in going into joint venture over this, Mike. As I see it, we have better facilities for debriefing this man, and that's a fact.'

'This man . . . ?'

Royston held out his glass. He waited until Gulland was busy at the drinks tray before he spoke again.

'I'm sorry, Joe, I'm not quite with you. Which man are we talking about?'

Gulland turned away from the table with Royston's drink in his hand and a glassy smile on his face.

'Bucharensky. You got him, right?'

'No', said Royston. 'We don't.'

'Aw, come on now . . .'

'We are expecting a man of that name', Royston explained politely. 'We would like to interview him.'

'Yeah', said Gulland. 'And we all know why, don't we.'

Such goodwill as had existed at the start of the meeting was now somewhere up by the ceiling with the dead smoke from their cigarettes.

'Why?'

'Because he knows the name of your precious damn source in Moscow.'

Royston was too tired to feign lack of concern. The shock must have been written all over his face, for Gulland went on, 'Don't act so surprised. It had to get back to us in the end. For years we've known you were sitting on something good but we played along, pretending to swallow it when you fed us some crap about what some guy said to some other guy in a brothel. Well now we know, see? That's what finally convinced us that Bucharensky's genuine. We have our source in Moscow too, and the word has gone out from Dzerzhinzky Square: Kyril left behind a diary which says he carries the name of a traitor. Right?'

Royston gave the matter some thought and decided to come clean. 'An officer in the rank of general', he said curtly. 'We've had him for years. C is the only person who knows his name.'

Gulland nodded. 'Okay', he said sourly. 'We can argue about that later when this shit's been cleared from off the front porch. What are you doing about it?'

Royston shrugged and said nothing.

'Why not let us give you a little help, Mike? We can do it.'

'Sure you can. Just like you did in Brussels . . . oh yes, Joe, we know about that. We wondered what the hell you were up to and now we know. A "covert operation"; everything left nice and clean and sanitised . . . and the next thing we hear, Bucharensky's living in New Mexico under an assumed name. We'll let you know whatever we get out of Kyril. It's the usual arrangement, Joe. Don't you trust us?'

'Not overly. He's here, in England. You snap your fingers and where does that leave us? An accident, you'll say, how unfortunate. He tripped in the can, broke his prick and bled to death.'

Royston was about to reply when the phone rang. Gulland snatched it up.

'Who? Yeah . . . put him on.'

He handed the instrument to Royston at arm's length as if wary of contamination. Royston raised his eyebrows and held the receiver to his ear.

'Royston', he heard a voice say. 'I want to see you. *Now*.'

32

_____

       Povin lay spreadeagled on the bed in the 'penthouse', his head turned towards the square of darkness, slightly softer than the rest, which was the window. He had been staring at it for some time, to the point where it now seemed to advance and retreat in a silent beat. He made several attempts to close his eyes, and failed.

He had been drinking since late afternoon. He was used to it and his constitution was strong, but he had long ago strayed over his normal outer limit. He wasn't sure whether he wanted to get up and couldn't, or no longer even had any desire to get up at all. Everything was undefined. The slightest movement made him giddy, so it was better to lie still and do nothing, except think about the names.

The bedroom was littered with tiny scraps of paper: on the bed, the dressing-table, the floor; it was as if someone had taken a full waste-paper basket and flung its contents about the place. Several scraps lay on Povin's chest, moving rhythmically up and down in time with his breathing. On each scrap was written a single name. There were hundreds of them. Inside Povin's head were hundreds more which he did not have time

247

to write down before the vodka disabled him.

Each tiny scrap of paper represented a death for which he had been responsible, in one way or another. It had started almost as a joke with himself, a simple exercise in memory. Who was the first, he asked himself as he tossed back the glass of petrovka. Let me write it down...

The first was Stanislav Petrovich Illyin. He could recall all three names quite clearly. Illyin had been a student with Povin at Officers' Training School. One day he had made some off-hand remark about Lenin at a time when he and Povin were alone together. Afterwards Povin became frightened that someone else might have overheard, and reported the matter. Next day, Illyin had gone. No one ever saw him again. After the celebration which followed the passing-out parade for his year the commanding officer of Ryazan summoned Povin and told him that because of his zealous and entirely correct conduct in regard to Illyin he had been singled out for special work. Povin asked what had happened to Illyin and the Colonel laughed. 'He was shot. What else do you expect? That's why Russia needs people like you, Povin.'

'People like you.' It was the memory of this phrase which made Povin take the first sheet of paper and write on it Illyin, S.P. Who was the second...?

Some of the scraps contained only initials or patronymics, all that Povin could remember of their former owners. Some merely had a bare description, such as 'Redhead', or 'Limp'. He could not remember many of the faces, but hundreds of names were there, ready to be summoned out of his subconscious mind with the vodka to act as solvent.

Some of the scraps contained merely a number, Povin's rough approximation of the extent of a particular group which he had consigned wholesale to extermination.

Some of them bore little crosses in the corner. They were the Christians.

Povin had long ago recognised the futility of penitence. Penitence, properly expressed, meant a martyr's death for which he was not prepared. To pray for absolution was pointless, unless you were willing and able to turn your back on sin. Povin relished the story by Camus of the man who went to the same prostitute every Friday, year in, year out, made confes-

sion, was absolved . . . Povin knew that God was not like that.
God did not read Camus . . .

In the early years particularly, when Povin was still working
under Major Oblensky, there had been many Christians to deal
with, mostly Orthodox. Their deaths had helped to mould Povin
into his present dilemma. If he did not repent he was damned;
if he turned his back on it all he was doomed. But for his early
association with the Russian Orthodox community he probably
would not have come to this pass.

He could not put a name to his first Christian martyr, only
a sense of atmosphere, of place. Povin had been detailed to
preside over an interrogation during a spell of duty in Minsk.
It turned into a kind of macabre game between the prisoner
and his torturers, to see if they could make him recant. This
was no part of the interrogation; the prisoner was suspected of
disseminating illegal literature, but what began as a sideline
soon developed into the main event.

The suspect knew something, that was obvious. Equally
obvious was that it could not be anything of great importance.
Povin remembered him as young, with everything to live for.
There was no reason to kill him: in those days it was not
uncommon to work someone over for a night and then toss
him out with the garbage next day, on the offchance that he
might let slip something useful. But this young man made a
mistake. He wanted to hide what he knew. When the pain grew
unbearable he started to sing a hymn, stifling his agony in a
soft, tuneless chant that somehow filled the smoky cellar to its
very corners . . . and so the game began. At first Povin merely
watched, detached from the heartless brutality inflicted before
his eyes. Don't be silly, he wanted to say, tell us what we
want to know; nothing is worth all this. But as the night pro-
gressed he gradually became drawn into the grim tableau, no
longer a disinterested, slightly bored spectator. The inquisitors
were oafs, two lusty peasant lads from the steppes assigned to
the task because they were brutish, unimaginative and strong.
Like bulls, they took time to work up their full fury. The more
they laboured over him, the harder the brave young man in the
chair chanted. It was provocation, a direct and inescapable
challenge.

Towards dawn the prisoner fell into a coma, exhausted. One

of the inquisitors poured cold water over him until he was
awake. As his eyes fluttered open his mouth began to writhe,
almost unconsciously, or so it seemed to Povin.

'Yes?'

The older lad was leaning close to catch the words, evidently
anticipating the breakthrough they had been waiting for: the
state secrets which could bring down the Soviet Union overnight, carried in the head of this hapless boy.

'Speak up, cretin!'

The boy shuddered. 'Our Father . . . Who art in heaven . . .'

The inquisitor shut him up with a clenched fist, then undid
the straps which held the prisoner in his chair. The boy collapsed on the floor. The first lout kicked him hard in the small
of the back, then bent down to pick him up by the legs.

'Ay, Volodiya!' squealed his companion excitedly, and Povin
realised that he was witnessing the repeat of an earlier incident.
He knew he should stop it, but remained in his chair by the
wall, mesmerised.

The larger soldier began to swing the boy round the room,
leaning backwards to steady himself and preserve momentum.
Faster and faster he turned, the boy's body now almost parallel
with the floor.

The second inquisitor was dancing about the cell, clapping
his hands to a beat which grew faster and faster.

'Ay-oh-la, ay-oh-la, ay-oh-la . . .'

Povin shrunk back, paralysed by the knowledge of what
was about to happen. Sweat was pouring off the first soldier's
face, his neck muscles stood out over his tight collar, the
physical effort required must have been enormous.

'Ay-oh-la, ayohla, ayohla, ayohlaayohlaayohLA!'

The soldier let go and the body went hurtling head first into
space, missing Povin by inches.

The wall of the cellar was solid brick.

Povin rose slowly to his feet and raised his arms above his
head in an exaggerated stretch. He was suddenly very tired.

'Sluice this place out', he said from the doorway. Then he
turned to go, and as his feet crossed the threshold he had a
sudden vision of himself entering a narrow corridor with no
exit: unable to be a Christian, unable not to.

The vision stuck and proved to be frighteningly prophetic.

He never did escape from that narrow corridor.

By making a great effort Povin moved his head to brush the scraps of paper off his chest, knowing that among them was one that bore the name of Vera Bradfield.

Illyin was the first name. Bradfield was the last.

Povin accepted full responsibility for her death the moment he learned of it. True, he had not dealt the blows, he had not even been there, but her murder was the natural consequence of his act in sending Sikarov after Bucharensky and so he took the blame. He did not attempt to split fine semantic hairs, or prevaricate. He prayed for her soul and went through the ritual of saying he was sorry in the knowledge that his words were empty: how could he repent of one out of so many? Death, for Povin, had become a habit, like Michaelov's papirosy cigarettes, and his own petrovka. It wasn't that he did not regret the scraps of paper, for he did; but what was the point of whining to God about things you couldn't change?

If it wasn't possible to bring Vera back to life, there was perhaps something he could yet do for her memory, a kind of invisible monument to be erected in her name.

The room had begun to revolve slowly around Povin's bed. His head ached. He thought longingly of cold water, but knew that it was beyond him to get up and go to the bathroom. Sleep. That was the only cure. Sleep and oblivion.

There was a way in which he could discharge the obligation. A kind of sin offering, Old Testament rather than New . . . Not all at once. Not Royston, not yet. But the Kommandant . . .

The last thought to cross his mind before temporarily giving up the ceaseless struggle with bootless conscience and remorse was that tomorrow he would send a message to Sir Richard Bryant and so, by betraying the brutal regime which had moulded him, perhaps take the first hesitant step towards redeeming his soul.

33

It was very cold in the loft which, as Royston vaguely recognised, meant that laying the Cosywrap last winter had been a worthwhile investment. As he rummaged about in the pile of wood-chippings under the cold water tank he was shivering: from the cold, and also from an uneasy feeling which bordered on panic that what he was looking for might have mysteriously vanished.

His groping hand made contact with an oilskin package and he nearly moaned aloud in relief. He drew it out of the wood-shavings and dusted it off in the feeble light of the torch which he had brought up with him when he climbed into the roofspace, muttering to his wife about leaking water-pipes. The package was intact; God knew why it should not be. Royston's fingers were numb with cold and tension. It took him a long time to unwrap the oilskin, wipe down the gun and test its mechanism.

The gun was a Police .45 Magnum. Royston had 'acquired' it early in his career, when he still occasionally went on the streets. No one else knew of its existence, the original owner now being dead, and Royston had kept it hidden in the roof for years, just in case.

On a visit to FBI headquarters in Washington, the part the public doesn't see, he had once watched a marksman blow down a solid wall, using just such a gun. The squat bludgeon of a weapon was difficult to hold in one hand, both were required to steady it, and even then its accuracy was poor. But if you were lucky enough to score a hit, the party stopped right there. Even the FBI armourer was in awe of what this gun could do.

Royston knew himself to be in mortal danger. Kyril was rumoured to have supplanted Yevchenko as Stanov's right hand man. It was inconceivable that he had not heard Royston's name spoken in the spacious, high-ceilinged office on the third floor in Dzerzhinsky Square. Whatever his motives in coming to England, he had to be silenced once and for all.

Royston looked down at the heavy gun lying in his hands. 'Don't fire it unless you intend to kill', that's what the FBI armourer had said, and Royston proposed to accept his advice.

'Michael . . .'

He looked up, startled to hear his wife's voice.

'Telephone!'

He stuffed the heavy weapon into his pocket and started to crawl back towards the ladder.

34

       The car swung on to the gravelled drive through large, ornate wrought-iron gates.

'What is this place?' asked Sculby.

'Crowden House. One of Surrey's finest country estates. Grade One listing, very good gardens, or so they tell me.'

'They?'

'National Trust. We have the use of one wing and share the running expenses.'

'Christ, there's people all over the place.'

The car was nearing the house and coaches were visible, drawn up in a neat line alongside the tennis courts.

'That's the point', replied Royston. 'Basically we use this place as a convalescent home for "difficult" cases—getting back to normality, and so on. But it's also useful for meetings with people like Kyril, who don't like closed doors. See that lot?'

Sculby followed the direction of Royston's pointing finger. Several people were straggling after a uniformed guide in the direction of some greenhouses.

'Loshkevoi needs reassuring as much as Kyril. What could

be more cosy than for the two of them to strike up a conversation on the lawn, in the open air, two tourists free to come and go as they please? With me? Thank God Easter was early this year. The place looks crowded enough for a bank holiday.'

Royston parked the car outside the main entrance next to a family of four picnicking out of the boot of an Allegro. Sculby looked at his watch. 'Nearly time.'

'Look . . . there he is.'

Sculby saw Loshkevoi come into view at the end of a grassed avenue winding in front of the house. Two men were with him but they kept their distance. It all looked very natural. Loshkevoi was wearing his own clothes and one of his companions had a camera slung round his neck.

From the front seat of Royston's car he and Sculby had an uninterrupted view of the main drive. Kyril was due to keep his appointment at three o'clock.

'No sign of him yet.'

Loshkevoi stopped as he reached the drive and turned back uneasily. One of his companions spoke to him and Sculby saw a look of panic-stricken protest appear on the face of his former client. The other man raised his hands in a calming, placatory gesture.

Royston picked up the radiophone and Sculby saw the third man raise the camera as if to adjust a setting.

'Tell him we've got marksmen all round the perimeter wall', said Royston softly. 'Tell him anything, but for Christ's sake ditch him. It's three o'clock.'

'Loshkevoi doesn't know . . .'

'That Kyril wants to meet him?' Royston snorted. 'Too damn right he doesn't.'

The man with the camera moved across to join the other two. A few seconds later the bodyguards sauntered off towards the main gate, leaving a bewildered and apprehensive Loshkevoi to stand on the drive alone.

Minutes passed. Kyril was late. Several people passed within a few feet of Loshkevoi but none of them made any attempt to speak to him. Royston looked at his watch for the umpteenth time and swore.

'Look!'

Royston watched curiously as a well-dressed woman picked

her way across the grass towards Loshkevoi. When she was almost touching him she spoke and Loshkevoi's lips moved in reply. Then the woman's hand moved in a tiny wave and she started to walk away, the encounter plainly at an end. Royston reached for the handset, his face tense. 'Right', Sculby heard him say. 'Pull them both in and bring them back to the house. Only for God's sake, do it quietly.'

He replaced the receiver and got out. Sculby followed. Royston led the way through the main hall and over a red rope carrying a 'private' sign. At once the decor became less elaborate. After a few minutes' walk they arrived in what Sculby guessed must have been part of the old kitchen, now partitioned off. Most of one wall was taken up with a large, sooty fireplace. The room was bare except for a table and half a dozen chairs, in one of which the woman they had seen on the drive was already seated. Royston lounged over to the fireplace, keeping his back to it, and put his right hand in his pocket.

'Introduce me', he said quietly.

Sculby now saw that the woman was young, pretty and extremely composed. She was smoking a cigarette, but apart from that slight indication of nervousness showed no sign of surprise at her situation. Sculby wondered why. On hearing Royston speak she crossed her legs and sat back.

'He said it would be just like this' she observed conversationally. 'How frightfully interesting.'

'He?'

The woman smiled and deposited some ash in the cocoa-tin lid on the table in front of her.

'That rather dishy man with the Slavonic-sounding name. Kyril.'

Her husky, well-bred voice conveyed that when she described Kyril as dishy she was speaking from intimate personal experience. Sculby was becoming more and more mystified.

'What's your name?' said Royston. Hearing the roughness in his voice the woman turned to him and smiled.

'Lucinda Bayliss, my sweet. What's yours?'

Royston said nothing. Sculby sensed that he was every bit as puzzled as the rest of them. The woman smoothed down her dress, drawing every eye in the room to long, attractive thighs.

'Is that all you're going to ask me?' she said lightly. 'How dreadfully disappointing. Kyril assured me there'd be lots of men in jackboots wielding rubber truncheons. It all sounded quite thrilling...'

'What are you?' interrupted Royston aggressively. The woman smiled at him.

'Expensive, my sweet. Very, very expensive indeed.'

Sculby watched comprehension dawn in all the other faces round him, and knew their expressions matched his own.

'So you're on the rent', said Royston. Lucinda shrugged, apparently quite unruffled by the sneer in his voice.

'You could say that. At my end of the profession we call it an honorarium, darling.' Seeing the look on his face she added, very softly, as if not to embarrass a thick child, 'From the Latin.'

Royston moved away from the fireplace. Like everyone else in the room he seemed partly mesmerised by this outstandingly cool performance.

'And how did you meet this... Kyril?'

'He rang me up, then came round later. At first I couldn't place him at all. He was refreshingly honest, you see.' She rolled her eyes upwards. 'My God, you don't know how refreshing honesty can be until you've done my job. He said some very nice things about my body but he didn't want to sleep with me, only to marry me. Look, isn't it nice?'

She held up her left hand, enjoying the effect which the sight of the gold band produced on the roomful of men.

'You married him?' said Royston incredulously.

'Oh no. Not really. Although he did say he'd rather like to...' She giggled. '... and he wanted me to keep the ring as a momento of the occasion. But no, I didn't actually marry him. He said he was playing a very elaborate joke on an old friend and if I helped him he'd pay me three times my usual hourly rate. He was a very generous man, was Mr Kyril. The kind who settles in advance without being asked...'

Sculby wanted to smile but the look on Royston's face deterred him.

'What exactly did Kyril want from you?'

'Well, he wanted me to go on a coach trip with him. As his wife, you understand. I'd never ridden in a coach before.

I know you shouldn't knock anything 'til you've tried it, especially in my line, but it was pretty disgusting, actually. Then, when we arrived . . .'

Royston sat down heavily in the nearest chair. 'Do you mean to tell me', he interrupted very quietly, 'that Kyril is here, now? In this house?'

The woman's eyes widened. 'Of course, my sweet. Didn't I just explain it all to you?'

For a moment nobody spoke, and Sculby fancied he could hear the sound of his own heart beating, it was so quiet in the room. Then Royston spread his hands in a gesture of hopeless inquiry and looked at the bodyguards, both of whom shook their heads. Sculby read consternation on every face, Loshkevoi's most of all.

'My God', said Royston. There was another awed silence. 'My God, and we never saw him. Go on.'

At a sign from Royston one of the bodyguards slipped from the room while Lucinda resumed her story.

'Well, after we got here he pointed him . . .' (a wave at Loshkevoi) '. . . out to me and asked me to go over and say a few words to him. First of all he said goodbye and gave me something extra, he really was terribly, terribly sweet about the whole thing . . .'

Royston drummed his fingers on the table.

'What . . . *exactly* mind you . . . did he tell you to say?'

'He told me to say: I'll be late, wait for me.'

'Those were his exact words?'

Lucinda nodded.

'You're sure?'

'Quite sure.'

'And nothing else?'

Lucinda shook her head. Royston turned to Loshkevoi. 'Is that right?'

Loshkevoi roused himself with an effort. He seemed dazed.

'Yes. It's what she said. Then I said something . . . I can't remember . . .'

Royston turned back to Lucinda Bayliss. 'What did he say?'

Lucinda's brow puckered in thought. 'He said: okay, thanks. At least, I think that's . . .'

'What were you supposed to do then?'

'Nothing. I'd earned my money and that was the end of it.'

The jerky, unpredictable silences were starting to get on Sculby's nerves. Loshkevoi's fingers played over his face, the remaining bodyguard frowned, Royston was lost in thought. Sculby wondered just how badly things were off course.

'What was he wearing?'

Royston's question seemed unnaturally loud after the long silence. Lucinda laughed, a soft ripple of sound which sent a tingle up Sculby's spine.

'I never look at what men *wear*, darling.'

Royston nodded, as if accepting a valid point made against him, and for a while nobody spoke. At last he seemed to make up his mind.

'That gentleman will give you tea and take you through this story of yours again.' Royston gestured at the remaining body-guard. 'Then you're free to go.'

The woman pouted and consulted what was obviously a very expensive gold watch.

'Can't I go now? I've been here simply ages.'

Royston stood up.

'Try thinking of it as helping the Police with their inquiries.'

Lucinda unfolded herself slowly from the chair in which she had been sitting, and the men saw that as well as being beautiful she was also very tall. Beside her Royston looked tense and shrunken, and for an instant Sculby was reminded of those countless fairy stories where the lovely princess falls into the hands of an ugly dwarf.

'You look as though you could use a little help', she said, casting a look of cold appraisal over Royston's unattractive body, and again Sculby wanted to smile but dare not. Royston's face remained impassive, as though he had heard nothing.

Sculby was nearest the door. He opened it for Lucinda Bayliss to pass through, and was rewarded by a delightful, lingering smile. Loshkevoi waited until the door had closed again, then said: 'What the hell is going on around here?'

'Shut up.'

'No. I won't shut up. First of all you give me this head-ache . . .'

Royston stirred impatiently in his chair.

'When you refused to get into the laundry basket you left

us no choice. The doctor says it'll soon wear off.'

'Would *you* have agreed to get into a basket? Too much like a coffin. Then who the hell is this Kyril?'

'Oh, for Christ's sake, leave it out. You know bloody well who he is.'

'Look, I . . .'

'We know about the arms in the garage, Loshkevoi. And the radio. And the money. And don't pretend you don't know what we're talking about, because we've got a lovely set of prints of you digging Kalashnikovs out of the rubble.'

Sculby had read about people going grey but had never seen it, until now. Loshkevoi looked as though he had gone into a state of suspended animation. Royston, on the other hand, seemed to be warming up.

'You want to know what's going on? All right, I'll fucking tell you. We have made a deal, see? If you say who you're working for, why, for how long and all the other details you know, it is just conceivable that we will not leave you in jail for the rest of your stinking, useless life. But that's for later. Right now, you're bait. Colonel Ivan Yevseevich Bucharensky wants to talk to you, very badly. So this is a trap and you're the lure. We're going to pot both of you.'

Loshkevoi shot Sculby a furious look. 'I should have known you were bent, all along. My *Christ*, but I should!'

Sculby turned his back on him and walked over to the fireplace.

'You're not very smart, are you?' Royston agreed. 'Next time, be a bit more choosy.'

Loshkevoi took no notice. 'You heard what that whore said', he gibbered. 'He's here! Inside this house . . .'

'So you *do* know what we're talking about.'

Loshkevoi's face fell and he mumbled something Sculby couldn't catch.

'Better start talking, Loshkevoi, if you want to buy some protection.' Royston's eyes were gleaming. 'It doesn't matter to me whether Kyril gets to you or not. You're not important. All we've got to do is watch your garage and sooner or later we'll have all the answers anyway. So if Kyril means to harm you, that's okay with me. He's another matter. It's true he's slipped through undetected so far, but even if we had spotted him we'd still have let him in. Don't be under any illusions about that.'

Royston stood opposite Loshkevoi, his hands resting on the table. The faces of the two men were very close.

'We'll gamble your life away, Loshkevoi, if we have to. You come cheap. It's Kyril we want, not you, and we want him so badly it's like a disease!'

It really is like a disease with you, thought Sculby wonderingly. Something pervasive and rotten. Syphilis, perhaps.

'Now you'd better start talking if you want us to help you.' Royston lowered himself into a chair.

'For a start, try explaining why Kyril needs to get to you so desperately. What's the big attraction?'

Loshkevoi opened his mouth and uttered some incoherent noises. He looked sick. For a few seconds of painful suspense Sculby thought that he was on the point of refusal. Then the damn broke and he started to babble.

'You keep Bucharensky away from me! All right, I'll grass, I'll say anything you want, but keep him off my back, you hear!'

He paused, gasping for breath, and loosened his collar. Royston nodded curtly. 'Go on.'

'I'm not part of the regular KGB. They pay my salary but Stanov's my boss.'

'You mean you report direct to Centre?' Royston interrupted him.

'No. I mean I report direct to the Chairman. He has this job for me. Terrorism. It's his pet game. He's been working on it for years. That's where I come in. I liaise for Centre with the Provisional IRA, National Liberation Army, a few others as well. I'm their banker. It's through me Stanov puts together his operations in this country. I'm telling you this as a guarantee of good faith, okay? To show that the source is impeccable. I can finger the men who killed Mountbatten...'

'Go on.' Royston's voice was still tired but now he was having to work to keep the emotion out of it.

'You want to know why Kyril's trying to see me? Because that's his real mission. Everything else is straight cover. This fabulous plan he's supposed to be carrying...' Loshkevoi did not attempt to conceal his scorn. '...It doesn't exist. Or if it does, Kyril hasn't got it, that's for sure.'

Royston had taken out a notebook and was busily writing in it, so that Loshkevoi couldn't see his face.

'That trek of his across Europe . . . a blind. It's me he wants . . .'

'How do you know that Kyril hasn't got the project-plan?' said Royston, looking up from his book.

'Because it's in Stanov's blue safe.'

'And how do you know that?'

'Because Nidus has seen it there, he told me.'

Royston held his pen up to the light and squinted at it, as if something was wrong with the nib. 'Nidus?' he said casually.

'Oh come on', said Loshkevoi wearily. 'You know who Nidus is. And I work for him on the side now. That's the trouble. Stanov suspects. You really don't know who Nidus is?'

Royston shook the pen a couple of times and tested it. 'No', he said, after a long pause, and Sculby saw a look of cunning suddenly appear on Loshkevoi's face.

'I forgot . . . of course, only Bryant knows . . . well, you ask him then. I'm not telling.'

The nib seemed to have cured itself, for Royston was writing again.

'Tell me this . . . why should Kyril want to see *you?*' Royston did not look up from his book while he waited for a reply. Sculby couldn't detect how important these answers were to him.

'Because I can identify Nidus. Stanov wants to know who he is.'

'And that matters?' Royston seemed befogged by his total ignorance of who or what Nidus might be. Loshkevoi sniggered.

'Ask Bryant. He'll tell you if it's important or not.'

'But you know the name . . . I mean the real name, of this Nidus?'

'No, I . . . When I said I knew who Nidus was, I meant I could identify him. I know what he looks like. And there's nothing Bucharensky wouldn't do to get that out of me. It's the whole point of his mission, I tell you. Bucharensky's loyal to Stanov, always was. Stanov suspects I know something. And he's damn right!' The rising note of panic was clearly audible now. 'He knows I couldn't stand the torture. Please! Give me a break, will you? Look, I can help you. I can...'

Royston started to interrupt but at that moment the door opened to admit one of the bodyguards. Royston looked up with annoyance and the man shrugged, spreading his hands to indicate that the search had drawn a blank. Royston appeared to deliberate for a moment.

'We'll go upstairs.' He looked at his watch. 'Five o'clock. There's not much daylight left. My guess is that he'll wait for nightfall before making a move, but I don't want to get caught down here.'

Royston nodded at the bodyguard. 'Take Loshkevoi upstairs to the first floor and wait there. I'm going to see if Franklin's had any more luck with the Bayliss girl, and then we'll all join you. Whatever happens, stay put.'

The man nodded, and beckoned Loshkevoi. Royston was about to follow them through the door when Sculby grasped his arm.

'Do you need me anymore?'

'For your own protection, Laurie, don't try to leave now.'

Sculby registered the note of anxiety in Royston's voice and his eyes narrowed. 'So there is a problem?'

Royston expelled some air in what might have been an expression of humour or annoyance.

'I don't know', he said at last. 'The theory went like this. There was no point in saturating the place because that would only scare Kyril away, right? But with four of us—Barnes, Franklin, you and me—five I suppose if you count Loshkevoi —he shouldn't have been able to give us any trouble. We put a few men on the outer wall, in the hope that they'd spot Kyril as he came in and after that we'd monitor him. Well, it didn't happen. It's obvious that Kyril's not going to keep to the deal he put up through you. But whether that spells danger, I don't know.'

Sculby swallowed. 'You think I'd be at risk if I tried to leave?'

'It's a long drive down to the main gate, Laurie, and I can't afford to send anyone with you. Frankly, I need you here, if you're prepared to stay. One extra body could make all the difference.'

Sculby nodded slowly, touched by Royston's evident concern.

'Okay, Michael. I suppose we've just got to sit it out and hope. Are you armed, by the way?'

Royston nodded reassuringly and patted his jacket pocket.

'Good. That makes me feel a whole lot better.'

Sculby led the way through the door into the hall as he spoke these words, and so unfortunately did not see the expression on Royston's face which they provoked.

35

Kyril's appearance had changed since his visit to Sculby's offices. Everything from the colour of his hair to the condition of his Bally casuals was different. No one who had only a photograph or a verbal description to go on could possibly have recognised him.

After he had said goodbye to Lucinda Bayliss he walked away without looking back once, leaving her to get on with the job. He was confident that she would not let him down. Kyril instinctively understood business people. He had chosen well there.

By joining one of the conducted tours he was able to build up in his mind a fairly accurate picture of the house. Upstairs, on the top floor, were the private rooms belonging to the family. Kyril wasn't interested in them. But the west wing was sealed off from the rest of the mansion by solid-looking oak doors, besides which sat a watchful attendant. Kyril subjected him to a long discreet scrutiny and concluded that he was more than a National Trust hack in uniform. So that's where the treasure was.

He wandered out to the terrace which flanked the south of the house, fixing the topography in his mind. At the west end of the terrace, paving stones had been taken up and a rough barrier erected to discourage the inquisitive, and the ground floor windows all had shutters across them. To the south, several acres of parkland rolled down to the road along which they had come earlier. He swung slowly round. To the east were the formal grounds, looking wasted and forlorn in the grey March light; beyond them an overgrown square of grass bordered by trees, a disused cricket pitch perhaps.

Somewhere inside the house a bell was ringing. Kyril looked at his watch. Three o'clock. They would be closing up, public viewing was restricted during the off-season, and about now Loshkevoi would be meeting Lucinda Bayliss on the other side of the house.

Someone was calling all visitors, reminding them that the house was closing. He did not have much time.

Kyril went in from the terrace and quickly made his way to the staircase. There was no one about. He slipped under the red rope and vanished into the upper regions of the house.

On the top floor he paused and looked about him. He was in a long corridor running the length of the north side of the mansion away from the terrace. Here the doors were of less substantial construction, and everything was covered with a heavy layer of dust. He cocked his head to listen. It was very quiet. He tried one of the doors but it was locked. He knelt down to the keyhole, which afforded a glimpse of off-white dust sheets and packing-cases. It was as he surmised: the family was away, for a long time too, by the look of it.

He stood up and began to pad down the corridor towards the west wing. Long before he came to the partition which blocked off the passage he could see that it was made of solid brick, a clumsy job, not like downstairs where the public went. The builder had simply run the masonry into the centre of a large mullion and coated it with paint.

Kyril rested his back to the partition wall and let himself slide down to his haunches. He needed time to plan the next move.

He had never visited Crowden before, although its functions were known to the London KGB, at least in outline. Unfortunately he had not had access to a plan of the interior, and he was having to rely on guesswork, which made for slow progress.

The light was failing and darkness would come quickly. Soon they would organise a search of the house; he must find deep cover before then. He stood up and retraced his steps along the passage, trying the doors. Most of them were locked but at last one gave under his hand; he looked through it to see a narrow staircase twisting away from him to an upper floor. The servants' quarters, under the eaves. And where there were eaves, you usually found access to the roof.

There were three rooms at the top of the narrow stairs, and he found what he was looking for in the last one he searched, just as he was starting to feel alarmed. A trapdoor led up into the roofspace. He took it down and with the help of a chair hauled himself through the tight opening.

He would need light. Fortunately he had had the foresight to bring with him a small torch capable of transmitting a thin beam, powerful enough to illuminate the darkest cavity.

Kyril closed his eyes, orientating the house in his mind. West was . . . over there. He began to crawl, painfully picking his way across the slats. The roof was filthy and before long he was having to stifle a cough. He rested for a moment, and studied the ceiling. Lathe and plaster, nothing unusual about that. No soundproofing . . . although of course, that might be on the other side. Well, he would have to risk it.

Kyril flashed the beam around. Ah! Another trapdoor, like the one he had come through in the east wing. He began to crawl towards it. When he reached it he laid his ear against the wood and listened.

Not a sound penetrated the constricted space beneath the roof. He ground his teeth. When the time came, that would be the risky part.

Kyril slowly lowered himself to a prone position and strove to make himself as comfortable as possible across the slats. For the moment he was safe. Now he would rest awhile. There was no danger of them leaving the house: wait, he had said, and he knew they would. He'd give them time to become drowsy, off their guard.

It was too painful to sleep. After a while he gave up trying to doze and began to review the plan he had made before leaving London.

Kyril was no longer working for Stanov, or anyone else. He was working for himself. If it had been a matter of simple loyalty, of doing the job, he would have gone back to Moscow in the hope that *Lisa* had been detected, and reported inability to complete the mission because Loshkevoi was being held incommunicado. However disappointed Stanov might have been at the outcome, he would not have blamed Kyril for something outside his control, no fault of his.

But it was no longer a matter of simple loyalty. Kyril had been lied to, used, squeezed into a role in a play which he never fully understood, one where the script was constantly being rewritten between and behind the scenes. Now he was looking for one thing only. The truth. If he owed Vera nothing else, he owed her that.

Somebody was trying to prevent him from talking to Loshkevoi. The same somebody who was responsible for Vera's death. But if Sculby could be believed, Loshkevoi was responsible for his own imprisonment, he had pleaded guilty, and that was, it could only have been, on someone's orders.

Who was Loshkevoi *really* working for?

However slight the chances of success, he had to make one last effort to see Loshkevoi. Then, well . . . even in Moscow he had never given much thought to the end of the ride.

After a while he grew bored with his thoughts. He used his torch to illumine the face of his watch. Late. It must be dark outside, the search would be over by now.

Time to go.

He was reluctant. The roof was cramped and stuffy, but it was cosy too—a haven before the last stage of his journey.

He crawled the final few inches to the trapdoor. This was the hard part. This was where it all mattered. Because if he lifted up the trap, and had guessed wrong about this house, a photo-cell beam would break and bring every guard within a mile racing to the top floor . . .

Kyril pressed down on the wood for greater purchase, clasped the cross-beam, and lifted.

36

One of the many spending cuts ordered by the Politburo involved an across-the-board reduction in staff. The Time and Motion people decreed that a particularly fruitful area for curtailment of overmanning was the nightshift, when little of importance came into Centre but the same number of employees sat around talking or playing cards. (High among the reasons for Michaelov's unpopularity with his subordinates was an irritating habit of coming in unexpectedly late at night and finding the duty officers monitoring Radio Luxembourg.) Now only two men staffed Radio Operations between eight at night and six the following morning, and they had little to do. The telex machine had vastly reduced the amount of cipher-traffic passing between Moscow and its far-flung embassies: a telex could be delivered at any time and unless it was urgent no one need read it until morning. Thus in another small respect did the KGB approximate more closely to the huge, inefficient capitalist conglomerates which it was dedicated to destroy.

Immediately beneath the small Union Jack which designated UK Sector two clocks showed the time in Moscow and London: nine and seven o'clock respectively.

One of the two officers on duty in Rad. Ops. had gone to the canteen for his break, leaving his colleague to concentrate on Playboy. He sat with his feet propped up on the desk in front of him, strategically placed to see if a 'call' sign lit up anywhere along the bank of receivers which lined the far wall of the European Division. When a 'pig' hissed through the pneumatic system and thudded into his In tray he did not hurry to pick it up. Without taking his eyes from the centrefold spread out on his knees he unscrewed the top of the cannister and felt for the message. Something else rolled out, an inch of evil-smelling black ash, and he wrinkled his nose in disgust. Something about the smell was familiar. He took a quick glance at the message, saw the green paper of the First Main Directorate with Michaelov's squiggle under 'Authorisation Code', and sat up abruptly, the magazine forgotten.

It was a long message and the transmission instructions were detailed and precise. It consisted of forty-nine groups with a specific but different number of seconds being allowed to elapse between each group. The transmission had to begin at exactly 2123 Moscow Time. That meant a computer job. The radio operator looked up at the clocks and swore. This was going to have to be done in a rush. Trust it to happen just when Aleksei had gone for his break, half an hour early, too.

By 2120 the message had been fed into the machine and was ready to go. All the officer had to do was set the automatic key, wait for the computer to send the transmission at the appointed time, and switch itself off. Yet he was troubled. There was scarcely any incoming traffic after six in the evening, and outgoing messages were rare enough to attract attention. That was one thing. But for a general to send a message under his own initials . . . well, that was extraordinary. The officer's hand hovered over the key. Should he send it? Obey orders and forget it . . . ?

His hand moved across from the console and picked up the telephone instead.

Someone answered, and the officer held the receiver away from his ear. Whoever was on the line had one hell of a cough.

'General Michaelov here.'

The officer, a non-smoker, waited patiently while the speaker got over another furious bout of coughing. Everyone knew that

Michaelov was smoking himself into an early grave with those damned 'papirosy' cigarettes of his. Filthy habit.

He took a deep breath. 'Forgive me, comrade General, but I wished to verify this message.'

'Yes, yes. What about it? Have you sent it yet?'

'No, I . . .'

'Well send it, idiot! What the hell do you mean by it, eh? Can't you read?'

'Yes, comrade General.' The officer was starting to feel wretched.

'Aren't the instructions clear enough?'

'Perfectly clear, comrade General.'

'Well then, don't make me come down there and sort you out. Damned insolence. Why if I . . .'

The call terminated amidst another bout of chesty coughing. The officer replaced the receiver and wiped the sweat from his forehead, wondering what he could salvage from the wreckage of his career. One thing was certain: he had better send that message before it was too late . . .

Outside in the corridor someone whistled. That must be Aleksei, returning from his break. Aleksei would know what to do. Every fucking night there was something: do this, do that, run here, go there, kiss my arse . . . Why couldn't Michaelov stay at home and poke his old woman like the rest of the brass did?

'What's up?' said Aleksei, catching the look on his colleague's face.

'Wait 'til you hear. It's the damndest thing . . .' The radio officer explained what had happened in his friend's absence. 'Do you think I should report it in the morning?'

'I shouldn't', said Aleksei knowingly. 'Forget it. Until you're asked. And maybe not even then.'

That sounded like good advice; and if Povin could have heard it as he walked slowly back along the corridor to his own office, his fingers convulsively squeezing the tiny crucifix in his pocket until it was slippery with sweat, he would certainly have endorsed Aleksei's opinion.

37

___

It was very hot in the first-floor room. Sculby and Loshkevoi sat at opposite ends of a long sofa like a couple of colonials who haven't been formally introduced. In front of them was the fireplace, where a modern gas-fire radiated uncomfortable amounts of heat. Sculby had tried to turn it down but the control was jammed. Heavy velour curtains were drawn across hermetically sealed windows; it was difficult to breathe.

The only light was provided by a single bulb encased in a glass bowl above the sofa, quite inadequate for such a large room. Sculby likened the whole experience to being in the ante-chamber of Hell, not yet dead and not quite burning either.

The door opened to admit Royston and Franklin.

'Aren't you hot?' asked Royston.

Sculby explained. Franklin went to kneel by the gas-fire and after a moment the orange glow abated.

'Can't we open a window? It's stifling in here.'

'Sorry. Too risky.'

'You really think he might come in through a first-floor window?'

Loshkevoi turned to look at him with an expression of unmitigated contempt on his face. Royston didn't even bother to answer.

'What about the girl?'

Royston was methodically working his way round the room's outer defences.

'Nothing more... except would you believe she had the best part of a thousand quid in her handbag? Jesus Christ... expensive, I should bloody well think she was.' He paused and looked up, as if struck by a sudden thought. 'I wonder if that's KGB money she had. Ah well...'

'Is she still here?'

'No. We called her a taxi.'

'You might have told me, Michael. I could have gone too.'

Royston sniggered. 'You don't think I'd risk you in the same cab with her, do you?'

Sculby was exasperated. 'Seriously, Michael...'

Loshkevoi stood up and began to pace around the room, hands clasped behind his back. Everyone turned to look at him.

'Do you have to do that?' asked Royston sourly, after a while. Loshkevoi stopped in mid-stride and flung himself down on the sofa again.

'Can't we have some more light in here?' he asked. 'There's too many shadows in this room. They make me nervous.'

'Shut up and sit quietly. Now listen...' Royston was addressing the room at large. 'You all know the set-up. The outer wall is guarded and floodlit, so Kyril can't get out. He's somewhere in the grounds, or possibly the house. Sooner or later he's going to show. We sit here, patiently, and wait. He *has* to make the first move and together we outnumber him conclusively, I'd say. So just make yourselves at home and relax, 'cos nobody's leaving. Here, you two...' He pointed at Barnes and Franklin. 'Pull up those chairs by the door, facing each other at an angle... that's right. Now you can cover the only entrance and exit.'

He rounded on Sculby.

'You keep to that sofa. You too, Loshkevoi. I'm over here in the corner. If you must talk, keep it low: I want to be able to hear anything that happens in the corridor.'

Royston took a final look round the room, checking that everything was in order. Apparently satisfied, he walked quietly over to the door and opened it, leaving a narrow rectangle through which Sculby, by looking over his shoulder, could see the passage outside.

Royston backed away from the door and retreated to the far corner of the room where he sat down by a low table, half opposite the lawyer. On the table was a phone. Sculby saw him lift the receiver and listen for a few seconds before replacing it on its cradle.

'Just testing', said Royston as he caught Sculby's eye. 'The line's okay.'

Silence fell. During the next few minutes Sculby discovered that he had three problems. He was nervous. He was hungry. And he was bored.

After twenty minutes of silence these problems seemed to have doubled in size. Instead of being nervous he was scared; his stomach ached with emptiness; his mind was darting from topic to topic in nightmare fashion. He cursed his folly in not bringing paperwork to keep himself occupied. Every few seconds his eye flew to his watch. Only half an hour gone. Christ. Perhaps he could sleep. He sat back and closed his eyes to find all three problems still there, only somehow worse for being in darkness. He opened his eyes again.

The room was hardly luxurious. It reminded Sculby of the dayroom in his house at school: all tat and second hand. The carpet was threadbare and stained; the walls were bare of pictures, in the corner stood an old radio, its aerial bent almost double. None of the chairs matched each other or the sofa. One of the curtains had a jagged tear in it. Pinned to the back of the door was a notice typed on yellow Ministry of Defence paper. 'Warning!' it said. 'Extinguish all power before leaving. Silence rules.' Sculby distracted himself by trying to work out the syntax. Was silence an adjective in this context? Or a noun—in which case should there not be an 'OK?' on the end? And why 'power'? Why not just say 'light' like everyone else, and have done with it?

Loshkevoi was sitting forward with his head in his hands, apparently absorbed by something on the floor. Royston reclined in the corner chair, looking vacantly at the ceiling. Sculby looked over his shoulder to see Barnes and Franklin both sitting upright, their faces tense with concentration. The two men had removed their jackets, revealing full shoulder-holsters.

Sculby closed his eyes again and tried to concentrate on a mantra. After a while he drifted into a light doze, pausing apprehensively to see if the Soviet officer with his swinging sword would invade his troubled brain. Nothing happened. Sculby slept.

He awoke what seemed like hours later and at once looked at his watch. It had stopped at five past seven. Other sensations began to make themselves felt. Somewhere nearby voices were being raised in disagreement.

'I'm telling you, I have to take a crap . . .'

Loshkevoi was by the door being restrained by Franklin while Barnes looked questioningly at his chief.

'Can't it wait?' snarled Royston.

'No it can't. I'm standing on one fucking leg as it is.'

Royston wiped a strand of hair away from his face, which was white with fatigue. You're not in control, thought Sculby, and then—Oh, God, Michael, don't give up now . . .

'All right, all right. Barnes, you go with him. Franklin, while they're away you sit in the doorway. And for God's sake, hurry up.'

'Get some sandwiches while you're at it', put in Sculby, and was rewarded with a furious look from Royston.

'Don't do anything of the kind. Just get on with it as fast as possible and come back here. Now move!'

Sculby swung his legs on to the sofa and rested his head on a cushion. 'Sorry Michael', he murmured. Royston grunted and was about to reply when suddenly the phone rang.

Everyone froze. Royston let it ring five times. Sculby reckoned he was trying to bring himself back under control after the initial shock had worn off. At last he reached out his hand to take the receiver.

'Yes? Yes, I recognise the voice.'

Royston listened in rapt silence. To Sculby the call seemed to go on forever. Only once did Royston speak, to say 'Repeat, please'; he terminated the call by hanging up without saying goodbye to whoever was on the other end. Sculby raised an inquiring eyebrow but Royston steadfastly refused to meet his gaze.

The lawyer was about to close his eyes again when Royston

did something which made him decide to stay awake after all.
From his coat pocket he took a large, ungainly gun and a box
of ammunition from which he proceeded to load the weapon.
Both gun and bullets looked enormous. Sculby watched with
growing apprehension. Royston's lack of familiarity with what
he was doing became more obvious by the minute, and in their
relative positions he looked far more likely to shoot Sculby
than any assailant bursting through the half-open door which
led to the passage.

Sculby heard a noise behind him and turned. Franklin was
standing in the doorway, gun in hand, facing outwards into the
corridor. He was listening with all his attention.

'What is it?'

Sculby stood up and went to stand behind him in the doorway. 'I don't know', Franklin whispered. 'I thought I heard a
noise. They'd been gone such a long time, I thought I'd take
a look.'

He laid his hands on the door, as if to open it further, but
as he did so Royston spoke.

'Stand still', was what he said.

38

Kyril squeezed a little closer to the wall, palms spread out against the panelled oak, eyes closed. His breathing had slowed, his heartbeat was way below normal and his hands were wet. He was listening. With every scrap of energy in his body concentrated on that one activity, he was listening.

He had been in the west wing, undisturbed, for several hours. It had taken him that long to descend from the topmost floor, testing every step before he took it, examining each door-jamb for the hidden beam that would break at a touch, forcing himself to be slow, slow, slow.

What *was* this place? He wished he had paid more attention to Crowden when he was in England six years ago. It was half-public and half-private, so obviously it did not rate a top-secret security classification. He vaguely remembered it as a retreat for agents who needed to recuperate in circumstances of peace and normality after a particularly gruelling tour of duty, a sort of hotel for washed-out staff. Also, it was useful for meetings which had to be 'open', because the target was feeling edgy. Kyril had known that to happen even in Moscow: a defector

would ask to roam the streets, looking in shop-windows, rub-
bing elbows with pedestrians just for the sake of human contact,
while KGB agents hovered nearby.

He was aware that round the next corner, ten metres away,
a door stood ajar, and through the gap light filtered into the
gloomy corridor. Kyril could occasionally catch the sound of
voices speaking quietly inside the room beyond the door. How
many people were inside? How many guards did SIS maintain
at Crowden? Not many, surely? Was Loshkevoi in that room?

Time ticked on. Kyril shuffled plans like cards, all discards.
Somehow he had to get inside that room. By a process of
exclusion he knew that this was where his target lay, had to
lie. A frontal attack would be certain suicide. But every second
he stayed where he was shortened the odds against his remaining undetected. He had to act, and soon, but . . . how?

Kyril opened his eyes. Inside the room was a sudden commotion, with voices raised in argument. He flattened himself
more closely against the wall and strove to listen. Suddenly
the voices grew louder: that must mean the door had
opened . . . people were coming out.

Opposite Kyril was another door. Without once pausing to
alert his conscious brain some crucial instinct of self-preservation sent him hurtling towards it. The door was unlocked. It
gave on to a short, dark passage at the end of which was another
door set with panels of frosted glass. And in that same split
second he realised that he had succeeded only in trapping himself, for someone inside that lighted room wanted to use the
lavatory where Kyril now was . . .

Footsteps outside. Kyril flashed his torch at the ceiling, saw
the bulb and jumped for it.

'Damn. Light's gone.'

From behind the door which led into the main passage Kyril
saw an arm feel along the wall oposite him, its owner guided
by the glimmer of light from outside. He heard voices. Two
men.

'Can you manage?'

'Yeah. Just.'

Loshkevoi had groped his way down the short, inner passage
almost to the door of the lavatory. Now the second man was
following him.

Kyril launched himself forward. The door slammed awkwardly against the body of the second man who drew a breath, about to cry out when Kyril's fist landed right in the centre of his adam's apple and he fell, the scream for ever lodged in his throat, unuttered. Kyril did not spare him another thought. His body was already twisting in a 90-degree vector so that by the time his right foot hit Loshkevoi in the stomach he was almost parallel with the floor. The fat man crumpled up double; Kyril bounced off the tiles and in a single co-ordinated movement had him rammed up against the glass-panelled door, forearm across the throat.

The precious moments he fought to control his breathing while his brain frantically re-ran the events of the past few seconds over and over again, trying to calculate how much noise they had made. The passage outside remained dark and empty. So far so good.

'Whaaaah . . .'

Kyril levered his arm a little more snugly into the folds of Loshkevoi's neck and whipped out the Stechkin, holding the cold metal to the prisoner's cheek.

'You know what this is.'

The rasping whisper seemed to reach Loshkevoi as from a great distance, so quiet it was.

'One squeal out of you and you're *dead*.'

If Kyril had shouted those words Loshkevoi would probably have screamed for help. But that whisper . . . something about it spoke directly to Loshkevoi's central nervous system, bypassing all rational thought. As long as Kyril continued to use that harsh, far-off whisper, little more than a breath in his ear, Loshkevoi was like a doll in the hands of a puppet-master.

'We're going out.'

Kyril removed his arm and swiftly used his free hand to wheel Loshkevoi round. His prisoner's foot collided with Barnes' body and he stumbled heavily.

'Careful!'

The two men, locked together in a tight embrace, picked their way over the corpse. Now they were in the main corridor.

'Left.'

Kyril guided Loshkevoi away from the room whence he had emerged a few minutes earlier.

'Wait.'

Kyril knew that a door at the far end of the corridor, by the stairs, was unlocked: he had checked it earlier as part of his cautious progress through the house. He hustled Loshkevoi into the room beyond and closed the door behind them, his fingers groping for the key.

Here there were no curtains. Through the windows opposite Kyril could see the glow from the floodlights along the perimeter wall.

'No lights. Stay where you are. I can see you silhouetted against the window. Make a move I don't like and I'll shoot.'

Kyril spoke quietly, but without using that terrible whisper, and Loshkevoi relaxed a fraction.

'I have no quarrel with you. I have no orders to kill you, either.' Kyril spoke rapidly. 'The quicker you tell me all I need to know, the sooner you'll be out of here.'

'I've been . . .' Loshkevoi's voice cracked with fear; he cleared his throat and began again. 'I've been expecting you. You must help me.' The pleading in his voice was unmistakable but there was cunning also. 'You have got to help me. Please. Please . . .'

'Stand still!' Loshkevoi had taken a step towards Kyril. 'What was that?'

Kyril pressed his ear against the wooden panel of the door. Was there a noise outside? Long seconds passed. Nothing. He turned back to see Loshkevoi's huge form high-lighted against the windows. His shoulders were heaving. Kyril could not see the man's face but with a stab of excitement he realised that Loshkevoi was in the grip of an emotion powerful enough to transcend even his fear.

'Yes, yes, I will help you. That is part of my message. We are going back to Moscow, you and I. Together. Tonight. Stanov knows that you have been troubled in your mind. That is why he sent me. But you'd better talk fast. Who is Nidus? Who sent Sikarov to England? Believe me, it's your only chance: to talk, tell everything.'

'Who? . . . Sikarov . . . I . . .'

'The A2 *gaybist*. Executioner.'

'I can guess who sent Sikarov', said Loshkevoi dully. 'There's only one candidate. It has to be . . .'

'Quiet!'

Had there been something, out there in the passage? Kyril flattened himself against the door, listening. The corridor was silent. He backed away from the door and felt his way towards Loshkevoi.

'You were saying', he hissed. 'It has to be . . .'

'The man in the suit. He came from Moscow. Not through the embassy, not the first time. He came from Stanov, he said. I believed him. He knew things that only someone next to the Chairman could know, details about my operations which Stanov was never supposed to confide in anyone. But this man knew them. I couldn't figure him out at all. He never wore a uniform, just a suit, the same suit every time we met. He asked me . . . if I was happy. Can you imagine that, eh? An officer of the KGB asking if you were happy?'

Kyril forced himself to be patient and swallow his anger. Loshkevoi was on the point of talking. Beyond all hope or expectation, he really did know something. The slightest interruption, the merest hint of irritation, and the delicate skein of understanding between them would be lost.

'I told him . . . no. Not the first time, but afterwards, when he came again. I said, the terrorism, it's getting so that I can't stand it. They're all mad, all insane. I was starting to drink a bottle a day, it scared me so. But . . . he understood. The man in the suit, he knew everything. He talked to me so . . . so kindly. And he kept coming, and every time he came he seemed to know more about me, what I did, how I felt. Until one day . . .'

'Yes?' Kyril could not keep the urgency out of his voice. Loshkevoi seemed not to hear.

'One day he just said . . . would you like to work for me, as well as Stanov, and I said . . . yes. I would.'

'You mean he was CIA, he was an agent?'

'No. You don't understand. He was one of us. Only he did things, he saw things differently from the rest. He understood, you see, he realised there were limits. *Human* limits.'

'So he was a traitor . . .'

'No!' Loshkevoi seemed genuinely surprised: Kyril detected shock as well as doubt in his voice. 'At least, I . . .'

Kyril had a sudden, sharp vision of Sikarov kneeling over Vera's body.

'It was he who mentioned Vera Bradfield?'

'Yes. That's right. How did you know that? He wanted me to go and see her, find out if you were coming . . . and he told me what to do when you finally arrived, so that I'd be sure to be sent to prison, and be safe. It was then I realised he meant to kill you. He wanted me out of the way, clear. I knew then there had to be a killer, somewhere.'

'His name. *What was his name?*'

In the second of silence that followed Kyril heard two shots, quite loud and close and then two more. He whirled round, mouth agape. Loshkevoi seemed not to notice.

'I don't know. He never told me. He wore this suit . . .'

Kyril moved quickly back to the door. The silence outside was unbroken. For five, ten, fifteen seconds he stood in exactly the same position, listening. Those *were* shots. He was sure of it, as sure as he was that Loshkevoi stood behind him, his hands held up to shield his face. Out there, along the passage, someone had fired.

Kyril crept back to his former position beside Loshkevoi. Why had nobody come to rescue Loshkevoi? Had they found the body in the lavatory yet? What was the shooting? *What was happening?*

Kyril shook his head angrily. *Think.*

'We haven't got much time.' His voice grated with tension. 'This man in the suit. The man from Moscow. Did you tell them anything about him next door?'

'No.'

'You're sure?'

'Sure.'

'Then describe him to me. Quickly.'

'Oh . . . cleanshaven. Blue eyes. Not much of a chin.'

'Blue eyes . . . did he have two deep clefts, here . . . ?'

Kyril traced them on Loshkevoi's own face with a finger.

'Yes. Where it shows if a man smiles a lot.'

'And the eyes . . .'

'Blue eyes.'

'Yes, yes I know, but how were they set?'

'Deep. The brows overshadowed them.'

Kyril slapped Loshkevoi's shoulders. He was almost sure. One more question and he would have it. He wanted to bounce up and down he was so excited.

'Think, Loshkevoi. Think harder than you've ever thought before in your life. His ears... *Tell me about his ears!*'

For a moment there was silence. Loshkevoi was swaying from side to side, as if the effort of concentration was too much for him. Kyril was suddenly glad he couldn't see through the darkness; the desire to smash out at the fleshy, petrified face would have been irresistible.

'Ah! You know him then...of course, you must do, to mention his ears.' Loshkevoi sounded awed. 'You know this man in the suit, too? Who was he, eh? What was his name?'

Kyril forced himself to count to ten, very slowly. Then— 'Tell me', he said, 'about his ears. You were going to say something about his ears.'

'Pointed. Like goblin's ears.'

Kyril leapt into the air, throwing his arms above his head as high as they could reach. He had the name. For a second he almost wanted to shriek it aloud. He wanted to kick off his shoes and dance, he wanted to laugh and cry, he wanted...he didn't even know any longer what he wanted. He had the name.

Povin.

Loshkevoi was speaking again, the note of pleading back in his voice. 'You will tell them in Moscow...I helped you, didn't I? And, and...you will be careful.'

Kyril was only half-listening. 'Careful?'

'He...he knew things only the Chairman is supposed to know.'

Kyril froze. 'What?'

'This man. In the suit. He knew things only Stanov knew. They were friends. He told me so. They... *liked* each other.'

An icy miasma distilled out of the four corners of the room, wreathing its slow way round Kyril's heart. Friends. They were friends. He wanted to think about that. But not yet. Later.

No, not later. Now.

Suppose Stanov was the traitor?

Kyril found himself staring at this thought, lacking the will to send it away. It had been waiting on the fringes of his subconscious for weeks.

What was the purpose of this...charade? Had Stanov been using him, and if so, why? What deep game was being played, what devious dealings at the heart of the Politburo had driven him here, to London, to be somebody's pawn? The more he struggled to keep a clear head, think his way through the maze, the less he understood. 'You will be flying very near the sun...', that was what Stanov told him at their first meeting. Did those words conceal some dark, ironic secret?

It was possible. Some little part of Kyril had always acknowledged it was possible. Now, however, it seemed more than just possible, it seemed likely. Kyril knew who the traitor was. Povin. It ranked among the world's more dangerous secrets. Suppose it really was Povin, just suppose for a moment... didn't the very name waft from person to person like a virus, fatally contaminating everyone it touched? Could Stanov afford to let him live?

Kyril took a fold of flesh between his teeth and bit it until tears sprang to his eyes.

39

The dimly-lit room was hazy with smoke and the throaty reek of cordite when Kyril stepped gingerly over the threshold. Royston had not moved. He still sat in the corner chair, the gun lying loosely in his lap.

As the two men saw each other they half-heartedly lifted their weapons, only to let them fall again.

'We have not much time' said Royston, putting the gun back in his coat-pocket. 'You saved me the trouble of coming to find you. My men have orders to stay on the outer wall come what may, but the shots are going to bring them to the house before long. Where are Loshkevoi and Barnes?'

Kyril looked up wonderingly from the scene of carnage at his feet. One man lay across the doorway, his back split open by some incredible force. Another, younger, man lay half over the arm of the sofa, most of his ribcage and neck smashed to pulp. Blood was everywhere, on the floor, the walls, the ceiling . . .

'Why . . . ?'

Royston hesitated. 'There was noise outside in the corridor. When I warned them not to go out they became suspicious, they wouldn't listen. Besides, we don't want any witnesses. It was necessary to get rid of them. Especially the younger one', he added bitterly. 'I ask you again . . . Loshkevoi and Barnes?'

'Loshkevoi is on his way out', Kyril said quietly. 'The other man is . . .' He gestured at the nearest body, and Royston nodded.

'A pity about Loshkevoi, then. My marksmen have orders to shoot anyone who doesn't have the password. If he tries to run for it he doesn't stand . . .'

Voices and the sudden crackle of gunfire outside brought very different expressions to the faces of the two men. The smoke had almost cleared now. Royston spoke rapidly.

'You know who I am?'

'Loshkevoi said they called you Michael. I guessed who it was. You're Royston.'

'You've heard of me?'

'Oh yes. I've heard of you.'

'Good. That saves us a lot of time. I guessed what was happening. These two wanted to go after you. I hope the sight of them will help you decide what is to happen next. You don't trust me, Bucharensky, and that's tough, because now you have to make up your mind about me faster than you've ever done anything before in your life. You heard the shots outside. In ten minutes, maybe less, this house will be overrun. In your mission, you have succeeded. Oh yes, I understand your mission very well. You were supposed to panic the traitor into making a mistake, weren't you. That and Loshkevoi . . . Stanov knew he'd lost control of Loshkevoi a long time ago. It was obvious you'd make for him. And it worked. The traitor sent Sikarov, to kill you before the regular KGB could catch up and twist the name out of you. But you won, all along the line. If you leave now, you can still make it back to Moscow as well. Here's a passport.' Royston reached into his coat pocket, looking to see if the gun jerked in Kyril's hand. It did not move. He read doubt in the man's face, doubt and exhaustion. 'Money. A credit card. You can be out of the country before daybreak. The password is 'Icepex', though I doubt if you'll need it . . .'

Kyril looked up sharply. 'What?'

'Icepex. As in Icepex G 17, Bucharensky. Oh yes, it's true. The Kremlin Kommandant, formerly the Palindrome Directive, before that Line 'H'. I've been attached to it for years. Seventeen because today is 30th March, work it out Bucharensky...'

'You're lying!'

Kyril was rocketed into a whirling, insane vortex of uncertainty. The Kommandant... no, it could not be true. But Icepex... *no one* knew about that, not even the Deputy Chairmen... or maybe the Deputy Chairmen did know, but...

'You have to be lying.'

Still the gun in Bucharensky's hand did not move.

'My casename is Pisa. Italy, Bucharensky. What does that tell you, eh? How many people know about the Kommandant and its casenames? You do, for one. You stood by Stanov's chair for months. You couldn't fail to know.'

Kyril held his hands to his eyes, trying to shut out the insidious voice. Royston knew all the details of his mission. Perhaps he could have deduced those, it wasn't so difficult, but... Pisa. G. 17. *Icepex*. They couldn't be faked. No one outside the Kremlin knew those things. Except perhaps a handful of the most senior Deputy Chairmen. Except *Stanov!*

'The name, Bucharensky, the name. I must have it. I know you wouldn't tell any mere defector in place, no one would, but you're looking at a member of the Kommandant, and I am ordering you to give me the name.'

There was a long silence. Kyril's head was going round and round. Could he afford to trust Royston? Could he afford not to? Three men only were in a position to identify the traitor: Povin, Bryant and himself. Why make a fourth? Besides, he had no proof. Povin, Michaelov, Stanov... He was at the centre of a maze, they were all using him.

'Think, Bucharensky. *Rodina*...'

Kyril looked up, his eyes widening. 'You... say that... to me?'

Rodina. Motherland... the very name had an aura about it; spoken aloud it made Kyril want to weep. For a second he saw the rolling green hills of his childhood, heard the river frothing down to the plain, could feel the sun on his back. Russia...

'What... what do you want me to do?'

Royston released his pent-up breath. 'This is the plan. I will turn my back on you. You use the gun to stun me: not so hard that I am killed but hard enough to make it convincing. They will come to find me. You overpowered me and got away, that is what they will think. But in case you do not make it, I must have the name. You must have a fall-back. I am all you have. The name, Bucharensky, *the name* . . .'

The room was going up and down. Kyril struggled to clear his head. He was so tired, all he could think of was sleep. Perhaps Royston was right. He *had* to be genuine; to offer to turn your back on a man and invite him to knock you out . . . But which name?

Povin.

Yes. Povin was the traitor. Loshkevoi said so, as Stanov had told him he would, right at the start. Stanov had not lied about Loshkevoi, after all.

And yet . . . what had Sikarov been trying to say in his last moments? Was it really Michaelov? If so, Michaelov was the traitor, for he had sent Sikarov to London. The First Deputy Chairman of the KGB, second only to . . .

Stanov.

Why had Stanov left him all alone in the field, defenceless, a running target? Why had he chosen Kyril out of so many others? Was it because of Vera? Did he forsee how Kyril would react, what Stanov would do? A cunning fox, Stanov . . .

Fox . . . *Lisa* . . .

Why did Vera have to die? *Why?*

Rodina. For the motherland. For Russia . . .

Kyril looked into Royston's eyes. It was all true. He really was a member of the dreaded Kommandant. Either that, or Stanov had told him its innermost secrets . . .

Stanov . . . Stanov . . . *Lisa* . . .

Kyril was surrounded, trapped. Royston might represent his last, his only chance of sending home the vital name.

Kyril swallowed, licked his lips and opened his mouth to emit the little puff of breath that would herald 'P . . .'

No.

He had not reached the end of his mission. This was only the beginning! Inspiration filled him, seemed to raise him a few inches off the floor. The truth lay elsewhere, in Moscow. And that was where he must go to find it.

Kyril's eyes narrowed to fine slits. The light hurt them, they were suddenly sore. *Think*. One thing at a time. Royston. It was necessary to get rid of Royston. Nothing dramatic, now. Nothing obvious. Reassure him. That's right, make him think you believe him. Win him over. Give him a name . . . any old name, except the prime, the number one suspect . . .

Somewhere inside Kyril's head Sikarov's dying scream reverberated.

'It was Michaelov', he said casually.

Royston nodded and turned his back. Kyril did not reverse his gun, as he would have to do if he were to stun the other man. Instead he stepped forward, his finger tightening on the trigger.

But as his brain commanded the final pressure that would trip the trigger mechanism his tired eyes saw the strange thing that was about to happen. A black, smoky hole exploding outwards from Royston's pocket as the gun, concealed there since shortly after Kyril first came in, was fired. A sudden pain, very sharp, very severe, in his chest. Kyril's eyes widened, then narrowed. Royston was rising up . . . no, that was wrong, he, Bucharensky, was sliding to the floor. It was very dark in the room, although he knew that the light was still burning. His brain transmitted its last message. Royston had stood with his hands in his pockets, and reversed the gun . . .

Bucharensky died.

Royston leaned against the wall and stayed like that for several minutes. From every angle it looked good.

Above all, Royston knew relief. Now Kyril could never betray him. The agony was over.

He knelt to the Russian's body and took the gun from his hand, exchanging it for his own. The coat with the black-fringed hole in the pocket he folded up carefully and placed by the door, ready to go with him when he left.

Kyril had committed suicide, that is what they would all think. The price of failure. Such a pity that before he took his own life he had to kill the foolhardy Sculby, whose overwhelming bravery got the better of him at last. That would go down well. The trendy lefty lawyer had nearly redeemed himself after all, no doubt in remorse for his duplicity in visiting the Bradfield woman (presumably on Stanov's orders) and his treachery in proposing a deal to Kyril. A good thing he had had the forethought to bug Sculby's offices. The tape of the lawyer's nocturnal conversation with Kyril played over very nicely. The phrase 'For love of the motherland' sounded particularly well.

Royston raised his arms above his head and stretched. Noises from below indicated that the rescue-party had reached the front door. Time to find a hiding-place from which to emerge, pale and trembling . . .

After the debriefings, the inquests, when things were quiet again, Royston would write a postcard. Michaelov, that is what the apparently innocent, coded message would say. Bucharensky got the name, and then he died before he could be interrogated. But he got the name. Michaelov.

Stanov had been right about so many things. Loshkevoi, himself turned traitor; Sikarov, sent by Michaelov. The Bradfield woman. Stanov had been right about that also.

Royston was looking at the future. And it worked.

40

It had been a false spring, after all. April came but in Moscow the nights were freezing once more, and brown slush coated the streets by day. The office on the third floor, however, was warm and fuggy. The Chairman had given orders for the central heating to be switched on again—and to hell with the Politburo, he thought privately to himself as he signed the chit. Let them save roubles some other year, after I've gone.

He had spent the past hour proof-reading a report, now ready for his signature. Its subject was the identity of 'Source *Lisa*', and the steps which Stanov had taken to uncover the traitor.

When he had finished reading the report he removed his spectacles and went to stand by the window in his favourite spot overlooking the square. He was smiling. Nowadays it was fashionable to decry the role of intuition in espionage. Take Kazin, for example; he would never have understood the subtle mental processes which had led Stanov to the traitor.

So many straws in the wind, so many hints over the years. A non-drinker. Daughter on the verge of becoming a dissident. No sense of humour, no gift of relaxation, no flair. Perfect material for the West. A Georgian. Stanov frowned. How the hell had they ever appointed a Georgian to be head of the First Main Directorate?

And the evidence! He was almost sure at the beginning when he briefed Bucharensky, but look at what had happened since then. Who sent an executioner to the UK? Michaelov. Who left traces all over Radio Operations, with those filthy papirosy cigarettes? Michaelov. Stanov shook his head sorrowfully. To betray the Inspectorate, the Kommandant itself: a bitter blow. But they had caught him, at least there was that consolation.

Intuition. That's what you needed. That's why he was going to remain head of the KGB for ten more years at least, while Kazin was going to the Ministry of Agriculture, there to rot with his own collective farm manure. Stanov shook his head again. Kazin would never have appreciated the value of men like Loshkevoi. Or Royston.

Royston stood particularly high in Stanov's good books that day. With advancing age the Chairman was growing tired of elderly Cambridge dons with their peculiar sexual habits. He found them faintly obscene. A meritocrat like Royston came as a refreshing change.

Yevchenko knocked and came in. Stanov turned away from the window.

'Strange', he said. 'Strange to think that Loshkevoi actually knew the name. I suspected many things of him, but never that.'

'A pity he did not live to confirm the identification, then.'

Stanov shrugged. 'What more could he have said? And this way it saves us the cost of a bullet. They are ready downstairs?'

Yevchenko nodded. In his hand he held a bunch of heavy keys. While Stanov watched with satisfaction he walked across to 'The Door' and unfastened the twin padlocks. It swung open to reveal a short, gloomy corridor, and a single light-bulb suspended from the ceiling by bare flex. Stanov rubbed his hands together.

'Come, Nikolai. It's been a while since I looked at the Lubianka cellars, and I'm sure the General doesn't want to be kept waiting. By the way, you remember what we were talking about yesterday? I've decided on Michaelov's successor and now we've finally got double-oh-seven-eight through, those bastards over the way can't stop me, eh? Normally I don't believe in promoting deputies at that level, but I'm going to make an exception. Povin it is. Excellent officer. Loyal. I like that, Nikolai. Remind me to tell Michaelov before they start . . .'

'A popular appointment, old man. I approve.'

Stanov paused on the threshold, struck by a sudden thought. He rested a hand on Yevchenko's shoulder and when he spoke there was genuine doubt in his voice.

'Nikolai . . . should I have told Kyril more, like you said? Would it have been better for him to die knowing all along that he was expendable, nothing more than a target? D'you still think I was wrong?'

Yevchenko smiled ruefully.

'If you'd told him the truth he would never have got to Loshkevoi. You were right not to trust him completely. I admit it. As it is, he was a good officer to the end. He died in the knowledge that he had not failed, that the name would get through.'

Stanov smiled, and removed his hand from Yevchenko's shoulder. They went through 'The Door' together. As Stanov turned to close it behind him he caught sight of 'The Chair' and it occurred to him that in say another ten years there would be a vacancy in the office of Chairman. Just time enough for Povin to show what he could really do. And then, perhaps . . . Who knows?

The Door closed behind him. In Dzerzhinsky Square the street lamps fizzled into life, illuminating the first snow of the night as it fell, untouched, through their incandescent blue circles. The room was silent and empty. As the natural light drained away, so one by one the features of the office dissolved into the surrounding darkness and became part of it. Andropov's vacant face was the first to disappear; then the quartz clocks, the telephones, the gigantic desk and, last to go, as if reluctant to surrender to the night, the ornate wooden chair . . .

The Chair . . . which, in the eyes of Soviet law, is never empty.

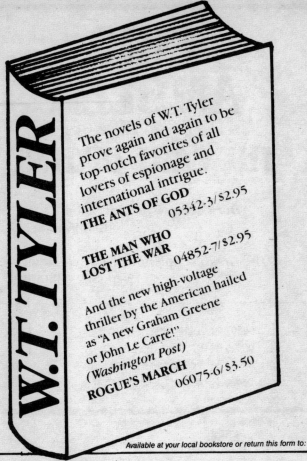

ERIC AMBLER

Author of the National Bestseller

THE CARE OF TIME

"Our Greatest Thriller Writer"
— GRAHAM GREENE

"The Greatest Spy Novelist of all Time!"
— SAN FRANCISCO CHRONICLE